# Unspoken Words

*Hope and a Future ~ Book 1*

Janna Halterman

UNSPOKEN WORDS (HOPE AND A FUTURE ~ BOOK 1)
Copywrite © 2019 Janna Halterman.
All rights reserved.
ISBN: 978-0-578-53577-7

First publication: July 2019

Edited by Liz Giertz: My Messy Desk

Unless otherwise indicated, all Scripture quotations are taken from the Holy Bible, New Living Translation, copyright © 1996, 2004, 2015 by Tyndale House Foundation. Used by permission of Tyndale House Publishers, Inc., Carol Stream, Illinois 60188. All rights reserved.

Scripture quotations marked (NIV) are taken from the Holy Bible, New International Version®, NIV®. Copyright © 1973, 1978, 1984, 2011 by Biblica, Inc.™ Used by permission of Zondervan. All rights reserved worldwide. www.zondervan.com The "NIV" and "New International Version" are trademarks registered in the United States Patent and Trademark Office by Biblica, Inc.™

This is a work of fiction. Names, characters, places, and incidents either are the product of the author's imagination or are used fictitiously. Any resemblance to actual persons, living or dead, businesses, companies, events, or locales is entirely coincidental.

# Dedication

To my sweet children, my dreams come true,
I pray you always know the depth of God's love for you.
Follow the dreams He puts in your heart.

Janna Halterman

# Prologue

## August 2161

She was happy in her work, surrounded by poetry, adventures, mysteries, history, and pages upon pages of wisdom. The quiet of the library that assaulted the nerves of many a student worked as a tonic to her, calming and soothing her; though at times giving voice to loneliness. Silence was her old, familiar friend. Today it was especially quiescent. Students who frequented her workplace remained away on summer break and she was able to focus on re-shelving, something that had backed up considerably over the summer while their staff was minimal. It was a time-consuming task.

Some time ago, the library had run out of room and when bookshelves could no longer expand outwards, they began to climb upwards. Re-shelving not only required carrying books all about the building, but also up and down ladders. But she loved climbing high up the ladders around the edges of the library. The tops of those ladders offered the best opportunity to admire the beautiful, stained glass windows; colorful mosaics depicting stories she'd never heard told. How odd it was to work surrounded by literature, having every sort of writing at her fingertips, and yet these window-trapped stories remained mysteries.

Before the last civil war, the war that ripped the country in two, this particular library had been a church. It escaped the cruel fate of destruction most churches suffered after the war. It was preserved; transformed. She was glad it had been saved. The almost three-hundred-year-old building was a statement of grand architecture, nothing like their modern construction. With vaulted ceilings, arches chiseled from aged stone, and those story-telling windows that cast a myriad of colors through the musky, dust-filled air as the sun rose and set each day, it was a work of art.

But the government had tried its best to hide the old building's majesty. The bookshelves attested to that. Made of harsh metal and formed with the sole intent of function, they brought a cold industrial air to the otherwise architectural masterpiece.

Not allowed to own property anymore, churches met quietly in peoples' homes. It wasn't against the law to be Christian, but she got the impression the government felt threatened by God and His people. Why else would they demolish and desecrate their places of worship?

What it would have been like to be here when it was still a church, to hear the hall filled with praises to this God. She knew nothing of what church had once been like, but every time a rowdy group came through the building, the acoustics came to life. She had to believe it was built for song, and in her heart, she knew it must have been beautiful.

She was lost in one of those moments of wonder when she met him. High up on a ladder, sightseeing in an era long gone in one of the glass pictures, she was startled.

\*\*\*

The book looked down at him, taunting him. His pride made him reach overhead for the ladder rung, and that pride was quickly smashed. His ribs groaned in protest, trapping his arm to his side, and flooding his mind with the unwelcome memories of the events which caused him this pain.

Extremists had been tearing New Mexico apart. Unhappy with the peace between the United States and the Texas Republic, they were targeting government officials, businesses, private citizens – anyone they saw as sympathizers to the Texas Republic. He had been sent there to deal with them.

And now he suffered the inconvenience of broken ribs because of them.

He shook the dark memory from his thoughts. His time in New Mexico was not all bad, though. It earned him a promotion to the rank of Captain, and he received his new assignment with his ticket home.

He was more than content to be home now. He much preferred heading up the Syracuse campus security, to dealing with the unreasonably violent and angry men and women of New Mexico.

Patrols had placed him on light-duty for a month; minimal hours spent mostly observing the new trainees. Hours upon hours preparing for an unexpected teaching position consumed the majority of his first three weeks of convalescence. Now only one more week remained. Meanwhile, the book continued to mock him from its lofty position. Frustrated, his eyes surveyed the options.

There was an older woman he could ask for help; a Mrs. Taaffe, by her name tag, who sat at the library's main desk. But his gaze was caught by the young lady presently on a ladder, with her own gaze entrapped in the stained-glass windows. She was a rare and beautiful flower...and he'd suffered his fair share of thorns of late.

He'd noticed her the first time he visited this library after his return from New Mexico. He wasn't sure what it was about her, but he was captivated. Completely. She looked to be young, but he couldn't be sure. In everything he'd seen of her, she didn't behave like other girls, even girls his age. Perhaps she was older than she looked. He didn't know. Maybe he noticed her because he saw others notice her, but he wasn't sure what drew their attention either.

She was beautiful, but you'd only notice if you took the time to look at her; which he did, often. Her posture was upright, yet somehow withdrawn. Her features were feminine and soft, though nothing was particularly striking enough to explain the stares she received. Her hair was a pretty color, an indefinable shade between blond and brunette, but was always up in a loose bun. If she wore it that way out of convenience or in an effort to evade attention, he didn't know. It did show off the slender curve of her neck. She almost always wore a skirt or dress, but the style was modest and in colors that almost begged to go unnoticed. Unlike other women who desperately flaunted their figures, she dressed as if she were trying to hide hers. But try as she might to camouflage herself, she failed.

# Unspoken Words

Her head stayed down as she worked, unless someone spoke to her. Then she would look up with a smile; not flirtatious, just kind. And there were times, like now, when she looked like an angel as she stood on a ladder with her eyes open wide and her chin tilted upward. The only time he saw her stare intently at anything was when she stared at the stained glass.

"Excuse me, Miss?" She jumped and he braced to catch the girl if she fell. Gripping the ladder to steady herself, she adjusted to the surprise. With a breath, she smiled down at him. "I'm sorry; I didn't mean to startle you. I was hoping you could help me. I've been searching for *Compromising to Peace*, but I've been unable to find it. Could you help me locate it?" That wasn't the truth, but he could live with that. He did need her help.

"Of course." Her soft voice was reserved, reflecting a gentleness he seldom heard. As she climbed down the ladder, he noticed she had perfected the art of ascending and descending ladders while holding her dress in such a way as to keep her figure safe from wandering eyes. Not that his eyes were wandering...

Her feet on the ground now, she picked up a stack of books that sat to the side of the ladder. "It's just this way." Leading him to the aisle he'd just come from, and setting the stack of books on the floor, the girl retrieved a ladder and climbed to the top. "Unfortunately," she called down in whisper to him, "you aren't quite tall enough to have seen it."

When her feet touched the ground again, her eyes didn't quite meet his, but she graced him with a smile as she handed him the book. He accepted the book, letting his fingers graze hers briefly. Judging by the soft blush in her cheeks, he easily discerned she was nervous. She had to be very young to blush so easily.

"Thank you very much. I would have been searching for this all day."

Well, he would have been at least staring up at it all day.

"I'm glad I could help you. Please let me know if you need anything else." She knelt to retrieve her books.

"I'm Jackson, by the way," he blurted out in an attempt to continue the conversation with her.

"It's very nice to meet you, Jackson." She smiled as she stood. "I'm Evelyn." And she was gone.

It was a few days later when Jackson learned Evelyn was only nineteen. How'd he get himself interested in a nineteen-year-old? Maybe that was part of what he found so attractive about her, her youthful innocence. He wouldn't act on his attraction, but that resolution couldn't keep her out of his head.

Between his own courses and the one he now taught, he had a heavy load of research to do; research he was happy to do in the library. That was the excuse he gave himself. But he caught himself looking at her, often, and always preferred seeking her help when he needed it. Even sometimes when he didn't. For that he didn't have an excuse. The pull on his heart to be near her was more than he could understand.

In the weeks after they met, vulgar conversations whispered about Evelyn plagued his ears. Nothing suggested she behaved in a manner to inspire these base comments and profane daydreams muttered cowardly from one lowlife to another. Jackson's blood boiled the first time he overheard something spoken. It was easy to imagine the horror coloring Evelyn's cheeks if she heard what these creeps were saying.

The second day it happened, it was officers serving under him who made the comments. He silenced them with a stern look and proceeded to work them over ruthlessly during their next shifts, just to make sure they understood. With a few of the other comments he heard, he forced patience on himself and used terse words to end the chatter.

His patience wore down. This needed to end.

"You think she's been with a man before?" Jackson's eyes jumped to Evelyn. A man at the table in front of him nudged the guy to his right but his eyes remained locked on her as well.

"How should I know?" Safe answer. Smart.

"Look at her."

Jackson watched Evelyn as she busied herself putting books away again. He couldn't recall ever seeing any of the other employees doing the heavy lifting she did. Her arms stretched up as she stood on tip-toe to slip a book into place. Her body was a perfect hourglass.

"I'll bet I could get her into bed." Jackson's knuckles went white. He needed to punch something. "The good girls are always the best."

He waited for Evelyn to walk down a row of books and out of sight before making his move. The cad's eyes grew two sizes when he saw it was Jackson who had him by the collar. Good. He knew who he was, and he was smart enough not to make a scene.

"You should've thought twice before talking about her like that." The air left the man's lungs with a whoosh. Jackson had to shake the aggression out of his fists once he had him pinned against the wall. He'd always had a temper that tended to get away from him. This time he thought it served a better purpose than just venting his anger, as the man looked like a scared kid now that Jackson had him cornered. Still, scared wasn't enough. He needed to be taught a lesson.

"I didn't know she was with you," the now repentant cad choked out.

"Now, what makes you think she's with me?" Jackson growled.

"I…you…" Too much stammering. Jackson threw his forearm into the kid's stomach, releasing his vice grip, and let him collapse like a sack of flour on the floor.

"I don't need to be with a woman to keep men from degrading her like you were." He shouldn't leave him on the ground. He rolled his shoulders out before he picked him up by his collar again. "You won't be speaking about ladies that way anymore. Am I understood?"

He nodded and hurried away as soon as Jackson gestured for him to do so. Jackson took a stroll around the library before returning to his seat. Evelyn was oblivious to the event, talking to an animated woman wearing bright pink high heels. He smiled and returned to his seat. The kid and his buddy were nowhere to be seen.

The library was silenced from such comments after that.

## FALL SEMESTER 2162

Evelyn sighed as she gripped the railing along the stairs leading up to her apartment. A day of lectures and debates left her in desperate need of a quiet night at home. Oh, and a bubble bath sounded delightful.

Her key turned too easily in the door, alerting her that the door had already been unlocked. They only left it unlocked when someone had company. Evelyn's spirits went through the floor as the chatter of a room full of people greeted her when she turned the doorknob and opened the door.

Sarah had friends over. Splendid.

Tall, voluptuous, with silky almost-black-hair, Sarah exuded sensuality. She'd been roommates with Evelyn and Bekah for about six months. She was gorgeous, and well aware of it.

Her friends were of the same mold; a pretentious and uncaring mix of people, most of them men.

Evelyn would be staying in her room.

She much more preferred Bekah to Sarah. She kept that to herself of course; it wasn't a kind thought. But she and Bekah had been roommates for the past three years and, like Bekah, her friends were a lot of fun. They were welcoming. Evelyn didn't feel like an intruder in her own apartment with Bekah's friends.

It was rare for Evelyn to know any of Sarah's friends. Those familiar to her, she only knew from a shared class and they never acknowledged her. Tonight, though, was different.

How long had it been since she'd seen him? Three? Four years? Thomas Williamson. The only boy she'd known as a child, he was the son of the government official who ran the orphan programs, including the one she grew up in. He begrudgingly tagged along with his father every time her home had an inspection. Tom was a few years older and had never been exactly nice to her. The Madames of her home insisted she be cordial with him. She didn't learn until later that it was because children who defended themselves against his cruelty managed to find themselves dismissed from the programs.

With Tom in Patrols now, and his father still being a powerful man, perhaps it would still be wise to play at being nice to him.

There were some advantages to her roommate having self-important friends; Evelyn was barely noticed when she walked in. Maybe he wouldn't recognize her. Maybe he would leave her alone. She smiled shyly to the one girl who looked in her direction and started making her way to her room.

"Evie?"

It was too much to ask for. But it was something that he bothered to remember her name. Inhaling deeply, she turned to face him, bracing for whatever sport he intended to make of her. She was awkward, standing still, not saying anything; but she didn't know what to say. Tom was relaxed, sitting on her couch next to Sarah.

Sarah looked irritated that Tom's attentions had strayed from her.

"I wondered if it was you when Sarah told me she had a roommate named Evelyn." Tom looked her up and down boldly. "You aren't the little girl I used to tease, are you? I'd say you're all grown up now."

Embarrassment burned her cheeks.

Sarah's hand ran over Tom's knee; an attempt to regain his attention. "Tom, leave her alone. You're embarrassing the little girl."

She failed.

"Get over here," Tom ordered Evelyn, nudging Sarah over to make room for her. Evelyn had never seen anyone nudge Sarah to do anything, and she didn't look happy about it.

There was simply no way out of it now. With every eye on her, Evelyn did as Tom asked and joined them, sitting right between him and Sarah. Sarah's annoyance was palpable. Tom's pleasure was…curious.

"Tell me," he started, "how old are you now?"

It was tricky sitting between Tom and Sarah, and talking with Tom. When Evelyn turned herself to talk to Tom directly, she had her back to Sarah, blocking her out of their conversation. If she kept her back against the couch, she ended up talking away from Tom, instead of to him. She hated the whole situation. "I'm twenty."

Tom laughed, a little too loudly. "She was nine years old when I met her! She was a scrawny little thing, too," he told the others. "You know, you were never any fun to tease. You always took it so well. I don't think I tried harder at anything than when I tried to rile you up. It made me so mad." He was laughing again.

"I assure you," Sarah said, attempting to steal into the conversation, "she's much easier to work up now."

Evelyn forced a smile and looked down at her restless hands, willing them to be still.

"Come on." Tom knocked Evelyn with his elbow. "Evie's a rock! I bet I could still pull at her braids all day and she'd just sit there." To her horror, he started tickling her, poking at her ribs! "Right, Evie? You're still a little rock." She gripped his hands to stop him and his bellowing laugh rang out. "Well, I guess I was right before; you're not that little girl anymore. But I bet you're a pretty fierce woman."

Her stomach twisted at the way he'd said it.

"Evie," Sarah used the name Tom called her. Bekah called her by it as well, but Sarah had never used it until now. "Didn't you say this morning you have a big assignment you need to work on tonight?"

Evelyn stood. She didn't care that it was a bold-faced lie on Sarah's part. She let her relief show when she smiled back at Sarah. "Yes, you're right." She turned back to Tom, not wanting to seem rude. The Madames' warning still rang clear in her mind. "Tom, it was nice seeing you again." She almost ran out of the room, hoping that would be the last time she would have Thomas Williamson in her apartment.

# Chapter 2

When days passed with no sight nor mention of Tom, Evelyn was content to think she wouldn't be seeing any more of him. Sure, he was handsome. And yes, he appeared to flirt with her. But the man was clearly the same little boy who tormented her as a child. That alone meant he was dangerous.

Sarah was spending more time away from the apartment than usual, confirming Evelyn's theory that she didn't want to bring Tom back after he ignored her in favor of Evelyn. That was fine with her.

Evelyn's walk to work was a wonderful time to think. Often times, when a car or bus would pass, her mind was set to wondering what it would have been like to live in a society where the masses drove cars. Streets lined with the busyness of traffic slowed after the Middle East closed their sales of oil to the U.S.A. It came almost to a halt when Texas split off, taking Alaska and all of its oil with them. The vast majority of the vehicles seen on the road now were electric, mostly buses, and only traveled up to forty miles an hour, at best. The government, and the very wealthy, used some of the old diesels, but pictures were about all that was left from the era of motor-vehicles.

The hairs on her arms rose at the thought of riding in one of those old-time vehicles. Driving one would be exhilarating. But she didn't drive, and that was the smallest hurdle she'd have to overcome to accomplish that. But that kind of speed, it was a dream.

Mrs. Taaffe was leaving for her break when Evelyn arrived at work. Evelyn guessed the older woman was in her late sixties. She was a simple woman with strict rules and Evelyn greatly enjoyed working for her. Taaffe's expectations of her employees were always clear, and she was not one for idle chatter. Unlike the other employees, Evelyn didn't mind that at all and liked Mrs. Taaffe very much. The woman didn't like nonsense and she didn't smile often, but was fair and honest and always treated people with respect. She was a good woman.

Last week's shipment of new books towered next to the library's ancient computer, waiting to be scanned into the system. After that rather tedious procedure, it would be Evelyn's job to find a way to make them fit on the shelves. She sighed and settled into the less physical work.

As was her custom, her eyes took an initial sweep of the building. Jackson was back. She smiled to herself, feeling silly though she couldn't help it. It felt better having him there. Safer.

Some time later, a bobbing blond head pulled Evelyn's eyes from her task. She set the book in her hand aside and smiled at the approaching little girl. Helping children was a treasured part of her job. They were always sweet and so very excited to check out their books. This little one was particularly adorable. Big green eyes shone from her sweet face and white-blond hair escaping her ponytail gave her face a carefree frame. Her walk had a happy little bounce to it as she came to the desk smiling widely.

"Hi, lady. I can't find my book." Just her head showed above the desk.

"Would you like me to help you find it?" Evelyn smiled down at her.

The girl smiled even wider, her eyes squinting under the pressure of her pink, adorably full, cheeks. "Yes, please!"

Evelyn stood and came around her desk to crouch next to the child. She found that the little ones enjoyed adults coming down to their level. She knew from her own childhood the confidence one could instill in a child with a simple gesture of respect. "Before I help you, I think we should properly introduce ourselves."

The little girl rocked on her heels, thrusting her hand in Evelyn's direction. "My name's Ashley. What's yours?"

"Ashley, that's a very pretty name." The little girl beamed at the compliment. "My name is Evelyn. Now that we're properly introduced, what book are you looking for?"

Ashley's eyebrows came together; clearly, she was frustrated. And adorable. "Well, I can't remember. But it's yellow and there's a doggy and a bunny snuggling on it. Oh, and the bunny is grey."

Evelyn smiled for the hundredth time at sweet Ashley. Mrs. Taaffe would have been annoyed with this precious girl not knowing the book's name. But like everything else about the girl, Evelyn found it adorable. "I think I know just the book you're talking about. Let's go find it together, shall we?"

Jackson was enjoying watching Evelyn interact with this little girl. He, of course, noticed her the moment she walked through the library doors, but his attempt to keep his eyes on his work dissolved when he saw the joy on her face at the approaching child. It wasn't the first time he'd seen her light up when a child went to her for help. She would make an excellent mother one day.

Thoughts about Evelyn as a wife and a mother had been invading his thoughts more and more since the first time he'd laid eyes on her. In all the relationships he'd been in, he never once thought about those girls in those roles. Now this girl, who he was quite certain held not a single romantic thought for him, was stirring the desire for a wife, a family, deep within him. It was more than a little frustrating, but a pleasurable frustration.

Still, he really didn't need to be thinking about her that way.

Evelyn led the skipping child by the hand to find her book. As usual, it took Evelyn only a moment to locate what she was looking for. When she crouched down with the child to hand her the book, the little girl threw her arms around Evelyn and knocked her back, sitting her quite flat on the floor. Jackson coughed to cover his laugh and forced his eyes back to his work.

"Tom!"

Tom grabbed her arm as she was walking back to the front desk and pinned her between himself and a bookshelf.

"Goodness, you scared me. Did you need help with something?"

"No," he answered casually. "I just wanted to talk to you. We didn't get to talk much the other night."

Evelyn focused her nervous energy into playing with a loose thread on her sleeve. "Was there something specific you wanted to talk about?" He stepped closer and she instinctively leaned into the bookshelf.

"I just wanted to see you again."

Had she heard him right? He wanted to see her again? Her eyes had been looking everywhere but his face until now; her hands, the floor, the shelves behind him. She looked at him now.

It was easy to see why Sarah was so possessive of him. Tom had been an attractive boy, but he too had grown up since they played – if you could call it that – together as children. His strong jaw was set with confidence and his blue eyes held such fierceness they seemed to pierce you. If your gaze managed to escape his, they landed on his broad shoulders, or firm chest, or his muscle-wrapped forearms protruding from his rolled sleeves.

Nowhere was safe to look on him.

"How are you?" Tom finally asked.

The man spoke as much through his body as through his words. Maybe more-so, if she was reading him correctly. But she read books better than she read men.

"I'm fine. I should get back to work though." She spoke slowly, trying to make sense of him, trying not to offend him. She had a difficult time separating this grown man from the boy who once tormented her so. It was more difficult still distinguishing the orphan girl she once was from the woman she had grown to be.

Tom shifted his body into her path. "Come on, Evie. You don't have five minutes for me?"

She eyed him skeptically, not sure if risking offending him was a good idea. Could he really have changed this much in just a few short years? "I'm sorry. I'm being rude. Of course I have five minutes for you."

His smile was triumphant, and she had to admit, also quite dazzling.

"So, tell me, are you seeing anyone?"

He was setting her up to be teased, she was sure of it and lost any confidence she might have had moments before. "I am not."

He laughed. "Too many to choose from, huh?"

She looked at him again, very confused. Too many had never been the problem.

His satisfied expression sent a chill down her spine. He apparently spoke and read body language fluently. "Well, that's good news for me. I won't have to deal with competition."

What was going on? "I…I need to get back to work." She was glad when he stepped out of her way, letting her return to work.

Evelyn blindly followed her feet along the well-worn carpet, desperate to escape Tom and his confusing messages. She pressed a shaking palm against her chest when she saw him leave the library, heaving a sigh of relief.

As her heart slowed to normal, her eyes settled upon a set of very white knuckles atop a clenched fist. She followed the tension up the arm, the shoulder…her feet had taken her to Jackson, and his head was aimed at the door Tom had just walked through.

Slowly, as if he sensed her presence – which was absurd – his fist relaxed. His arm and back followed suit and in a steady motion, he peered over his shoulder with a smile for her.

Her eyes dropped, but she returned his smile with one of her own before returning to her work.

# Chapter 3

"Guess who's in a good mood tonight?" Bekah greeted Evelyn with rolling eyes.

Bekah was sporting one of her signature outfits that night; oversized sweatshirt, ripped jeans, and neon-yellow stilettos. According to Bekah, your shoes didn't make the outfit, they were the outfit…everything else was just accessories. Unlike Sarah, Bekah wasn't sultry, but rather a natural beauty wrapped up in a quirky package. The bright yellow stilettos testified to that. She had small facial features, except for her eyes that were alive with joy and mischief. Her espresso hair was chopped short. She was always saying she liked the way it felt when she swished her head around. She wasn't tall, but her personality – and her heels – made her seem bigger than she was.

Bekah was the liveliest girl Evelyn had ever met. One never had to guess at how she felt or what she was thinking because Bekah wore her heart on her sleeve and if asked – even sometimes when she wasn't – she would tell anyone exactly what she thought. Everyone liked her. She was fun, upbeat, unconventional, and a flirt. But most of all, she was good.

"Do you know what she's mad about?" Evelyn asked in a low voice, worried a petulant Sarah would hear her and bring her ruckus to them.

Bekah grabbed the glass of milk she was drinking off the counter and sat at the kitchen table, putting her feet up on the chair next to hers. "She's probably just upset the sun was out today."

Evelyn wondered if it didn't have something to do with her talking to Tom at the library earlier that day. The woman had a way of knowing too much.

Sarah's door opened and closed with a thud. Their conversation halted just before Sarah appeared, dressed for a night out. She was the kind of woman whose presence made other women suddenly self-conscious and men's mouths hang open. Tonight's ensemble would tempt a lot of men. Though, judging by the way she had behaved the other night, and the hostility her eyes held for Evelyn, she was probably only out for Tom. Evelyn couldn't help but wonder if she'd be successful. How could she not? She was Sarah. Still…

"Where you off to, Sunshine?" Bekah asked, poking at Sarah's already irritated disposition. At least it took her eyes off of Evelyn.

Sarah had an astounding way of composing herself. In fact, other than irritation, she seemed a woman void of emotion. Sarah stood a bit taller as she scrutinized Bekah. Evelyn winced at the thought of her roommates' unspoken peace-treaty dissolving…or rather, exploding.

"I'll be back late."

That was it. Thank goodness. Sarah checked her purse for something and left. Evelyn and Bekah both smiled with pleasure.

"Have you eaten dinner yet?" Evelyn asked, rummaging through the fridge.

"Nope," Bekah answered. "Just got home a little before you."

She kept staring at the contents of the fridge. "Would it be horrible if we just ate nachos?"

"Yes, but who cares? That sounds amazing."

Bekah chatted happily about her day as she helped Evelyn dice, chop, arrange chips, onions, meat, jalapeños…which was something of an amazement because Bekah hated cooking. After everything was assembled, they collapsed on the couch with their plates piled high.

"I like evenings like this," Bekah said with a mouth full of chips and toppings. "Why'd we ever decide to get another roommate?" Her words were followed by the crunching of a well-loaded chip.

"Bekah!" Evelyn scolded, trying not to laugh. "That's not nice."

Bekah smiled shamefully. "I know, but neither is she. But," another sigh, "she does help with rent, so that's something I guess."

Evelyn shook her head. Sarah wasn't her favorite person either, but she'd never been comfortable speaking behind others' backs. "Just eat your food and be quiet."

"Oh yeah, like that's going to happen," Bekah retorted. "But, I'll stop talking about Miss Priss. Mmm," she said, taking another bite. "So good! Oh, speaking of so good, have you seen some of the guys on Patrols? One of the trainers, well, I think he's a trainer...who knows? Who cares? Anyway, he is gorgeous! Do you know the one I'm talking about?"

Evelyn kept her reply to a laugh.

"That's right, you avoid their training course. I don't know any woman in her right mind who would avoid that. Besides the eye-candy," she winked, "they had a flyer posted about the school race this spring! They're using the training course as part of it. You're still running with me, right?

A heavy sigh escaped, her head falling back against the couch. The school race...a time for friendly competition and campus camaraderie. Her cup of tea exactly.

They had run the last two years together. Evelyn did enjoy the actual running and the challenge of the obstacles. Bekah liked it for the crowds and always found a way to draw attention to them. Evelyn did not like attention.

Bekah pursed her lips. "Big baby. You know it's fun."

"I have always wanted to run their course." Just not with people watching.

They both cleaned their plates and Bekah offered to clean the kitchen, so Evelyn headed to her room. She had a heavy load of studying and homework to finish before bed.

## Chapter 4

The smell of desperation and alcohol thickened the air as Jackson maneuvered through the horde of people crowding the dance floor. His eyes stayed on his target, hoping to discourage the women trying to bait him. If their half-dressed figures weren't enough to entice a man, their hands gliding over him were more than sufficient to break most men's resolve. But not his.

He still wasn't sure why he let his friends convince him to come out. He'd been to plenty of places like this, but since returning from New Mexico, he no longer enjoyed them. Too often the night ended with him having to break up a fight because some drunken idiot looked at some other drunken idiot's woman the wrong way. Even worse was when the drunken idiots were women, degraded and enflamed by the liquor running through their veins.

That was the downside of working for Patrols; you were never officially off-duty.

"Jack, you made it," George called out, shaking his hand when Jackson reached their table.

Jackson met George his first semester of college. They were in the same training group for Patrols and became easy friends. George was witty and entertaining, but their friendship lasted because he was more than that. He was smart and had an uncanny ability to discern situations and people. And more than that, George was honest. He was one of the few men who didn't let Jackson intimidate him. George held him accountable, even when Jackson didn't want him to. They were brothers in arms, and brothers in faith.

Now George rented a room from him and Jackson couldn't ask for a better housemate. George was incredibly laid back and rarely home. The running joke was that they saw each other more at work than at the house.

"Yeah," Jackson said, taking the empty seat next to George. "Figured I could use a night off." He'd worked every night for the past three weeks. Evidence of extremist activity had been turning up, and with his experience in New Mexico landing him the label of 'Extremist Expert,' he was thrown into meeting after meeting because of it. Their overly complacent commanders were in an upheaval over the chaos plaguing their usually peaceful town. They weren't accustomed to being hassled by extremists; or rather, they were intentionally and blissfully ignorant of them.

In the past year of being a captain, Jackson had found too many trails of extremist activities that had gone unnoticed. He suspected it was more likely that they'd been ignored. Break-ins were occurring with higher frequency and becoming increasingly violent. Something was going on, but with no leads, he couldn't get a glimpse of the big picture.

George had been in many of those counter-extremist meetings. It was after a particularly wearisome meeting, teeming with panicked officials, that George invited him to this.

"Let me introduce you to everyone," George called over the noise. Starting with the man on the other side of him, George named them off. "You know Liam. This is Will, Everret, and Chase." He pointed to a familiar looking woman chatting at the bar. "And that's Candice, Will's wife."

The men all nodded their greetings and George waved a waitress over to order a round of drinks. The waitress was dressed more modestly than the others working that night, but wore the usual look of confusion Jackson received when he ordered black coffee. To her credit, she didn't question it. Since his homecoming, it became a rarity for Jackson to drink. He preferred the stimulant of caffeine to the haze of alcohol.

The waitress returned quickly with their drinks and laughed with the men, clearly enjoying their attention. Jackson could understand her friendliness. She looked to be about his age and it was easy to assume she would be irritated with the drunks and young philanderers who made up a large number of her customers. He didn't, however, like the way her hand slid across his shoulders when she placed his drink on the table. A muscle in his arm flinched at the smirk on George's face. The man saw too much, as brothers often do.

"You men let me know if you need anything else," the waitress said, directing her smile at Jackson before turning to serve another table.

He was glad to have her gone.

He'd spent the majority of his college life enjoying the flirtations of women, now he was irked by them. He had become all too aware of how weak he was against fleshly desires and he never wanted to be a slave to them again. Sitting back, he listened to the conversation at his table and tried to ignore the rest of the bar. Their talk was focused on trouble they had run into on a bank run. He guessed they worked Armed Transports.

It was too soon when a pair of young females – he couldn't bring himself to call ladies – approached their table. Jackson watched the girls sizing up each of the men at his table, deciding who would be their ticket to a good time. The golden-blond trained her eyes on Jackson.

Fortunately for her, or not, golden-blonde was not his type. Nor was desperate. Jackson was grateful when Candice and the two women she was talking with joined them; even more for Candice making it clear that the young girls were unwelcome.

Liam and Chase didn't look as grateful for the rescue. He took another sip of his coffee to hide his amusement over their loss.

"I've heard a lot about you, Jack," Candice said, after her husband introduced them. "You're spoken very highly of in my office."

"It's nice to know I have a good name somewhere. Where do you work?" He stood while speaking, offering his chair to Candice's friend who had her eye on George.

Candice put her hand on her hip and glared at her husband. "William, how is it that this man is offering his chair to a woman who's practically a stranger before you offer yours to your wife?"

Putting his hands up in surrender, Will gave his wife his seat, wrapping his arms around her from behind. "Hey," he argued. "He's gotta do what he can to impress the ladies. I already have you."

"Yeah, yeah, yeah," Candice said, playfully waving him off. "To answer your question, Jack, I'm a Government Lawyer. My office is the building just east of the Cell Building."

"That's where I must have seen you before, then," Jackson commented. "I thought you looked familiar when George pointed you out. To be honest, I didn't think that office was too fond of me."

Candice smirked a little. "Well, maybe if half of the staff weren't single ladies, then that might be true. But even so, any case you're involved in is an easy win for us. You don't leave any loose ends. We all appreciate it."

"That's Jack for you," George teased. "Always making the rest of us look bad."

Jackson just rolled his eyes and let the conversation drift to another topic. When he spotted Tom dancing with a woman, he lost the conversation entirely. What he could only describe as jealous anger coursed through him at the possibility of Tom bringing Evelyn to such a place. But the woman he was with now was not Evelyn. Confident. Indiscrete. Arrogant. She wasn't anything at all like Evelyn, nor did she look the type to let Tom's interests wander. And Tom looked rather enthralled with her.

When his eyes made it back to their table, he noticed Liam was locked on to Tom and the woman as well, and it wasn't desire nor lust that darkened his gaze. They made eye-contact for a moment, and Liam's intensity was gone, masterly disguised behind his previous laid-back persona. He clearly had some insight on the pair. The question was, was it just insight, or did he have a history with them?

The evening continued with minor disturbances, and Jackson relaxed and joined into the boisterous conversations around him. But as his defenses lowered, the women grew bolder. A few different girls looked like they had just worked up the courage to approach him, when he decided to leave. There was only one woman who's interest he'd welcome, and she wasn't present.

## Chapter 5

He was waiting for Evelyn when she got out of class. Tom. Two weeks had passed since he cornered her at work, and even though she never told him what classes she was taking, there he was. Sarah. She's the only one who would have told him anything. Strange considering her previous behavior. The girl was surely up to something.

Tom, walking straight for her, snapped her back to reality.

"Hey Evie." Tom greeted her with a suspicious tilt to his lips.

She smiled, but if felt tight. "Good morning, Tom. What are you doing here?"

"Are you always going to sound so annoyed when you see me?" he asked, falling into step with her. "I wanted to see you. I thought that'd be easy enough for you to figure out."

"I'm sorry," she quickly apologized. "You surprised me is all." And worried her.

"What are you doing tonight?" Tom asked, sounding indifferent enough.

"I plan on being home. Why?"

"It just so happens," he began, "that I'll be coming by this evening. Sarah invited a couple of us over. I just wanted to make you admit you'd be home before I told you."

Evelyn grimaced. "I don't think Sarah's planning on me being part of that."

"I don't think she cares," Tom argued. "Besides, you live there too."

Evelyn stopped to look at him. "Listen, Tom, it's nice that you want to include me, but I really don't think I'd be welcome, and I really don't mind it."

# Unspoken Words

Something in his eyes made her suddenly very nervous. When he spoke, his tone was low and forceful. "If you don't want me there, just tell me, and I won't go. I'm only going to see you, Evie."

She felt her own eyes widen in surprise. "No, I didn't...I didn't mean to offend you. I didn't know...I just..." She shook her head. Why couldn't she think straight? Should she be nervous? Confused? Flattered? "I'll be there."

"Good. I'll see you tonight then." His eyes flickered over her, making her blush, before he turned and left.

As Sarah's friends arrived, Evelyn hid in the safety of the kitchen. A rare few acknowledged her existence with a raised brow, but mostly she remained invisible.

Tom was the last to show up. His scan of the room was cut short by the few women who were present, each taking their turn hugging him tightly in greeting. Lingering touches and flirtatious smiles made their hopes of catching his attentions obvious. Each of them failed.

His jaw set a line of irritation when he didn't see Evelyn among his friends. Sarah waited for him with a look of impish delight. Powerful strides crossed him to her quickly.

Sarah nodded Evelyn's direction and Tom's eyes finally spotted his target.

Standing quietly in her kitchen, Evelyn looked like the little girl he'd met eleven years ago. Tom couldn't believe he hadn't noticed Evelyn standing there, though it was clearly what she wanted. That didn't surprise him. She didn't dress to attract attention, she didn't make eye contact with anyone, and she didn't make a sound. Their eyes only met for a moment before she smiled shyly and lowered her lashes. He smiled to himself as he watched her shift her weight nervously at his approach.

He knew how to seduce a woman, but Evie was different. It didn't take a suggestive touch or a seductive comment to make her nervous; it was just him, and he reveled in it. He always had. When she was a child, he marveled at the calm she could cloak herself in, even as he teased her; though her hands always gave her nerves away. And that courageous fire he saw in her eyes when she came to another's defense impressed him.

He didn't know anyone could be so powerful and yet so still in the same moment until he met her.

She was a bewitching mixture of things he'd previously known impossible to coexist. Meek but strong. Female but honest. Serene...but he could make her nervous. Now that she was a woman, he desperately wanted her for himself. He hungered to see that fire in her eyes again, but it was a new game now.

His senses awoke as he felt her tense at his closeness. He wouldn't say anything. Not yet. Instead, he joined her in leaning against the counter and draped his arm across her shoulders. It was a casual gesture, but her response was anything but. She was nervous indeed.

Tom looked down at Evelyn, flashing a less-than-pleased look. "Everyone here is going to think you hate me if you stand like that." He studied her for a minute. "You have no idea how to act with a man, do you?" He laughed as heat flooded her face. "Just relax, I'll teach you. You can start by leaning into me instead of acting like the thought of touching me hurts you."

Through her trembling, Evelyn obeyed. It would be a challenge for him to move slowly enough to not scare her away, especially with his hunger for her growing as it was. But he'd do it. She was one woman worth the work.

The others, always so slow to catch on to anything, finally noticed he'd shown his favor for her. The nasty looks from the other girls he didn't care about. They were idiots for thinking they had a chance with him anyway. Sarah's smug smile rubbed him a bit, but it was the other guys who were challenging his temper. More than one set of eyes laid claim to her body. Time would tell if any of them would make the mistake of trying to take what was now his.

Tiring of pretending he actually cared what the others were talking about, Tom dropped his lips to Evelyn's ear.

"You're beautiful today. I meant to tell you when I saw you earlier. I haven't stopped thinking about you since the first time I saw you here." He paused to steady himself. Lust was taking over. "And don't worry, it makes you even more attractive, how pure you are...your not knowing what to do with a man."

Evelyn's eyes fluttered. His words were honey and she couldn't help but savor them.

Tom smiled wickedly at her fidgeting hands, a telltale sign of her nerves. He didn't have to say any more, but he couldn't stop his hand from slipping down to her hip. If she were any other woman, he'd take her to a back room that moment. But she was Evie. She was different.

Evelyn quickly realized her apartment was just their meeting place before heading out dancing. Sarah flashed a deceptively sweet smile at Tom and Evelyn while putting on her jacket. The shudder Evelyn tried to suppress wasn't hidden from Tom, but it did surprise him. Apparently, little Evie saw Sarah for the viper she was.

"Evie, you're coming out with us, right?" Sarah mocked in disguise.

"Sorry, not tonight. I have work early tomorrow." Evelyn shrugged, trying to make it look like she was disappointed and that there was nothing she could do about it.

"Come on, Evie," Tom pushed, turning his hips toward her. Her attempt to hide her panic was adorable. "Come out with us. Come out with me."

Somehow…somehow...she stood her ground. "Honestly, I do have work tomorrow."

"Ok, not tonight," he conceded after a heavy silence, but he wasn't about to let her off the hook. Instead, he slid his arms around her waist and pulled her against him. She tensed but didn't reject him. "Evie, this is where you would hug me back." He spoke with his lips against her ear, smiling at her obedience. "You'll come out with me next time, won't you?"

Evelyn tried to back away from him, but he held her tighter. He was a solid wall of warmth against her.

"I'm not letting go until you promise you'll go dancing with me."

She could barely breathe, and not just from the strength of his arms surrounding her. "I will," she whispered. "I promise."

Tom's breath caught when he let her go. She was a vision of purity and goodness…and her eyes were on him. "Next Saturday, then." She wouldn't have been safe from him tonight.

She swallowed hard. "Next Saturday."

## Chapter 6

The days before the nerve-wracking Saturday flew by. Tom waited for Evelyn at the end of every class after that to walk her home, always flirting and with his arm over her shoulders. But she never invited him in. She would thank him, and he would leave looking frustrated, but determined. Always determined. There was something, still, she hadn't figured out about him, though she couldn't begin to know what it was.

Then Saturday came. Evelyn had work early again and was grateful Tom had work as well so he couldn't walk her. She was nervous enough as it was. With knots in her stomach, she dressed in a black long-sleeved blouse tucked into a high-waisted, loose gray skirt that fell mid-calf, slipped into her black flats and her jacket, and set off for work.

The library was teeming with frantic undergraduates studying for midterms, and as she assumed it would be, her day entailed helping student after student locate their oh-so-needed but waited-until-the-last-second-to-read books. After hours of scaling ladders and finding and returning books to their shelves, her arms and feet ached. It had been a wise decision to not wear heels today. A weak sigh escaped Evelyn's lips when she finally found a moment to rest from her weariness. What a relief it was to see that only twenty minutes of work remained…until she remembered what her evening held. Her shoulders slumped in exhaustion.

"Long day?"

"Jackson." She never knew if the inability to steady her breathing was from being startled, or if it was just the effect he had on her.

Since their first meeting over a year ago, his face had become a familiar, and very welcome one, at the library. He wasn't like the other students. Aside from his physicality setting him apart, he was a real gentleman. He always looked her in the eyes, though she rarely met those deep eyes with her own. After that first day, he never let her climb a ladder to retrieve his books. She had the impression he was hurt when they had met. His face would strain when he used his right arm to reach for anything, but she was too shy to ask, and he never acknowledged it. But that was long gone now.

Her mind fluttered back to a bitter storm that had blown in at the end of their last winter break. It was the sort of storm one only braved if you had to, so the library was empty. Evelyn didn't enjoy her commute to work on such mornings. Walking the whole way in the brutal conditions would be absurd; even the short walks to and from the bus left her shivering.

The holidays never held enough work to keep Evelyn busy. She typically ended up reading the books as she re-shelved them. As a result, she added a minor degree to her education with ease. On the day of the storm, she had knocked into a full cart of books. Loneliness sounded as the scattering books echoed through the vaulted room. Kneeling down, she allowed her head to hang in discouragement, just for a moment. When she reached for one of the fallen books, her hand landed on Jackson's. It was just one of the many times his presence startled her. He had smiled a friendly smile, sending heat through her, and made pleasant conversation as he helped pick up all the books. She wasn't used to people helping her and she left work that day with a warmth she couldn't explain.

"You have a tendency to sneak up on me." She smiled up at the man. "And yes, it has been a long day. But it's been a good day too."

Jackson eyed her with kind suspicion. He could see that she was exhausted, but he wasn't surprised that she didn't complain. She never complained. "Do you at least get to go home and rest soon?"

"Yes…well, I get to go home, but I'm not sure if I'll be getting any rest."

Jackson leaned against the counter that she sat behind. Her stomach did a little flip. "What do you have going on that'll keep you from resting?"

"A friend made me promise to go out dancing tonight." She tried to hide her grimace. For a minute it looked like he was going to ask her something. She hoped he wouldn't ask her who that friend was. The idea of admitting to Jackson that she was going out with Tom was unsettling.

"I'm sure you will have a great time. Just promise me you'll be safe."

"I will do my best." Evelyn frowned. She was neglecting her job. "I'm so sorry, Jackson. I'm talking too much about myself. Is there something I can help you with?"

"No. I just wanted to say hi on my way out. Have fun tonight." He smiled and turned to leave. Evelyn was still looking at him when he stopped and turned back. "Evelyn, please be careful tonight."

And he left. Evelyn was left with ridiculous butterflies in her stomach from the way he had smiled at her, and blushing with embarrassment from having been caught watching him leave.

The knot in her stomach grew as she walked home, and things only got worse when she got home.

"Good, you're home," Sarah snapped.

*What a greeting.*

Sarah's critical eye looked her up and down. "You can't wear that, or anything you own for that matter. Come on."

Evelyn followed her without a word and watched Sarah flip through her closet, throwing a couple pieces on the bed.

"There," she indicated. "Pick from those."

There was no way she could wear any of it. The tops were too low, the bottoms too short, and everything too tight!

"Oh gosh, Sarah!" Bekah materialized in the doorway. "What are you trying to do to our roommate?"

"She can't wear what she's got on," Sarah argued.

Bekah rolled her eyes. "Evelyn, put on your dark grey leggings and meet me in my room. You'll die from embarrassment if you have to wear any of this."

Evelyn obeyed gladly.

Bekah already had a few things out for her to look at when she got to her room. They decided on a black dress that hung comfortably but tight enough to blend in with Sarah's crowd, with a pair of black ankle boots.

"Why are you even going?" Bekah asked, as she began on her makeup.

"I promised Tom I'd go."

"Do you like Tom?" Bekah sounded like she hoped she would say no.

"I think so. I think he likes me. He says a lot of nice things, and he is very cute. But, I don't know. I thought it'd all be different. Sometimes I still have a hard time not seeing the boy who used to tease me." She didn't add that she liked feeling liked, or that it was nice to have someone flirt with her. It was embarrassing and Bekah wouldn't understand.

Bekah finished with her and Evelyn looked at her reflection in the mirror. She didn't look like herself, but she didn't look like Sarah either, and that was a good thing.

Bekah was silent for a minute. "Just be smart about him. Be careful. Ok?"

Evelyn smiled at her friend. "Don't worry, I'm good at careful."

## Chapter 7

George and Liam were the only two who had the evening free, and they welcomed a night out. After speaking with Evelyn, Jackson had decided it would be a good night for him to hang out with the guys. She was going dancing... maybe he'd get lucky and end up at the same place. Why couldn't he get her off his mind?

The crowd was rough tonight, and Jackson found himself hoping he wouldn't run into Evelyn.

"So, what do you think, Jack?" Liam was speaking to him.

"I'm sorry, I was thinking about something else. What do I think about what?"

"I never took you as a day dreamer, Jack," George laughed, slapping his shoulder. "We were talking about those two guys over there. I say they're planning something. Liam thinks I'm wrong."

He followed George's nod. The scheming twosome were easy to spot. "I hope you're wrong, George. I really wanted the night off."

Liam shook his head. "You two are just paranoid from all your top-secret meeting nonsense. You'd probably look at the three of us and think the same thing."

George and Liam continued to talk while Jackson used the two men as an excuse for continually scanning the room. It was close to eight when he saw Tom, flanked by a crowd of people. The woman he'd seen Tom with before was back as well, but it was clear now that they weren't together. Something about that disturbed him. A different girl stuck close to his side tonight. She seemed uncomfortable. His spirits dropped when he realized it was Evelyn.

She didn't look like herself tonight. She was done-up enough to blend in, but not enough to hide that she didn't fit in. He'd never seen her with her hair down, and he was sure he'd never seen her in anything like what she was wearing. Stunning. Even from his distance, he could tell she didn't like the attention she was drawing, but a change of outfit wouldn't hide her any better. She was too good for a place like this. Her innocence was something lewd men hunted after, and judging by the looks on more than a few men's faces, their target was her. The only comfort he had was knowing Tom wouldn't let another man touch her; but that boy was a danger in himself.

Jackson had to look away. The way Tom looked at her was enough to make Jackson want to hit him. Tom's hands on her as he guided her to the dance floor didn't help Jackson's mood, either.

Stepping into the bar had terrified Evelyn. If not for Tom's tugging hand, her feet would never have crossed the threshold. Walking in behind Sarah drew every man's eye to her. She couldn't hide her blush when Tom pulled her tightly to his side. Apparently he didn't like other men looking at her either.

Tom was saying something but the booming music drowned out his words.

"What?" she yelled.

Tom leaned in with an inviting smile, sending a tingle into her stomach. Being the center of his attention, or any man for that matter, was strange. If not for the fear she still fought for him, she'd even say it was nice.

"Dance with me."

Before she could protest, he had her on the dance floor. Laughter and music drowned out her fear. Tom smiled and winked graciously as her body slowly began to breathe in the rhythm of the songs.

When her feet finally managed to master the task of dancing with someone, Tom pulled her against him.

"It's better to not have to yell, don't you think?" he spoke against her ear. She hadn't ever danced with a man before, let alone so close. His hands moved down her side and she was suddenly overwhelmed by their closeness. Dancing this close was all about feeling, not thinking, and with his hands on her, she couldn't turn her mind off.

"You okay?" Tom asked. They were so close she knew he felt her muscles tense.

"I don't know," she admitted. "I mean, yes. I think so."

"I want to be gentle with you, Evie," he encouraged her, running a hand through her hair. "I don't want to scare you away."

Oh goodness, his hands... "I just don't know how to dance like this," she lied. All she had to do was follow his lead, and with their bodies against each other, she could feel his next step before he took it. Still, she wasn't sure if she wanted his hands on her like that.

"I would never have known if you didn't tell me," Tom reassured her. "You're very good at it."

Chills. There was so much unfamiliar tenderness in his voice. "Why are you paying so much attention to me?"

"Because," Tom said, kissing her shoulder. "You're different than any other girl I've known. You're sweet, and innocent." His hands found her hips, thighs... "And beautiful."

Bekah's warning voice echoed in her mind. "I think I'm going to get some water."

"Alright," he relented. "I'll get us drinks. You just want water?"

Evelyn forced a reassuring smile and nodded as he turned, headed for the bar. She couldn't have followed even if she had wanted to. The bar was sectioned off and you were only allowed past with an ID showing that you were twenty-one or older. She was still only twenty.

Every woman noticed Tom, but only a few were brave enough to join him where he stood. He didn't seem to encourage their attentions, but he didn't discourage them either. Evelyn wasn't sure how she felt about his nonchalance.

Leaning against a wall while watching Tom, she felt safer with support behind her, the unsettling feeling that someone was watching her pricked her skin. When she turned to see who it was, the stranger took it as his cue to make his move. Not wanting to show any sign of her nerves or her tendency to be intimidated, she stood taller as he walked towards her. A sudden longing for Jackson to be near ran through her. Curious longing to have at such a moment.

The stranger came and stood much too close. He was average in height and build, and looked to be in his later thirties. Some women probably found him attractive; he acted as if that's what he was used to. Though he wasn't old by any means, she had a strong distaste for older men preying on younger women. Even more so when they hung around college hangouts. It was creepy.

"I haven't seen you here before," the man said. The whiskey and peanuts mixing in his breath competed with the spice of his cologne. "This your first time out dancin'?"

"No." She lied, desperately hoping to discourage him.

"My name's Tyler." His tone suggested that she should feel privileged to be spoken to by him, and that she needed to show him the respect he expected.

"It's nice to meet you, Tyler."

Tom was still at the bar.

Jackson watched with indignation as one of the suspicious men pursued Evelyn's attention. What was Tom thinking leaving her alone? Each movement the man made moved him closer to her. His intentions were clear. When the man put his hands on her, Jackson stood to go remove him from her. To Jackson's surprise, and dissatisfaction, George had stood with him, digging his fingers into Jackson's arm with a death grip.

"Let Tom take care of it," George warned.

Jackson looked at his friend, willing to hit him to get to Evelyn. Ever-discerning, George must have sensed it because he stood taller and squared his shoulders.

"Jack, you've got no business there. Now sit down."

Tom noticed the unwelcome stranger and was making his way, determinedly, to Evelyn. Jackson huffed and sat down before looking at his friend again. "Am I that obvious?" He was still tense.

George laughed and took his seat next to him. It was astounding how quickly he could shake off a tense situation. "You've been watching her for some time; so yeah, you're that obvious. How do you know her, anyway? She looks pretty young."

"She is. I don't know her, not really. She works at the library down the road. I just know her from there."

George laughed again. "Jack and a sweet little librarian. I hate to tell you this, but I think you waited too long to make your move."

"I never intended to make one."

"So, what you're telling me is, you come out here to keep an eye on her, ready to knock a guy out just for looking at her the wrong way, willing to hit *me* for getting in your way…and you never intended to make a move?" George shook his head. "You know that doesn't make any sense, right?"

"Yep, I know it." Jackson and George looked up when they heard a crash. Hot-head-Tom had thrown the man into a table. Jackson would have been fine with that, applauded him even, except for the fact that now Tom had five other guys ready to fight him. One of them was bound to go for Evelyn since she was with him. *Idiots looking at other idiot's women…and the woman had to be her…*

"Alright," George said, standing with him. "Now it's your business."

Jackson jumped over the rail and headed straight for Tom. The first guy had already made his move at Tom. Jackson and George intercepted the others. As soon as Jackson knocked one of the attackers on the ground, he grabbed Tom's arm and swung him around. "You get Evelyn out of here, now!" To his relief, Tom nodded, grabbed Evelyn, and left.

Jackson usually fought clean and fair, but tonight he didn't mind leaving these men bruised and hurting. Security finally got involved in time to clean up the mess and throw the now bleeding men out.

"I'll let Liam know we're done for the night," George said after the chaos subsided.

"That's probably best." He didn't want to deal with anyone else that night. Violence was still boiling in him. It had felt too good to vent his frustration – and his temper – through his fists, which meant he probably had a lot of praying to do about it.

Evelyn clung to Tom's hand as they walked the final stretch of businesses that led to their campus. Now with the old highway separating them from the noise of local nightlife, the silence punctuated Tom's brooding intensity.

"Thank you," she tried, hoping to break through the tension. "For getting that man away from me."

It had all happened so fast. All Evelyn could really remember were snapshots. Tom's arm around her waist. Tyler's hand shoving Tom's shoulder back. Then Tyler flying over a table. She'd never been so close to a fight, and she disliked it as much as she thought she would. She was, however, grateful Tom was on her side that night. A shiver ran through her at the thought of being on the wrong side of his temper.

Tom didn't respond to her gratitude. Instead, he led her to the shadows underneath a tree and stood in front of her. She swallowed hard. Fire still swam in his eyes from the fight, but she was right to think it was not the only fire brewing in him.

"You've always done that; looked down when you're nervous," Tom said when she dropped her eyes. "When we were younger, you'd only look at me once I made you good and mad. Your eyes were so beautiful when you were angry. Sometimes I'd make you mad just so you would look at me. It took me a while to figure you out though. It wasn't until you caught me teasing another girl that you finally looked me in the eyes for the first time." He stepped closer to her. "Don't make me find someone to pick on right now just so you'll look at me."

Evelyn looked up at him and instinctively stepped back. She'd never seen that expression before, not directed at her. "I didn't realize I was so easy to read. I'll have to work on that." She took a deep breath, trying to steady her breathing. "I probably should be getting home." She went to step around him, but he captured her arm and gently pulled her back.

"I'm not an idiot," he said, his voice velvet. "As soon as we get to your place, you'll thank me for walking you home and then lock yourself safely away behind your door. We stopped here for a reason."

Her heart was in her throat. She liked Tom. She liked the way he looked at her, liked that he could protect her, but she wasn't ready for things to be anything more. She still didn't trust him. Her lips trembled as she tried to smile and not sound terrified. "I don't know what you're talking about."

"Evie," he said, putting his hands on her hips, guiding her closer to him. "You may be sweet and innocent, but you can't be that naïve. You know I like you. You should know I want you."

Her hands shot to his chest to stop him from bringing her closer. Most girls had their whole adolescence to prepare for moments like these. She hadn't had that luxury. This was too much. "Tom, please don't do this. Not yet, not now."

"Why not now?"

"Please, just be patient with me."

He wrapped his arms around her, trapping her. "I am being patient. I just want to kiss you right now." He saw her terror and began rubbing her back in an attempt to comfort her, but all it did was make her want to be further away from him. "You've never even kissed anyone before, have you?"

"No, Tom, I haven't, and I'm not ready to start now." She meant to sound assertive. It would have helped if she could speak louder than a whisper.

He smiled wickedly. "You don't need to be so nervous. I promise it doesn't hurt. It's just a kiss."

He wasn't listening. She forced herself to speak louder. "Tom, please, not tonight. Not after what happened at the bar." A muscle in his jaw clenched. She was pushing his patience.

"Yes," he practically growled. "Let's talk about the bar. Just a minute ago you were thanking me about getting that man away from you. Were you lying when you said that?"

"No! Of course not! I'm very thankful."

His hands were back on her hips, gripping her forcefully. He was trying to reign in his temper, but it was a losing battle. "Then show me you're thankful."

"Tom!" She gasped at his order. What happened to his gentleness? To his not wanting to scare her away?

"Evie, I've been at you for weeks now. It's the longest I've ever had to chase a woman. I'm starting to think you're just a tease, and I'm getting tired of waiting on you!"

Before she could think better of it, she slapped him. He'd lit a fire under her, calling her a tease. She didn't think after that. She didn't wait for his reaction. She didn't try to apologize. She just ran.

## Chapter 8

Evelyn awoke to tear-swollen eyes. Dragging herself down the hallway to the shower, she still wore the clothes she'd gone dancing in. Bekah was doing her hair in the bathroom. The floor was a good place to sit and wait.

"Did you just get home?" Bekah asked in a shocked, high-pitched voice.

"No. I was home before curfew." She could feel her roommate's eyes burning into her.

"You look like... What happened?"

Evelyn wished she wasn't so tired, maybe then it would have been possible to stop the tears. "It was horrible, Bekah. It was wonderful, and then it was horrible."

Bekah sat down on the floor with her, worried for her housemate. Evelyn had never cried in front of her before. "What did he do?" Her voice sounded carefully controlled.

"Nothing. All he wanted to do was kiss me, or at least that's what he said. But he got so mean when I said no, and he started scaring me, so I slapped him and ran. He probably hates me now."

Bekah was silent for a moment and Evelyn imagined she probably thought she was as ridiculous as Tom did. She was wrong. Habitually-bubbly Bekah spoke very seriously. "I'm proud of you, Evelyn. No one else would have the guts to do that. You did the right thing by running."

She wasn't so sure. If she had stayed, she could have apologized, or at least dealt with his anger then. As it was, there was no telling what he had planned. She knew him well enough to know he didn't allow people to get away with upsetting him. "He's never going to forgive me."

Bekah patted her hand. "You'll feel better after a shower."

She wasn't sure a shower would help much, but it did a little. She at least felt like the night was behind her now.

The first time she heard the lies Tom had spread was the next morning in her first class. A girl who sat near her, Mia if she remembered correctly, leaned towards her, telling her how lucky she was to get to do those things with Tom. When she asked the girl what things she was talking about, the girl listed them, bluntly. She spoke as if Evelyn had won some amazing prize. They were lies, but even so, Evelyn was ashamed of them.

*It's just Tom,* Evelyn told herself. *He just wants to get a rise out of me, that's all.*

No matter how many times she told herself that, it never helped, and she still hurt. It didn't take long for Tom to spread the rumors about her, but in his version, instead of running home, she'd gone to bed with him. She was horrified at the detailed lies whispered about her. Even for Tom, this seemed extreme. The worst part, if there could be anything worse, was that Sarah still invited him to their apartment, as she had tonight. He sat on her couch, much the same way as when she first saw him in her home, and he winked at her as she came in the door. His cruel mockery cut her deeply. She had to bite her lip to keep it from quivering. She should have known he was still the same bully he had always been, but instead she had chosen to turn a blind eye and drank in his poison.

He had told her once her purity made her more beautiful; now he told people her purity was all he had wanted. Now that he allegedly had it, he was done with her. She quickly retreated to her room and locked her door for good measure. She was a prisoner in her own apartment, imprisoned in her room by Tom's physical presence, and held captive in her mind by his lies.

Three weeks had passed now since that awful night, and Evelyn had managed to sit in class and go to work, trying in vain to ignore what was being said. Tom had ruined her and there was nothing she could say to stop the lies.

Today, Evelyn just wanted to escape to the gardens and hide away in them. She needed to work on a paper, but she was suffocating indoors and longed desperately to get out, to not think, if only for a little while. This garden was her favorite place to be on campus, though she rarely found time for it anymore. Almost always empty of people, it was tranquil and beautiful. Hidden among ivy-covered buildings, it was so easy to forget the city and chaos surrounding them. It was easier to see life clearly when she was there. Easier to remember that Tom and his lies did not direct her path.

Peace settled over her as she walked through the gardens, enjoying the roses, letting their fragrance fill her lungs. But that peace was not meant to last. Movement caught her eye and when she looked up, a group of people were just entering the garden, and Tom was with them; in her sanctuary.

Everything she had been trying to run away from caught up with her in that instant, slamming into her, burying her. All of her feelings of embarrassment and worthlessness came rushing over her; and if she was honest with herself, feelings of desire too. That made everything worse. Unwelcome sensations rose as memories of the flattering words he had spoken came to her unbidden. Those words had proven lies, just bait to reel her in because he wanted things she wouldn't give. How quickly his sweet gaze had turned bitter. She only asked him to wait, but he wouldn't. Her body shivered remembering the rage in his eyes even before she slapped him. She got away then, but here he was coming towards her now, and he looked determined.

Evelyn turned to leave as quickly as she could, wanting to flee, but he was still approaching. Their eyes met just long enough for him to know she had seen him. Why did he have to be there? Why did she have to have these feelings? Why did his lies still tempt her? The man was dangerous. His words poison.

Quickly scanning for the quickest route away from Tom and his entourage, she spotted him. Jackson. Maybe it was genius, maybe it was desperation, but an escape plan began to take form.

No one questioned Jackson. She'd seen him settle heated arguments with a single comment. Tom wouldn't dare anything if Jackson were near, would he? Tom was intimidating and powerfully built; but Jackson was too, even more-so.

He would know the stories of what people said had happened between her and Tom. Who didn't know her pathetic story? And she knew she probably looked crazy with desperation as she stepped into his path. This was an insane idea. She was so close to letting herself run away as she pleaded to him, "Please just play along…please?"

Jackson was puzzled for a moment, until he glanced behind Evelyn and saw Tom striding towards her. Understanding settled upon him as she slid her arm around his waist and her body begged him to keep walking with her, feigning the idea that they were, at least, intimate friends.

They knew each other, but not well. The library she worked at was his favorite study spot and he always went to her when he couldn't find a particular book or article. She seemed to have the entire library memorized, and she always helped him with a smile. Sometimes when his eyes needed a break from the pages of books, he would watch her work; never with lust, but she was beautiful. He'd never been caught looking. He credited that to her modesty and not to his ability to be sly.

Today she looked like a rose, in her cream dress, petal-pink sweater, and lace tights. His fingers itched to test the fabrics, wondering if they were as soft as they looked…if she was. She was a vision of sweetness.

She wasn't like other girls. She never looked to see if she was being watched. Jackson didn't know if it was because she simply wasn't curious, or if she thought no one would be watching. If she weren't a good six years his junior, he wouldn't have been able to keep his distance from her. It was still hard. Most young girls flirted with him, some even pursued him; but not Evelyn. She always treated him with sweetness and respect, but it was the same way she treated everyone, and nothing more.

Yet here she was asking for his help. His prayer life overflowed with petitions for her. Strange he'd feel such a burden for someone he barely knew. He wanted to help her however he could and it tugged at his heart to protect her.

*Tom's an idiot*, Jackson thought. Evelyn was beautiful and sweet-tempered. He didn't know if the rumors were true or not, but he wouldn't judge her either way. He'd made enough mistakes of his own. How Tom could have hurt her the way he did, he just didn't understand. So he hugged her to his side and matched his steps to hers. Panic may have been the only thing to convince her to turn to him for help.

Having Evelyn so close to him made him realize how drawn to her he was. The most they had ever touched were the times he brushed her hand with his when she handed him a book; but it was so comfortable. No, comfortable wasn't right. It was tantalizing to have her arm around his waist and his about her shoulders. He was thinking about how beautiful she was when they passed a couple, obviously in love, and the idea came into Jackson's mind; an idea he knew would make Tom's blood run hot and stop him in his steps. He was an idiot, but he wouldn't dare confront Jackson, at least not publicly.

Jackson stopped and turned to her. Glancing at the couple and then quickly in Tom's direction, he hoped his gaze would explain to her that what he was about to do was for Tom to see.

Their eyes locked. Had she ever looked into his eyes before? She couldn't have, he would certainly have remembered, and he would have kissed her before now for other, more personal, reasons than to upset Tom. But that was the plan, for Tom to see. So why was he savoring each second? He captured a strand of her hair that had escaped its pinned place and tucked it back behind her ear. His hand refused to leave her and slid down to cradle her neck while his thumb traced her chin.

He had his answer. She was softer than she looked.

Her eyes never left his, except for an occasional flicker to his mouth. She was warm and soft, but frozen under his touch. Her eyes, round with a timid look of anticipation, were focused on his as their lips met. Her lips were hesitant as her eyes fluttered shut. She tasted of honey and springtime.

Her honeyed lips parted as he wrapped his free arm around her, pulling her against himself. She was trembling. He pulled back and saw a tear streak her sweet face.

*What have I done?*

He wanted to protect her, but her downcast eyes told him he'd hurt her. He was a grown man, a Captain in Patrols! What right did he have to kiss her, even if it was to put Tom in his place? He sighed. It may have started as a show, but he couldn't lie to himself. It ended with his own desires taking over.

*I'm as bad as Tom.*

Taking her face in both of his hands, he wiped the tears away with his thumbs. She wouldn't look at him, and still she trembled. He wrapped her in his arms, hugging her tightly. "I am so sorry, Evelyn," he whispered.

He held her for just a moment before he brought her to his side again and led her away, out of Tom's view. As they walked, he wondered about the truth behind the stories he'd heard about her. Her lips had pressed against his with the uncertainty of inexperience. But he knew Tom. He didn't take a girl out without taking something from her. It couldn't have been her first kiss.

# Chapter 9

It was a beautiful kiss. As they walked, Evelyn tucked against Jackson's side, her thoughts jumped back and forth from panic to disbelief in a frenzy. Her emotions were worse. She was sure she would crumble if not for Jackson's arm around her.

How could she have been so stupid to ask for his help? Jackson, of all people. He'd always been such a calming presence for her, now things would be strained and awkward. Oh, but that kiss… she put her hand over her stomach in an attempt to calm the butterflies.

Jackson had communicated clearly enough through his look that the plan was for Tom to see, for him to think she had moved on, that he had no power over her. In that moment it had been true. She couldn't have forced herself to think about Tom if she wanted to. Jackson was so handsome, far too handsome for her to ever hope to catch his eye. The way he had looked at her, the way he had touched her… He had to be very well practiced with women. He may be the only man she'd ever kissed, but it didn't take experience to know when a man knew what he was doing.

They walked in silence until they reached the school's outdoor theatre. Jackson led her, keeping her tucked into his side, down the steps of the amphitheater to the front row of benches. He gestured for her to sit then joined her, staying an arm's length away. She wasn't expecting to find herself alone with him; she hadn't thought past getting away from Tom.

She focused on the stage. A play was scheduled for that evening, and the set was a very good distraction. It was a funny display, with mirrors everywhere, all distorted but for one. Beautiful ribbons and fabrics of gold, whites, and purples were draped all about.

Silence surrounded them until Evelyn mustered up her courage. She was still trying to process everything, but it was rude to make Jackson sit so long without saying anything.

"Evelyn," he beat her to it. "Are you alright?"

She lied and nodded.

"Did I hurt you?" The tenderness he spoke with gave her a glimpse at the depth of his kindness.

"No," she answered. "I really appreciate you helping me. I'm sorry I dragged you into my mess, and for my behavior."

"You have nothing to be sorry for, and you didn't drag me into anything." He put his hand on the back of her neck, sending a shiver through her. He moved his hand to the bench-back instead. "I'm sorry. I won't touch you."

"Oh, no Jackson," she turned, facing his pained expression. "That's not it. That's not it at all." How could she make him understand without making a further fool of herself? She closed her eyes and buried her face in her hands. "This is so embarrassing." She didn't mean to say that. She sat up, glancing at him but mostly looking at the stage, holding her trembling hands in her lap. "I'm just a very silly girl. I'm not used to… I don't get close to… Tom was the first boy that I ever went out with. I'm not used to men touching me. I just wasn't expecting it is all. And I keep thinking about…" She was sharing too much.

"About what?" Jackson encouraged her.

She let out a sigh. "I keep thinking about my first kiss, and that it… goodness, I'm sorry, you don't need to be bored by this."

"Nothing about this is boring, Evelyn. I'm enjoying getting to talk to you."

She felt her cheeks go hot. "Thank you."

"So, what about your first kiss are you thinking about?"

What if he realized he was her first kiss? No, he wouldn't. What twenty-year-old hadn't kissed a boy before? "I always wanted my first kiss to be special, or to at least mean something to the other person. Anyway, I realized it didn't mean anything to the other person. It was all just a lie," a lie to deceive Tom, "and it hurts more than I expected." But she was still grateful to Jackson. He was kind to her. She didn't know anyone else who would have helped her as he did.

Jackson was quiet for a minute, provoking Evelyn to steal a glance at him. His eyes were focused on the stage. He seemed to be thinking, or rather lost in thought, so she felt safe looking at him. She was caught up again by how handsome he was.

She reminded herself that a handsome face can be deceiving. She'd focus on his character, because that's what made a man. Though his character seemed as honorable as his face was handsome.

"What are you thinking?" What could it hurt to ask? She had already kissed the man. What worse could she really do?

He remained looking at the stage. "Tom's an idiot." He snuck a look at Evelyn and saw she wore a small smile. "See, you agree!"

She sighed again. "No. He's smart, and calculated, sometimes cruel, and unfortunately very attractive; but no idiot." And in her heart, she believed it to be true. "Why do you think that, anyway? I thought most guys thought he was, well, something."

"Oh, he's something alright, but I won't say what kind of something. And you're wrong. He is an idiot. He has to be, to hurt you, to let you go."

Evelyn hadn't realized it until heat spread from her chest up to her cheeks that they had been speaking face to face. She had gotten lost in his eyes. But when the reminder of the rumors of her character rushed back, she couldn't hold his gaze any longer. The gossip about her and Tom oppressed her with underserved shame. No one believed she was pure, even though she was.

What was the harm in telling him the truth? She always denied the rumors, but no one ever believed her. There really was no proof, and Tom was a convincing story teller. She just looked like a little girl who had given away too much and was trying to save whatever she could. She wanted someone to believe her. She wanted him to believe her.

And then it came blundering out of her mouth.

"He left me because I wouldn't do what he wanted me to." Her lip began to quiver as tears flooded her eyes. She didn't want to cry now, not again, but tears were disobedient creatures and spilled over. She quickly wiped them away. "None of the stories are true, the ones about what he says I did for him, did with him." Shame of the accusations flooded her, but even in the tears there was a peace. It was amazing the effect of truth, no matter what other people believed. "I know everyone believes him, but they aren't true."

Jackson thanked God in his heart that the stories weren't true. She was too precious to lose her purity to the likes of Tom; to the likes of anyone. A hot anger boiled in him at the lies, and at the man who had spread them. "How long were you guys together?"

"That's the thing," she said, her heart aching, thinking he didn't believe her, "we never were actually together. We've known each other for a while, and I guess we flirted for a few weeks, at least he did. But I freaked out and ruined it when he wanted more. He was the first boy to ever say he liked me like that, to think I was beautiful…well, to say he thought I was beautiful. He knew it too, and used those lies to draw me in." She was amazed, and a little embarrassed, at how easy it was to admit these things to Jackson. Maybe it was just nice to be able to talk to someone, or maybe she kept talking about those things to keep away from talking about their kiss. Either way, the more they talked, the calmer she became, and the more comfortable she was with him.

"He may have used those things against you," he said after some thought, "but they weren't lies."

"They were lies," she answered softly. She was watching her reflection in one of the distorted mirrors and suddenly let out a small, almost sad, laugh. "Just look at me."

Jackson obeyed with pleasure. "I am."

His eyes were so intense. Evelyn found it quite difficult to breathe again, so she closed her eyes and shook her head. "Then you know, I may not be a zero, but Tom has beautiful women seeking him out. Compared to them, compared to him, it never made any sense."

She jumped when he grabbed her hand.

"Come with me," he said after standing. He tugged her along the short distance to the stage and let go of her hand. "Pardon me," he smiled and scooped her up, setting her on her feet on the stage. She was immediately grateful for the length of her dress, hitting her mid-calf, and for his averting his eyes as soon as she was above him. He was a gentleman. He easily jumped up to join her, his strength and agility shining through the ease of his movements; and the fact that he had lifted her like she weighed no more than a small child.

Taking her hand again, he took her to the only undistorted mirror and stood her in front of him. "What do you see?" he asked, releasing her hand.

She looked at his reflection behind hers. "I see me, of course, with you standing behind me."

He became suddenly serious and it set her hands to fidgeting in her nervousness again. "Look at yourself, Evelyn Carter. What do you see?"

She sighed – it was a day of sighs – and looked at herself. What did she see? "I see myself. A face, hair, a body, arms, hands, legs, feet. I see me." The use of her last name sounded funny coming from him, strange too. She didn't know he knew her last name. It was on her desk at work, though. He must have noticed it there. The way he said it made her feel like a child being spoken at by a school teacher. That was probably exactly how he felt next to her. "What else should I see, Mr. Monroe?"

Jackson stepped closer, just inches away from her; maybe less. "May I tell you what I see?"

Fear. From head to toe, fear ran through her like a river of lava. Alarms were sounding, telling her to escape, to run. But she couldn't move.

"I see a young woman," he began, "who, somehow, has bought into some very cruel lies about herself. I see a girl who is gentle, and slow to anger, one who doesn't seek out revenge or cruelty on others. Every day I have seen you at the library, I've seen a woman who is a hard worker, compassionate, and respectful." He gently placed his hands on her shoulders. Her frame felt fragile under his touch and the strength of his hands. She couldn't stop the slight tremble coursing through her at the unfamiliarity of his touch. "I see a woman who doesn't complain about the burdens she carries." His reflected gaze held hers.

Evelyn smiled shyly. "Thank you." It was kind of him to say those things, and it brought her so much happiness knowing someone thought well of her, that she wasn't what the rumors suggested. His hands tightened slightly on her shoulders, cutting her thoughts short.

"I am not finished." Jackson cleared his voice and continued. "You are kind and able." He slid his hands down her arms and held her hands. "Your arms and hands are delicate, but strong." He could feel her trembling again, but someone needed to speak against these lies she believed. "Your body is alluring and feminine, but you remain modest and humble and carry yourself with a grace I've never seen." He turned her around and took her face in his hands. When she tried to look away, he gently encouraged her. "Evelyn, it is safe to look at me." When she looked up, both tears and embarrassment once more lined her eyes. "Your face is radiant with beauty. Your eyes are sweet and thoughtful, and your lips…" He closed his eyes and touched his forehead to hers for a moment, having difficulty focusing while remembering their kiss. "Your lips are very pleasant. Everything about you is breathtaking. If you dressed like other girls, or behaved like them, you could have any man you want. Tom pretends those things are lies for his own selfish reasons. He yearns for you and cannot have you, and I pray he never will." Tears slipped down her cheeks and he wiped them away once more. "Evelyn, that is what you must see when you see yourself."

She couldn't move, and she'd completely given up on breathing. She meant to say thank you, but tears choked her. She gave into them only for a moment before she shook her head and took what felt like her first real breath. Looking up at the man who had so quickly come to mean so much to her, she tried to speak. "Jackson…" but she couldn't find the words to express everything she wanted him to know.

"My friends call me Jack," he smiled, wiping the last of her tears away. He made her tremble. It was partly from being terrified, though not wholly from fear. In truth, he took her breath away.

She returned his smile. "Yes, but before today, I really only knew you through your library card."

"That's true," he conceded, "but I hope we can be friends now."

"I would like that very much."

"Now what to do about this situation we're in," he said, giving her shoulders one last squeeze before turning to sit on the edge of the stage. She followed and he continued once she was seated next to him. "We have a very angry Tom, and that's putting it lightly, and a handful of other people who now think you and I are more than friends. I can see two ways to go. The first, when asked, we just answer honestly, saying that we're just friends and that the kiss was a one-time, uh, misunderstanding of sorts. The other, we keep up the pretenses of being a couple, until we realize we just work better as friends, or until you fall desperately in love with me and we run away together." He smiled and winked at her. "Of course, I would be much, much more respectful toward you than before. We could let people assume we kiss, rather than me stealing them from you…until you fall in love with me, that is. And then I will kiss you very often."

Her face burned hot with his comments about kissing. "Selfishly, I want people to assume we're together," she admitted. "I don't think anyone would question me if they thought you would hear about it. But falling in love with you would be too easy, and unfortunately, love has to be a two-way deal." She looked up at him, blushing, realizing what she had just blurted out. He laughed and she sighed. "But keeping up a lie would be wrong. So I guess we should go with friends."

"I wouldn't mind playing along for a while longer, if you wanted to," he teased. "But, if we hang out, even as friends, people shouldn't bother you."

Evelyn couldn't help but smile. "You really don't mind? Being friends, I mean! Not playing at being a couple."

"I insist."

"Thank you Jacks…Jack."

Something unfamiliar played in Jackson's eyes.

"We should probably get out of here," he blurted out. He was too close to doing something stupid, like kissing her again. "Don't want people talking. But tomorrow I'll be at your library to see how you're doing. I expect you to smile at me, and chat with me, and maybe even throw in a few giggles." She laughed, which was what he had hoped to accomplish. "If you need me before then," he continued, taking out a pen, "you can find me here."

# Chapter 10

"See, I told you it was true."

Evelyn looked up from the task of copying Jackson's address onto paper to see Sarah's glare and Bekah's gaping mouth.

"Evie!" Bekah practically squealed, stealing her hand. "Why didn't you tell us about Jack? That's the trainer I was telling you about. Oh, he's gorgeous. But we thought you were still hung up on Tom. What happened? When did it happen?"

*Here we go*, Evelyn thought. "We're just friends."

"Yeah right," Sarah snorted. Of course she had been one of Tom's shadows in the garden. "And that kiss was what? His way of saying hello?"

"No." Evelyn tried so hard to keep herself from blushing, but failed miserably. "We really are just friends. It was a one-time, huge, misunderstanding."

Bekah threw herself on the couch. "I bet it was great. Was it great? You think I could get him to misunderstand me? Wait..." She rolled over to look at Evelyn. "You're friends...that means you can have him over. We could host a dinner...I hate cooking. Well, we could host a something. Just bring him by to hang out. I can take it from there."

Oh, Bekah. The girl was harmless; but Evelyn was much too jealous of this imaginary future Bekah was envisioning. "If he ever asks to hang out here, and you girls are here, I will be sure to let him come." Really, what were the chances of that actually happening?

Sarah's eyes surveyed Evelyn suspiciously. Evelyn didn't think she truly disbelieved the gossip about her.

It wasn't long before Sarah's bad mood and Bekah's daydreams of Jackson drove Evelyn from her apartment. Her library was closed, but the campus library was open late this week, so she grabbed her books and headed across campus. She hadn't realized how cold it had gotten already, and her sweater wasn't nearly thick enough to keep her warm. Picking up the pace in her little brown ankle boots, she walked briskly the remainder of the way.

A little too briskly.

As she crossed from the cold to the warmth of the school library, with teeth still chattering, she almost bumped straight into Tom! What luck she was having. In her attempt to escape the judgment and questions of her roommates, she walked smack into him.

"Hey Evie." Tom greeted. She wasn't sure she liked this new way he was looking at her.

"Hello, Tom." There. She managed a hello. Now she just wanted by him, but of course he had pre-calculated her move and adjusted himself into her path.

"You don't usually come here." His eyes began to study her in a possessive manner she now was sure she did not like.

Even with all the people around them, the intimacy of their closeness scared her. And everyone was watching, which made it worse. She should have stayed home. "I need to work on a paper and couldn't focus at home."

Tom stepped even closer to her; he always used his body to intimidate her. "Do you think we could go somewhere, and talk a while? I..."

She was in danger now of panicking and needed to get away, but he broke off whatever he was going to say. He stepped back quickly, his body taking on a rigidness uncharacteristic of him, as his eyes locked on something behind her.

Evelyn turned to see what he was looking at and almost jumped. Whether it was from the shock of him being so close without her knowing or the joy of seeing him, she didn't know or care. There was Jackson.

She hadn't realized how incredibly tense she was until he put his arm around her shoulder and she relaxed into his side. He looked down at her and smiled, and it was easy to smile back; she was so glad to see him. He was turning into her knight in shining armor.

"Hey Tom. How are you?" Jackson took his time looking at him.

For the first time in her memory, Tom looked uncomfortable, nervous even. "Hey Jack. Yeah, I'm fine. I was just catching up with Evie. Uh, I'll see you in class tomorrow."

Evelyn could tell that Tom was angry about being thwarted, but he left without argument.

"See you tomorrow," Jackson called after him, keeping his arm around Evelyn even after Tom walked away. "Evie, huh?" he asked, and tugged her along with him as he started walking towards an empty table.

"Yeah," she breathed out. "My roommates and Tom call me that." With the immediate threat of Tom gone, her closeness to Jackson began to affect her in strange ways, causing her heart to skip about nervously. "I didn't know you guys have a class together."

Jackson smiled what Evelyn thought to be a wicked, but very handsome, smile. "Well, we're in the same classroom at the same time, but we're not really in the same class." Evelyn was very confused by his answer, and he knew it. His smile became even more wicked. "I'm his professor."

Evelyn ducked out from under his arm. "You're his what?" She thought he was still working on his masters…older, sure, but still a student! Oh, she'd kissed a professor. What if she had to take his class next semester? Embarrassment didn't begin to describe the humiliation that was coloring her red.

He laughed light-heartedly and sat in one of the chairs. "Sit down, *Evie*," he teased. "I only teach one class. They were short a professor and I happened to be in the right place at the right time. They only have to pay me half a normal professor's salary since I'm technically a student teacher, so they were eager to hire me instead of finding an actual professor."

A student teacher was easier to take. She sat in the chair opposite of him, grateful she didn't have to rely on her wobbly legs to keep her standing any longer. "I thought we were taking the 'friends who had a misunderstanding' road."

Jackson smiled a self-satisfied smile. "Tom doesn't need to know that. All he needs to know is that I'm around. I feel better with him thinking we're more than we are."

Evelyn's head tilted with the effort of trying to process that comment.

"If he asks," he said, leaning closer, "I promise I will be honest. If he doesn't ask, though, I'm not going to make a point of telling him." It was all he could promise. "So, what are you studying?"

She had forgotten all about her paper. "U.S.A. Hostilities." The class was on their most recent war and the conflicts that led up to it. It had been a violent time, but she loved learning about how different life was back then, before the country was split in two.

She read once that citizens commonly carried phones around with them, whenever they wanted. She was fascinated by that, since now it was illegal for a private citizen to own a personal phone. They had phones in their homes linked to Patrols for emergencies, but that was it. The government said it was to help minimize chaos. She wasn't entirely sure what that meant.

"Are you a history major?" he asked, intrigue lining his tone.

"No," she admitted. "Literature major, but I'm minoring in history. It helps me appreciate literature better when I know about the world the authors lived in."

"So you're using history to get closer to literature…not very nice of you." She smiled at his teasing but didn't respond. She was transforming into the woman he watched at the library. Quiet and diligent. As she opened her laptop, he saw that the books she had with her were some of the books he referenced frequently in his own papers. "You've chosen excellent books to help you."

Evelyn smiled a little and glanced up at him. "It's one of the many perks of working at the library. A lot of books pass through my hands. It's helped me a lot in my own studies."

"Do you know I reference these books a lot?"

Evelyn smiled and blushed in response.

"Do you use these books because I use them?" he questioned suspiciously.

Evelyn put her hands in her lap so as to hide her fidgeting and forced her eyes up to his. "I promise I wasn't trying to remember what books you use. You are just at the library a lot, and I help you find books more than anyone else. One day when I was putting your books away, I decided to read one, and couldn't put it down. So, I decided to add on a minor and figured you were a good reference to go by." The heat of embarrassment painted her cheeks at her confession. She giggled nervously and buried her head in her arms on the table. "I know, it's terribly shameful of me to use you like that."

Jackson laughed, too loudly for a library, and she looked up and shushed him with a smile. "I think you're being a little hard on yourself. Anyone who's stumbled across my course syllabus would have a list of my favorite books. But it's nice to know you noticed." He knew she'd be flustered by his last comment, so he unbound the papers he brought to grade and started reading, closing the conversation.

Evelyn released a grateful sigh and set herself to her own studies.

They sat across from each other for some while, silently working. As was his usual habit, Jackson watched her when he needed a break from looking at the papers, and she kept her eyes on her work, completely devoted to the task in front of her. Somehow she had stolen a tender place in his heart. His intentions towards her worried him some, but he convinced himself, for the moment, that he could be content being her friend. Just her friend.

He had a horrible feeling he was lying to himself.

He watched her work and wondered what it would be like to have her kind of focus. But as the hours went by, he noticed her eyes becoming heavier and heavier as she read through the books she had brought until she rested her head on her arm and fell asleep.

As he watched her, he also wondered about what sort of man would sweep her off her feet one day. As quickly as the thought came into his mind, he forced it out…but he couldn't help thinking how much he would like to try and be that man. He prayed it wouldn't be Tom, though, or anyone like him, and wondered how he ever got close enough to get his claws into her. She had told him they'd known each other for a while. How long was that?

It was late now, and she needed to go home. Jackson ran his fingers over the soft back of her hand. Her hand was so cold. The temptation to hold it and warm it with kisses almost overtook him, but he fought it back. Instead, he whispered quietly, "Evelyn. Evelyn."

## Chapter 11

Sleep tugged at Evelyn, but it was losing the battle for her consciousness. A warm hand was gently resting on hers. And there was a voice…a man's voice…

Urgent panic sat her up too quickly, as she tried to piece together the memory of where she was. Across the table sat Jackson, wearing a sweet smile. In her groggy state, she couldn't fight the desire to stare at him. She took in his dark eyes, and perfect nose; he looked as if he hadn't shaved in a couple days, but that just seemed to add to his allure. She couldn't suppress her smile when she looked at his lips. Finally, awareness of what she was doing settled upon her, and she quickly looked down at her things to begin collecting them. How stupid she was. "What time is it?" she asked him as she rose with her things.

Jackson hadn't missed her stare, but he wouldn't embarrass her by mentioning it right then. "Just about ten."

She looked up at him with wide eyes. "How close to ten?"

"About five 'til. What's wrong?"

"Jack, I'm not 21."

The curfew. He had forgotten how young she was, but he still didn't understand why she was so worried. The curfew was easily dealt with; he would just take her home. It was true, the Patrols had a reputation of being rough when they found someone breaking curfew, and there were worse stories of their treatment of young ladies. Patrol officers would be dealt with, severely, if they were ever found out, but unfortunately the few he suspected to be the offenders kept out of sight and managed to keep their victims from turning them in. He always assumed Tom was one of them. One day soon he would catch him. But as for Evelyn, as long as she was chaperoned, she would be fine. "I'll take you home."

Evelyn paused to consider his words.

"Evelyn, I won't let anyone bother you."

She didn't realize until later how comforted she was by his words or by the deep tone of his voice. All she knew then was how relieved she was that she wouldn't have to ask an officer to escort her home. She knew they couldn't all be bad, but she still didn't trust any of them. They were there to keep everyone safe, but she knew the ones who worked the Campus Patrols were young and often looking for trouble. She just hoped Bekah and Sarah wouldn't see Jackson walking her home.

"Thank you, Jack. I really would be very grateful." She was already in his debt so much, and just from one day! They finished gathering their things and walked toward the doors. The two attending officers at the doors nodded to Jackson as they left.

Even just outside the library, where you could still feel the heat from the room, it was freezing. Evelyn hugged her books and computer tight to her chest in an effort to keep warm. As her teeth set to chattering, Jackson put his papers on a bench next to him and shrugged out of his jacket. Without a word, he snatched away her things and wrapped his jacket around her.

"Jack, no. You'll be so cold! It's not your fault I wasn't thinking when I left without a jacket." But he had put her things on the bench with his and was zipping his jacket up, trapping her inside.

"I'm sorry, you just don't get a say in this." He smiled and picked up their things. He was enjoying the sight of her in his jacket. "So, which way to home?"

Evelyn slid her arms into the sleeves. "The apartments south of the gardens…" The same gardens where she reached out to him for help. The same gardens where he kissed her.

They began to walk, her in his jacket, and him carrying their things. The jacket was still warm with his body heat and it pushed the chill out of her own body. She didn't understand Jackson. He had become so complex in just one day, and she had so many unanswered questions about him. Why was he helping her, and why was he so kind about it? How was he so confident in everything? And why had those officers acknowledged him as they left?

It was a dark night. There was no moon out and the sky was clear of any clouds. Almost every building was completely dark as well;

everything had been shut down for the night. The only other people who were out were the officers patrolling the campus.

Evelyn was uneasy as they walked by the first set of officers they passed on their way to her apartment. The officers slowed when they saw her and Jackson walking, in what she thought showed more curiosity on their part than anything else. But Jackson was right; no one bothered them. They nodded and continued on their way.

The gardens were completely empty. Even in the gray palette of night, they were beautiful. All the plants seemed to sleep in sweet serenity, lulled by quiet trickles from the fountains. The heated water prevented freezing and sent wispy fingers of steam dancing into the air. It felt like a dream.

"Would you mind if I called you Jackson, instead of Jack?"

"No, not at all," Jackson laughed. "May I ask why?"

"I think it fits you better. Jack is too casual. Jackson sounds important. It's a name people would listen too. People listen to you. Like with Tom, he doesn't listen to anyone, but he listens to you…and I don't think he wants to. Why is that, do you think? Just because you're his professor?" She did find it peculiar, how everyone seemed to respect him, almost to a point of fear. Was there a mean part of him she hadn't yet met? She was confident no one else could hurt her when he was with her, but should she be afraid of *him*?

"Evelyn, you will always be perfectly safe when you are with me." Curious emotions rose in Evelyn at that statement. "I know you don't fully trust me yet. I appreciate you trying to figure me out."

He thought a moment before answering her question. "You don't know what I do, besides teaching that is, do you?" he asked. She shook her head. "You'll notice, I'm sure, that it isn't everyone who listens to me, it's mostly just the men. You see, every male that comes to this school is required to serve at least one semester on Patrols. So, every male who has served their term in the last year and a half has had me as their Captain. I'm sure some of them have wanted to challenge me, but the fun part is, if they have an issue with me, they'd have to report to the Colonel…my father. That is why they listen to me. And as for Tom, he's been on Patrols for four years, and didn't like it when I came on as Captain. We've never been on good terms."

Most officers served because it was required. Evelyn guessed only a handful of campus Patrol officers were like Tom, making their career out of it. But to be a Captain, and at Jackson's age, that was remarkable. She knew the tests required for that title took tremendous strength and agility, as well as skill with weapons and an extensive knowledge of the laws. Her own feelings of inadequacy began to overwhelm her as she stood next to him. "Jackson, would you be honest with me for a moment?"

"I always am."

They stood just outside her door now. "Why have you been so nice to me today?"

Jackson looked over her head at the wall behind her and exhaled. He couldn't tell her it was because he couldn't get her out of his head and wanted to be near her, but he didn't want to lie either. "Because you're worth it."

"Come on, Jackson. You're amazing, and I'm just me. Yet, you've saved me from embarrassment and from Tom multiple times, sat with me while I was practically falling apart, walked me home in the freezing cold after curfew, and…" she blushed thinking about their kiss and what he said at the theatre. "…and a lot more. You said you would be honest."

"A lot more," Jackson laughed. "That's one way to put it." He had thoroughly enjoyed the *a lot more* and was currently enjoying the blush tinting Evelyn's cheeks with the memory of it. He couldn't help but smile and pull her into a hug with his free arm. She instantly became a statue in his arms. He tried not to laugh. "Evelyn, I know you're not going to invite me in, but I'm freezing. Just give me a little break on this."

Guilt dropped in her stomach like a rock. She was warm and content in his jacket, and behaving like a little girl. That fact didn't stop her nerves from rattling, or her heart from racing, but she wrapped her arms around him tightly and, resting her chin on his chest, looked up at him. "I'm sorry."

He was pushing his self-control to the limit. He could feel her body, statue turned flesh, nervous in his arms. He wouldn't risk losing her; he couldn't ask for more than her friendship. "You're shaking."

"You scare me…this scares me." She didn't mean to tell him that. For the first time, though, she was able to keep her eyes on his.

"You never need to fear me…and I wasn't lying. You are worth it."

Just then the door opened and Sarah materialized in the doorway. She leaned against the doorframe, sliding her arm up against it in an overtly seductive manner. Evelyn's arms fell to her side and she quickly stepped away from Jackson. Jackson was the poster-child for calm.

"Just friends, huh?" Sarah asked. "Tom was here just a few minutes ago, looking for you, Evie. He seemed pretty upset you weren't home." Even as she spoke to Evelyn, Sarah never stopped looking at Jackson.

Evelyn didn't like it and was caught off guard as jealousy coursed through her. Sarah looked like a goddess as she stood in the doorway. Her nightclothes weren't inappropriate, necessarily, but they showed off more than Evelyn wanted Jackson to see. Her heart sank when she saw his eyes distracted by her body.

"He knew we were in the library," Jackson answered for Evelyn. "There was no reason for him to come to here. It was his mistake for attempting to seek her out."

Sarah stepped forward, extending her hand. Her long fingers were adorned with gold rings. "Since Evie seems to have forgotten her manners and has failed to introduce us, I'm Sarah."

Sarah's body language was anything but innocent, and though annoyed by it, he couldn't help but notice her. He shook her hand once and dropped it. "Evelyn's had a rather interesting day and I'm sure she is exhausted. I assure you, her manners are more than what they should be." He turned to Evelyn. "I think I have kept you long enough. I should be going. It was nice to meet you, Sarah," he said, only glancing in her direction. Sarah rolled her eyes and went back inside, leaving the door cracked. They both assumed she was still listening.

A chill ran over Evelyn as she handed Jackson back his jacket and took her things. She wished they could have talked longer. She didn't think she would be able to speak so freely with him tomorrow. "I'm not working tomorrow," she remembered. "Earlier you said you'd see me tomorrow at my library, but I had to take the day off."

Jackson put his jacket back on, and though its warmth was welcome, he had enjoyed the warmth of her in his arms more. "Is everything ok?"

Evelyn was already beginning to shiver again. Tomorrow was her mother's birthday. She never really knew her mother. She had been addicted to drugs until her death, while Evelyn grew up in a government home, but she still liked to visit her grave every year. Her mother managed to stay clean during her pregnancy, and Evelyn was born healthy, so the government was willing to house her. Babies who were born addicted to their mother's drugs weren't accepted by the government housing, and more often than not, the mothers weren't able to help them survive. It was one of the worst things about their world. But her mother gave her a clean start and Evelyn was very grateful to her for that. She wasn't ready to share all of that with Jackson. "Oh, yes," she answered. "I just have someplace I have to go. I don't like missing class, so I have to miss work instead."

Jackson seemed hesitant to leave, but Sarah was listening. "Ok. Well get inside before you freeze. I'll see you later." He smiled at her and added with a wink, "Just make sure you're home before curfew tomorrow." He turned and left.

"Good night, Jackson," she called after him.

As she walked into the apartment, she heard Sarah's door close. At least she wouldn't have to deal with her tonight.

Evelyn's head was spinning. She was exhausted, but even as she curled up in bed, thoughts of Jackson were intoxicating. It was a good thing that she didn't work tomorrow. Perhaps after a day of not seeing him, she could return to her normal self. She didn't doubt this was the end of their friendship. He had been nice for the day but would forget about her tomorrow. Her heart weighed heavily in her chest at that thought. She wanted him around, but her heart would be safer with some distance between them. She just hoped that Tom would leave her alone, too.

"She's still mine." Tom's seething voice came from a dark corner of the building. Jackson wasn't surprised to find Tom lurking around; though he was surprised he would challenge him so soon, and so alone. Jackson stopped walking and turned as Tom approached him from the shadows.

"Hello, Thomas." Jackson wasn't one to rush into confrontations. It wasn't that he was afraid of them; it was just that he always finished them. He didn't like Tom, but he knew Tom was angry and he didn't want to have to hurt him if he attempted to fight. If he was honest with himself, he didn't want to get hurt either. He knew he could beat Tom in a fair fight, but fights over women were rarely fought fair.

Tom was what every Captain coveted in an officer, except Jackson. Jackson knew the reasons Tom made a good officer were the same reasons girls swooned after him; powerfully built, assertive, showed no signs of fear. But Tom was cruel and had a defiant heart. Jackson wondered for a moment why Tom would be so invested in Evelyn. His blood ran hot as he realized why he was after her. She was pure...her purity would be a trophy for his pride.

The stories weren't rumors. They were goals.

"Do you understand me, *Jack?*" Tom continued, stopping a few feet from him.

Jackson took a deep breath, hoping the cold air would calm him. "Thomas, I believe you are wrong, and I would encourage you to leave her alone from now on."

"If you want her, you can have her if I tire of her. But she is mine."

It took every ounce of Jackson's self-control not to knock Tom out, right where he stood. "Thomas, let me be clear. Evelyn is no one's property and will never be anything to you. If you touch her, or I hear that you have upset her in any way, you will answer to me and no one will be able to help you. She is under my protection now, as her friend...and as your Captain. Do you understand me, Thomas?"

Tom eyed him with wariness. "Yes." He had no intentions of losing Evelyn to Jackson, but he needed time to learn this new game; especially now that there was a new player involved.

Jackson turned and began to walk away. "And Thomas," he added, "You will address me as sir from now on. If I hear you use my name, you will be reprimanded for disrespect to your Captain." He left then, leaving Tom behind him. He didn't think this was over, though. Like he had told Evelyn before, Tom was an idiot.

## Chapter 12

Evelyn awoke the next morning to Bekah jumping on her bed.

"So," Bekah chirped, much too cheerfully, "I know he was here last night. You didn't invite him in. You said you would invite him in." She looked at her expectantly.

Evelyn pulled the covers over her head and moaned.

"Come on!" Bekah pleaded, pulling the covers back down. "What happened? You can't just bring Mr. Gorgeous to our doorstep, after curfew, and not tell me what happened!"

Evelyn liked Bekah, even early-morning Bekah. She was silly, and a hopeless flirt, but harmless. Sarah, however, was not to be trusted.

"I'm sorry, Bekah, nothing happened. I promise. We were both at the library and I didn't keep track of time, so he walked me home. Nothing exciting at all." Of course, there was also that little part about Jackson saving her from Tom again, and having his arm around her, and wearing his jacket home. But Bekah didn't need to know those parts.

"Tom was here, ya know?" Bekah wrinkled her nose. There were things she knew about Tom, things that were impossible to share with Evelyn. "He seemed pretty upset. He talked to Sarah for a while. I really don't like him." She threw herself back on Evelyn's bed. "I know, I know, you like him. But he's so creepy. I like Jack much better."

Evelyn sighed and sat up, looking at Bekah sprawled across her bed. She wondered if this is what it would have been like to have a sister; talking casually about boys or whatever you wanted to talk about in your nightclothes? She liked it. "I don't like Tom. I think I just liked the idea." That wasn't the truth, but maybe if she kept telling herself that, she could convince herself too.

Bekah sat up. "But you're so weird around him. I thought you still liked him?"

"I don't know how to behave around him. He spread all those lies about me. I've never had to deal with boys before." Bekah smiled. "I know, you think it's so funny. But I have no idea what to do with a boy, let alone a boy that everyone thinks…well, thinks things about. Bekah, you believe me, right? That I didn't actually do those things?"

"Oh sure," Bekah answered. "Anyone who really knows you couldn't believe those things, even if you didn't argue that they're lies."

"I don't think Sarah believes me."

"She does. But I wouldn't trust her if I were you. There's something weird about her and Tom. I sometimes wonder…" but she didn't finish her sentence. Secretly, she wondered if Sarah didn't have something to do with what happened between Evelyn and Tom. "It doesn't matter. So, do you like Jack?"

Evelyn's blush betrayed her again. "I could. He is so incredibly handsome. I've never met anyone like him. Did you know he's a Captain in Patrols? Not a trainer." She paused a moment. "What does it matter, though? He'd never like me. I just hope we stop running into each other."

"What? Why? Aren't you friends?"

Evelyn looked down. She wanted to be his friend. She wanted him to be around all the time, but that was the problem. "He seems like the best friend anyone could ask for, but I think it would end up being too difficult for me."

"Oh Evelyn, I hate to tell you, but you do like him, and I'm willing to bet you like him a lot."

Evelyn sank back into her pillows. Bekah was right, however much she didn't want her to be. What was the point of liking someone you knew would never return those feelings? Time away would help her forget.

"So," Bekah continued, "visiting your mom today?"

Evelyn stared at the ceiling. "Yes. Right after class. Speaking of which, I guess I should get ready. Don't want to be late."

Bekah stood up with a huge smile. "Last day of class before Thanksgiving break! I'm glad we still celebrate Thanksgiving." She turned to leave but stopped in the doorway. "You're always welcome to come home with me for break. You know that, right?"

Evelyn sat on the edge of her bed. Bekah was really a good friend to her, and she was overwhelmed with thankfulness for her. "Thank you. I'll be alright. Can't miss what I've never had."

With that, Bekah left.

Evelyn sat a moment longer thinking about the holiday. A Thanksgiving meal was something the government homes simply couldn't do. The ladies who worked with them were kind and tried their best to make it special. She had been blessed to be in a home with such kind women. She smiled. She already had two things to be thankful for this Thanksgiving.

Class went quickly enough. After they submitted their papers, the professor began his very animated lecture. She enjoyed this class. Her professor was a dear older gentleman who lit up every time he taught. It was evident he was passionate about teaching, and about what he was teaching. She wondered what type of professor Jackson was, but she wasn't supposed to be thinking about Jackson, so she pushed it from her mind.

After class Evelyn walked to the station and waited for the bus. She wished she had brought a book to read while she waited, but instead filled her time people watching. Most of the people she saw were Patrol officers. She didn't mind the city's officers as much as she minded the school's. They were men who chose Patrolling as their career. They weren't young men looking to prove themselves.

The bus finally came and it was a peaceful ride to the cemetery. As always, the cemetery was empty when she arrived. She walked between rows and rows of graves, some decorated, and some so old she could barely make out what they said. She enjoyed reading them as she walked. There were so many she didn't think she had ever read the same one twice. Then she came to her mother's.

*Justine Evelyn Thompson, 2122-2151*

Evelyn sat down on the grass next to her mother and tucked her feet under her gray dress. "Hi Mom. Happy birthday." She knew it was silly to talk to her mother, but she always did. "School's going well. I think you'd be proud of me. After this semester, I just have one more and I'll have my schooling completed. I'm hoping to stay on at the library when I'm done. It's not adventurous, I know, but it's safe and I do love it." She thought over everything that had happened with Tom, and Jackson.

"It's been difficult lately. There was this boy, Tom. I was a fool to believe he felt anything kind for me. When I didn't...I guess when I didn't please him...he made it clear he had never liked me and spread some pretty horrible lies about me. Now there's this other man, Jackson. I think you would like him; everyone likes him. He comes to my work a lot, and yesterday he kind of saved me, and he kissed me. It was wonderful, but I know he was just doing it to make Tom angry. Mom, I don't know what to do. He wants to be my friend, but I don't think I can be that. I'm sure it will all just blow over. I'm sure he hasn't thought of me once since yesterday." Her heart hurt as she remembered how Jackson's eyes moved over Sarah's figure last night. If he was thinking of anyone, he would be thinking of her.

Evelyn sat with her mother a while longer, until time demanded she return to the bus station.

"Happy birthday, Mom. I love you. Thank you for giving me a life." She meant it.

As she looked at her mother's grave, she wondered, as she always did, why her mother had chosen to give her, what she assumed, was her father's last name. She didn't even know her father's first name; he was never listed on her files.

When she got up to leave, she noticed a man sitting at the bus station. She had never seen anyone at that station before. As she walked back through the cemetery and closer to the bus station, anxiety began to overtake her. She knew the man at the bus station and knew it couldn't be a coincidence he was here.

Tom.

There was nothing she could do about it. She had to get home and it was too far to walk, so the bus was her only option.

Tom turned and when he saw her, he stood. She became very self-conscious as he let his eyes wander over her. She forced herself to continue to the bus stop and sat down on the bench. Tom sat down too close. She didn't speak and kept her eyes on her fidgeting hands in her lap. She wished she was brave and that she could talk to him and pretend she wasn't afraid of him, or hurt by him. How did other girls have such confidence around him? He reached over and took one of her hands. She tried to take it back, but he would not let go of it. "Please, Tom," she whispered. "Please let me go."

He refused to obey. "Evie, why won't you look at me?" His voice was sweet and tender.

Evelyn looked up, surprised. He caught her eyes with his and held them. Uncertainty paralyzed her. She wanted to leave...wanted to say something, or look away...anything...but couldn't.

"I'm sorry Evie. You have to believe me. I'm so sorry."

"Why did you do it?" She asked him. It was hard not to have feelings for him with her hand in his and with his blue eyes pleading with her.

"I don't know. I guess my pride was hurt when you rejected me."

"Tom, I wasn't rejecting you. I was scared of you! You know I've never kissed anyone." She bit her lip...that wasn't true anymore, and Tom knew it.

"You kissed Jackson Monroe." Where she expected to hear anger, she heard sadness.

"Because I was scared of you again. I panicked, and I didn't think you'd actually care." She saw now that he did. "I'm sorry, Tom. I honestly never wanted to hurt you, or make you angry. Please forgive me."

Tom couldn't remember a time that he'd received an honest apology, and even he knew Evelyn had nothing to apologize for. He'd seen the shock on her face when Jackson kissed her. He laid every ounce of blame for that kiss on his Captain. He was lost in this game, but he was slowly realizing that, unlike other girls, Evelyn wasn't playing a game.

"Evie." He squeezed her hand. "Evie, look me in the eyes." Evelyn obeyed. "I still want you."

She didn't want to be wanted; not like he meant. She wanted to be loved before anyone took what he was asking for. He had to stop. She would not sit and listen to the lies she was too close to believing. Today was supposed to be her private time with her mother; not a time for him. Her frustration at his interruption was the only thing keeping her mind focused.

"No, Tom, you don't want me. I could never be what you want. I can't give you the things you want from a relationship." She was relieved to see the bus just down the street. "I need to be left alone. I need you to leave me alone. We've known each other a long time; can't you grant me this one request?"

His look went cold. "He'll be worse than me. I hope you know that."

The bus was almost there.

"He's older than me, Evie, and you don't think he'll want more, or be willing to take it?" Everything about Tom was threatening now, but the bus had stopped and was opening its doors.

"We're just friends, nothing more." With that she slipped her hand from his and stepped onto the bus. She exhaled as the doors closed behind her, leaving Tom at the station. He must have had an alternate way home, in case things didn't go as he wanted. The trip home wasn't as peaceful as it was on the trip out. She knew Tom liked to tell lies, but the quiet of the bus let her mind agonize over the possibility of what he'd said about Jackson being true.

## Chapter 13

Jackson's fists clenched every time he looked at Tom while teaching. Eventually he had to just stop looking at him. It was a relief, though not a surprise, that Tom vanished as soon as class was dismissed. Now that he'd sobered up, he undoubtedly wised up too.

His original plan was to use the remainder of the day to work on papers at the library. However, when he found out Evelyn wouldn't be working, he decided to occupy his time with work instead. Today's Patrol work required a focused mind, so he didn't have to worry about his mind wandering a lot to thoughts of Evelyn. It almost worked.

By the time he was off, it was late. Most students had either left campus for the break or were home packing to leave in the morning. What if she already left for the break? Temptation got the best of him, and he headed in the direction of Evelyn's apartment.

Lights were on in the windows as he knocked on the door. He hoped she was home, but wasn't sure what his excuse would be for being there if she was. Before he could think of anything, an unfamiliar girl answered the door.

"Jackson!" She practically yelled at him before clamping her hand over her mouth giggling. "Sorry, I meant to say, hi! Are you looking for Evelyn?"

He laughed easily with her. "Hi. Yes, is she in?"

"Yes." She smiled ear to ear. "Yes, she is. Why don't you come in, and I will let her know you're here?" She opened the door and stepped aside making way for him to come in. She was up to something, but he went in all the same, eager to see Evelyn. "Feel free to sit anywhere. She'll be just a minute." He sat on the couch as she disappeared down the hall.

Evelyn had heard voices and wondered who would be visiting Bekah this late, when Bekah walked into her room. Her face communicated distress. "What's wrong?"

"You have a visitor."

Her body in its entirety tensed. She thought she had made herself clear to Tom. She gathered her wits about her and walked out to the front room, grateful it was Bekah home and not Sarah. "Tom, I told you I..." but it wasn't Tom. Her heart leaping into her throat cut off the reprimand intended for Tom. There sat Jackson, impressive and striking, still in his uniform, sitting, on her couch. And she was in her nightclothes. He stood as soon as she entered the room.

"Jackson," she corrected herself. "Is everything ok?"

He smiled warmly at her. "Good evening, Evelyn. Yes, everything's fine."

"I'm sorry..." Evelyn stated in confusion. "Why are you here?" Suspicion pricked at her when she saw him hesitate. He'd never been nervous around her before. What would cause a man of Jackson's fortitude unrest? She still battled with what Tom had said and worried that Jackson had come with lies and unwelcome intentions. But no, Tom was lying. He had to be. She was sure of it.

"Well," Jackson began, "I just got off work and, to be honest, I was just curious if you had left for break yet or not, so I thought I would come by and see."

"Evie," Bekah butted in. "Isn't that nice of him? Now, aren't you going to offer him something to drink? Jackson, would you like something to drink? Evie and I were about to have hot chocolate." She smiled gleefully at Evelyn and added, "Sarah's already left so we're allowed to act like kids now and giggle and drink hot chocolate in our nightclothes. Well," she looked Jackson up and down with a look of unmasked appreciation. "You're not in your nightclothes, but you can still be invited."

"Thank you, but I shouldn't impose. It looks like you two have the night planned out already."

Evelyn didn't miss the glare that Bekah shot her. She had promised to invite him if he ever asked. He wasn't technically asking, but in Bekah's mind, this was pretty much the same thing. She smiled reassuringly at

Jackson. "I would love to make you some hot chocolate as well, if you could stay." Bekah was beaming.

"I would really enjoy that. Can I help you?"

Bekah plopped herself into a chair and answered for Evelyn. "You might as well sit down and relax. She doesn't allow us to help."

Jackson sat down and looked at Evelyn as she busied herself in the kitchen.

"She always tells me," Bekah continued, "that cooking, or in this case brewing, is how she shows people she loves them." She giggled and pretended like Evelyn couldn't hear them, "But don't tell her I told you. She'd be embarrassed."

"Thank you, Bekah, for giving away my secrets."

Jackson looked at Bekah. "Bekah, it's nice to know your name."

Bekah threw her head back against the chair. "Jackson, I am so sorry! Yes, I'm Bekah!"

Evelyn was pleased to have the conversation go between Bekah and Jackson. Bekah did most of the talking, with Jackson asking questions about her classes and work. Evelyn graciously used the time it took to make their drinks to collect herself as best she could. When the drinks were done, she arranged the mugs of steaming cocoa on a tray and adorned each mug with her homemade whipped cream and shavings of dark chocolate. She carried the tray to her friends and set it on the coffee table. She wasn't surprised that Bekah had taken the chair, leaving her to sit on the couch with Jackson. She handed out the drinks and hoped Jackson didn't notice her hand shaking when she gave him his mug.

"Mmmmm. Thanks, Evie!" Bekah said through her sipping.

"This looks amazing," Jackson complimented.

Evelyn smiled her thanks.

"So where are you two off to for break?" Jackson asked, looking to both of them.

Bekah, unsurprisingly, answered. "I'm headed home tomorrow. My parents live a couple hours south of here in Binghamton."

Evelyn shouldn't have been surprised when Bekah answered for her as well.

"Evelyn is staying here, for the whole break! I've tried to convince her to come home with me, but she won't."

She almost choked on her hot chocolate. She didn't like people knowing she stayed during breaks because she didn't like having to explain why she had nowhere else to be.

Jackson sat patiently as the drama unfolded before him.

"Evie," Bekah continued on. "It's not my fault you refuse to come with me. If you were, I could have said that *we* were going to Binghamton tomorrow." She took another sip of her hot chocolate then stood up. "Well, I'm tired. I think I'll just finish this in my room. It was a pleasure meeting you, Jackson. I hope you have a good break. Evie, thank you for this. It's delicious, as usual."

She skipped off to bed.

Jackson really liked Bekah, and the fact that she appeared to be on his side. Now alone with the woman he was there to see, he shifted to better face Evelyn. "Are you really staying here for break?"

Evelyn was not normally a violent person, but she could hit Bekah for doing this to her. She wasn't ready to tell him her life story. "Yes. I enjoy having the apartment to myself," she lied.

"Evelyn," he tried again. "Why won't you tell me?"

Her resolve was pathetic around him. Putting her drink down, she took a deep breath and answered. "I have nowhere else to go." She paused to consider her next words. The decision to tell him everything was easy. Bekah would come bounding back in to help fill in the blanks if she didn't. Evelyn never heard her door close, so Bekah was probably listening in. Though it was an easy decision, it was not an enjoyable one.

"My mother and father are both dead. I was told my father died a couple months before I was born; got into a fight with the wrong people, or something like that. My mother died when I was 9, but I never knew her either. She died from an overdose of drugs. Today is her birthday, or was her birthday; she would have been forty. I visit her every year, that's where I was today. I have no other family." She didn't want him feeling sorry for her. "But I don't mind staying here. It's what I've always done. I think that it's easier, anyway, to be alone rather than see what I'm missing."

Jackson had an impressive poker face, but his voice revealed his emotions. "What do you mean, see what you're missing?"

"If I never have to see a family together in their home, it's easier not to ache for it." She could tell he pitied her. Pity always made her feel small and worthless. "I have everything in the world to be thankful for. I have a home, a job, and am getting a wonderful education. That's more than a lot of people can say, and more than most of those brought up as I was." She stood and took their empty cups to the kitchen to wash them. "Enough about me. How was your day?" The subject of her life was closed.

It felt good to busy her hands with a familiar task. That, and doing the dishes kept her in the kitchen, a safe distance from Jackson. Yet even while hiding away in the kitchen, his deep voice soothed the tension from her body as he told her about his day.

Too soon the task was completed, and Evelyn was left wondering what to do with herself.

"I think I've overstayed my welcome. I should leave," he said, standing suddenly.

"You're welcome to stay," she said quickly, knowing it was her behavior that gave him the false cue to leave. She blushed knowing her voice sounded too eager. "It is late, though, I understand if you need to leave."

"I want to stay, but I probably should leave. It is getting late." He smiled. "And I think your friend probably wants her roommate back."

Bekah's voice came down the hall, "No I don't!"

They both laughed. With timid steps, Evelyn walked Jackson out. Though she wanted so badly to be near him, without Bekah listening, even for just a moment, she simply didn't possess the courage to close the door behind her.

But she didn't need to be brave. Jackson reached behind her and closed it, shrinking the space between them. Their breath mixed in the cold air.

"Thank you for my hot chocolate. It was best I've had, I think ever."

Evelyn smiled up at him. It had to be cold outside, but standing so close to him warmed her from the inside. Was he radiating the same heat she felt?

"I'm glad I could make it for you, and that you liked it."

Jackson watched her, trying to figure her out, as her eyes flickered to his mouth. He had a good idea what thoughts consumed her when fear leapt into those lovely eyes, causing her to withdraw from him, and bump into the door.

The war inside her was evident on her face. "Why are you so scared of me?" Jackson finally asked.

"I ran into Tom today," she quietly confessed. Jackson's jaw went tight. "He said you'd be worse than him and that you're lying about just wanting friendship. That you'd want more from me...that you'd take things from me." She looked down again, too ashamed and embarrassed to look him in the eyes. The hurt was all too evident on his face. "I told him to leave me alone."

She expected a growl in response, as Tom would have done. Instead, his voice was low and gentle.

"I wasn't lying to you when I told you that you will always be safe with me. Is it so hard for you to believe me?" He wanted to hug her, and to punch Tom in the face.

"I want to, Jackson, it's just difficult." The words spilled out before she could stop them. "I mean, you've kissed me! Tom never even did that!" She bit her lip, silencing her admission.

Jackson didn't say anything. Evelyn could see his eyes shifting, replaying their time in the garden...and the amphitheater...and the library...

"Evelyn, be very clear please. Who was your first kiss?"

Her red-hot cheeks gave her away.

"You." It was barely a whisper.

"Geez, Evelyn!" Jackson backed up, grabbing his head in panic. "It was hard enough to believe Tom was your first kiss...but me?"

"Please, Jackson," she pleaded, grasping his lowered hand. "Don't let this be the last thing I tell you, and please tell me I don't need to be ashamed in front of you. If we truly are friends, please show me that we are."

He pulled her to him and wrapped his arms around her. This time, she didn't tense at his touch; but rather rested her head on his chest, hugging him back, tightly around his waist. She'd never felt safer.

"How'd a woman as beautiful as you get to college without ever being kissed?" Evelyn's knees almost gave under her. "I'm proud of you for speaking to me like that. You never need to be ashamed in front of me, and this will not be the last thing we say to each other. I'm sorry I took that from you. I never would have done it if I had known."

She forced herself to let go of him and moved back just a step. "I know."

"You could have stopped me if you had wanted to," he teased. He began laughing before she could respond. "No wonder Tom's ready to kill me!"

"Yeah, I did stop him." She closed her eyes and shook her head slightly, dismissing the memory of Tom. "I should go inside."

Jackson tucked her comment away for another time. "I work tomorrow. I won't be off until after your curfew, but I'd like to come see you when I'm off, if you don't mind."

"Bekah will have left by then," she thought aloud.

"We can stay out here," Jackson offered. "If that'd help."

She nodded with a smile trying to press through her pursed lips.

"Then I'll see you tomorrow," he replied, winking as he continued. "Now get inside and save Bekah from her torment. I'm sure she's waiting to hear from you."

## Chapter 14

Evelyn was glad she didn't start work until ten that morning. Even with the thirty-five-minute walk, she was able to sleep in and have a lazy start to her day. It surprised her that Bekah was already gone by the time she woke up, but Bekah left a note telling her goodbye and that she expected lots of exciting news when she returned next week. She laughed her response. Jackson didn't see her as anything but a little girl who needed looking after. Still, he was the most wonderful man she'd ever had the privilege to know. She suspected he could indeed be the most wonderful man alive, but had not enough knowledge of any others to prove that theory.

Plenty of people needing help at her library kept the day from being monotonous. Tall stacks of books requiring re-shelving kept her moving the entire day. However, there'd never be enough of anything to keep her mind off of Jackson, at least not today.

It was dark, but still early, when she left, and the clouds that had threatened rain all day finally released a downpour. She walked home as quickly as she could but still managed to get soaked through completely by the time she arrived at her door. She still had hours until Jackson would be there. After making some tea while the bath filled up, she peeled off her wet clothes and relaxed into the tub, enjoying some much-appreciated quiet time. Knowing she didn't need to hurry to free the bathroom for her roommates, she soaked a long time, letting the hot water and tea warm her.

The rest of her afternoon and evening ticked by. She busied herself around the apartment, cleaning this and tidying that, and finally settled on making cookies for her and Jackson for that night.

Baking was a delight. The ladies who raised her taught her how preparing food for people was an act of love when done with joy in your heart. It was one of the lessons she treasured from her childhood. She hoped Jackson would enjoy them.

As time crept closer to Jackson getting off work, Evelyn's anxiety grew. Outside, rain continued its downpour and was eventually joined by thunder. She wondered in amusement if the weather had some connection to the turmoil of emotions stirring within her. She gathered a few blankets for them to use and waited. But eleven o'clock came and left, and Jackson didn't come. She wondered if perhaps he had just been delayed by the rain, but by midnight she gave up and went to bed. She felt like a fool as tears ran onto her pillow.

Frustrated, Jackson finished briefing the leading officer who had just arrived at the scene. Someone had been breaking into campus apartments sporadically the last few months and, just as he suspected, as fall break was upon them, there was another break-in. Luckily there hadn't been anyone home this time. Whoever this person or persons were, they were violent, fast, and elusive. It was midnight by the time he was off.

He felt horrible for standing up Evelyn, but there was nothing he could have done. He was sure she would be asleep by now; but still he decided to go by her apartment just in case a light was on. He also didn't like the idea of her being alone when they hadn't caught this guy yet. If nothing else than to assure himself of her safety, the walk would be worth it.

He grabbed an umbrella from his office and made his way to her apartment. As he suspected, her lights were off, but he was relieved to see that everything looked undisturbed.

Taking out a pen and paper, he set to leaving her a note. He owed her an apology and an explanation.

> *I'm so sorry I missed our evening together.*
> *We had a situation at work that I couldn't escape from.*
> *I want to see you. I'll come by at 9:00pm.*
> *I'll understand if you are unavailable.*
>     *Jackson*

He hoped she'd get it.

The sound of rain pelting her apartment roof was the first thing to penetrate her waking senses in the morning. Apparently, it was still coming down hard. Throwing off her covers, Evelyn stretched the sleep from her limbs and sat up.

It was Sunday.

Her face plopped into her hands. Her library was closed on Sundays, which meant no work. And rain meant no running. She'd be stuck inside with nothing to do but wonder why Jackson hadn't come over the night before.

"Ugh," she gasped at her reflection. Her eyes were a puffy mess. The consequences of her foolish tears over Jackson's no-show. "You're quite the killjoy this morning," she scolded herself. Being pessimistic wasn't in her nature, so she splashed cold water over her face, patted it dry with her towel, and determined not to spend the day thinking glumly about Jackson.

Late in the morning, she made herself some tea and, grabbing one of last night's cookies, decided that she'd watch the rain. She'd still be stuck at home, but at least she'd be outside. She needed a distraction from the quiet of the apartment. While stepping out her door, her bare foot landed on something. Curious, she reached down and picked up what turned out to be a note. She leaned against the wall, happiness curling her mouth into a smile, as she read his note. He had come by after all.

Work was getting busy, and crime was on the rise. Syracuse wasn't the same town it was when Jackson started college, or even the same town as when he left for New Mexico. Violence had made its way into his city. Patrols managed to keep things discreet, citizens panicking wouldn't help anything, but violence was there and getting worse.

His position was growing to encompass not just the campus, but the city as a whole. Captain Rogers, the man who oversaw the city's Patrols, was due to retire in a few short months. No one had said anything yet, but Jackson sensed that instead of hiring another Captain, that they were going to make his enlarged territory permanent. And that was fine with him. With all the high-ranking positions being steadily filled, he had been content assuming he'd have to look outside of Syracuse when he finished his masters. Now with Evelyn in his life, he would prefer to stay on in

Syracuse, at least while he processed his feelings for her, and hers for him. For the time-being, at least the rise in crime was providing decent job-security. And if Rogers' position merged with his, he'd be set for a good long while.

Jackson checked his bandage again before putting on his jacket. A fight had broken out just at the end of his shift and while breaking it up he managed to get cut by one of the idiots. The fact that both parties would be sleeping in cells tonight helped his mood, but only slightly. For the most part, he was running low on sleep and patience, and now his arm hurt. It didn't help things that his umbrella was in his office, and he was at the holding cells...a block off campus. He was tempted to run home before going to Evelyn's, but it was already a quarter to nine, and after last night, he didn't want to be late. It looked like soggy was going to be added to his list of complaints.

He'd been thinking a lot about the things he'd recently learned about Evelyn; mostly the fact that she was an orphan. The thought made him feel empty. How could such a precious girl be an orphan; to never know the love of her mother and father?

He didn't remember until after he had left her that Tom's father ran the orphan's government homes. He recalled Evelyn telling him that she had known Tom for a while. Did she mean she met him when she started college, or could she have meant she'd known him since she was a child?

The rain slowed long enough for Jackson to make it to Evelyn's apartment with only his face and jacket getting soaked; the rest of him was damp, but he could deal with that. As he knocked on her door, he was glad to see his note was missing.

The thunk of the deadbolt sliding to open brought his eyes up.

"You look pitiful."

It wasn't the greeting Jackson had hoped for, but looking at her standing in the doorway with her head leaned against the door, he didn't care what she said. He was just glad to see her. "Well thanks, Evelyn. It's so nice to see you too," he bantered.

She opened the door so there was space enough for him to come in. "You're going to get sick. Come in and we'll try to get you dry."

Jackson was grateful. He would have been more than willing to stay outside like they had agreed, but he also didn't enjoy being wet and would welcome any opportunity to get dry. He almost made a comment about the *we* she used, but perhaps tonight was too soon to tease her like that. Though he did wonder what she meant. "Thanks," he said, walking past her, trying to keep his inappropriate thoughts from showing on his face.

"Take off your jacket. I'll go get you a towel." Evelyn spoke while disappearing down the hall. He was grateful he managed to get his coat off before she returned so she wouldn't see the strain it was. He hung his jacket on the back of a kitchen chair as she returned, handing him a towel.

A groan slipped out as he lifted the towel to his face.

Stupid arm.

Stupid pride.

"Are you ok?" Evelyn asked at his side. She'd never expected to hear the sound of pain escape his lips. Now seeing a bandage soaked through with blood, every thought was for his care.

"Yeah," he answered. "Just a cut, that's all."

"You're tired," she said, fingering his bandage.

"It's been a long day."

Leaving his bandage alone, she looked up. The weight of Jackson's day eased as they looked at each other. She was so beautiful. His life would be good if he could come home to her every day.

He scolded himself. That was a dangerous thought to entertain.

"Has anyone looked at that?" she asked, her eyes rounded with concern.

"It's fine. Like I said, just a cut. Thank you for the towel." He handed it back to her.

"I'll take that as a no," she retorted, surprising him. "Sit down and let me look at it."

He raised his eyebrows at her adorable attempt at being stern, doubting she had any ability to deal with blood.

"Sit down," she ordered, and he did as she said. She pushed his sleeve up and undid his bandage, being careful not to hurt him. The cut was still bleeding a lot. She pressed the bandage against his cut again and looked at him. "Can you hold this while I go get some things?"

"I think I can manage," he answered smiling.

Evelyn went to the bathroom and came back with a fresh bandage, towels, alcohol, and something in a dark glass bottle. Sitting next to him, she put some alcohol on a rag and slid her hand under his, relieving him of his duty of holding the soaked-through bandage.

"You're lucky Bekah's a klutz," she commented, "or I might not have this stuff."

She had become a completely different person before his eyes. Where she normally was cautious, nervous, she now had steady, confident hands. Her lips pursed together as she concentrated, but he could find no sign of squeamishness in her.

In typical Jackson behavior, he hadn't taken the time to check how deeply he'd been cut. He regretted his carelessness now, seeing his blood on Evelyn's hands.

"You should have gloves on, Evelyn."

"And you should have had a doctor look at this," little miss feisty-pants countered. She glanced up, meeting his eyes for just a moment.

"Perhaps," he conceded. "But then I wouldn't have had this pleasure of having you as my beautiful nurse." He smiled to himself seeing her focus falter.

Neither acknowledged her blush.

Quicker than he'd expected, Evelyn had his arm cleaned and re-wrapped. He didn't miss the lingering of her fingers on his arm when she pulled his sleeve down.

"All done," she concluded, standing away from him.

Jackson looked over his new clean bandage. "Thank you," he said and then looked at Evelyn washing her hands. "What was that liquid you used?"

"Tea tree oil," she almost laughed. "You let me apply something and didn't know what it was?"

*Good point*, he thought. "I have to admit, I'm really impressed. Normally you seem so terrified of touching me, and here you are tonight mending my wound, getting my blood on you, and you're fine."

"I'm still plenty terrified of you," she admitted with a shy smile. "You don't need to stay, you know, if you are too tired. It seems like you could use some rest."

"I'd rather be with you right now." He hoped that wasn't too forward. "But," he added, hoping to calm her, "I did promise I'd stay on your patio since no one's home. I think it's about time we moved out there."

"Yes," she nodded, "you did promise that." Jackson stood up and opened the door for Evelyn and the armful of blankets she'd gathered. She quickly laid one of the blankets down as a barrier between them and the cold concrete, and motioned for him to sit.

"I feel like a little kid," he said as she placed the blanket over him. "Being all tucked in by my mom." He suddenly felt like a fool, remembering that she'd never had a mother, and didn't know what to say to amend his careless statement.

Evelyn laughed down at him. "So, your confidence can falter," she observed aloud. "You don't have to be so careful with me. I'm not going to get upset when you talk about moms. Just because I never had one doesn't mean it is a difficult subject for me. It's just the way it was. Besides, it's nice hearing that I have a motherly trait…I'll be right back." She stepped back in her apartment and reappeared with a plate of cookies. "I almost forgot," she told him, sitting and placing the plate between them. "I made cookies for us yesterday."

She made him smile. He had showed up at her door wet and in a foul mood. She helped him get dry, fixed his cut, practically tucked him in, and now was feeding him cookies. She was like a sweet balm, refreshing and healing to his aggravated spirit. "Thank you," he said and took a bite of a cookie. "Is everything you make this delicious?"

She pulled the remaining blanket over her, grinning at his question. "There are a few things that, I'll admit, I can make quite well." She kept her hands tucked under her blanket to hide her nervous energy. "So what happened last night?" she hesitantly asked.

Jackson leaned his head back against the wall. "There was another break-in, and this one left a lot to clean up. I'm worried the break-ins are just going to get worse, though, especially with so many people away right now. Makes the school an easy target." It also made beautiful young women easy targets, but he didn't voice that concern.

"What about tonight? How'd you get hurt?"

"Oh, tonight was nothing. Just two guys who got in a fight and I was careless when breaking it up. I'd rather not talk about work right now."

"Sorry, I didn't mean to pry."

He felt like an idiot. Again. "That's not it. I'm just tired is all and don't want to bore you. I'd really like to know more about you. Like what your childhood was like, if you wouldn't mind telling me."

"No," she smiled. "I don't mind. No one's ever asked me about it before. There's not much to tell. I grew up in a government home. My mother was able to stay off drugs through her pregnancy, but she dropped me off just days after I was born. I don't think she was strong enough to live free of them." Jackson closed his eyes as she talked. She told him about the other girls in the home, and the joy and sorrow that she felt each time someone was adopted, or the rare occasion of someone being reunited with their parents. She talked about her schooling, how working hard at it and doing well helped her to see value in herself. As she got older, she was taught how to help with the babies that were brought to the home. There was nothing she enjoyed more than the babies, but nothing made her sadder either. She never could understand how someone could abandon a baby to be raised without a home.

She finished telling him of the wonderful ladies who raised her, working at the home. They were the ones who taught her that being kind and helping people was a way to love them.

"Jackson?"

He opened his eyes and looked down at her, waiting for her question.

"I've always wondered, why do people who know love so deeply, act with so little kindness?"

"That's a good question," Jackson thought aloud. Conviction hit him harder than he wanted to admit. "I suppose it's because we're selfish."

"I don't understand."

"Well," Jackson tried again, "I think you understand that love is more than an emotion; it's something you give, like a gift. Most people never learn that. To them, love is all about the feeling they have, and if someone doesn't make them feel a certain way, they don't think they need to treat them with kindness." He glanced at Evelyn in time to see a mix of sadness and confusion run over her features.

The more Jackson knew of Evelyn, the more she was turning into a jigsaw puzzle in his mind. She was an orphan who managed to remain innocent of the world, even naïve to it. She acted with courageous kindness, but was terrified to make eye-contact with him; not to mention touch him. And she'd never known the love of parents, but couldn't understand others' inability to extend love. No matter how he tried, he couldn't get the pieces of her to fit together.

"Would you tell me about your childhood, about your family?" she asked, interrupting his ponderings.

He closed his eyes again and leaned his head back against the wall. He began where he thought she was actually asking about, by telling her about his parents.

"Before I was born, my dad served for the government. Since he started so young, by the time I was born, he was able to get a permanent station overseeing the cities surrounding his and my mom's. Dad was pretty strict. Disrespect of any sort wasn't tolerated, but he's a very kind man. Mother was the complete opposite. She's kind," he amended, "but not at all strict. She's always singing and still encourages me to dream and explore, like she did when I was a kid. Some people saw my parents as a strange couple, but no one can deny the love between them. I've never once seen my father take a harsh tone with Mother. He's always treated her with gentleness and respect. And Mother adores him, even when he's difficult."

The rustling of blankets turned Jackson's head, curious to see what was causing the noise.

The poor girl was trying to keep from shivering. Her legs were pulled up to her chest and she was pulling the blanket in more tightly around herself to keep the chill out.

Not being one to miss an opportunity, Jackson picked up the plate of cookies and, placing them on his other side, slid over to her. Her confusion was adorable when he took the blanket off his legs. He waited to explain until he had his arm around her and his blanket wrapped around the both of them. "You looked cold."

Evelyn's body spoke of her apprehension. Eyes fluttering shut on her inhale, she then exhaled slowly, and with the release of her breath, her body relaxed into his.

"Thank you. I am cold." She opened her eyes, blushing up at him. "This is better."

Their faces were so very close…close enough to easily close the distance between their lips.

"Would you tell me more?"

Evelyn turned and watched the rain, and Jackson put his desires in check before telling her more of his childhood.

Somewhere between talking about his schooling and telling stories of getting into mischief, his fingers begin to stroke her arm. Evelyn's breath caught at the surprise of it, but as he continued a story about his father, ever so slowly she melted back into the warmth of his side.

The storm had seized its passionate downpour, and now all that remained was a steady mist.

"We grew up rather differently," Jackson said, after finishing his story, enjoying the feel of her arm as he stroked it.

"Yes," Evelyn agreed, "very differently. I like hearing you talk about your family. Your parents sound wonderful. I'm glad you have parents who love you."

Jackson could only nod in response. His mind had wandered to less pleasurable thoughts.

"Are you okay?"

He nodded again. "Yes. Why do you ask?"

"You look like something's on your mind."

"I have been wondering about something," he admitted, "but I'm worried the subject will upset you." Evelyn gave him a look that was full of compassion and appreciation. More pieces to the puzzle. He had everything she lacked, yet she held compassion for him.

"I don't mind you asking me things. Even if it's difficult for me to answer, I will. If it's been bothering you, it's probably important."

Jackson looked down at Evelyn who was looking up at him with expectant eyes. He needed to do something with his mouth before he kissed her, so he asked her what he was wondering. "Did you know that Tom's father runs the government homes for children?"

"Of course I do," Evelyn answered. "Why have you been thinking about that?"

Jackson had to look away. Her mouth was far too tempting, and the look of waiting in her eyes – even if just waiting for his response – was moments from driving him to taste of her mouth once more. "That's not exactly what I've been thinking about. I'm curious how you met Tom, how long you've known him."

"Tom actually reminded me of that when I first ran into him some weeks back. I was nine when I met him. His dad brought him along on his monthly visits to our home. He always picked on me when I was little, but I hadn't seen him in the past three years. He wasn't nice to me until Sarah had him over earlier this semester. Well," she corrected herself, "I guess he's still picking on me…it's just different now."

It still didn't make sense to Jackson how Tom got close to her. If he'd always been mean, how did he change her opinion of him? "What was he like as a kid?"

Evelyn laid her head against Jackson's shoulder, shocking him into stillness. They sat like that while she thought back on Tom…and then she realized what she was doing.

"Jackson! I'm so sorry," she apologized, sitting up. "I didn't mean to do that."

"I don't mind it. I'm sure it's more comfortable than sitting straight up like that." He wasn't being honest, and he knew that, but he couldn't tell her that he preferred her closer. She looked doubtful, so he encouraged her still. "Really Evelyn, please lean back. I don't mind."

Evelyn leaned back against him again but was clearly not planning on resting her head on him. Jackson, knowing that full well, put his hand gently on her hair and brought her head against him.

"I really didn't know Tom when we were kids," she began. "I don't even know if the time I remember meeting him was his first time visiting or not. He always picked on someone when he came, so maybe I just remember when I became his target. He pulled my hair; not hard. I think he was just trying to test me. He said a lot of things I guess he meant to be mean, but they were true, so they didn't bother me. He…"

"What things did he say?" Jackson interrupted her.

"Oh, he just teased me about not having parents and not being loved; things like that. But like I said, it was true, and I already knew that, so it didn't bother me."

Jackson was shocked into silence. Not by what Tom had said to her, he could see him saying cruel things, but that it didn't bother her that he said those things.

Evelyn continued, seemingly unaffected by the memories. "He tried to hurt me over his next handful of visits, but I think he eventually gave up.

Then, I saw him making a girl cry and didn't like it, so I stood in between them. I thought maybe if I stood in front of the other girl, his words would hurt me instead. He didn't like being challenged, even then. I didn't mean to challenge him, though. I just meant to divert his attention. Anyway," she realized she had been rambling. "Does that answer your question?"

"Yes. But can I ask you something else?"

"Mmm-hmm."

"Why did you ever trust him enough for him to get so close to you?" Stillness overtook her. "I'm sorry, Evelyn. You don't need to answer that."

"No," she answered quietly. "I told you I'd answer you. To be honest, I ask myself the same question. I knew he was dangerous, but like I told you the other day, he was the first boy to compliment me or flir…" Embarrassment was getting the better of her.

Jackson squeezed her arm gently. "Don't worry, I understand. We've all been there at one time or another." And he really did understand, all too well.

Two Patrol officers were walking by and saw them. They stopped and called over to them. "It's almost eleven, you two."

"Thank you, officers," Jackson called back, and their eyes widened when they realized who he was. He almost shook his head. Was his reputation really so intimidating?

"Sorry, sir, we didn't see that it was you."

Jackson knew it was time for him to leave. They both needed sleep, and he had a long week ahead of him. "Are you two going to headquarters?" he called to them.

"Yes, sir."

"I'll join you. Just give me a minute, would you?"

"Of course, sir. Take your time." They turned away, pretending not to be interested in who their Captain was spending time with.

Jackson turned to Evelyn. "I really should be going."

Evelyn nodded and stretched out her legs, not wanting to leave the warmth of the blankets, or lose the closeness between them.

He stood and helped her up before he picked up the plate of cookies and the blankets and placed them inside her door, being sure to stay in view of the officers. He didn't need to give anyone another reason to gossip about her. "Thank you for allowing me over tonight."

"I'm glad you came." Evelyn wanted to ask him when she would see him again, but hesitated, not knowing how to ask such a thing. "I work the next couple days," she tried. "Will you be by at all, do you think? I just mean…" but she trailed off.

Jackson smiled. "I'll be away for a couple of days for work. I should be back Wednesday."

The idea of Jackson being away was not a pleasant one in Evelyn's mind. He made her feel safe, not just when he was with her, but from simply knowing he was around. "Will you visit me," she asked quietly, not daring to be any bolder, "when you get back?" Her fingers played with the hem of her shirt as she spoke.

"Yes." His answer was quiet, but in an intimate, sure manner.

Wonderful butterflies flitted around in her stomach. "I work until four thirty on Wednesday. I'll be home after that." She peeked at the two officers waiting for Jackson. When they saw her looking, they quickly looked away and pretended to not have been caught watching. "You should probably go," she said, looking back to Jackson. "They're waiting for you."

"You're probably right. I'll see you Wednesday." He turned to leave but stopped, facing her again, the previous nights' break-ins suddenly invading his mind. "Evelyn, please be careful while I'm away." He left with that, falling into stride with his officers as he caught up with them.

Evelyn closed the door and locked it. The next couple of days were going to be lonely.

## Chapter 15

Little rays of sunlight came jabbing through her blinds the next morning. Evelyn rolled out of bed and threw the blinds up.

"Yes," sighed out of her. Not a cloud in sight. Not that she disliked clouds, but when the silence of loneliness overwhelmed life, a cloudless sky meant a day she could escape for a run.

She tried to avoid campus over breaks. It was too quiet, and anyone she passed noticed her. She much preferred being unnoticed. But Bekah's excitement about the spring run continued to play on repeat in her mind. She needed to check out the Patrol's course.

Patrol Headquarters was one of the only offices operating over break, but even they ran on a skeleton crew, so no one was using the course when she got there. Sure enough, there was the flyer Bekah had told her about, confirming the use of the course for the race. Evelyn took her time looking it over. The ropes were going to prove a challenge; she didn't have any experience on those. Maybe Jackson could give her some advice…

No. She certainly wouldn't be informing him that she would be running. She didn't need his eyes on her through it. She wouldn't be able to move if he was watching. But the course would be near impossible if the crowd was the same size as last year's.

It was easier to be alone during the day, and with the sun shining. By night, she was lonely with not enough to do. Books and studying only took up so much time, and every night ended with Evelyn going to bed early, only to wake earlier that she hoped the next day.

Wednesday finally came. Her body woke her early, which she knew would happen. She lay in bed as long as she could, but eventually gave in to the restlessness and threw off the covers. She at least had plenty of time to get ready for work.

Jackson claimed most of her thoughts on her walk to work. It was silly to be so eager to see him, but they were friends. She justified her eagerness by deciding all friends got excited to see each other.

Of course, she was lying to herself.

Her day ticked by slower than a snail's pace. She was quite sure no other day had ever taken so long. Time and time again, she would be certain that she had waited a half hour before checking the clock, but would find that she had only waited five minutes. Never before had she been so impatient to get home!

Four thirty finally arrived and she gathered her things and locked up quicker than she ever had. The hope of seeing Jackson that night bubbled excitedly within her. Anxiety quickly followed, flooding her with doubts.

Selecting her outfit consumed most of her attention. She wore her long brown skirt and the green sweater she liked. Bekah, she thought, would have been a world of help to her, as fashion was just one of the many areas of life where she was completely hopeless. Looking into the mirror one last time, she sighed and willed herself to believe her clothes were fine. Then, she let her hair down, pinning a few pieces back like Bekah always encouraged her to do. She hoped Jackson would like it, too.

After that, there was nothing to do but wait. She had already cleaned the apartment, twice, having so much time to herself over the past couple of days, so she sat on the couch and tried not to watch the clock. At long last there was a knock at the door. Jumping to her feet, she hurried to answer it. She should have waited, so as not to give the impression that she was just waiting around for him. But the knob was turning and the door opening before she could think.

Evelyn stared at him for a moment, unsettled by his appearance. He looked upset; unstable. "Tom, what are you doing here?"

"You answered quickly. Were you expecting someone else?" Tom glanced past her and she knew he saw the jacket. She hadn't even realized Jackson had left it until Monday morning, but he saw it right away. "Jackson, maybe?"

"Tom, why don't you come back later? I'm not feeling well," she lied. Her skin was tingling and her heart thundering. She tried to close the door, but he was too quick and too strong for her.

Tom pushed the door open and grabbed her arm, moving her back as he forced his way in. Her mind focused on the door. She couldn't let it close. Closed doors were harder to get through, and she desperately wanted to escape. By a stroke of luck, her jacket hung next to the door and she was able to hit it down as he threw the door back to close it. The door closed but didn't latch.

He smelt of alcohol. "I know what you've been up to, Evie. You've been a busy girl." He glared at her as he spoke, tightening his grip on her arm.

"I don't know what you're talking about. I've been alone all week." Evelyn tried to calm the panic pressing in on her, tried to keep her mind clear, hoping to find a solution that got her away from him. Panic didn't solve problems.

Tom struck her across her face. The force made her fall, and panic burrowed closer to her heart. Before she could recover, Tom jerked her back up. She was a rag doll at his mercy. "You know, everyone already thinks we've done this. So really, I'm not taking anything that wasn't already gone." He spit the words out at her and grabbed her face, putting his mouth on hers and letting his free hand explore her.

"Tom, no!" Evelyn tried to scream, pushing and hitting at him. She'd try anything to get away from him. Somehow, she managed to get a hand to his face. She had meant to claw him, but her scratch still caused his grip to falter. Now she needed to run.

Tom's violent shove sent her slamming into a wall, rattling her insides. All she managed was to make him angrier…and so much more determined. He covered her scream with his hand, the sound almost completely muffled. She heard her shirt ripping as he pulled at the shoulder while he defiled her exposed skin with his mouth. Still, she tried to fight him off, but it was no use. All of her strength was futile against him.

And then she saw him, and tears flooded her eyes as relief washed over her.

Jackson.

Evelyn had never seen rage like that which was emanating from Jackson as he went at Tom.

Jackson pulled Tom off of Evelyn and threw him against the counter, sending the fruit bowl scattering to the ground. Grabbing him again, Jackson ran his knee into Tom's stomach and as Tom doubled over, he drove his elbow between his shoulders, causing Tom to fall to the ground.

Tom laughed as he stood back up, breathing heavily. "I'm sorry; did I blemish your precious child, sir? I don't know why you're even wasting your time on her; she's just a revolting tease!" His words were pungent with malice.

Tom's voice sickened Jackson, and he decided he was done hearing it. He silenced him, punching him in the mouth.

Evelyn was watching it all in horror. She needed to do something. She hated Tom in that moment, but she didn't want to see anyone beat unconscious before her eyes, and Jackson was showing no signs of slowing his assault.

"Jackson!" She cried as he struck Tom again. "Please, Jackson, no more," she begged. Jackson kept his eyes on Tom, and Tom looked defiantly back, but he was on the ground, not attempting to get up, and not talking. Evelyn walked to Jackson and took his hand in both of hers, hoping she could calm him down. He was shaking.

His anger scared her. She'd never seen him out of control, but the look in his eyes said he was teetering over the line. She held tighter to his hand, needing his strength to steady her, and hoping her touch would somehow communicate that need.

Slowly, he turned to face her, but as soon as his eyes were off of Tom, Tom used the opportunity to strike, kicking Jackson in the stomach and knocking him off balance.

Tom was up in an instant. Evelyn couldn't bear the thought of Jackson getting hurt. It was her fault he'd taken his eyes off Tom. "Please Tom…" She jumped between the men. Stepping closer to Tom, she thought she saw his face soften with a glimpse of the Tom she'd gotten to know before he tried to kiss her. "Please don't hurt him." But his face hardened again, and he pushed her hard out of his way.

Everything was a blur of pain for a few moments. By the time Evelyn could focus again, Jackson had taken Tom outside her door and had him pinned to the ground under his knee. Tom was bleeding profusely, but he was still conscious.

Evelyn felt behind her. She'd landed against the table. No blood, but she was going to hurt for a while from this.

Jackson whistled and a group of officers came clamoring up her steps. As soon as another officer had a hold of Tom, Jackson was at her side.

"Miss Carter?"

Her eyes met his. His face was void of emotion, but his eyes, something was in them.

"I need you to lay still. This is officer " She missed the name. "He's going to see to your injuries." Jackson returned to the group of officers leaving her with whoever this man was.

"I'm fine," she assured the officer. She probably wasn't fine, but the last thing she wanted was another man's hands on her. Bile threatened, stinging her throat, at the thought. "I was just a little shaken by it all." The officer wasn't getting the clue. "Please don't touch me," she asked quietly, fearing Jackson would overhear. "I don't want you to touch me."

"I understand," the officer answered with a gentleness she didn't notice. "Just don't try…"

Evelyn watched as other men, officers, combed through her apartment. She felt exposed. Violated. And not just by Tom. She didn't invite men, or anyone, to look so closely into her home.

"Miss Carter." That officer was still there. Evelyn's eyes shifted to acknowledge him. "You're in shock, Miss Carter. Physically, you'll be fine, but I'm only going to sign you off if you promise to not move until we all leave and Jack takes a look at you. If you can't do that," he spoke to her confusion, "I'll be forced to take you to a doctor. Can I trust you to do that?"

She nodded.

"Then, I just need one more thing. I can't leave you on the floor, so I'm going to help you into a chair. You only need to take my hand, and I'll hold your arm to steady you. Then you'll be rid of me." He did a curious thing then and smiled. Compassion and sadness lined his eyes as he looked at her. No mockery or teasing. Not even a hardness.

Evelyn nodded once more and allowed the officer…she should have listened better to his name…help her into the chair. Honest to his word, he left her side as soon as she was seated. Somehow she knew he'd been a kind man.

As the other officers turned to leave with Tom, Jackson's parting words drifted almost too quietly to her ears.

"I told you what would happen. If you so much as look at her again, you won't have the luxury of walking away."

The cold hatred in his voice sent a shiver down her spine.

## Chapter 16

Evelyn watched Jackson as he came in and closed the door behind him, her eyes refusing to break away. She wanted to memorize this man who had rescued her. His hands. His arms. His chest and shoulders. His face. He was so capable at everything. Tom, who was powerful and practiced in hurting people, never stood a chance against him. Jackson was the embodiment of strength.

With every deeply-drawn breath, Jackson's body relaxed a little more. He was still tight, still tense, but under control now.

"Thank you, Jackson." Evelyn shook her head. "I wish I knew how to better say it." Thank you didn't begin to express what she felt toward him.

Jackson remained standing by the door. "How are you?"

Evelyn tried to smile, but it felt more like a frown. "I'm fine," she lied again. Because of him, she was safe, but the feeling of powerlessness and horror lingered. She could still feel Tom's hands on her, his mouth on her neck. She was not fine.

"George said he wanted me to take a second look at your head."

She nodded her head in agreement, but only a little because she was slowly becoming aware to the pain pulsating through it.

Jackson moved slowly toward her, not knowing if his own touch would frighten her. He knelt at her side, noting the dilation of her pupils at his approach. If not for her tattered clothes and disheveled hair, she would have the appearance that everything was as she said, fine. But as she sat perfectly straight, her hands shook as they mindlessly fiddled with the fabric of her skirt, giving light to her emotions.

"Do you trust me not to hurt you?" He needed her assurance before he laid a hand on her. She swallowed harder than she nodded, but he'd take it. He slowly began his exam of her, checking her head and looking at the bruising already beginning to show on her face. "Did he…" he paused to collect his thoughts and suppress his boiling rage. "Did he hurt you in any way before I got here, that I should know about? Or that you'd need a doctor for?"

Her paled skin assured him she knew what he was asking. He thanked God when she shook her head.

He wanted desperately to hold her and tell her it was over, that everything was okay, but he worried his touch, any man's touch, was the last thing she wanted. He'd made his mind up about something, though, and he knew she would be opposed to it. "I need you to pack whatever things you'll need to get you through to whenever Bekah and Sarah return."

Evelyn didn't want to be here, but where else would she go? "I've already explained to you, I have nowhere else to go."

"You can't stay here," Jackson stated. His tone softened, but his eyes remained adamant. "I'm taking you to my parents' home. We'll stay with them until I know you won't be alone here anymore. I would have you stay at my house, because it's closer, but I know you wouldn't allow it."

Evelyn was taken aback by his plan. What was he thinking? Who was she to him that he'd take her to his family's house? Who was he to even suggest it? "I can't just go and impose on your parents, Jackson. Tom is in a cell; he won't be able to bother me. I'll be fine here."

"Then you'd rather stay at my house?"

"No! I can't stay with you, and I can't stay with your family either!" She had never yelled at him before and wasn't sure why she was yelling now.

Jackson walked to the couch and sat down, wiping the sweat from his palms on his knees. The adrenaline was beginning to clear out of his veins, and it left him feeling nervous, weak, and desperate. "You don't understand. I can't leave you here. I won't. It would be unbearable for me, not knowing if you were okay. And I know you don't want to be here alone, so please do not lie to me and say that you do."

Evelyn was trying to make sense of her situation. There had to be a solution that didn't involve her imposing on him or his family.

"Please," he was begging. "Please come with me, Evelyn. We don't have much time. I instructed the officers to arrange transportation for us. I promise you, my parents will be like-minded with me. My mother would shoot me if she found out I left you here alone, and my father and I are almost exactly the same in how we think. They wouldn't expect me to do any differently. Now please go get your things."

Evelyn's head was pounding now. She was too tired to argue anymore. So she nodded and went to pack her things.

Her reflection in the bathroom mirror flooded her with embarrassment. She'd wanted so much to look nice tonight, and now she was a disaster. Her hair and clothes were a mess, a bruise was already appearing over her eye, and marks of her defilement colored her shoulder and neck. Shame pierced her.

She packed her clothes and what personal items she thought she would need and changed into warm clothes, throwing her discarded ones in the trash. She would never be able to wear them again without thinking about tonight; and besides, her sweater was ruined. She pulled the pins out of her hair and draped it around her shoulders, trying to hide the marks of her shame. Nothing else could be done. She took up her bag and walked back to the front room where Jackson was waiting for her.

"Ok," was all she could say. With her ruined reflection fresh in her mind, she felt dirty and worthless before him.

Jackson took her bag and put it over his shoulder as she put on her jacket, and they left. It was the coldest night they'd had so far this winter and the air bit at Evelyn's face. She hoped in vain it would numb the pain Tom's hand left behind, but instead it just added to it.

"You don't need to carry my bag, Jackson. I don't mind carrying it," she spoke to Jackson's back as she followed him.

"It's fine."

Jackson was angry with her; she was sure of it. Tears stung her eyes as a sob rose in her throat, but she had put him through so much already…she refused to add another burden, and she forced herself to stay composed. Once she was alone, there'd be plenty of time for tears.

Jackson looked back and saw that Evelyn was struggling to keep up with his pace. He stopped and waited for her to catch up. When she did, she stopped next to him and kept her eyes down. He took her hand gently in his and started walking again, slower this time. The fever his anger was burning in him began to subside with her hand in his.

Evelyn had assumed they would go to the Patrol Headquarters, but they were walking the opposite direction. It took her two blocks to work up the courage to speak. "Where are we going?"

"The Cell Building," Jackson answered. Worry creased Evelyn's forehead. "We won't need to go in. Our transportation should be waiting for us outside."

Evelyn had never traveled by anything but her two feet and the city buses. Only military and the very rich, or very important, had access to private vehicles. A bus wouldn't alter its route for them, so she figured they must be taking a Patrol car, but she was wrong.

An unmarked car and driver were waiting for them. Jackson was much more important than he let on. Having a private vehicle and driver available at his beck and call meant one of two things: he was either very rich or very distinguished. Either way, Jackson was a powerful man.

"Thanks for being here," Jackson spoke to the driver as they approached and handed off Evelyn's bag. "I owe you."

"Don't mention it, Jack," the driver replied. "I was glad you had the mind to request me." The driver, a slightly older gentleman, turned his kind face to Evelyn and held out his free hand. "I'm Jim, Miss…?"

"Evelyn," she supplied, reluctantly slipping her hand from Jackson's to shake Jim's.

"It's very nice to meet you, Evelyn," he smiled kindly. "Should be a quiet drive up to the Monroe's. Not much traffic, and the weather seems to be behaving."

She smiled. He seemed to understand her silence, or at least respect it.

Jackson held the door open for her, gesturing for her to get in. She hesitated for a moment. She would be getting into a car with a driver she'd only just met, and a man she realized she really knew almost nothing about, except that he made her feel safe. That would have to be enough.

Jackson slid in after her and sat across from her. The inside of the vehicle was spacious, very spacious, with two bench-length leather seats facing each other. At a quick glance, she found a blanket folded on each seat, bottles of water in the cup-holders, and more buttons than she thought any vehicle ever needed. Never had she imagined transportation to be so luxurious.

Jackson stared out the window as they drove. Evelyn watched him openly from her seat, thinking him unaware of her gaze. She noticed his hands were clean now, his knuckle still looked raw, but wasn't bleeding. He must have washed his hands while she had packed.

His eyes met hers when she gazed back up at his face.

"What?" He didn't mean for it to come out so short.

"I'm so sorry I've put you in this situation."

"You have nothing to be sorry for. It's not your fault that Tom did what he did."

She wasn't so sure of that. Even so, she knew Tom was mad. She knew revenge was coming. "I was worried about you. That's why I asked you to stop; not for his sake."

"Worried about me?" Jackson wondered. "Why were you worried about me?"

"You seemed so angry," Evelyn answered. "I didn't want you to do something you'd regret later."

"I don't think I've ever been so angry before," Jackson admitted. He had wanted to kill Tom when he saw him with his hands on Evelyn and kissing her neck, and when he saw the terror on her face. He was still praying against the desire to murder him. "But I assure you, I knew what I was doing."

"I'm s…sorry," she stammered. "I…I didn't mean to say I doubted you." She didn't know what else to say, so she stayed quiet.

"Evelyn," Jackson said, allowing gentleness into his voice. He hated hearing the tremor in her speech. "I told you, you have nothing to be sorry for, and I meant it. You did nothing wrong, except…"

"Except what?"

"Nothing."

"Jackson, except what?" She asked again.

He sighed. "Except you put yourself between us. Why on earth would you do that?" His voice was tense again.

She looked down to her fidgeting hands. "I didn't want him to hurt you."

Jackson leaned over, putting his head in his hands and running his fingers through his hair. He was ashamed to admit, even to himself, that he was angry with her. He was angry she'd put herself in harm's way, that she thought her own safety was less important than his. "It was a very stupid thing to do." He tried to steady his voice, but he knew it came out harsh. "I'm sorry," he quickly added. "Please forgive me. I didn't mean that. But it made me sick when I saw you hurt. Walking in and finding him there, and then seeing you hit the table the way you did, it was worse than any harm he could have done to me."

"I'm so sorry," Evelyn uttered. She didn't want to think about Tom anymore. She didn't want to think about any of it. But there was no escaping it.

"Evelyn, you're safe now," Jackson spoke, trying to comfort her. "Why don't you try to get some rest? It'll be a little while before we arrive."

Evelyn was tired, and the pounding in her head was getting steadily worse. She didn't want to sleep, though, terrified by what her dreams might hold, but closed her eyes and eventually lost the battle, dozing off.

Once she was asleep, Jackson felt it was safe to look at her. His heart ached for her. His mind wandered over the evening's events. He'd noticed her jacket in the door when he arrived at her apartment. He didn't think it was an accident that it was there. She was smart to try and keep the door open. When he tested the door, it moved without a sound, opening the scene to his worst nightmare.

He still didn't know how he'd kept himself from killing Tom. The truth was, he didn't restrain himself. The three-word-prayer, God help me, he'd sent up when he went after Tom had been answered. Every ounce of self-control was the grace of God poured over him. Even now, it was only that prayer, repeated over and over again in his mind, keeping him steady.

All he wanted to do now was hold Evelyn and tell her, convince her, she was safe. Not just safe, but treasured and protected. But experience reminded him that his touch may prove too much.

*Oh God,* he prayed, *You're a God of mercy and grace and healing. Thank you, God thank you, for getting me to her before it was too late; before Tom got what he was there for. Thank you for giving her the wisdom to put her jacket into the doorway, that Tom wasn't thinking enough to lock the door behind him. And thank you for keeping me from murder. You know my thoughts, oh Lord. You know my anger, and you know my feelings for this woman. Thank you for being there with all of us, for being here with us now. But God, how do I comfort her? How do I show her she's safe with me? How do I keep her safe now?*

Jackson couldn't tear his eyes from the woman across from him. She looked so uncomfortable sitting up as she was. What was the harm in letting her sleep comfortably? And she had let him hold her hand. That was all the prompting he needed.

Sliding into the seat next to her, he gently put his arm around her, tipping her into himself and away from the frigid window. In her sleepy state, she snuggled into him and brought her hand to his chest as she would if he were her pillow. He smiled and closed his eyes, happy knowing she was safe and in his arms.

# Chapter 17

"Oh goodness! Jackson!" Evelyn gasped, sitting up too quickly. How long had her head been on his chest? "I'm so sorry! I just…" But she didn't. It dawned on her, "You moved."

He gave a guilty smirk. "Do you mind?"

"No," she answered honestly. Her head was throbbing now. His arm was still around her and his fingers began stroking her arm like he had on her porch the night of the storm, but the events with Tom were still too fresh and she slid over to put more space between them.

"I'm sorry."

She tried to smile reassuringly at him, but the pain in her head made it impossible.

"Evelyn?" The concern in Jackson's voice confirmed her failure to hide her pain. "Evelyn, are you ok?"

"Yes." She hoped. Maybe she should have let the officer, or at least Jackson, check her over better. "I just have a headache."

"Did George give you anything for the pain?"

"No," she confessed. "I sort of told him to leave me alone." She felt like a little girl regretting her temper-tantrum.

"That's fine." He shouldn't find any of this amusing, but he would have enjoyed seeing her order George around. Seems she did have a little spark in her.

Evelyn peeked through one eye and watched him sort through a compartment of medicine.

"Take these." He handed her two pills. She put them in her mouth without question. She'd do anything to make the pain go away. "And drink as much as you can of this," he said, handing her a bottle of water.

She managed to drink half the bottle, but stopped at the protest of her stomach. Jackson graciously took the bottle from her. She kept her eyes closed, trying to shut out the pain.

"Evelyn?" His tone was careful. "How hard did you hit the table?"

"Hard," she answered. "But it didn't knock me out. You don't need to worry. I can think fine. No concussion. Just a headache."

"We have about an hour left to my parents' house. You should sleep if you can."

She nodded and obeyed, fighting the yearning to let Jackson hold her, and instead leaning the opposite direction of him.

The car took a sharp turn and slowed down drastically, rousing Evelyn from her sleep. "We're here," Jackson said, as he looked out the window.

Jackson held the door open for Evelyn again and helped her out of the car. Jim greeted her with a smile and handed Jackson her bag. Only then did she realize Jackson didn't have anything with him, and that her head was feeling much better.

"You didn't bring anything?" she asked.

He looked down and smiled. "I have things here so I don't have to worry about packing. You ready?"

She looked up at the huge house before them. Even in the dark it was beautiful. "Not in the slightest." She tried to smooth the rumples out of her brown sweater. When they were leaving, her only thoughts were for warmth and to cover as much of her skin and shame as she could. Now she wished she'd chosen something a bit nicer.

They walked up a number of steps and through beautifully foreboding, French, wooden doors. Evelyn's eyes tried to take in everything, but the shadows of night concealed the home and its surroundings. The inside was dimly lit, yet stunning. Warm, sweet smelling air flowed through it and, even though the house was the largest Evelyn had ever been in, she found it charming and cozy. She didn't belong here, with these vast ceilings and fine things, nor was she worthy of Jackson's kindness or hospitality.

"Mom? Dad?" Jackson called out.

"In here," came a man's voice from another room.

Evelyn couldn't tell which direction it came from, but Jackson did and began walking toward one of the open doors. She couldn't convince her feet to move.

Jackson looked back and saw Evelyn rooted in place. He went to her, took her hand, and gently led her forward. "You have nothing to be nervous about."

His parents waited for them in the study. His father sat at a table next to a fire, going through documents while his mother sat in a chair reading a book.

"You've brought a guest," his mother said delightfully, getting up to hug her son. His father stood at the sight of Evelyn and came to greet them.

Evelyn let go of Jackson's hand when she saw his mother notice them. She wished she had let go sooner.

"This is Evelyn Carter," Jackson gestured to her. "Evelyn, these are my parents, Natalie and Charles."

Jackson's parents couldn't have looked less alike. Mr. Monroe was very handsome, with fair skin and dark brown hair worn short and neat. Mrs. Monroe was about Evelyn's height, but built stronger with a very petite waist. She had thick, blond, wavy hair that complimented her olive skin beautifully. They were a very handsome couple.

"It's very good to meet you, Mr. & Mrs. Monroe," Evelyn said, shaking Jackson's mother's extended hand.

"You will call us Natalie and Charlie," his father replied, winking as he gently took her hand in his.

"So, to what do we owe the pleasure of our son coming home a day early, and with a guest?" Natalie asked, smiling at Evelyn but clearly directing her question to her son.

"Evelyn was involved in an unfortunate situation…" Jackson began. He looked down at her. "I can explain later, if you'd like, so you don't have to hear it all again."

Evelyn's cheeks burned with embarrassment, but she shook her head. Neither parent had asked, but since there was no hiding the marks already showing on her skin, they had to be curious about her story and she'd prefer it come from her. She touched her hair, making sure enough hung over her shoulder to conceal at least some of her shame.

"Thank you, but no. I'd rather explain. I'm so sorry; it's really all my fault. I managed to become…acquainted with someone who, well, with someone rather noxious." She looked up at Jackson. "I don't deserve it, but your son saved me." She looked back to his parents. "Jackson knew I didn't have anywhere else to go and invited me here. I'm so sorry to impose."

"That's not really the whole truth," Jackson added, looking at his dad. "It was an officer, Thomas Williamson," his father raised an eyebrow, "who assaulted her. And I didn't invite her here. I made her come."

Evelyn was shocked when Jackson's mother threw her arms around her, hugging her so tight that she almost couldn't breathe.

"I'm so glad he made you come, dear! We'll have so much fun together!" Natalie exclaimed.

Evelyn already liked his family, very much. She fought back her tears, refusing to let a single one drop. If she let them go now, there'd be no stopping them.

Natalie reluctantly let go of her. "Well, let's get you something to eat, and then we'll show you to your room. I'm sure you're both hungry."

"Starving!" Jackson exclaimed. He took Evelyn's hand again as they followed his parents to the kitchen. It felt awkward, but she couldn't deny the comfort it gave her.

Natalie laid out a small feast. Evelyn snacked on a biscuit, dipping it in delicious gravy, as she watched Jackson. He was speaking to his mother quietly while eating more food than she thought any one person could consume on his own. They both seemed to be guarding their expressions, but every so often, Natalie would glance in her direction. Charles, who was sitting close by, smiled at her.

"There's no trusting those two," he said loudly, so as to tease his son and wife. "They're always up to no good."

Evelyn smiled with their laughter.

After they had their fill, Natalie offered to show Evelyn to her room while Jackson and his father excused themselves back to the study. Having seen the look his father gave Jackson when he said Tom's name, Evelyn assumed more would be said about Tom privately.

"I just need to grab my bag," she said as she started following Natalie.

Natalie waved her off. "Jackson will bring it up," she explained, and led her up a flight of stairs.

The room Natalie took her to was lovely. The walls were a delicate pink, and the bed looked like a cloud, decorated with soft, white linens. "This room is lovely, Mrs. Monroe. Your whole house is beautiful."

"Thank you, Evelyn, but if you call me Mrs. Monroe again, I will be forced to call for Charlie." Natalie replied lightheartedly. She sat in one of the two wicker chairs in the room and invited Evelyn to take the other. "Jackson cares for you, and he's worried about you as well. He's convinced you lied to him when you told him you were okay."

Evelyn looked down. She didn't wonder what the two of them had been speaking about any more. "He's been very kind to me and more attentive than I deserve. I confess I am struggling right now, but I will be fine, thanks to him."

"I know we've only just met, but you're welcome to come to me anytime if you need someone to talk to," Natalie comforted her. "But just know, Jackson wants to be here for you." She stood. "I'll let you get some rest. If you need anything, Jackson will be in the next room, and we are at the end of the hall. The restroom is across the hall, and the kitchen is always open. Please consider this your home while you're here."

Evelyn stood with her. "Thank you, Natalie."

Natalie smiled and left, leaving the door cracked behind her.

Evelyn sat at the vanity and looked at herself in the mirror. She touched her eye where she'd been hit. It was bruised, but not black like she thought it'd be. She moved her hair to look at her other bruises. Images of Tom replayed in her mind. She hadn't washed since he'd attacked her. She could feel him still on her, still claiming her. Panic was swallowing her. She rose to find the restroom so she could wash Tom off of her and literally ran into Jackson when she opened the door.

Jackson saw the panic on her face. "What's wrong?"

Too many emotions pulsed through Evelyn when she looked into his caring eyes. He'd done too much for her, and all she'd brought him was trouble. "I'm so, so sorry, Jackson." He started to tell her again that she had nothing to be sorry for, but she cut him off. "I know what you're going to say, but I hate what I've put you through. From the moment I asked you for help in the gardens, I have been nothing but trouble for you, and you've saved me from so much..." She was very near tears. "I don't understand you at all, Jackson Monroe. Why are you so nice to me?"

He walked towards her, but she backed up with each step he took. She was scared; scared by what had happened to her, scared of letting that fear overtake her, scared of him.

"Why won't you let me near you?"

"Because I don't deserve to be near you! I'm dirty! I'm covered with him! I can still feel him on me," she cried out, touching her neck, disgusted with herself. Jackson reached out and brushed her hair from her shoulder, exposing her bruises. She trembled under his fingertips. The marks would fade and eventually disappear from sight, but she'd carry them with her nonetheless. He moved toward her, slowly bringing her to him, and wrapped his arms around her.

"I'm so sorry I wasn't there sooner. I'm so sorry I couldn't stop him from hurting you."

Evelyn couldn't stop the tears now and she sobbed. She curled into his arms and he held her close as she released the flood of emotions she had been holding back over everything that had happened. His fingers ran through her hair and gently rubbed her back, trying to comfort her.

After a long time, the tears stopped and her breathing calmed, but still he held her. She wiggled her arms out from between their bodies and wrapped them around his waist. "I don't deserve this."

He sighed quietly into her hair. "I already told you, you're very worth it." A while later, but still too soon, he released her. "I'm sure you'd like to get ready for bed now. I brought your things up." He grabbed her bag from outside her door and placed it on her bed. Even in his parents' home, and after all she'd been through, temptation attacked him being alone with her. "My mother probably told you, but I'm in the next room. If you need anything, please let me know." He turned and left, not wanting to leave her, but needing to. He hated himself for being so weak.

Evelyn wished she could have stayed in his arms for always. She was safe there. It was such a new feeling for her to find safety in someone else. She'd never had anyone care for her or comfort her. Not like Jackson did. Of course, she had the Madames who raised her, but it was their job. It was Jackson's job too, she realized, to keep people safe. He'd said his parents would agree with him in bringing her with him, and he was right;

but it was Charles' job, as well. Maybe all of what they were doing for her was because it was their duty. The thought left her feeling a bit hollow, but she held fast to her gratefulness for all of them.

She took what she needed from her bag and found the restroom. The shower was hot; washing Tom off seemed hopeless, but maybe she could burn him off. Her skin was red and tender when she was done, but she didn't care. She dressed for bed and tried in vain to sleep. Hours later, when she finally drifted off, Tom waited for her in her dreams.

When she woke the next morning, her eyes were swollen and her pillow was wet.

# Chapter 18

Jackson rose early. He spent his sleepless night in prayer and poring over scripture. Experience taught him that his best rest came from spending time alone with God, and though his body was moving a little slower, his heart and mind were refreshed.

He wisely anticipated Evelyn's uncertainty of waking in a strange home, so kept an attentive ear to her room. When he heard movement, he went to greet her.

He kept his knock quiet.

She'd been crying. His heart ached for her. He gave her a moment to focus her thoughts before he spoke. The way her eyes took him in stroked his pride. Of course, she could just be adjusting to seeing him in flannel instead of a uniform or his teaching attire.

Her eyes found his.

"Good morning," she said as she opened the door further, taking a step back to put more space between them. She instinctively draped her hair over her shoulder, trying to hide the marks on her neck.

Jackson smiled warmly. "Do you know where you are?"

"We're at your parents' home. I didn't hit my head that hard!"

"I know you know that, but do you know where my parents' home is?"

"Oh," she blushed. "No, I don't know where we are. Where are we?"

"Well, at my parents' house, of course." He teased, rolling his eyes. "What a silly question." He smiled again and took her hand, leading her out of her room and towards the stairs.

Jackson had taken her hand a number of times since they left her apartment, and thus far she hadn't protested. But this morning she didn't hold on. Instead, she slipped her hand from his.

That was a bit discouraging.

"Just follow me." He led her down the stairs, to the back doors, and out onto the back deck.

The view was breathtaking. The Monroe home sat at the edge of a lake, surrounded by trees with their leaves on fire with reds and oranges. Jackson smiled seeing Evelyn lose herself in the beauty around them. She walked to the edge of the deck and rested her arms on the railing.

Jackson always felt God's presence and His peace here, at his parents' home. He watched Evelyn gazing out at the lake, happy to see her appear carefree and at ease for once. He knew she wouldn't notice him stepping away, so he slipped back into the house for blankets and coffee.

He held both cups of coffee out for her choosing when he returned. "I didn't know how you take your coffee."

"I like it sweet," she replied, her smile sweeter than the sugar in her coffee.

Preferring his black, he gladly relinquished the sweetened cup. As he had done in the library so many times when giving or receiving a book from her, he let his fingers brush over hers as she took the mug. Unlike at the library, she acknowledged his touch, though he knew she didn't mean to. Her eyes fluttered up to his, wide with questions, but quickly fell down to her coffee, then focused back on the lake. She stayed leaning against the deck's railing as he draped a blanket about her shoulders, then sat on a patio couch. He enjoyed watching her. The wind blew lightly and played in her hair. She didn't seem to notice the chill. He thanked God again for her, and that he had made it to her before any worse had happened.

Charles and Natalie quietly joined him, both bundled in warm jackets and scarves, carrying coffee. Natalie set a plate of breakfast pastries silently on a table and snuggled against Charles' side, taking his hand. Jackson smiled at them and prayed one day he could have a marriage like theirs. If he was lucky, maybe it could be with the woman standing before him.

He tried to push that thought away. She needed a friend right now, nothing more.

"It's beautiful here." Evelyn said.

"Just wait until tonight when the sun sets," Natalie answered. "Everything glows just before it disappears behind the trees."

Evelyn jumped at Natalie's voice, somehow managing to not spill her coffee, and turned to see the three of them sitting. "I didn't realize you were there!"

Natalie smiled at her new friend. She could see why her son was so attracted to her. She was young and beautiful and had a sweetness about her, even as guarded as she was. "Come sit with us, Evelyn."

Evelyn sat in a chair next to the patio sofa Jackson sat in. Natalie saw the disappointment in her son's face. He needed to be patient. It was a mark of respect for Natalie and Charles that Evelyn didn't sit with him, not rejection.

Evelyn looked at Jackson and his family, and her heart ached. This was why she never agreed to go with Bekah during school breaks. One night here was enough to stab her heart with the loneliness and longing she thought she'd learned to ignore.

"Were you comfortable last night, Evelyn?" Natalie asked, offering the pastries.

"Yes," she answered honestly. "Very comfortable. Thank you."

Jackson knew she was nervous. He wondered what she was thinking, but knew not to ask. Turning to his mom, he steered the conversation to that night's feast. "So, Mom, it's been a while since I've had your cooking. I hope you're prepared for my appetite!"

"Of course!" Natalie exclaimed. "I've been looking forward to this day all week! You boys will have to entertain our guest, though. I'll be busy cooking all day for it."

"I think you may find a worthy helper in Evelyn. I believe she loves the kitchen as much as you do," Jackson said, gesturing to Evelyn.

Natalie turned to her with a wide smile. "Well, you're more than welcome to join me, dear! I'd love the help, and Charlie and Jackson have never proven anything but a hindrance when it comes to cooking."

"I think that would be very fun, if you're sure you don't mind."

Natalie was thrilled. "Well then, I'll run in and get properly dressed and we can get started!"

Charles smiled after his wife as she skipped into the house. "You've made her very happy, young lady," he said, looking at Evelyn.

## Chapter 19

Evelyn and Natalie spent the entire, wonderful day cooking together. Evelyn didn't know where the boys had disappeared to. She only saw them briefly when they came in to inhale lunch. Jackson had run his hand along her lower back when he greeted her with a very charming smile. She was once again amazed at how much he could eat. She'd make a mental note of that in case she ever got to cook for him at home.

Natalie was easy to talk to. She told lots of stories about everything from her childhood to marrying Charles and having Jackson, to the raccoon that broke into their house just two days ago. She asked a lot of questions, too, but it never felt like she was prying or judging.

Cooking with Natalie was the most fun Evelyn could remember having in a long time. The events of the previous night were all but forgotten, until she began putting her hair up to keep it from her face. She promptly dropped her hair back around her shoulders.

"Oh, Evelyn, dear!" Natalie exclaimed, having noticed. "You don't need to worry about those. Just tie your hair back already. No one here is going to judge you, so you might as well be comfortable while we work." She talked about it like she was talking about something no more scandalous than the weather.

Evelyn decided to listen to her and tied her hair back and set quickly back to her work.

It was sometime later when Natalie finally brought up Jackson. "So, tell me, how did you and my son meet?"

"We met at my work. I work at the library just off campus and he needed help finding a few books."

"And you two just became friends after that?"

"Not exactly. Until last week, we only saw or talked to each other if he needed help with something at the library." They had just finished setting the table and she was happy to hear the men coming into the house, not leaving them with enough privacy to finish their conversation.

The men walked in, and though they talked quietly, their presence filled the room. Both men carried themselves with such confidence. Both were tall and broad-shouldered and shared many of the same features. Their skin tone was their main distinguishing feature. Jackson had a warmer olive color like his mother's. Both men, though, were handsome, and when Natalie looked at Charles, Evelyn could tell she was still mad about him.

The men laughed when they looked at Natalie. Somehow she had managed to cover herself in flour. Charles pretended to dust it off her shoulder. "It never fails," he said smiling down affectionately at his wife. "Each year you manage to make a bigger mess of yourself than the last. What am I going to do with you?"

Natalie grabbed her tidy husband around the waist. "Love me forever, I guess," and wiped her flour-covered face all over his clean shirt. She looked back at Evelyn and Jackson. "We'll have dinner in thirty minutes," and she and her husband left the room chuckling to themselves.

Jackson laughed lightly and looked at Evelyn. "How was your day with my mother? And you have to tell me how you managed to stay so tidy while she covered herself completely."

Evelyn laughed relating all the details about the pies and how Natalie talked with her hands even while measuring out flour.

"Are you okay, now, that I made you come with me?" he asked when she was finished.

She nodded and smiled. "Yes, of course. There have been a few difficult moments, like this morning." The look Jackson wore told her she'd lost him. "Staying with a family is a learning experience," she explained. "But I've already had so much fun. Do you know this will be my first real Thanksgiving?" Excitement had been bubbling in her stomach all day and she now felt as though she'd boil over with it. She was nervous, too, but after waiting twenty years, her excitement over joining a traditional Thanksgiving dinner won out.

He raised his eyebrows in surprise. "No, I didn't know that. I'm glad I get to share it with you."

"I'm glad too," she replied honestly. She looked at him then, thinking about his parents and all the love she had already experienced in their home. "You're incredibly lucky. I know I don't have any other families to compare yours to, but yours is special. I think this whole house must be so filled with love it's ready to burst at its seams." She spread her hands referring to the whole house. "The world would be a better place if everyone was like your family," she thought aloud.

Before Jackson could respond, his parents returned.

All four of them helped bring the food to the table and then sat. Evelyn sat next to Natalie and across from Jackson. She was confused as to why Natalie took her hand, but she didn't hesitate to accept Jackson's hand when he extended his. Without voicing her questions, she slipped her hand into his and followed along as they bowed their heads. Charles began to speak, to God.

"Thank You, God, for Your Son, Jesus, and all He did for us on the cross. We praise You and thank You for all that You've given us this year. We especially thank You for our family, and for bringing Evelyn into our home and our lives. Thank You for this food. Please bless it to our bodies, and help us to bless others. In Your Son's holy name we pray, Amen."

Natalie and Jackson both gently squeezed her hands before they let go. Evelyn wasn't sure what mixture of excitement and shock had struck her, but as they began passing the food around, she processed the fact that she had indeed experienced her first prayer. The Monroes were Christians! Evelyn tucked that treasure away in her heart and hoped maybe, just maybe, she'd get the answers to the so many questions she'd had from the stained-glass-windows of her library.

Natalie began talking joyfully about all the fun she'd had with Evelyn and how she'd always wanted a daughter and Jackson was never up to playing the part. Both Charles and Jackson treated Natalie with a special tenderness. It wasn't in a way that made her seem weak, but in a way that showed her honor and love. Evelyn knew it was something very precious, something she was sad to say she'd never have herself. But it was beautiful to behold.

Thanksgiving as a whole was beautiful, and Evelyn was thankful to be a part of it.

*This*, she thought, *this must be what home feels like.*

## Chapter 20

"I think you're just going to have to join the family, Evelyn," Charles chuckled as the last plate was cleared from the table. Natalie hadn't stopped chattering about the joy it was cooking with Evelyn. "My wife doesn't seem willing to give you up, now that she's had a taste of having another lady in the house."

Evelyn smiled easily. "I wouldn't mind in the slightest. But I think Jackson may eventually protest against sharing you with me."

"Oh, he's had us to himself for his whole life," Natalie called from the kitchen sink. "It's about time he learned to share!"

"Are you kidding?" Jackson butted in. "As long as you two keep busy in the kitchen, you won't hear any complaint from me." He winked at Evelyn.

Natalie came bursting into the dining room. "It's settled then! Evelyn, you must join us for Christmas!"

Evelyn wasn't expecting that. She had been enjoying their banter and felt quite welcome, but Christmas? This family was far too generous to her, and she couldn't see Jackson being overjoyed about the idea. She'd already been enough of an inconvenience to him.

"Natalie," Charles raised his voice to his wife. Evelyn thought it was because he didn't want her invited to Christmas, but his eyes were smiling, and Natalie didn't seem the least affected by his tone. "You can't just tell the girl where she's going for Christmas. What are you thinking?" He turned to Evelyn, "But just so you know, you will be breaking my wife's heart if you don't come now."

She looked to Jackson who was laughing. It was clear he had no objections. "Well..." There was no getting out of it. "I suppose I should say thank you?"

Natalie squealed and threw her arms about Evelyn as the two men laughed heartily. "Oh Evelyn! I'm so excited! You'll be here for Christmas and then we can all ride back to Syracuse together for the New Year's Ball and it will be such fun!" She reminded Evelyn of a child with all of her excitement.

Natalie finally managed to calm her excitement and shooed Evelyn and Charles from the kitchen. "It's our tradition that Jackson helps me clean up after our Thanksgiving meal."

"You have an amazing wife," Evelyn told Charles as they sat down in what Evelyn could only describe as their library, while Natalie and Jackson set to work. "Is she always so happy?"

Charles smiled and leaned against the high-backed chair. "Not this happy, but yes, she is very good at filling our home with joy." He had a special tenderness in his tone when he spoke of his wife.

She looked around the room. It was a masculine room, decorated with dark leathers and wood, but Natalie had brought her feminine touch, even here. Across from Charles' chair and next to a couch was another chair, in a light tan fabric, in contrast to the rich leather of the other pieces. Over one of the arms hung a light green throw and white ballet-style slippers hid tucked under the chair. The rest of the room was entirely Charles. The walls were a dark cherry and bookshelves were built into them. She skimmed the titles of the books; most of them were books on law and government.

"Jackson said you're his Colonel. I'd love to hear about what you do, if you wouldn't mind telling me."

"I'm afraid my particular position isn't very exciting to talk about. It's mostly a lot of meetings - meetings with the Patrol Offices, meetings with other Colonels, and meetings with Canadian officials. Since we're a border state, we have to be sure to maintain those borders. Canada is a very peaceful nation, so there's never much trouble. What trouble there is, is usually from our own citizens."

"Have you always been stationed here in New York?"

"No. When I graduated, I was stationed in Louisiana, patrolling the Texas border. As you can imagine, I was very busy."

Evelyn was dumbfounded. Louisiana was the most violent state in their country. Texas had separated from the United States after they banned guns, and it wasn't long after that the war broke out. Arkansas, Mississippi, and Alabama all joined with Texas; Louisiana was surrounded by the Texas Republic. Alaska, Colorado, Kansas, Kentucky, Missouri, Oklahoma, and Tennessee also sided with Texas and eventually those eleven states became the Texas Republic. Completely surrounded by the Texas Republic, only the highest-ranking officers were stationed in Louisiana.

"That's where I met Natalie. I knew I would marry her the moment I laid eyes on her. I was on duty when we met. She hadn't made it home before curfew and asked to be escorted. Curfew's different there; it was dangerous to be out late. The next day I took her flowers and asked her to marry me. She laughed so hard she cried, but I kept asking. Every day for a month I took her flowers and asked her to marry me. She finally said yes."

"What brought you to New York?" Grief ran through Charles' eyes; it disappeared quickly, but Evelyn had seen it. "I'm sorry, I'm being nosey."

Charles shook his head. "No, no; it's fine. Natalie became pregnant soon after we were married, with a little girl. Some rebels sought me out at home and Natalie got between us. She was fine, but she miscarried a few days later." Evelyn thought about how angry Jackson was with her when she had gone between him and Tom. Now she understood. "I worked as hard as I could so that, by the time we found out she was pregnant with Jackson, I was guaranteed my transfer. It's still very dangerous there. The Texans respect the borders and are good people, but Louisiana is split. There are some very angry people who think they should be in the Texas Republic and not the US, and some even angrier who feel we should not have stopped fighting against Texas. They're the real danger."

Evelyn felt even closer to Natalie in light of what Charles had shared. She had never known her daughter, and Evelyn had never known her mother. "Do you think we'll all ever be united again? A lot's changed since Texas left. We can own guns again, that's important to them, right?"

"Not enough has changed. If we ever are united again, it will be under the Texas flag. They're a strong country now, and they have even stronger beliefs. Their country still runs on 'In God we trust.' Ours tolerates God, at best. I sometimes wonder if we shouldn't have run to Texas instead."

Boldness came upon Evelyn as she listened. "I'm glad you didn't. There's a lot of darkness in our country, and we need people like you and your son to protect us. And, who knows where I'd be if your family didn't take me in this Thanksgiving?"

She meant to ask Charles about the God Texas trusted in, the one he had prayed to, but Jackson and Natalie joined them, and she closed her mouth.

For the remainder of the evening, they enjoyed wonderful conversation and the most joyous laughter Evelyn had ever had the privilege of hearing. Natalie, to Jackson's mortification, shared a story about his childhood.

"He was four years old at the time. Some of the officers Charlie was training were over for a visit that night. Jackson kept refusing to keep his socks on. I don't know why it bothered me so much, maybe because it was such a cold evening, but I insisted that if he wanted to be able to stay up and sit with the men, he needed to keep his socks on. Oh," she laughed, "he'd looked at me like I was the worst thing that ever happened to him and stomped up the stairs. I should have known that wasn't the last of him. I took the men some coffee, in this very room, and in came Jackson. He sat down with the men, wearing nothing but his socks!" She had to stop talking to regain her composure; she had started laughing so hard. "Oh dear, what a night that was. I was so proud of Charlie! I was so embarrassed and could have spanked his bare little cheeks right then and there. But not Charlie. He took his coffee and looked over his son and remarked, very pompously too, I must say, 'I see you've found your socks.' The officers crumbled into laughter and Jackson stomped off, so upset that he hadn't gotten a rise out of us!"

The three of them laughed at Jackson's expense, and he looked completely uncomfortable, which made them laugh all the more. Evelyn felt so happy, and whole, sitting with Jackson and his parents. These people welcomed her and made her feel like family, something she'd never had before. She always thought seeing others with their family would make her hurt, but here with the Monroes it was completely the opposite.

Eventually Charles and Natalie said goodnight, leaving Jackson and Evelyn to themselves.

"You seem like you've changed a lot since you were little," Evelyn smiled at Jackson. "I think it would have been fun to know you then."

Jackson's mouth tipped up on one side, giving him a very mischievous look. "I haven't changed that much. You just don't know me very well yet."

Yet? "I don't know, I think I know you pretty well now. I haven't seen you up to any shenanigans since we've been friends. You're always so calm and collected, like your father."

He chuckled. "Have you forgotten how we became friends?" He loved her blush. She didn't acknowledge his statement. "A lot of people say that about me, but those people only know me by my work. I'll admit, in uniform, my father and I are very alike, but I think that's where the similarities end."

Evelyn disagreed. She may not know either of them as well as she thought, but she knew they had more in common than that. "No. It's not just when you're at work. But I'm guessing there's no point in arguing with you."

"I knew you were a smart girl." He flashed a wide grin. "Were you able to sleep at all last night?"

"Not really," she answered, yawning. "I'm so tired tonight, though, I don't think I'll have any trouble falling asleep. Speaking of which…" Fatigue was weighing on her and she knew she wouldn't be able to fight it long, so she stood to go upstairs. "I think it's time for me to go up to bed. Thank you for a wonderful first Thanksgiving." She expected him to offer to walk her up, or try to hug her, or something. She had even hoped it; but he just looked up at her and smiled.

"You're welcome. Get some good rest." He grabbed a booklet from the table next to him and began reading.

"Good night." Evelyn left with a longing in her stomach, and she didn't like it. But she forgot about everything as soon as her head touched the pillows and fell into a deep and peacefully dreamless sleep.

What Evelyn didn't know was that if Jackson had moved any closer to her, he wouldn't have been able to keep himself from kissing her. So instead he stayed seated right where he was, determined to read God's Word and to pray desperately for wisdom and self-control.

# Unspoken Words

Jackson looked down to the book of Luke open in his lap. Every time he reread the story of the prodigal son; it tore at his heart.

*Lord,* he prayed, *You've forgiven me so much. I knew You, yet still I turned from You. But You brought me back to You and I'm striving to follow You. You know my heart; You know my feelings towards Evelyn. Help me to keep my thoughts and motives for her pure. Please God, help me to keep her safe. I feel like the enemy has surrounded her. I can't fight this enemy on my own. God, please, keep her safe. And help me to trust You with her safety, and with my feelings. You guide my path; help me to remember that.*

## Chapter 21

It was still dark when Jackson woke the next morning. He listened for movement from the room next to his and was happy to hear silence. Evelyn needed rest.

Thoughts of her had been consuming him. He tried to take those thoughts to God. His prayer life had spiked in the last few days.

Jackson made his way downstairs to start the coffee, all the while working over his feelings for the woman asleep upstairs. His flesh had always been a bit of a struggle, and Evelyn was beautiful…very beautiful…but for whatever reason, he didn't think that could be all that was causing these unexpected feelings. She was young and innocent…two things he had no right to. She was selfless, a rare quality in any person. Watching her with children while she worked proved she cared for them. She was by far the hardest worker at the library; the girl was smart.

He poured himself a cup of black coffee and headed back up the staircase to his room.

Evelyn was everything he'd ever hoped to find in a wife. That explained everything. And the cherry on top was her physical need for protection. What man didn't want to protect his woman; to supply that safety for her?

But she was not his, and he most definitely didn't deserve her. He'd done too much… She deserved someone so pure and good.

A light knock sounded on his door. His mother must be up.

"It's open."

The door opened just a crack. "Hey. Sorry. I didn't mean to wake you. I just –"

"Evelyn?" He cut her off, yanking the door all the way open. "Are you OK?"

Jackson's worry subsided looking down at Evelyn. Oh sweet, sheltered, Evelyn. He hadn't put on his shirt yet and, seeing how distracted she was by his bare chest, he wondered if she'd even ever seen a man without his shirt on. Her cheeks flushed as she tried to keep her eyes focused on his face. His initial worry was unwarranted; she was just fine.

He leaned against the door, flexing a little. He couldn't help himself. "You know, if you wanted to get me out here half dressed, you could have just asked." Her reaction was priceless. Her cheeks went from a soft pink to a deep red in the time it took her to gasp.

"Jackson Monroe!" Evelyn scolded as quietly as she could manage, trying not to choke. How dare he insinuate… "For your information, I was trying to be polite by letting you know I was going out for a run! And now that you know, I'm leaving." She was more upset with herself than she was with his comment, but she was angry all the same. At least it'd help keep her warm during the long, hard run she now had planned.

"Wait, wait, wait," Jackson called after her, laughing to himself. "Give me two minutes, I'll go with you."

Jackson threw clothes and shoes on as fast as he could, knowing Evelyn had no intentions of waiting for him.

He caught up with her about a quarter mile down the lake trail. She didn't greet him, so he kept quiet as well, figuring she'd eventually break the silence. But the only sounds for some time were the birds and the water gently lapping against the rocky bank.

"What?" Evelyn didn't mean to sound so mean, but she was becoming winded. She estimated they'd run about two miles already, and she was not accustomed to trail running. She should be turning back by now.

"I didn't know you run."

"Well," she exhaled. "There are a lot of things you don't know about me."

Jackson slowed with her as she eased into a walk. He stood and watched her pace. He'd seen her embarrassed before, but never mad over it. "You don't like being teased, do you?"

She finally looked at him. Her cheeks and nose were bright red from the cold, her eyes vibrant from the run. It was the most alive he'd ever seen her.

He took in her bruises. She'd been hurt pretty badly when Tom went at her, but she hadn't complained once. It had been hours later when she finally let herself cry, and he knew it had nothing to do with the physical pain. The girl was strong.

Her physical strength was impressive. Her emotional strength astonishing. It'd be a long road to healing from the damage Tom had done, but she was putting on a brave face. Some of it had to be a mask to keep herself guarded, mostly from him.

She was different with his mother. His mother had a way of calming hurt souls. With her, Evelyn knew she was free from judgment, and gave no signs of hurt, other than the bruises Tom inflicted on her. Jackson was beginning to think maybe he'd misjudged her strength all together.

"I don't mind being teased," Evelyn spoke at last. "I just don't like being caught."

Jackson raised a puzzled eyebrow at her. "Yeah, I have no idea what you're talking about."

"Oh come on!" Evelyn exclaimed, rolling her eyes. "It was like being a kid and getting caught drooling in the candy-shop window. It's just embarrassing!" She sat down on a rock, gazing out at the lake.

"I've never been referred to as a candy shop, but I'll take it as a compliment." He sat next to her. "I was just teasing you, though; I didn't think you'd get so mad. But really," he nudged her with his shoulder, "any time you want my shirt off, just let me know."

Evelyn pushed him and he fell over laughing.

"Oh my word! You really are so full of yourself, aren't you?" Without helping him up, she started toward the house.

"I bet I can make it back before you," he challenged when the house came into view.

She slowed to a stop. "What are you betting?"

"Breakfast. If I win, you make me breakfast. If you win, I'll make you breakfast."

"What kind of bet is that? Your mother probably has breakfast waiting for us already. When I win, I expect breakfast Monday morning."

That was probably true. "Then we'll bet Monday's breakfast. Deal?" He held his hand out to her.

"Ok," Evelyn agreed, shaking his hand. "Let me just catch my breath for a minute."

Jackson used the pause to look over the lake. There was no way Evelyn was going to win this bet, but he was glad she'd taken the challenge.

A thrill ran through Jackson. He could feel Evelyn's breath on the back of his neck, just before she bumped the back of his knees, causing them to buckle under him.

A giggle squealed out of the little cheat as she took off running for the house. He couldn't stop his own laughter. This girl was full of surprises, and he was thoroughly enjoying every one of them.

Evelyn threw her shoulder into him when he caught her. She grunted as she tried it a second time. He laughed all the more and left her in his wake.

"Jackson!"

The pain in her voice stopped him cold. Turning back, he saw her limping to a tree.

"Evelyn," he moaned, running back to her. "I am so sorry. What happened?"

"I rolled my ankle. I just need a minute to rest," she got out in between heavy breaths.

"It could be sprained," he voiced, dropping to his knees. He felt like an idiot for challenging her. He reached for her ankle, determined to be gentle, when the woman threw her whole weight into him, successfully knocking him onto his back. She laughed and sprinted for the house.

"You've got to be kidding me!" Jackson yelled after her. He couldn't believe he'd fallen for that! More than that, he couldn't believe she'd done it!

Evelyn made it to the house first, but Jackson was right on her heels. She turned, just in time for him to scoop her up and throw her over his shoulder.

"Jackson, you put me down right now," she giggled out.

Jackson did not obey.

"I didn't know you had it in you," he said, carrying her into the house. "Mother, Father," he said, entering the kitchen and retrieving a muffin. "We've had the wool pulled right over our eyes. You've been housing a cheater all this time, and we didn't even know it!"

"I didn't know you were such a sore loser," Evelyn teased. "Now could you please put me down?"

He let her go for a second and let her slip further down his back. He grabbed hold of her again, but not before she screamed and threw her arms tightly around his body. He didn't mind those arms around him one bit.

Natalie walked behind Jackson with the bowl of muffins. "Good morning, dear," she giggled. "Would you like a muffin?"

Evelyn smiled upside-down and took one. "Thank you, Natalie. I'm sorry I concealed my cheating ways."

"Oh, we're all cheats in this family, so you fit right in." She poked Jackson's side. "Now go put her down so she doesn't choke."

Jackson grabbed two cups of coffee and carried Evelyn upstairs. He managed to get both mugs of coffee and her up the stairs without dripping a drop of coffee on the floor, or Evelyn on her head. He finally proved to be human though and had to put her down so they could kick their shoes in their rooms before he led her to the sunroom.

Jackson set the coffees down before plopping down on the couch and pulling Evelyn down with him.

Evelyn tucked her feet up under her and leaned her head against the couch, sighing. "That was fun. And French toast is my favorite; in case you were wondering."

"I don't think so," he snorted. "No breakfast for you. You cheated!"

"You, Jackson Monroe," she stated, "are such a wretched loser."

"Just be quiet and eat your breakfast," he laughed back. He didn't tell her he had every intention of bringing her breakfast. It would be much more fun to surprise her.

"This room is beautiful," Evelyn commented as she ate her muffin and sipped her coffee.

"It's Mother's favorite."

The room was just about the complete opposite of the room they had sat in the night before. This room had no harshness to it. The furniture was soft and comfortable; the carpet thick and rich. Light coming in through the wall of windows flooded the room decorated in light yellows, creams, and whites.

"She says sitting in here is like sitting in sunshine."

"Mmm," Evelyn sighed, closing her eyes. "That's the perfect way to describe it."

Peace floated in the silence between them.

"I wish we didn't have to go back to school," she confessed. "Is that bad?"

"Nope." He wished the same thing. "Nothing bad about that."

He had been putting off thinking about going back home. Tom was back in Syracuse, and he didn't want to deal with or even see him; but duty called. He was scheduled to work Sunday night.

Things in Syracuse, especially on campus, didn't feel right. With crime on the rise, he wondered if it wasn't just idiots getting into trouble, but something more threatening. Taking Evelyn back to that didn't sit well with him.

"When do we need to head home?"

"We'll need to leave Sunday by noon so I can get to work on time." He paused, hesitating to ask what he knew she wouldn't agree to. "I've been thinking. Bekah may not be back when we get home. If she's not, I'd like you to stay at my house until she is."

"You're very sweet," she sighed again, "and the best kind of friend any girl could ask for."

He knew she meant it as a compliment, but it hit him like a punch in the stomach. "Please, Evelyn." He looked her square in the eyes, willing her to say yes. "If Bekah is not home when we get back, please stay with me."

"I'm sure either Bekah or Sarah will be back, but even if they're not, you know I can't stay with you. You already have a handful of officers who know we left town together. You don't need any more talk about you than you'll already face from that."

He didn't have anything to say after that. He couldn't tell her he didn't trust Sarah. He couldn't tell her how crazy it made him to think of her alone and unprotected. She was right, too. There would already be plenty of gossip awaiting them as it was. He'd silence it quickly enough from the Patrols, but there would be no stopping it if it made it to the campus.

Evelyn stretched her foot out and poked him in the side. "Are you always such a pouter when you don't get your way?"

"Don't kick me." He sounded like a two-year-old, and had to force himself not to laugh. She poked him again. "Evelyn. I said don't kick me." He raised his voice that time. He knew she wouldn't be able to resist poking him again, and he caught her foot when she did. He flashed her a smile and pulled her roughly across the couch to him, pinning her down and tickling her sides. "I told you, young lady, not to kick me."

Evelyn screamed her laughter as she tried to force him away. Her efforts were adorable, but futile.

"Now," Jackson said, continuing his torment of her. "Tell me you're sorry for cheating and for kicking me."

"Never!"

He laughed and just tickled her all the more. "Come on," he coaxed, "swallow your pride and say you're sorry."

"My pride! My pride? You're the one who's so full of himself, remember?" she cried through her laughter.

"Ok, death by tickling it is."

The woman was fast. In an instant, she wrapped her legs around his waist, threw her arms around his chest, and pulled herself as tightly against him as she could, effectively minimizing his accessibility to her.

Evelyn realized her idea was a bad one just a moment too late. Jackson's body was tense under her touch. He stopped tickling her the moment she pressed toward him. He kept one hand against the couch, keeping himself from crushing her with his body. His other hand was frozen against her side, managing somehow to hold her steady.

For not the first time in his life since meeting her, Jackson had no idea what to do. Having her so close was paradise and agony all at once. After holding her in silence for what felt like forever but was probably only seconds, he finally spoke. "You really don't play fair, do you?"

"When I'm against you," she breathed, "anything I can do should count as fair."

Well, two could play that game. A small gasp escaped Evelyn when Jackson slid his hand a bit suggestively around her, changing his hold so his arm cradled her back while his fingers wrapped around to her stomach.

He let her go and she loosened her arms and legs, falling onto the cushions.

He smiled down at her. "See. It's not nice when others play dirty, is it?"

Her cheeks went hot with embarrassment. The look in her eyes suggested maybe some desire helped tint her cheeks as well.

"Alright," she relented. "I'm sorry, but not about beating you in the race." Jackson sat up and pulled her up with him. "I won that fair enough."

"Fine," he yielded. "You won. But loser gets to shower first. So I guess that's me." He stood with a smile and turned, not wanting to leave, but again needing too. His weakness against his flesh was pathetic.

"Jackson?" He stopped at the door and looked back. A childlike innocence radiated in her eyes that captured him completely. "Is this what it's always like?"

"What?"

"I've never had a boy friend." She shook her head. "A boy for a friend. Is it always this much fun?"

"No, it's not always this much fun. In fact, I've never had so much fun with a *girlfriend*." He covered his mouth with his hand in mock embarrassment, making Evelyn laugh. "I've never had so much fun with a girl before. You're very special, Evelyn. I'm glad you're having fun." They smiled at each other and he turned again for the shower. He hoped a cold shower would wash the feeling of her body against his away.

## Chapter 22

Evelyn inspected her bruises in a mirror the next day. She was relieved to see the marks on her neck and shoulder were already beginning to fade. Scarves and high-necked sweaters would cover them up easily enough for now. She was extremely grateful for the cold weather; it gave her an excuse to hide her neck. The back of her head was still tender to the touch, but no one could see that bruise. Her eye, however, remained quite discolored. Chances were, Sarah wouldn't ask much about it. Bekah, on the other hand, would want to know every detail. She wasn't looking forward to explaining it all to her, in part because relating the incident with Tom would require her to confess she'd spent the last few days with Jackson and his family. She didn't want to share these precious memories with anyone else. She wanted to keep them safely tucked away in her heart.

"Oh good," Natalie exclaimed in greeting as Evelyn exited her room. "I was just coming to look for you. I was hoping you could do me a favor. I have a horrid dinner to go to tomorrow night and need a woman's opinion on what to wear. Charlie tries his best, but let's be honest, men prefer their women in less, rather than appropriate clothing." Evelyn blushed at her frankness. "Sorry dear, I didn't mean to shock you. It's just how it is, though. Even the most straitlaced men like to see skin; just make sure you marry one who only wants to look at yours. Anyway, would you mind helping me?"

Evelyn smiled at Jackson's mother. She was quite a woman. Surprisingly, her confident bluntness drew Evelyn in, rather than shocking her away.

"I'd love to help," she replied. "I just don't know how helpful I'll actually be. Fashion isn't really my forte."

"Oh pish-posh!" Natalie said, grabbing Evelyn's hand and walking her towards her room. The gesture seemed to run in the family. "You have to be better than the men in this house. And besides, it'll give us a chance to chat some more."

They walked into Natalie and Charles' room and Natalie motioned her to sit on the bed. The room was remarkable. The walls were a light sage green and the bed was draped in ornate linens and taupe coverings that complimented the walls nicely. A wonderful plush rug warmed the wooden floor and a stone fireplace climbed to the ceiling in the corner of the room. Natalie had thrown open a set of double doors revealing a small room, which apparently was her closet, and began flipping through clothes, taking down dresses she wanted Evelyn's opinion on. As she sifted through her clothes, she began chatting again. "I heard a lot of laughter a little while ago. May I ask what tickled the two of you so much?"

"It was your son, actually," Evelyn tried not to blush at the memory of his hands on her. "He was trying to make me confess my cheating ways, so he decided to try and tickle it out of me."

"I see. I hope he didn't succeed." She gave Evelyn a devious smile.

"Not completely."

Evelyn couldn't see Natalie's expression, but she seemed to be thinking something over. "So, tell me, what kind of man are you attracted to?" Natalie laughed at Evelyn's startled expression.

"I've never really taken the time to think about it," she answered honestly.

"Why don't you think about it now," Natalie pushed gently, "with me?"

"Well," she swallowed. "To be honest, I've only taken notice of a few boys. For the most part, I've kept busy with school and work. And then growing up with all girls, boys just weren't on my radar. But after everything with Tom… I hope I've learned my lesson about what's important. But even Tom's appearance pales in…" She shook herself. She'd almost blurted out that Tom was no comparison to her son!

"I suppose," she started again, "I'd be attracted to the sort of man who is strong, but uses his strength to protect people; not hurt them. Someone kind, and who can make me laugh, and helps me forget about all the bad in the world. Someone slow to anger, and honest. But finding all that, and hoping he'd feel the same about me. Well, it sounds like a bit of a fairytale."

"You like my Jackson, don't you?"

Natalie didn't even look at Evelyn when she said it. Evelyn's jaw dropped and she knew her face was bright red. Had she been that obvious? How was she supposed to answer? "We seem to have become good friends." There, that was honest, wasn't it?

Natalie had an armful of dresses and walked back to Evelyn. "You're not getting out of this that easy. You know what I mean. You like him more than just friends." It wasn't a question anymore, but she was smiling sweetly. "I had my suspicions you were falling for him, and fighting it. But what you just said confirmed it."

Evelyn looked down at her fidgeting hands. Natalie had been so kind to her, she owed it to her to be honest. "I think you're right. I am trying to fight it, though, and I would never act on it. I promise. I know he doesn't need a little girl like me making things uncomfortable for him."

Natalie laughed, startling her. "I wasn't going to reprimand you! And I didn't mean to embarrass you. I just wanted to make sure I was right. I wouldn't call you a little girl, though. Jackson says you have a lot of admirers, and he didn't seem too happy about it."

"Jackson's a liar, then, or very misinformed. There was only Tom, and he was rather two-faced."

"Just because there's only been one bold enough to say something, doesn't mean you don't have more admirers," Natalie countered.

"I hate to disappoint, but I think that's exactly the case. But enough about me and boys, we need to pick you out a dress."

Natalie looked like she wanted to say more, but she kept it to herself. They looked through the dresses and Natalie put on a fashion show of their favorites. She had sensational dresses. They chose a crimson long-sleeved tea-length dress that wrapped tight around the waist and flowed away from her body at the hips in a full skirt. She looked incredible in it. As Natalie was putting her dresses away, she asked Evelyn, "Do you know what you're wearing to the New Year's Ball?"

Of course she didn't know what she was wearing. She wasn't going. It required an invitation from an officer. "Natalie, I don't think I'll be going. I don't get asked to those sorts of things."

"Oh," Natalie responded, confused in light of a previous conversation with her son. "You would love it! There are plenty of officers in want of a date, just tell Jackson you want to go. And if we're all riding back from Christmas together for it, it would only make sense for you to join us."

Evelyn was sure Jackson could find someone to take her; he would probably order an officer to do it and he'd be forced to follow orders. But who wanted to be taken by someone who was forced to ask you? And, she didn't want to have to see Jackson with another woman. "Maybe. We'll see."

Natalie hoped her son would rectify this situation quickly and ask the girl already. If he was right about her having many admirers, someone else may ask her before she realizes his affection for her. "I do hope it works out for you to come," she said while putting her dresses away and closing the closet doors. "It would be so much fun to have you there."

Evelyn was fidgeting again. Their conversation evoked uncomfortable emotions, making her jealous of whoever Jackson would take. She needed to change the subject. "You're going to be lovely at your dinner tomorrow night. I think Charlie will be pleased with our choice of dress, don't you?"

"Yes, I believe he will like it. And speaking of Charlie, I bet he's hungry. It's about lunch time now. Would you mind helping me in the kitchen?"

She exhaled, letting the tension leave her body. She was glad Natalie dropped the subject of the ball, and Jackson. "I'd love to." She followed her out of the room. Before they got to the kitchen, she asked quietly, in case there were listening ears nearby, "Could you not say anything to Jackson, about anything we talked about?"

Natalie frowned, but agreed. "My lips are sealed."

They busied themselves in the kitchen and had lunch ready quickly. The men joined them; Charles coming in from outside and Jackson from upstairs. Evelyn wondered what he'd been up to.

The four of them spent the remainder of the afternoon in the library together. Evelyn and Natalie read while Jackson and Charles talked about government things and protection details they thought were needed. Once in a while they disagreed, but for the most part, they saw eye to eye on things. From what Evelyn caught of their conversation, trouble was coming. It was just one more thing that made her want to stay with the Monroes.

That evening, Natalie surprised Evelyn by having everyone eat dinner in the sun room upstairs, where Jackson had taken Evelyn after their run. Natalie insisted she didn't want Evelyn to miss the sunset.

It was glorious. Evelyn had never seen anything like it in all her life. With the sun burning through the already flame-colored trees, and all of it reflecting off the glass-like lake, it really did look like it all was on fire.

Jackson knew she was captivated by the beauty before her, so watched her freely without fear of getting caught. His mother gave him a strange look; he thought she looked frustrated with him, but he didn't know why. She knew how he felt about Evelyn, and he knew his mother loved her already; so he went back to watching her.

She fit into his family so well. She had spent time with both of his parents and got along with them better than he could have ever hoped. His mother had found the daughter she'd always wanted in her, and his father already respected her greatly.

His attraction to her went beyond her outward beauty. She was beautiful, but she was so much more too, and he was drawn to her more and more each time he learned something new about her. He wasn't sure how much longer he'd be able to bear being just friends. He worried, though. What if his feelings drove her away? He decided to wait until after Christmas to say anything. He didn't want to jeopardize her coming back with him for Christmas.

Natalie brought out family albums after dinner, and after the sun had set, ending its fiery show for the night. Evelyn delighted in seeing pictures of Jackson as a little boy. He had been a sturdy boy since the day he was born. They all stayed up late into the night listening to Charles and Natalie tell stories and looking through their pictures, as Evelyn and Jackson stole hidden glances at each other whenever they could.

## Chapter 23

Evelyn woke screaming. She had been dreading the return to Syracuse before she fell asleep, and her nightmares were full of all the horrible things that haunted her; Tom was a recurring theme, but not the worst.

She was sitting straight up, gasping, clutching her covers with tears streaming down her face when she finally woke up. She tried to push the nightmare away, but she couldn't shake it. She jumped when her door cracked open.

"Hey," a shirtless Jackson whispered from the door. "You okay?" All she could do was lie and nod. "Mind if I come in?" She nodded again, he stopped. He looked down at his half-dressed self before looking back to her. "I'm coming back in two minutes. If you don't want me in there, meet me out here."

Evelyn was scared. Her nightmare still gnawing at her. She could feel herself shaking and was fighting back nausea. She knew Jackson was safe, but she didn't want to be alone with him in her room. Reluctantly, and hoping more for a steady stomach than steady nerves, she got up and waited for him in her doorway.

When Jackson came back, he wasn't shirtless. That was good. He also didn't look anything like he had in her nightmare, which helped her a great deal.

There was no point trying to hide that she'd been crying. Try as she had to dry her cheeks before Jackson returned, steadying her quivering lip was a losing battle. She settled for wrapping herself with her arms and let her eyes fall to the floor. He'd have to be the one to break the silence this time.

Jackson took her hand and led her down to the sun room. Her hand was ice cold and clammy in his; just one more embarrassing thing she couldn't hide from him.

When they got to the room, he let go of her hand and went to a chest containing blankets and took one out. When he turned back, he studied Evelyn who was still standing in the doorway. His eyes ran over her, evaluating her, trying to decode her.

He walked back to her, took her hand in his, and sat her on the couch. Putting the blanket over her, he sat facing her on the couch. She refused to look up at him and watched her fidgeting hands instead.

"You're not okay. What's wrong?"

Evelyn just shook her head, trying to guard herself from the tenderness in his voice. She didn't want to be next to him, or for him to ask why she didn't want to be next to him. Alone in her room, or here on the couch with him didn't matter though, she'd be thinking about her nightmare either way.

He put his hand over hers, causing her breathing to flutter. "Evelyn, it's just me. What's wrong?"

She took her hands from under his and wrapped her arms around herself again. "I just had a bad dream. That's all. I'm sorry; I didn't mean to wake you. You shouldn't have gotten up."

"What was it about?" There wasn't any room for arguing in the tone he used. It wasn't mean, just sure.

"Tom, and you."

Dread began to prick at Jackson. "What about me and Tom?"

She looked up at him, pleading. "Jackson, please don't ask me to tell you."

"What about me and Tom?" He forced his voice stern, needing her answer.

Evelyn looked down again. If he insisted on knowing, she would tell him, but she didn't have to look him in the eye when she did. "It was about the night Tom attacked me, but it was different. It was worse."

"How was it worse?"

"You didn't stop him, you helped him." She knew it was a nightmare, it wasn't real, but silent tears fell anyway. She hoped he couldn't see them in the dark; but he did.

"That is worse," he thought aloud and he reached out to wipe a tear away. She didn't mean to recoil from his touch. "You know I'd never do that." She nodded. "And you know I'll always stop him."

Nodding seemed to be all she could manage.

"Please look at me." His voice was very gentle, and very sad.

She looked up. Pain was evident on his face, but his eyes said something more, something she didn't know how to hear.

"You're so precious to me. I'll never do anything to hurt you."

His words tugged at her heart and drew her to him. "I don't want to be alone." He didn't know she meant more than just in that moment. Evelyn went willingly when he pulled her to his side and wrapped his arms protectively around her. It was the first time anyone saved her from her nightmares, and she welcomed the safety of his arms. His arms calmed the turmoil in her body, easing the fear and the nausea, but giving way to a flood of hurt. "Why'd he do it?"

"I don't know."

"Did I do something to make him think I wanted him to do that?"

"No," he spoke into her hair. "It wasn't anything you did. He'd been drinking that night, and I don't think he's used to not getting what he wants."

"Are all men that way? Would you take something that wasn't yours, just because you wanted it?"

Jackson could feel her body shaking as her tears began to fall again and he held her tighter. "I think all men, or at least most men, struggle with their desires. But not all men are like Tom. Evelyn, I can't tell you I've never taken something that wasn't mine…I did kiss you after all. But I can tell you that I'd never do more than that."

Evelyn slowly relaxed into him again. She thought about his answer and was glad he'd been honest with her. She began to wonder how many other kisses he'd stolen when she decided she liked thinking about how firm his arms and chest were more. Sleep began to claim her as she rested in the safety of his arms, listening to the steady drum of his heart.

"Do you drink?" she asked, sounding half asleep to Jackson.

"Yes, once in a while. But I don't get drunk." Evelyn's head was getting heavier against his shoulder. She would be asleep soon.

"I don't want to be around you when you drink. Bekah doesn't drink. I always feel safe with Bekah."

"Do you feel safe with me?"

"No," she sighed. "I mean yes. I don't know. But what will I do when you forget about me?" Her words were slurred together, but Jackson heard it quite clearly. Evelyn pulled the blanket around her and fell asleep.

When Jackson was sure she was asleep, he kissed the top of her head. "I'll never forget about you," he whispered. He began to think that Christmas may be too long for him to wait, and he decided he'd never touch alcohol again.

It was almost five now, and Jackson knew his parents would be up soon. He didn't have to wait long to find out what they thought when they found them. He lifted his finger to his lips when they walked in. "She had a nightmare," he whispered.

His mother looked sad; his father looked angry. Jackson hadn't seen that face in a long time. "We'll talk about this later, before you leave." His father put his arm about his mother and they excused themselves silently from the room.

Jackson didn't care that he'd have to report to his father about this; though he wasn't sure why he needed to. He wasn't even sharing the blanket with her. Even though it was his father's home, he was a grown man. But whatever the reason, having her nestled against him was worth it.

He looked down at the angel in his arms. She'd whimpered once since she'd fallen asleep. He whispered to her that she was safe, and he was almost certain she'd whispered his name before settling back into a peaceful sleep.

*God*, his heart cried out. *What would You have me do? It feels so right holding her, being here to fight her nightmares with her. How am I going to leave her alone back home? I know Your Word says to give You all of our worries because You care for us... Please build my faith and help me live those words. Please be Evelyn's safety.*

Evelyn's cheek rubbed against his chest just as the sun was peaking over the east side of the lake, bathing everything the light touched in gold.

He hadn't thought about how she'd react waking in his arms. She'd all but fallen over when they were in the limo on the drive over, but of course she hadn't willingly fallen asleep on him then.

Her breathing altered just enough to signal that she was awake then. Apparently, she was content where she was because she wasn't moving. He didn't have any problem with that.

Her hand that had been on his chest, under her chin, ran, palm down, across his chest and around to his side. Something he was beginning to notice, tired Evelyn didn't have the self-control that awake Evelyn did. He smiled to himself. He didn't really mind that either.

"Good morning," he greeted when he was finally sure his voice wouldn't scare her. He laughed when she turned her face into his chest. "I'm sorry. Go back to sleep."

"No." Evelyn spoke into Jackson's chest, refusing to let the light of day spoil the closeness between them. "I should get up."

"Why?"

She tilted her head back just enough to reveal her eyes. "Well," she tried to focus. "For starters, it's completely inappropriate of me to be sleeping against you like this. And, because I'm sure you would like me off of you."

Jackson held her tight to stop her retreat. "As to this being inappropriate: you had a nightmare, a bad one. You didn't need to face that alone. And for you thinking I want to get up…I cannot think of anywhere I'd like to be more than here holding you." His hand rubbed her back. "When you told me about your dream, I was scared you wouldn't let me near you again."

She sat there looking at him, weighing the argument for getting up against staying with him.

"And," he added. "It's still early." He almost had to pinch himself to keep from kissing her pink lips before she settled back down, resting her head against his shoulder.

"I'm really sorry I woke you up last night."

"You don't need to be sorry." This was worth being woken up for.

"You should have just gone back to bed. You didn't need to come to my room."

He caved and kissed the top of her head. "I'm glad I did."

"You're very strange sometimes," Evelyn thought aloud. Jackson left the comment untouched, except for a soft chuckle. Moments later though, his misbehaving stomach growled. Loudly.

"Why didn't you say you were hungry?"

*Stupid stomach,* he thought. "I didn't know I was."

She stood up and stretched, then extended her hands to him. "Come on, let's go get breakfast."

Jackson let her help him up and waited for her as she folded and put away the blanket. They walked through the kitchen door to find Charles holding Natalie in his arms; they were talking quietly about something. Jackson observed Evelyn's blush at the scene and wondered if it was a difficult scene for her to see. Just in case, he cleared his voice, startling his mother.

"Oh! Jackson, Evelyn, we didn't see you there," Natalie said.

Charles turned and kept one arm around his wife. His voice didn't show any sign of surprise. "Good morning, you two. I hope you slept well." He smiled at Evelyn but aimed his pointed look at Jackson when he said the last part.

"Yes, just fine," Jackson answered quickly, stepping slightly in front of her.

Evelyn looked between the two men. An unsettling feeling bubbled up suggesting there were a lot of unspoken words between them, and she hoped she wasn't the cause of it.

Natalie bumped her husband with her hip. "Don't you two get started until you're out of my kitchen. Take your breakfast to the library so Evelyn and I can have our eggs and coffee in peace."

The two men obeyed her and took their food and left. Once they were gone Natalie rolled her eyes. "Those two always manage to have something to argue about."

Evelyn poured herself a cup of coffee and sat at the counter. "I hope I didn't cause it." She was uneasy about the whole situation. Since coming to the Monroes' home, she hadn't seen anything but ease and kindness between them.

Natalie brought her coffee and sat next to her. "You don't need to worry. Even if you're brought up, it's only because they like a good argument. Charlie likes to challenge his son. Says it keeps him tough and on his toes. I say rubbish! He's just looking for a fight and knows he can't win one against me." She laughed as she talked. Natalie had a wonderful way of reassuring Evelyn, but something in her was still uneasy. "Jackson said you had a nightmare. Would you like to talk about it?"

Evelyn was glad she hadn't been taking a drink of her coffee at that moment, or she would have choked. "No. I mean, yes, I had a nightmare, but no, I don't want to talk about it."

"I used to get nightmares. I would wake, and I knew they weren't real, but they held enough truth in them to make them feel real. Old memories haunted me when I would wake, mixing with the lies that tormented me in my nightmares." Natalie put her hand on Evelyn's arm. "You don't have to tell me about it, I just want you to know I understand."

Evelyn remembered the story Charles had told her about them being attacked. Natalie understood better than anyone, and had gone through much worse. Still, she didn't want to talk about it. "Thank you, Natalie."

Natalie changed the subject for her. "So what time are you guys heading home today?"

"Jackson said by noon. I wish it wasn't so soon."

"I wish that too," Natalie said. Evelyn hurt at the disappointment on her face. "Did Jackson tell you we hold church here on Sunday mornings?"

"No," she said excitedly. "Would you mind if I joined you guys? It's something I've always been curious about!"

"Oh, I'm glad you want to come!" Natalie exclaimed. "And, of course, you can come. It's church; everyone's welcome. There are just a few of us, and we meet in the library at nine. Actually," she said, looking at the clock, "I should head upstairs and get dressed." She took another sip of her coffee and excused herself from the kitchen.

Evelyn could hardly contain herself. Church! She had always wanted to attend a church group, but never knew how to find one. What a wonderful way to end her time with the Monroes. She had so many questions, and now she had an opening for asking Jackson.

## Chapter 24

"That was very rude of you to say that in front of Evelyn!" Jackson stormed. "If you're upset, you take it out on me, and not when she's around!"

Charles sat calmly and drank his coffee. "Sit down, son, and we can have our talk."

Jackson watched his father, looking completely unaffected by his words. His father's calm demeanor made Jackson boil, but he knew yelling wouldn't do any good, so he obeyed his father and sat.

"I'm sorry," Charles began, surprising Jackson, "You're right, it was rude of me to say anything in front of Evelyn. But Jackson, you need to control your actions a lot better, especially if you plan on bringing her here again for Christmas." He saw that his comment angered his son. "I'm not saying she would become unwelcome. I'm saying that *you* might. You're in danger of hurting that poor girl very badly."

Jackson's shock didn't help his anger. "You know I have no intentions of hurting her! I told you how I feel about her."

"I do know how you feel about her. She, however, has no idea. Do you know she has no clue that you even plan on taking her to the New Year's Ball? She's a sweet, innocent, and extremely naïve girl and you are taking advantage of her! I won't sit by and let my son hurt her."

Jackson didn't know if he should still be angry, or just confused. "How could she not know that I feel something for her?"

"Have you told her?" his father asked harshly, as a father defending his own daughter.

"Of course I have! Not everything, but she knows I care for her." She had to know.

Charles shook his head. His son was just as naïve as this girl. "Son, from what that girl has shared with your mother, it sounds like she is falling in love with you; but she is desperately trying to fight those feelings. I swear to you, she is oblivious to your feelings for her. If anything, she thinks you see her as a little sister. If you don't intend on pursuing her, then holding her hand, comforting her, even protecting her to the extent you have been is just hurting her."

His father was right; he was always right. "She's afraid of me, Dad. How do I make my feelings known to her when I already scare her?"

"Just take it slow, and minimize the physical until you've made your feelings clear to her." Charles looked at his son firmly. "And even after that, minimize the physical. You had better remember she's a lady, and since she doesn't have a father, you'll answer to me twice over if you cross that line. Do you understand?"

Jackson laughed, even though he knew his father was serious. "Yes, Father. I understand."

After finishing his long-turned-cold breakfast, Jackson found Evelyn alone in the kitchen. Both hands were set to the task of holding her coffee as she stood looking out a window in the kitchen, humming a very old hymn very quietly. He'd never heard her sing, though even now she was only humming, but the noise he heard was angelic. He hesitated to say anything, not wanting her to stop, but knew it would be rude of him not to let her know he was there.

"That's one of my favorites," he said, "the song you were just humming."

Evelyn stopped humming and gave him a reproachful look. "You didn't tell me your parents held church." She couldn't keep her smile from peeking through.

Jackson leaned against the counter opposite her. "I'm sorry. I just came to tell you, though, if that helps my cause at all."

"I'm really excited," she said, smiling widely now. "Have they always opened their home for that? Did you get to grow up going to church?"

He didn't expect her to sound so joyful over it, or so curious. "Every Sunday my whole life. It's very important to my parents, and to me. I'm assuming you're joining us?"

"Of course! I've always wanted to attend one. I was thinking about church the first time we met. Do you remember when you scared me while I was up on that ladder?"

Jackson smiled remembering. "Yes. I had to ask you for help finding a book."

"Well," she continued, "I was looking at the stained glass and thinking about what church must have been like when the library was still a church. I had no idea you had walked up to me, until you spoke. You actually do that a lot, sneak up on me." Jackson didn't know why that statement caused her to blush. "Anyway, it's kind of neat, don't you think, that I was thinking about church when we met and now, I get to go to church with you in your parents' home?"

"Yes," he agreed. "It's kind of neat." He often times took it for granted that he was so blessed to grow up with God-fearing parents who raised him in God's Word. Seeing the hunger for it in her eyes reminded him, and humbled him, too.

Evelyn looked at the clock; it was a half hour until nine now and they both were in sweats still. "We need to get ready. What do people wear for church?"

Jackson gestured for her to follow him as he answered. "My parents never want anyone to feel out of place when they join them in their home, so they've made it a habit to dress casually."

He saw relief wash over her. "You have amazing parents," she commented. "They must be the most wonderful people I've ever met." When they arrived at her room, she stopped, looking up at him, and surprised him by taking his hand in both of hers.

"Thank you."

He got a little lost in those big doe-eyes. "For what?"

"For everything. For being my friend, for caring about me. For bringing me here and sharing your family with me." Her eyes dropped before meeting his again. "For sitting with me last night. I'm not sure what I would have done... I know it's your job to keep people safe –"

He almost interrupted her, but she moved a hand to his chest, silencing his argument.

"I know it's your job, but I also know that what you've done for me...well, it doesn't make any sense. But thank you."

Just as quickly as she had grabbed him, she let him go and pushed through the door into her room. Jackson blinked after her door clicked shut. He was entirely convinced the woman had put him in a trance, as he hadn't moved or breathed since she took his hand.

## Chapter 25

Excitement and anxiety pulsed through Evelyn as they entered the library for church. She wished she could hold Jackson's hand to still her fidgeting and borrow some of his strength. Then every eye turned to her, and every mouth smiled, and she was instantly glad she gave no reason for further attention.

Nine other adults were present, and three children; two boys and a girl. The girl looked to be about five, and the boys about three and maybe one. They seemed rather well-tempered, happily playing in a corner until their parents called for them. Several of the men had brought chairs in from the dining room, but everyone was gathering into a circle, instead of sitting in them.

"Why aren't they sitting down?" Evelyn whispered to Jackson, confused.

"We always begin with prayer," he answered her. He took her hand – she decided holding hands was better than not – and led her to the others.

The older of the two boys smiled up at her and took her other hand without question. She bowed her head when she saw the others do so and listened to Charles lead them in prayer.

There was undeniable power in that moment, in the unity of these people who, as she heard from Charles' lips as he prayed, gave their allegiance to God before and above all else. She understood then how the government could see these people as a threat. If their God was against them, these people would stand against them as well.

But Charles and Jackson both worked for the government and strove to protect their country. She thought it'd be a better idea for the government to side with God instead of trying to push Him away. But perhaps there was more to it, more to this God.

Charles finished his prayer and everyone echoed him with, "Amen," then took their seats. Evelyn retreated to the back of the room and sat away from the others. It wasn't that she wanted to keep herself separate from the people gathered; she just wanted to see everything. A hunger for understanding had been awoken in her. Jackson brought a chair over and joined her. Charles opened what looked like a notebook, very similar to what she'd seen Jackson read the night before last, and began reading. "What's he reading?"

She missed the look of astonishment he gaped at her.

"He's reading from Matthew today, it's one of the books from the Bible."

At one time, the Bible had been printed as one whole book, but that had been before the last civil war. Ever since, the government had restricted the printing of it and each of the books were published individually in cheap bindings. Evelyn nodded when he answered her and leaned forward resting her elbows on her knees and her chin on her hands. These were the first words she'd ever heard from God's Book.

She couldn't help but drink in every word Charles read. The Madames who raised her told her about God, and she believed in Him. Anyone with eyes to see should have no excuse to not believe. The world proclaimed His existence. But she had never heard this, as it was against the law for the Madames to bring religious books into the home or for the library she worked at to own any. These words Charles read told a story about Jesus and a man named Nicodemus. Jesus was telling him how God sent His son to save the world, and something about being born again she didn't understand.

After Charles finished, the people talked openly about what he read and how it affected them. Evelyn had difficulty focusing on what the others were saying because she kept thinking about what she had heard. After a while, the people took turns asking the others to pray about specific things for them. Then something very curious happened. Natalie brought out a tray holding a loaf of bread and small glasses filled with a red liquid. The tray was passed and Evelyn watched in wonder as each person took a glass and broke off a piece of the bread. After the tray passed from their hands, their heads bowed in silence.

Evelyn looked up at Jackson. "It's communion," he answered her unspoken question. Evelyn's brows came together in puzzlement.

"I don't know what that is," she whispered to him.

"It's a symbol of our faith. The bread symbolizes Christ's body that was broken for us and the wine…or in this case juice…symbolizes His blood that was spilled for our sins. Eating and drinking is a memorial of His death and proclaims our faith in Him."

Evelyn decided it was best she didn't join them in this. She didn't understand it and thought she shouldn't take something from God that she didn't understand. "You don't eat and drink with them?" she whispered again.

"I do," he answered. "But I didn't want to leave you alone back here by yourself."

"No," she whispered back while shaking her head. "I want you to join them. I'm okay by myself." Jackson studied her for a moment, but she'd been purposely strategic in her wording. *I want you to join them.* He hesitated still. "Really, Jackson," she said, placing her hand on the top of his knee. "I don't want to be the reason you don't join them. It doesn't feel right to get between you and this."

He patted her hand with his own, then stood and joined the others. Evelyn watched Jackson break bread with his father and take one of the glasses of juice, then bow his own head. She had a pretty good idea that they were each speaking silently to God. What did one say to God before communion? What did Jackson say? But silent prayers were private matters, and she would never ask.

After a moment, Charles spoke. "This is the body and blood of Jesus Christ our Lord and Savior which was given for you. Eat and drink in remembrance of what the Lord has done for you." And they ate and they drank.

When everyone finished, they stood to pray once more. Evelyn joined them, taking Jackson's waiting hand. They finished again with "Amen" and squeezed hands.

Now that church seemed to be over, everyone was interested in Evelyn. Jackson stood loyal by her side, smiling as everyone introduced themselves to her. He was proud of his church family for the way they accepted Evelyn so immediately, for the gentle kindness they bestowed on her, and for their discretion in not asking about her bruised eye.

The couple with the children were the last to introduce themselves. The youngest snuggled in his mother's arms, while the older boy and girl stood quietly smiling between their mother and father. "Hi," the mother greeted, extending her free hand to Evelyn, "I'm Claire."

"I'm Evelyn," she replied, shaking Claire's hand.

"I'm Lillian," the little girl stated, making herself heard, and smiled.

"It's very nice to meet you Lillian," Evelyn said as she smiled down at her.

Claire shook her head, smirking at her daughter. "This," she said, referring to her son in her arms, "is Joshua." She put her hand on her older son's head. "This is Ryan, and this," she motioned to her husband and he extended his hand, "is Nathan."

"It's nice to meet you, Evelyn," Nathan said, shaking her hand with a firm but gentle grip.

"We all grew up together," Jackson said, joining the conversation. "We used to have lots of fun until they decided to fall in love and get married."

"Hey," Nathan responded, raising his hands in defense, "Don't blame me! It was all her idea."

Claire laughed. "He's kind of right. But in my defense, I waited eighteen years for him to make a move. I got tired of waiting."

Evelyn enjoyed their banter and laughed easily along with them.

"So," Claire continued, "How do you two know each other?"

The question gave Evelyn pause. Though they weren't in a romantic relationship, their friendship came from unusual – personal – circumstances. "Oh, well…"

"School." Jackson answered for her. "She's a librarian and helps with my studies."

Evelyn wasn't sure, but she thought she saw Jackson give Claire a stern look and shake his head.

"Jackson always did need help with his studies," Nathan laughed, teasing Jackson and breaking the tension that was momentarily present.

Jackson laughed sarcastically.

"How long are you guys in town for?" Nathan asked.

"Leaving today. Actually," Jackson said. "We're leaving in about an hour."

Ryan began pulling on Claire's arm. All three of the kids were getting restless. "That's too bad," Claire said. "It would have been nice to get to catch up and get to know you, Evelyn."

"I wish we could stay longer," Evelyn admitted, smiling sadly, "but Jackson says he has work."

Joshua began to whine and rub his eyes, making it clear that he was ready to leave. "We should probably go," Claire said. "We need to catch up next time you're in town, Jackson. Evelyn, it was really nice meeting you."

"You too," Evelyn smiled back.

The men shook hands and Jackson hugged Claire and the kids. They were the last of the guests to leave and Evelyn was once again alone with the Monroes.

"Charlie," Evelyn began. The questions she had about his reading were becoming a storm inside of her. An unnatural urgency pressed her to find the answers. "Could I ask you about what you read?"

"Of course," Charles replied eagerly. "What do you want to know?"

Natalie put her hands up to pause them. "Wait," she said. "Chat at the dinner table so you can talk while you eat."

Charles and Jackson returned the chairs that had been brought into the library into the dining room, and the three of them sat down while Natalie disappeared into the kitchen to prepare lunch.

"Okay," Charles continued their conversation, "what did you want to ask me?"

Evelyn was silent for a moment, trying to organize her thoughts as best she could. "I guess my first question is, was that story real? I mean, did it really happen that way? Jesus really said those words to that man?"

"Yes, the story is real. Are you not familiar with the Word of God?" Charles asked. He understood better than his son did that many people didn't have access to God's Word.

Evelyn shook her head. "The women who raised me told me about God, but only that He created us and that we should believe in him and worship him. They taught us a couple songs they sang for God, too." She was glad Charles didn't look shocked; it made her feel less embarrassed for admitting her ignorance.

"I read from a book called 'Matthew.' Matthew, and the other books that make up the whole Bible, were written by, and about, real people and they record what actually happened. Matthew was one of Jesus' closest friends, so he was likely there for this conversation."

Evelyn's spirit was comforted by that somehow, but she still didn't understand the story he had read. "Jesus…that's God's son, right?" Charles nodded. At least she had that right. "He was telling Nicodemus about being born again, and I don't know what that means, but I got the feeling it is important."

Charles nodded. "You're right, it is important. Jesus was talking about a spiritual birth. When we are born, physically, we are alive; but we are not alive spiritually until we are born again." Her left eye narrowed and her mouth creased into a frown. Her look of confusion prompted Charles to continue. "I know, it's still confusing. We are all born sinners. Sin is our imperfection, or disobedience from God's perfect law. The consequence for sin is death and an eternity away from God. It's what we call hell. Jesus came down to us to fix that, though. He offered himself as a sacrifice and died for us. The Good News is, He didn't stay dead. He defeated death and came to life again and offers His life for anyone who believes in Him. Jesus offers us a rebirth into life forever with Him, if we choose to believe and obey Him. We have to choose to, as we are led by His Spirit, be born into his family. Does that make sense?"

Evelyn thought about it for a minute. She had always believed in God, at least in what she knew of Him, but this rebirth Charles was talking about was new. "Jesus *chose* to die for us?"

"Yes."

But He was God, she thought. "Why?"

Charles was silent a moment before he answered, "I don't mean to be insensitive, please forgive me if I offend you, but I'm thinking it may be more difficult for you to understand because you grew up without parents. You see, Evelyn, I would gladly die for Jackson or Natalie, because he is my son and she is my wife; I would do anything I could to protect them and take care of them. I think that's a piece of Himself He puts in a Christian father and husband, to give us an example of His love for us,

His children. But remember, I am just a human, imperfect and broken. If I would die for them, would it not make sense for our Heavenly Father to send his Son, who is God the Son, to die for us, His children?"

"He must love us a lot," she pondered aloud. "It still doesn't make sense to me, though. The story does, but His love doesn't. It's too much. I don't deserve it."

"None of us do," Jackson responded. "That's why it's a gift. You just have to decide if you want to accept that gift."

Evelyn looked at Jackson and Charles. This is what made them so similar, she decided, their faith. She saw now that everything they did, everything they thought, was grounded in this faith, this relationship with the Creator of the world who died to save humanity. "I've always believed in God, does that count?"

Jackson took over answering her questions. "Do you believe what my dad just told you; that Jesus is the Son of God and died and rose again to save you and forgive you of your sins?"

She nodded. Though she had only just learned this, something inside her knew it to be true. "Is belief all it takes? That seems too easy."

"No," Jackson replied, "Even demons believe; you can believe in Him and still reject Him. You have to confess to Him that you are a sinner, that you're imperfect, and that you need Him."

"I do!" she exclaimed, hope bubbling inside her. "Of course I do! But really, that's all it takes?" Excitement was bubbling within her.

Jackson smiled tenderly. "Yes, that's all it takes."

A frown overtook her features. As always, she was cautious with hope, and what Jackson and Charles were saying…well, it didn't seem fair. "But He did all the work, and I get all the gain."

Jackson put his hand over hers. "He is your great reward, and you are His treasured and precious child. Never again will you be Fatherless. He loves you and delights in you and your love for Him."

Tears sprang to her eyes as Jackson's words poured God's love into her heart. She was loved. She had a Father!

Natalie walked in then. Evelyn saw the worry her tears were causing.

"We have a new sister in Christ," Charles explained.

Natalie's arms flew up. "Praise Jesus!" She squealed as she ran to Evelyn, throwing her arms around her in a mama bear hug. "Welcome to the family, dear."

Evelyn was overwhelmed by this love. God's love. She had found a Father, and an entire family in Him. As Natalie hugged her, she wept tears of joy and hope.

Jackson still held her hand, and Charles put his hand on her arm and prayed over her. "Father we thank You for Your daughter, and her new life in You. Thank You for bringing her into our son's life and ours and we look forward to an eternity together with You. We pray protection over her, and steadfastness in her heart for knowing You more. Please clothe her with Your strength and help her find her beauty in You. And we ask for blessings to pour over her, and that Your will, will be the desire of her heart. We pray this in Jesus' name. Amen."

## Chapter 26

Jackson watched Evelyn in the seat across from him, as she watched his parents' home fade from sight. Though he wasn't looking himself, the bend in the road told him it was out of sight. Evelyn's eyes lingered out the window a minute longer before she settled back against her seat with a sigh.

"Goodbyes are hard," he commented. Her eyes met his and he saw the tears she was holding back. Her lips parted as if she might say something, but instead she closed them with a weak smile, and dropped her eyes to her hands.

His attention followed hers, and the silence stretched on as they watched Evelyn's nervous energy escape through her hands.

"You're still nervous around me."

She tossed him an amused expression. "I think I'll always be nervous with you. But," she continued, reading between the lines. "Right now, I'm just trying to process everything from the last couple of days. And from this morning."

Guilt and regret weighed on him as he sat there watching her. He'd let a year and a half go by...

"I'm–" His voice cracked. Weird. And a little embarrassing. "I'm sorry I never spoke to you about God, or about my faith, until today."

Her hands stilled. "You've shown me God, even if you never said anything. But next time someone asks you why you're so nice, it might be a good opening to tell them about Jesus."

Jackson laughed lightly but felt a heaviness in his heart that wasn't there earlier. She was right, in one sense; but in another way she was wrong. He should have told her about God's love when she asked him why he was kind to her, but in reality, he hadn't been consciously acting out God's love for her. He'd been acting on his feelings for her. He could see now God had given him so many opportunities to share His love with her, His salvation. But his eyes had been focused on Evelyn; not God.

"It's amazing, isn't it?" she asked. "God's love, I mean."

"Yes, it is," he answered assuredly.

"Just look at us." Her words came like thoughts trying to work themselves out. "You needed help finding a book, and so we met. I'm a complete fool and got mixed up with Tom and needed you to rescue me, and somehow, we became friends. I got attacked and m-" she stuttered and couldn't finish. Shaking her head, she continued. "You rescued me, again, and took me to your parents' home and, for some unfathomable reason, I got to meet God! Happenchance meetings. Heartbreak. Even injury. And it all brought me here, with you."

Their whole relationship had been marked out by God to bring her to Him. *Thank You for saving her*, he prayed. *Rejoice with me because I have found my lost sheep...* The words from Luke 15 ran through his mind. *I rejoice with you, Lord. You are good.*

"It's humbling to see Him work."

"You mean God?" she asked, her eyebrows furrowed in an adorable way.

"Yes, God." He saw questions bouncing in her head, so he stayed quiet and waited for her to voice them.

"Do you believe God set it all up?" she asked with sincere confusion.

"Well," Jackson thought aloud. "It's clear God had you marked as His. Jeremiah 29:11 says God knows the plans He has for us, for a hope and a future. And Romans 8:28 says He uses all things for the good of those who love Him and are called according to His purpose. I think He's a good God who didn't want to see you live without Him for another day. I believe He took Tom's ill intent, and even my failure to speak to you about my faith, and used it all to bring you to Him."

Evelyn mulled this over, thinking back over other things that had worked to prepare her to hear and receive God. The Madames, the stained-glass-windows, even things Bekah had said. Hindsight was always better, and she saw now the arrows God had placed throughout her life, pointing her to Him.

"Evelyn, how old are you?" Jackson asked suddenly.

"Twenty. I thought you knew that?"

"That's what I thought. I've just never asked you."
"How old are you?"
"I turned twenty-seven last Monday. When do you turn twenty-one?"
"June second."
"Do you have a middle name?"
She smiled playfully. "Yes, do you?"
"Charles, after my father. Will you tell me yours?"
"Evelyn." She laughed at the face he made. "I go by my middle name. I don't know when, or why, they started calling me Evelyn, but when they told me it was my mother's middle name too, I didn't mind. My first name is Ayanna."
"What does it mean?"
"Beautiful flower." Her face scrunched at the confession.
"I think that's a perfect name for you," Jackson said, remembering how he'd thought of her as a flower among thorns the first time he saw her. "So, now I know your full name, and your birthday, and how old you are. What else don't I know?"
"I don't know," she said shrugging. "I'm not really used to telling people things about myself. You already know more than most people. What do you want to know?"
"You've never had a boyfriend?"
Her cheeks flushed. "Correct."
"And you really don't know of anyone else who's ever liked you, like that, I mean?"
"No. Remember, before college I was pretty much surrounded by girls, living in a government home and all. The only boy I ever saw regularly was Tom since his dad manages the orphan program. Why are you asking?"
"Well," Jackson continued, not answering her question. The reminder of how long Tom had been in her life chaffed his nerves. He tried to not think about it. "You've been in college for a while now. You really, honestly, have no knowledge of men being attracted to you?" He smiled as she turned into a tomato.
With her hands clasped tight, Evelyn shook her head.
"You're oblivious to the world around you," he said, laughing. "Do you know how many guys I've overheard talking about you? And not in

relation to Tom, either. I almost hit a guy this past spring because of the way he was talking about you!" Okay, maybe he had hit a guy because of it, but she didn't need to know that. Besides, it was more of a shove.

"Being talked about isn't the same as being liked," she said quietly.

He sobered. "You're very right, it's not. But you're still oblivious."

She rolled her eyes. *He* was oblivious. "Do you have any more questions?"

"Oh, I have more. Have you ever liked anyone, more than just their looks I mean? Liked them the way you want to be liked?"

"You ask very personal questions."

He just kept looking at her, waiting for her to answer.

"No."

"Liar."

"Yes," she conceded under the pressure of his gaze. "Yes, of course I've liked someone."

"Who is he?" he asked, undaunted.

"Jackson, even if I wanted to, I wouldn't tell you." She gave him the cutest pointed look. "How far is it to Syracuse?"

"Maybe a little over an hour." They'd been driving around thirty minutes already. "You can ask me questions, too, if you'd like."

"How many women have you dated?"

Obviously payback for his questions.

"Since starting college, I've had four girlfriends, none of them very serious, or at least not very long. Before college, well, that shouldn't count."

"How many before college?"

"Twelve."

"Twelve?" She almost choked. If their difference in age didn't make her feel like a child, her lack of experience did. "Were you in love with any of them?"

He inhaled a deep breath and exhaled slowly. "There was one I thought I loved; but I was foolish. So, no, I wasn't in love with any of them." He was curious when her hands began fidgeting again.

"Evelyn," he coaxed after a period of silence. "What is it you want to know?"

"What was she like?"

*Poison,* he thought. "Much like your friend Sarah. She enjoyed seducing men, and when she decided she wanted me, I wasn't strong enough then to resist."

There was such shame and bitterness in the way he spoke about this woman. But she could understand. She knew Sarah.

She also knew Sarah was like Tom in what she wanted from a relationship.

"Sarah tends to leave a trail of broken hearts," she commented. "If your woman is truly like her..." She paused, not knowing if her words were appropriate.

Jackson smiled a self-conscious smile. "Thanks, I think? Do you mind if I ask some more questions?"

"Sure," she answered, "But I have one more for you first. What were you and your dad talking about during breakfast? He seemed upset and I couldn't help feel that I had something to do with it."

"Well, we were discussing the New Year's Ball, if you must know." It was true; they had spoken, briefly, about the ball.

*Thank goodness,* she thought. She could relax. She had worried all day that she had upset Charles and was glad to know it had to do with something completely unrelated to her. "Okay, go ahead, ask your questions."

"What's your favorite color?"

"That's easy, green."

"What's your favorite food?"

"Chocolate chip peanut butter cookies and French toast are pretty high on my list. But always fresh fruit. Growing up, any fruit we had was canned, so fresh still tastes like a luxury to me."

"Really?"

Evelyn nodded, looking as if growing up with no fresh fruit was the most normal thing in the world.

"Okay, one more question and you'll be off the hook for today. Will you go to the New Year's Ball with me?"

Evelyn's lips turned into a tight frown. "It's not nice to tease, Jackson."

"I'm not sure if I should be offended or not. I'm really asking you to the ball. I'm not teasing you."

"Is this what you and your father were talking about? Did he tell you to ask me, because your mother wants me to go? I should have told her not to say anything to your father either."

"No! We did talk about me taking you, and he was frustrated that I hadn't asked you, but only because I was assuming you knew I wanted you to go with me. He said you didn't have the slightest idea about it; I can see he was right. If you don't want to go with me, just say so. But don't act like I'm the one not wanting you to go." This wasn't going how he thought it would. Evelyn had a way of making it hard to think, and hard to say what he meant. It appeared that she was as unaware of his feelings as his father suggested.

"I'm so sorry, Jackson. I'm not sure why you're upset," she stuttered in sincere concern. "I'm so confused…Isn't there someone else you'd rather go with?"

"Don't you think if there was someone else, you would have heard about her by now?"

She shrugged. "I don't know. Is that the kind of thing we'd talk about?"

"Oh, Evelyn," he laughed, moving to her side and scooping her into a hug. "Please forgive me for being a jerk. I honestly want to go with you, and only you. Please, please say you'll go with me?"

She was stone in his arms for a long moment before he felt her sigh, her body relaxing against his.

"I'll go with you on one condition," she said, playfully smiling up at him as he loosened his hold on her. "I'll go if you have a date for Bekah, too. She really wants to go…" *She could easily find her own date,* Evelyn thought, "and it'd be nice to have her with us…with me." She bit her bottom lip as she waited for his answer.

That was easy enough. George had been asking about her since he found out Jackson knew her. "You have a deal," he said, releasing her and moving over just enough to be respectful. "But, if I said I couldn't, would you really not go with me?"

"Of course, I'd still go." Her smile was radiant. "I'm really excited. A lot of girls are going to hate me after this."

He delighted in her happiness. "You're excited that a lot of girls are going to hate you?"

"No!" A giggle escaped her. "I'm so excited to go. With you. But a lot of girls are going to hate me for going with you...oh goodness," she went a bit pale. "I'm going to be hated by the entire school; maybe the whole city."

His laugh rang through the car. "They're not all going to hate you."

"I'm quite serious. Every unattached female is going to despise me for getting to go with you, instead of them getting to go with you. Then everyone thinks I...you know...with Tom, so of course no one will think I deserve to go with you. Of course, really, they're right about that, but not for those reasons. I'm not even certain Bekah won't loathe me for this! You should have heard her when she found out I kissed you! She actually asked if I thought you could 'misunderstand her?' Because that's what I told her, that it was all just a big misunderstanding. It's a good thing I'm graduating in the spring...I might have to move after this!" Evelyn paused finally to breathe. "Sorry...I'm rambling."

There were only two things he really heard her say in all of that: the first, that she said she kissed him; it was the first time she didn't say he was the one who kissed her. The second, that she was graduating in the spring.

"You're only twenty years old. How do you have only one semester left?"

Alluring was not the look she meant to give, but it's the one he received. "I worked very hard...and I'm a genius." Her face cracked. "I started when I was sixteen. The Head Madame at my home had me take some tests and recommended me for an early-start program. I think it came down to money. It was cheaper for them to put me in school and let me start working than to keep me in the home."

That wasn't true. Jackson knew those programs were incredibly difficult to get into. You had to be extraordinarily smart and show overwhelming evidence that you could live responsibly away from your parents, or in her case, her orphanage. "What are you planning on doing after you graduate?"

"I'm not entirely sure, to be honest. I've been putting off any decisions until after this semester is over. I've been thinking I'd like to stay on at the library, but I don't know if I would be able to afford to work there once I'm not in campus housing. How much longer until you're finished?"

"This is my last semester," he answered while thinking over her words. "I'll be staying in Syracuse, though, with my job; unless they were to transfer me somewhere else. But the way things are, I don't see them doing that." He didn't want to mention the rising crime. He was still hoping against the odds that they were just random incidents.

They were back in Syracuse now. Evelyn only noticed the fact when she spotted her mother's cemetery. That was a topic she would not be bringing up, at least not today.

The driver dropped them off at Patrol Headquarters, instead of the Cell Building where they had been picked up. Evelyn was grateful for the shorter walk to her apartment since the snow had just begun to fall.

"I guess I'm done running for the winter," Evelyn commented, catching a snowflake in her hand. Jackson took her bag and showed no sign of letting her carry it. She thought about trying to convince him he didn't need to walk her home, but she knew he wouldn't listen to her. "Did you have a good time at your parents?" she asked as they began their walk to her apartment.

"Yes," he answered. He wished the car ride had been longer though; he wasn't ready to give her up. But he knew he needed to trust God to protect her now, and He was better at it anyway. "Did you?"

"Yes," she said, smiling. "Your dad called me a, 'sister in Christ'?" Jackson nodded. "Does that mean I'm your sister too, and you're my brother?"

He wasn't sure if he liked being called that by her, but it was true; in Christ they were brother and sister. "Yes, I suppose that's what it means."

She looped her arm with his and looked up at him grinning. "I always wanted a brother."

He smiled at her, and she made him laugh, but a rock landed in his stomach at her comment. He wanted to be more than a brother to her. *Lord, did you bring us together, just to keep us apart?*

It was a short walk and they arrived at her apartment too quickly. If Bekah or Sarah were home, she wouldn't be able to talk to Jackson. Not like she could alone.

"You have something on your mind," he stated.

"Do you have the books of the Bible?"

"Yes, I have them."

"Do you think I could visit you, at your house sometime, and you could teach me about them like your dad did at church?"

"You're welcome over any time you'd like," he answered. "I'm not sure how good of a teacher I'll be, but I'll try my best."

"When's your next night off?"

Her boldness was a wonder, especially in light of his most recent question to God. "Wednesday. As much as I'd love to have you to myself, you should invite Bekah. My roommate would like to meet her."

He waited as he once again saw her working something out in her mind. Not wanting to rush her, he kept quiet. Instead of a question, though, she stepped suddenly to him and wrapped her arms tightly around him.

Evelyn hugged him tighter than ever and breathed in his scent. The thud of her bag dropping to the ground sounded just before his arms surrounded her, cocooning her in his strength. She let herself enjoy the embrace; she didn't know for how long. She never wanted to let go of him. The thought brought her back to her senses.

"Thank you," she finally forced herself to speak, though still clinging to him.

"You're welcome," he replied in whisper.

"I'm scared to go in," she admitted. Even in Jackson's arms, the memories of Tom tormented her.

He ran his hand over her hair, cherishing their closeness, both physically and emotionally. "Invite me in, and you won't have to face it alone."

Evelyn leaned back to look at him. "Would you like to come in?"

"I'd love to," he smiled down at her. "Thank you."

Everything looked normal inside the apartment, but it felt all wrong. It would be a while until Evelyn felt safe here again. Jackson closed the door behind them.

"Hello?" Bekah called, coming down the hall. Her eyes immediately fell on Jackson and Evelyn's bag in his hand. "Evie, you have some serious explaining to do...Evie!" Bekah exploded at the sight of her. "What happened to you?"

"It's kind of a long story," Evelyn grimaced, touching her forgotten black eye.

"Jackson," Bekah barked, her violent expression now trained on Jackson. "You had better not be the one responsible for this; or so help me, I don't care who you are or how strong you are, I'll…"

"Bekah!" Evelyn interrupted, appalled by her questioning Jackson's character. "It wasn't him!"

A darkness Evelyn had never seen overcame Bekah's whole person. "Tom."

"Jackson got here before…" Evelyn stopped and looked up at Jackson.

She didn't see the way Bekah looked at the two of them, but Jackson did. He couldn't decide if she looked curious or upset, but there was no questioning that they'd be having a conversation in the near future. He was happy to learn he was not the only one looking out for Evelyn, and got the distinct feeling the little spitfire staring him down was more lethal than she appeared. He looked back to Evelyn. "Will you be okay?"

"Yes, I'll be fine." She hoped that was true. "Thank you, again."

He turned his smile to Bekah. He might as well get it over with then. He needed her help getting in for breakfast the following morning anyway. "Bekah, could I talk with you outside? It'll just take a minute."

She grabbed her coat and marched to the door in reply.

Jackson looked back at Evelyn. "I'll see you Wednesday, if not before." He opened the door for Bekah and followed her out, closing it behind them.

Bekah stood with her arms crossed and her toe tapping.

"You know," he started, "at one point you were on my side."

"At one point, Evie wasn't coming home from who-knows-where with you, sporting a black eye," Bekah snapped back. "Is this where you make excuses, or are you going to just tell me what happened?"

"I'm glad Evelyn has you," he commented before filling her in. "I had been away with work and came over as soon as I could when I got back. I found Tom here with her. It was pretty easy to see he planned to rape her if she wasn't willing to give herself to him; and she wasn't willing." Bekah's face showed the horror he felt retelling the story. "Tom ended up in a cell, and I couldn't bring myself to let Evelyn out of my sight, so I made her go with me to my parents' home. We left that night and just got back."

"But you got here in time, right?" she asked. "Before Tom…"

By the grace of God, "Yes."

She shook her head. "I'm gonna kill him."

"I understand the feeling," he admitted. His veins still ran hot with rage against Tom. "It was the hardest thing I've ever had to do, keeping myself from killing him. He should be very glad I got here when I did. Any further…" He was ashamed to say he'd have willingly killed the man if he'd hurt Evelyn further.

"Thank you for being there for her." Bekah looked straight at him when she spoke, saving him from finishing his confession. "So, what are you and her now?" she asked, curiosity climbing into her eyes.

"We're friends."

"Is that all you feel for her? Just friendship?" The motherly tone she used managed to amuse him from his vengeful thoughts.

"No," he answered honestly.

"Good," she said, nodding. "You seem like someone who will treat her the way she deserves to be treated. But if you break her heart, I'll break you."

"I won't," he promised, somehow not doubting this pixie's ability to inflict pain. "I'd appreciate it if you didn't say anything to her about it, not yet. But I actually asked you out here because I need your help. I lost a bet and owe her breakfast tomorrow. I'm pretty sure she thinks I'm not planning on living up to my end of the deal, so I'm hoping you could let me in tomorrow morning so I can surprise her."

Bekah put her hands on her hips. "Only if I get some of this breakfast, too."

"I already planned on that."

She smiled. "Good. Then we'll see you tomorrow morning."

"Four thirty."

Bekah closed the door with a groan. Apparently early mornings weren't her thing.

## Chapter 27

Whatever it was that Jackson was talking with Bekah about, she knew they were outside so she wouldn't hear them. Not wanting to be tempted to listen in, she took her bag to her room to unpack. Her normally tidy room looked like it had been rummaged through; evidence of her rushed departure and her panicked state of mind. At least she remembered being the one doing the rummaging.

It was strange…unsettling…to be back in her room. Only four nights had passed, but it felt like a lifetime since she'd slept in her own bed.

"He didn't even hug me goodbye," slipped out as she unzipped her bag. Bekah's footsteps zipped her lips and refocused her thoughts.

"I've been filled in about Tom," Bekah said, plopping onto her bed. "I won't ask anything about him. But," she gave Evelyn an expecting look. "I will ask you about that man who just dropped you off. What's the story with him, huh?"

Evelyn couldn't keep herself from smiling, even though she tried with great effort to keep herself from doing so. "There's really no story, but I did have a nice time with him."

"'There's really no story, but I did have a nice time with him,'" Bekah mocked her. "Come on, Evie! You can't come strolling through the door with Mr. Gorgeous and not give me some details."

It was pointless trying to keep everything from Bekah, so she joined her sitting on the bed and began telling her some of what happened over the past four days. "I'm sure Jackson told you, but once he dealt with Tom, he invited me…made me…go with him to his parents' house. But I hate to disappoint you. Nothing romantic happened." She was almost convinced of that herself. "But, though I am quite sure his parents put the thought in his head, he invited me to the Officer's New Year's Eve Ball. And," she had to take a breath. "I got to go to church! A real church service! Mr. Monroe leads one every Sunday in their home. Have you ever been to one?"

"Yes, I've been to a couple of them," Bekah answered in a cautious tone.

The admission shocked Evelyn. Bekah had never mentioned church to her before. "Well, Jackson invited us, me and you, over on Wednesday so he could tell me more about the Bible and stuff. You'll go with me, right?"

"Yes." It was Bekah's turn to be taken aback. "Are you sure he invited both of us though? I barely know him."

"Yes," Evelyn confirmed. "He specifically said that I should invite you. You are quite surprising. Do you know that?"

Bekah laughed. "How so?"

"Most of the time you're so laid back and happy-go-lucky, then all of a sudden you get like you were tonight. Intense. Intimidating even. Surprising or not, I appreciate you looking after me."

"Well, someone has to look after you, especially now that you have boys pursuing you," Bekah teased. She stood to leave but paused with a troubled look. "Do me a favor, Evie. Don't go around telling people you went to church, or that Jackson did. Don't get me wrong, I'm glad you got to go. It's just, you may find that not so many people around here agree with us on the idea of church."

That was a curious thing to say, Evelyn thought, but she nodded anyway and watched as Bekah left her room.

Outside, snow was falling steadily, and her thoughts drifted back to Jackson. She hoped he'd be working inside, instead of patrolling the campus, tonight. She sighed deeply. She needed to stop thinking about the man. They were home now and back in reality, and just because he had found his way into her heart, didn't mean she'd found her way into his. Friend. Brother. No more, she smiled, but no less.

Jackson was irate. Tom had been released the same night he had been arrested. His father had gone to the Cell Building and used his government title to get him out. The officer on duty informed Jackson that Tom had been placed on probation, but he didn't care. Probation still let him out, and put Evelyn in danger. Hopefully Tom was in too much pain to try anything for a while.

After the report on Tom, Jackson pulled George into a meeting to get updated on everything else.

"I've got a bad feeling, Jackson," George started. They closed the door to Jackson's office. The last thing they needed were intruding ears. "Something's just not right. These break-ins don't feel random."

Jackson felt the same way. "Has there been anything new this week?"

"There were break-ins every day except Wednesday."

Jackson got the feeling George was holding something back. "What are you thinking?"

George looked at the door, hesitating even with it closed. "There's a particular officer who has been in town for every break-in, and was preoccupied on Wednesday. And I'm not positive, but I think there is a connection between the victims."

"Do you mean to say you think extremists are involved, or something else?" He never liked Tom, but had never entertained the idea of him being an extremist. Thinking about it now, he couldn't refute the idea.

"I mean to say," George continued, "things don't seem right, and I think it's time we start being very careful about who we trust, even within the officers. And I think there's a particular lady in your life who's going to need a little extra watching out for."

A chill ran through him hearing those words. "I've been thinking the same thing," he admitted. "Do you think she fits the victim profile though?"

"No. I think you do. But you're not really a realistic target. Anyone dumb enough to enter your house runs the risk of meeting both of us. Even with just one of us, they're not likely to get away, now are they? But your friend…"

Jackson nodded, understanding. "I've made it plenty clear I care for her…to everyone but her." How could he have been so stupid to make her a target? He needed to stay focused. Dealing with the entire problem was the best way to keep her safe. "You really think that officer's involved?"

There was no doubt in George's voice when he spoke. "Yes."

"And do you think this is extremist activities?"

"Yes."

"Alright," Jackson said, thinking aloud, "First we need to re-route Patrols with the officers we trust. I won't be able to focus on much else until I know someone's watching her building at all times." They set to work on the new routes immediately after George filled him in on the details from the other break-ins.

## Chapter 28

Morning came too quickly. Jackson was grateful the few hours of sleep he got were deep, but after the excitement of surprising Evelyn wore off, caffeine would be the only thing getting him through the day.

The snow had stopped falling and had only dusted the ground in white, making his walk to Evelyn's an easy one. After a soft knock, a very tired Bekah opened the door.

"Thanks," he said, smiling at her. She didn't return his smile.

"Please tell me that you don't need my help cooking?" she asked groggily.

"No. Go back to bed, I'll be fine." She collapsed on the couch and pulled a blanket over her head. He laughed to himself.

Before long, he had hot French toast with strawberries and whipped cream plated for the girls, with steaming coffee to go along.

"I need your help again," he whispered, peeking under Bekah's blanket.

She whined and pulled the blanket back down, covering her face.

"Come on Bekah," he pestered. "You know I can't just walk into her room; she'll freak out."

"That's true," came from under the blanket. Slowly, Bekah stretched and sat up, removing the blanket from her disheveled head. "You know you owe me for this, right?" He nodded. "You're lucky I'm so awesome." And with that, she stood up and dragged herself down to Evelyn's room.

Bekah opened the door and gave Jackson time to put the plates on the dresser and retrieve the coffees before she climbed into bed with Evelyn.

"What in the world are you doing?" Evelyn asked as Bekah shoved her over.

"Breakfast," was all Bekah said.

"I'm not making you breakfast, Bekah," Evelyn complained. "I'm sleeping." She refused to open her eyes and allow her slumber to be interrupted.

"Not you, dummy. Him."

Evelyn's eyes shot open. "Jackson." His name was but a breath, and she slid deeper into her bed, covering her face with her hands. "Why are you here? I cheated."

"If you don't start eating, Evelyn," Bekah said through bites and sips of coffee, "I'm going to eat it all."

"Hey," Evelyn retorted. "I worked very hard for this food. You're lucky you even get any." She looked at Jackson who held out her plate to her. She almost cried. "My favorites? You really didn't have to do this."

Sitting up, she accepted the plate of food and took a bite. The moan that escaped her was a little embarrassing. "You inherited your mother's gift of cooking."

Jackson smiled at her, leaning against her dresser. "I'm glad you like it."

"Aren't you going to eat?" Evelyn asked.

"Oh," he replied, "I'm gonna eat. You think I'd miss out on my own home cooking?" He winked at her. "I have some in the kitchen. Do you ladies want anything before I go eat?"

Evelyn didn't trust her voice at the moment. His wink just about did her in. So instead, she shook her head in response.

"I'm not allowed to have you, so no, I'm good." Bekah was back to her old self.

Jackson laughed at Bekah's comment, and Evelyn's reaction, then left the girls to eat.

Jackson was doing the dishes when Evelyn brought both empty plates out.

"Where's Bekah?" Jackson asked, taking the plates from her hands.

"Wherever her dreams take her." She smiled. "You know, I can take dish duty. You did feed me."

Jackson dried his hands, prompting Evelyn to take over, but she didn't make it further than a step before Jackson's hands found her waist, lifting and sitting her on the counter.

"Just let me take care of you, okay?" He winked again and refilled her coffee, adding cream and sugar.

"Thank you," she whispered before taking a sip of her coffee. "You really didn't have to do all this."

"We made a bet and I lost," he said, glancing up at her with another smile. "So, I really did have to do this." He finished the few dishes he had left and, after drying his hands, took up his coffee and leaned against the opposite counter.

She had a bad habit of not controlling herself when she was tired and around him and caught herself staring. It really wasn't safe for her to be around him after so little sleep. She quickly looked down and took another sip of her coffee.

He noticed. "It doesn't bother me when you do that," he said.

"What doesn't bother you?" she asked, red with embarrassment. He gave her a knowing look and she knew for sure she had been caught. "I'm sorry. I promise I don't mean to do it."

"I told you, it doesn't bother me," he repeated. It was all pride, but he enjoyed catching her looking at him that way. "And you don't need to be embarrassed about it. I've been just as bad with you. You just never notice, because I'm so sneaky."

Evelyn almost choked. "You're such a liar, Jackson, but thank you for trying to make me feel better. I guess I shouldn't really blame myself though; you are Mr. Gorgeous." There she went again, not censoring herself with him, saying things she didn't mean to tell him.

"Mr. Gorgeous, huh?" he teased, looking very pleased. "Not such a bad name. I'll take it."

Evelyn slid from the counter and Jackson followed her to the couch, sitting close to her. "Don't give me credit for that," she said. "That's just what Bekah calls you." She wasn't sure why she was telling him that. She decided to blame him. He made it so difficult to think sometimes, and editing her thoughts before speaking was becoming just plain impossible.

Jackson kicked his feet up and put his hands behind his head, giving himself an air of cockiness. "So, I'm Mr. Gorgeous to Bekah and a candy shop to you? And you can't give credit to anyone but yourself for that. I've got to say, if I ever need a boost to my ego, I'm just going to come over here."

Evelyn pulled a blanket over her from the back of the couch and laid down, leaning away from Jackson. "Yeah, that's just what you need, a boost to your ego," she joked. "More like you should avoid us so you don't become one of those horrible self-absorbed ego-maniacs."

Jackson found her feet and pulled them on his lap, rubbing them as he battled his feelings for her. "Evelyn," he spoke after a spell of silence. "Do you feel safe with me?" He had asked her this just two nights ago, but he didn't think she remembered; and she was much more coherent now.

"That's a strange thing to ask," she thought aloud, indeed not remembering the previous time he'd asked. "Of course I do. You've protected me from so much."

"I don't mean do you feel safe because of me," he countered. "It's my job to make people feel safe and make this town safe for them to live in. What I mean is, right now, do you feel safe with me touching you this way? Or if we were alone, and Bekah wasn't in the back room, would you still be okay with me being here?"

"I've never felt safer with anyone else in my entire life," she answered, completely naïve to what he was really asking. "I'd never lay like this with someone else, or fall asleep on anyone besides you. Actually, there are a lot of things I've done with you that I've never done, and probably would never do, with anyone else: ride in a car, visit your family, be thrown over your shoulder and carried around like a sack of potatoes, have breakfast in bed." She wiggled her toes. "Have my feet rubbed. But you're safe. I'm too young for you to like me…so maybe that's it." Her nose wrinkled. She didn't like remembering how childlike she was to him, and she certainly didn't enjoy saying it out loud.

He watched her for another minute. How could he show her that he did not see her as too young, but as a woman that he had fallen for. For as many relationships as he had been in, he was completely unsure of himself with her.

"It hasn't even been a week since Tom attacked you," he commented. "I don't want to scare you away."

Evelyn's lips parted to answer just as the door opened. Sarah was home.

"He came over this morning," Evelyn explained, sitting up and stealing her feet away from Jackson. "That's all."

Sarah didn't acknowledge Evelyn or her words. Her eyes were focused on him alone, and he was all too familiar with the look he saw there. Ice ran through his veins, for in that moment he knew, Sarah was an extremist.

Terror gripped his heart. Evelyn had the enemy under her own roof.

"What a convenient surprise." Sarah wore a faint, mocking smile. "I don't think I could manage to carry my bag another step. Jackson, would you mind taking it to my room for me?"

Jackson kept his expression uninterested and didn't respond to Sarah. She couldn't see his fear, or she'd know he'd figured her out. Instead, he turned to Evelyn. "I'll be right back."

He retrieved Sarah's dropped bag and followed her down the hall. When he reached her door, he was careful to keep his feet outside of her room as he leaned in to drop off her bag. He turned around and left without speaking to her.

When Jackson retuned, he found Evelyn with her knees pulled up to her chest, leaning her head against them. It was the look of defeat. She'd probably seen too many men disappear in Sarah's wake, not to reappear so quickly. It hurt more than he imagined realizing Evelyn thought he'd fall prey to Sarah, or would ever choose Sarah over her.

Swallowing the pride he had no right to have, he set his path to the fridge. His mission: strawberries.

Her pretty little head turned to him when he sat next to her. Her surprised smile lit up the room.

"I didn't expect you to come back so quickly."

"Do you have that little faith in me?" And there went her smile. He was an idiot. "I came over this morning because I wanted to see you, not Sarah."

Her smile almost returned. "Can I have a strawberry?"

Jackson looked up, pretending to consider his response. "Hmm…ok." He tossed one up in the air and was astounded when she caught it in her mouth. "Um, that was kind of awesome."

"Well," she said, smiling and chewing. "I am kind of awesome." The strawberry was ripe and sweet, drawing her across the couch to sit close to him. "It's still really early. What time did you get here?" she asked, stealing another strawberry.

"Four thirty."

"Is there more whipped cream?" she asked, thinking about the strawberries again.

He laughed at her and started getting up, but she tugged him back down.

"No, no," she said. "You've done enough and must be exhausted. I'll get it." She retrieved the whipped cream and returned, sitting closer to him and tucking her feet back under his legs because she was cold now from leaving her blanket. "Have you slept at all since being back?" She dipped a strawberry in the whipped cream and ate it.

He swallowed hard at her closeness. She had no idea the power she had over him. He had to force the thoughts of taking her face and kissing her away from his mind. "I slept a little, but I don't work again until tonight. I'll have time to sleep some more after class." He wondered if Tom would be in class today. He wanted to force the thought away, but it was time to update her on the varmint. "Speaking of work," he added. "I need to talk to you about a couple things."

The look in his eyes. The line his jaw drew. The way he spoke. Evelyn didn't like it. "What?"

"First," he eased in. "You're going to notice more officers around your building. George and I set a new Patrol route with officers stationed very close to you."

"Why?" she asked, unease unfurling in her chest.

"That's the second thing I need to talk to you about. I got back to work last night and was informed that Tom has been released." He saw the chill run through her, but she kept a brave face. "He's on probation, and George and I hand-picked the officers who will be on your route. Evelyn, I have to be completely honest with you." Even if he didn't want to be. "George and I have been tracking a streak of break-ins, and we don't think they're random. We both believe I've been targeted by the same people responsible for those break-ins."

"Wouldn't it be really unwise of someone to target you?" she asked, interrupting him. "I can't see you as being an easy target."

"That's the problem," he continued. "I think they're trying to get at me, by going through you." He expected her to shudder, or show some sign of concern, but she looked perfectly calm. He could almost hear her thoughts. She'd become a target because of him. It was cause for concern, but she wasn't afraid. At least not yet. Something else had drawn her focus.

"Okay," she said finally. "What about Bekah and Sarah? Do you think they're safe?"

He stared. It was all he could do.

"Jackson," she said, more insistently. "What about Bekah and Sarah?"

"I don't think they're in any danger," he admitted. Sarah, being the danger, was most definitely safe. He prayed Bekah would be safe. He couldn't see a good reason for her to be targeted. But being collateral damage was always an issue…

Evelyn exhaled. "Good. Then just tell me what I need to do, how to be careful."

He shook his head. Her calm baffled him. "I'll tell you how to be careful, but promise me, if this person comes at you, you won't try to fight. Promise me you'll yell for help as you run away as fast as you can."

Evelyn understood; whoever was after him, and therefore after her, she wouldn't be able to fight off. She knew who it was; of course, she knew who it was. "It's Tom, isn't it?" Fear was pressing in on her now.

"Yes. George and I believe he is involved, and he has a personal grudge against me, so I believe he'll try something again."

She retreated into her thoughts for a moment. "It's so weird," she said, thinking allowed. "When we were little, Tom picked on everyone, but especially me. Then when we ran into each other here, it was all so different. He said he only teased me and the others so I would look at him. It had to all have been lies, but even looking back now, it really seemed like he had changed; well, changed towards me. It wasn't until later…" She trailed off, lost in her thoughts.

Jackson watched her while she spoke. She was trying to figure something out, something she hadn't mentioned to him before. He didn't want to ask her. He didn't want to hear about Tom and her; but he needed to. She had already told him some about her and Tom. At the time he heard it, he thought that was the end of it. Now, he could see there was more. "What happened between the two of you?"

She slid away from him, closing off from him, sitting with her legs crossed, thinking. "The first time I saw him was here, on this couch. I tried to sneak past him, but he saw me and had me sit between him and Sarah. Sarah wasn't ecstatic. He acted like we were old friends, and when he looked at me..." Her eyes found Jackson, and she hesitated. "He just looked at me differently. And then he showed up at my work, and after my classes, and would walk me home. He was always touching me; not inappropriately though. I just mean, he'd always have his arm over my shoulders, or would..."

She looked at Jackson who was watching her carefully with his jaw clenched tight. "I don't want to talk to you about this. It's very uncomfortable."

"I don't want to talk to you about it either," he admitted. "But I think you need to talk through it to work through whatever it is you're trying to figure out. And I need to hear it. I need to know as much as I can about him."

She nodded and began playing with her nails. As she spoke, she only glanced at Jackson. "The next time he was over, he stood with me in the kitchen. He put his arm around me, in front of everyone. I didn't know what to do. He told me to lean against him, so I did. He told me..." She tried to push through the embarrassment and humiliation of sharing everything with Jackson. "He told me that my purity made me more attractive. He only found out that night I hadn't ever dated anyone or been with a man before. And he said he'd teach me how to be with one...with a man." She looked up, wide-eyed, hoping to convince Jackson, "I didn't know what he meant! I thought he just meant how he told me to lean against him when he had his arm around me, stuff like that." But that wasn't entirely true. Her eyes fell.

Jackson could see she was holding something back, and he was sure he didn't want to hear it. "I won't judge you for anything you tell me, and you don't need to be ashamed; but I won't force you to tell me more than you want to."

Evelyn nodded again. "A part of me hoped he meant a little more than that. But I promise, I never wanted him to teach me to..." She was panicking. "I didn't...never...I just..."

Jackson put the bowl of strawberries on the table and put his hand on hers, causing her to look up. "You don't have to explain that," he said, trying to soothe her. "I think I know you pretty well, and I know the kind of woman you are." He left his hand on hers and she began to trace his fingers, which made having to hear everything about Tom a little better.

"He wanted me to go out with him and Sarah's friends dancing that night, but I said no. So, he made me promise I'd go later. I told you about that, remember? At the library. You told me to be careful. You and Bekah both told me to be careful that night. Anyway, I went out with him, and we danced. Then this guy came over and was being too...I'm not sure I even know. He just seemed like he was up to something. I didn't like him near me. Tom apparently didn't like him near me either, because before I knew it, the guy was lying on a table and Tom was ready to fight everyone all at once. Right then was when everything changed. He hit another guy, then grabbed my arm and took me out of the bar. Something was different in him then. It was on the walk back to my apartment that he tried to kiss me. He wanted me to prove I liked him. It felt like he was afraid there was someone else. I couldn't understand any of it. I got scared, and he called me a tease, so I hit him and ran. He could have caught me if he wanted to, but he let me go. The rumors started the next day."

Jackson took his hand away. It didn't make sense to her, because she was missing a part of the story.

It was all his fault.

He looked at her. Her hair. Her face. Her eye that had mostly healed since Tom assaulted her. Her shoulders and arms. Her hands now fiddling with her pajama pant leg. "I should have never spoken to you." She looked up as he spoke, startled and confused.

How could he explain? "I should have asked the other woman to help me find that book. I shouldn't have asked about your day or told you to be careful. I should have turned from you in the garden and I should never have kissed you. I should have stayed away from you completely."

Evelyn didn't respond. She couldn't. Tears filled her eyes and spilled over. She didn't understand why he was saying those things. Weren't they friends?

Jackson wanted to hold her and comfort her, but he didn't know if he should. Everything he had done to try and help her ended up bringing her pain. He knew he needed to explain better, but didn't know what to do or how to say it.

Silence stretched between them as tears streamed down her face. "I'm sorry I told you about Tom," she finally managed to get out. "I completely understand you feeling that way." She stood. "Don't feel like you need to stay any longer. And don't worry; I'll leave you alone from now on." She couldn't look at him.

He couldn't keep himself from her. "Evelyn, that's not what I meant!"

She backed away from him, holding a hand out to keep distance between them.

"Evelyn, do you really think anything you could tell me would make me not want to be near you? I meant I should have left you alone for your own sake. Everything Tom's done to you was because of me, starting that night at the bar."

"That doesn't make any sense. We weren't even friends then."

"Evelyn I was there. I knew you were going out and I went to a bar with George, hoping it would be the one you were going to. I saw the whole thing. I saw you dancing with Tom. I saw him leave you to get your drinks, I saw the women at the bar talking with him, and the man approach you and put his hands on you. I almost went at him myself, but George stopped me. And then when Tom hit him, George and I went to help, and I ordered him to get you out of there. He already didn't like me, and I didn't like him, and because I knew who you were and was worried about you, he must have thought I was the other man. So he tried to kiss you. Then, I confirmed his suspicions when I kissed you. He even waited for me after I walked you home from the campus library and I ordered him to stay away from you.

"I lied to you, Evelyn. I told you that you'd be safe with me, that just being friends with me would keep people away from you; but I was wrong. Everything, every last horrible thing, was my doing." He sat on the couch and held his head in his hands, completely defeated. How could he have been so blind and caused her so much pain? She would have been safer with Tom. At least then she'd be in his care, and not his wrath.

The logic of what he said made sense to Evelyn, but some of the details didn't. She didn't care about the details at that moment, though; she just wanted to comfort him. She knelt down at his feet and rubbed her hand gently over his hair. "Jackson," she cooed. "Do you remember what we talked about yesterday on the way home from your parents?"

He rested his arms on his knees and looked at her. If he hadn't been sitting, his knees would have given beneath him from the way she was looking at him. "Yes, Evelyn, of course I remember. I remember everything we talk about."

She put her hand on his arm. "Tell me what I said."

His brows furrowed. "Which part? We talked about a lot of things."

She smiled, her face still wet from crying. "When we first got in the car, before you started interrogating me."

"You were talking about God."

She began stroking his arm with her thumb. "Good. What about God?"

"You were talking about His love."

"Yes," she said, "and you said that it was humbling to see Him work. You and I can look at all of this in two ways. We can look at it with hope or despair, and I choose hope. It's not your fault Tom is lost, or that he is striking out because he doesn't like you and thinks you stole his toy. I have gained everything because you chose to talk to me. Without you, who would have introduced me to Jesus? Sure, you kissed me in front of a crazy person," she smiled mischievously, "but I can't say I didn't enjoy it."

It took everything in him not to grab her face and kiss her hard and fierce. She suffered everything because of him, and was facing more still, yet she saw nothing but hope. When he looked at her, it was as if her heart was radiating from within her, making her glow.

Instead of kissing her lips, he took her hands in his and kissed them. "Then you don't hate me?" he asked.

"How could I ever hate you?"

He wiped the tears that still wet her cheeks. "I'm so sorry I made you cry."

She laughed lightly. "That's another thing I don't do with other people. Cry." In a moment of courage, driven by her love for him and wanting to calm the fire she saw burning in him, she reached up and touched his face. They were already close, but she thought he leaned forward a bit more. "I don't want you to blame yourself, Jackson, and I don't want you to worry."

"You have the most beautiful heart I've ever known, Evelyn."

She gave him a smile that said she didn't believe him. "Are you alright?"

"No," he answered honestly, "but you're helping."

They sat there for a moment longer, then she slid into the chair and took a deep breath, letting it out slowly. She was a mess inside, but was determined not to show it. "So, what do we do about Tom?"

"We won't have to worry about him for a little while. As long as he's on probation, he's being watched. But I'll pick up more Patrol shifts, and I'll try and be on the route that watches you on nights he's off as often as possible." He'd work every night if he had to, to keep her safe.

"You don't need to do that," she protested.

He wasn't going to argue with her about this. "Like I said, I don't think we need to worry about him while he's on probation. Right now, just don't talk about me to anyone, and if people ask about us, just shrug them off."

"What do you mean, *us*?" she interrupted.

Jackson's look made her feel like she had been reprimanded, but what had she said wrong?

"Just do it, okay?" he said. He knew they were just friends, but he also knew Tom was well aware he wanted more. And then there was Sarah... "I want you to go out with Bekah, too, and make it a point to talk with other guys; especially if Tom's around. If Sarah invites him over, and you can't figure out an excuse to leave, pick one of the other guys and show interest in him."

He could see she didn't like what he was telling her to do. He didn't like it himself. She looked like she was somewhere between about to throw up and freaking out.

"Evelyn, I know it sounds weird, but Tom knows I'm with you a lot. He saw me kiss you, and I've said things to him that insinuate you and I are...more... I thought I was protecting you. It's important that he, and others, see you aren't interested in me." And there went his plan to court her.

*Lord, please help me trust her to You; her safety and our future, if there is a future for us.*

Evelyn was about to argue with him, but Bekah bounced into the room, silencing her protest. "Gosh, what'd I just walk into?"

"I was just telling Evelyn that she needs to spend less time with me and more time going out with you and flirting with boys…" His insides twisted "…to help keep her safe from Tom."

"Ah," Bekah said, leaning against the wall. "Well Evie, looks like we're going out tomorrow night."

"No!" Evelyn exclaimed. "I'm not going out with anyone, and I'm definitely not flirting!"

"You will if it keeps you safe!" Jackson almost yelled. He instantly regretted his tone. Evelyn had cowered away from him. What was he doing? He looked at Bekah, silently pleading for help.

"It'll be fine, Evie," Bekah said, calmly. "Jackson's right. *If* you two are determined to be just friends, then Tom needs to see that. We'll go out with some of my friends a couple times, maybe Jackson could send a few of his friends with us. You'll dance or bat your eyes or whatever at a couple harmless boys and the word will get out. Really," she spoke quietly now. "All we have to do is put on a show for Miss Priss and it'll all get back to Tom. And Jackson," she shot him a hot look. "Stop leaving your stuff around our place. It doesn't help anything." She grabbed his jacket that still draped over one of the kitchen chairs and threw it at him.

# Chapter 29

"It's getting bad around here," George said.

They had just returned from an off-campus call. A man had been murdered. They normally wouldn't be called out for something off campus, but this had all the markings of extremist activity, so the local authorities called for backup. Jackson knew Tom couldn't have been responsible for this; he worked last night, and it was too far from campus for him to have been able to get there and return without someone noticing his absence. He hoped Tom wasn't capable of something like what he had seen. Jackson knew, though, that if this was the work of extremists, they should be looking for a female. Most, if not all, of the extremely violent murders were done by the women; huntresses, as they called themselves. He still couldn't believe he'd practically lived with one for three months; and he now was almost positive Evelyn lived with one.

"It doesn't make sense, though," Jackson said, forcing himself back to the present. "I can't find any connections between the victim and Texas. Are we sure this is the work of extremists, and not some other group acting out?"

George was looking through the report; he didn't look up as he spoke. "I don't know. I guess it could be. Maybe we'll get lucky and be wrong."

Jackson laughed sardonically. "Yeah, this is one thing I'd love to be wrong about." It was beginning to feel like New Mexico to him, just colder.

George put the report on Jackson's desk and sat across from him. "I don't think Tom's the only danger we have among our officers, or even our commanders."

It was something, that all of the crimes were happening unseen. "It would seem someone's been shielding them. You don't think officers are doing these things on duty, do you?"

"Could be," George answered. "But I think we're missing some of the puzzle, and I'm getting the feeling it's an important part."

Jackson spent the rest of the day going over the files of all the previous break-ins and tried to find a link between them and the murder. Before he left, he checked over the schedule for the EV Route; that was the name he'd given the Patrol route covering Evelyn's building.

As much as she loved her classes, Evelyn couldn't pay attention in either of them. The week had begun so wonderfully, being surprised by Jackson on Monday morning, but it had already turned sour. Bekah and Jackson ganged up on her over what they thought would keep her safe, and she hated all their ideas.

Bekah invited friends over Tuesday night and introduced Evelyn to a man named Everret. He smiled at her too much, and sat too close, but he wasn't horrible to be around. He proved to be as harmless as Bekah had promised, and he managed to single-handedly keep their conversation running. She tried her best to do as she had been ordered, but she wasn't sure how good she was at actually flirting. It did help, however, that she was angry with Jackson for ordering her around like she was a little girl or one of his officers. She wanted to make him jealous but, unfortunately, she had never been a manipulative person. Sarah saw her, though, and that was the plan.

To make everything worse, her nightmares had stolen her sleep for the last two nights. She managed to battle her fears back during the day, but both nights she had woken soaked with sweat, screaming into her pillow, and her knight seemed to have disappeared. Jackson left frustrated Monday morning, and he hadn't visited her since; at home or work. She wasn't even entirely sure if he was still expecting her and Bekah to go over that night.

Bundled warmly in boots and her knee-length winter jacket, she walked to work after her classes. Snow shovelers were still working at clearing the snow from the sidewalks. The first real snow-fall of the season blanketed the city in white. She was very glad the skies had cleared. She loved snow, but didn't enjoy walking in a blizzard and hated having to take the bus.

Work held a pleasant surprise for her. One of the local schools brought their younger students to visit. They only stayed a half hour into Evelyn's shift, but their smiling faces and sweet chatter filled her with joy. After they left, the library seemed much too quiet.

Her final hour of work stretched out before her. To fight off the drowsiness of working the desk, she set herself to putting books away. She didn't realize she had disappeared into the stained glass again until she was startled, grasping the ladder she was standing on so she wouldn't fall.

Jackson.

She climbed down the ladder and stood looking up at him. He was in uniform and, even though she was still mad at him, she couldn't help but appreciate how handsome he was.

He glanced around them. No one was watching, but they were close to the main hall, open to anyone who happened to look up. He took her hand and led her further down the aisle and further from peoples' eyes, until they were alone.

Evelyn pulled her hand free. If he wanted everyone to know there was nothing between them, then she was determined to show them. "Hello Officer Monroe," she said, trying to sound indifferent. "Can I help you with something?"

She looked exhausted, and his heart ached for her. "How are you Evelyn?"

She fought against the tenderness in his voice. "I'm fine, sir." He grimaced.

"Evelyn, please don't call me that."

She stared defiantly back at him.

"I'd hoped you'd be happy to see me."

"If there's nothing I can help you with, *sir*, I have a lot of work to get done before I'm off." He caught her about the waist when she turned to leave. His touch threatened to break her anger, so she pushed him away. She didn't want to let go of her anger yet. "Jackson!" she hissed at him in whisper.

He let her go but stepped closer. "Evelyn, why are you so mad at me?"

"I'm at work, Jackson. You already tell me what to do at home, but please don't come here and treat me like a child." She was losing her resolve to be closed off to him and dropped her eyes.

He tried to hide his smile. "I'm not here to tell you what to do. I'm here to ask if you'll still come over tonight." He shifted his weight, bringing himself closer to her. "I've been looking forward to it all week."

She stepped towards him and looked up at him, tilting her head slightly. "It's only been a couple days." She was so weak; her anger was already melting.

"It's felt longer."

His closeness, and her lack of sleep, made her head foggy.

"Then will you still come?" he asked. He was as distracted by her as she was by him.

"Yes," she said, smiling slightly. "I will come if you want me." She had meant to say 'to'…she would go if he wanted her to.

"I hope you were easier on Everret," he laughed.

Completely confused, Evelyn asked, "What do you mean?"

Jackson raised his eyebrows suggestively. "I mean, I'm away from you for a couple of days and you seem to have mastered flirting. I just hope you weren't so convincing with Everret the other night."

"How do you know about Everret?" she asked. As soon as the words passed her lips, she knew. She should be embarrassed, but she was angry. "You told him to be there! He's not even Bekah's friend, is he? He's yours!" Her anger mounted. She had been caught flirting with Jackson, when he was the one sending guys to flirt with her!

Jackson couldn't contain his laughter. "You're right. I'm sorry. I'll still see you tonight, though, right?"

She glared at him. "Yes, you'll see me tonight."

He smiled. "Okay," he said. "But really, poor Everret. I should have warned him." He winked at her and left before she could retort.

## Chapter 30

Evelyn was almost asleep, forehead on the table, with a half-eaten sandwich in her hand, when Bekah got home.

"So, we're off to Jackson's tonight," Bekah said as she took and ate a banana. "Are you excited to see him?"

"You didn't tell me you didn't know Everret."

"Bah," Bekah opened her mouth showing her thoroughly chewed banana. "Who cares? Jackson wanted someone he trusted. To be honest, I don't even know how well he knows him. I think he knows one of Jackson's friends better, or something like that."

"I'm mad at him," she grumbled. Exhaustion made her grumpy.

Bekah smiled knowingly. "You're just mad because you're being told to flirt with people who aren't Jackson."

Evelyn put her head on the table, face down. "You're right. I'm so pathetic!"

"You're not pathetic," Bekah laughed. "You do have good taste in men though. Well, this time around you do."

"What good does good taste do? Sometimes I think there's something there," she finally admitted, "but then he gets all big-brother-like. There's no future for us beyond that."

Bekah shook her head at Evelyn. "You're ridiculous. Now get up." She grabbed Evelyn's coat and held it out for her. "We should be going."

They knocked and a dark, handsome man with a grand smile and happy eyes answered the door; George, she assumed. He looked familiar, but Evelyn couldn't place his face. She smiled and looked at her friend who, she was pleased to see, looked very taken with the man before them.

"Come in," the man said in a rich, almost melodic voice, as he opened the door wider so they could enter the home. "I think Jack's getting out of the shower. He just got home." He closed the door and took their coats. "I'm George."

Bekah waited for him to put their coats down on the bench behind the door and extended her hand to him. "I'm Bekah," she said, still smiling.

They shook hands a little longer than was necessary, and Evelyn smiled at them. Bekah was so much better with men than she was.

George looked to Evelyn and extended his hand to her. "And you're Evelyn," he said, shaking her hand. "It's nice to officially meet you. I've heard a lot about you."

She tried to hide her blush. "It's nice to meet you too, George."

Jackson came out of a room then, pulling a shirt over his head. "Good," he said. "You've met. Thanks for coming, Bekah," he said, hugging her.

"Thanks for inviting me," Bekah commented, hugging him back.

Evelyn was ashamed of the jealousy she felt as she watched them embrace.

Jackson let go of Bekah and turned to Evelyn. "Are you still mad at me?" he asked with a teasing tone.

"Yes," she tried, looking him over. His hair was still wet from his shower. He was too handsome to stay mad at, and that wasn't rational at all. She shook her head, defeated. "I guess not."

"Good," he said, and moved at her quickly. He lifted her from the ground, hugging her. "I'm glad you came." He set her down and took her hand. "Come on. No reason for us to hang out at the door."

Evelyn was thrilled to have her hand in his again as he led her, and George and Bekah, to their living room. The home was modestly furnished, and remarkably clean, but warm and comfortable, too. On the coffee table sat a stack of booklets.

"Are these all books from the Bible?" Evelyn asked, releasing Jackson's hand to get a closer look.

"Yes," he answered. "That's not even all of them. There are sixty-six in all."

"Sixty-six!" She was amazed. "I had no idea there were so many. What are we reading tonight?" she asked, anxious and excited to learn.

"That's up to you," he said.

She was kneeling on the floor and looked up at him. "Do you have a favorite?"

"I do. I have two favorites," he told her, "but I don't think that either of them would make the best start. Maybe we should just start at the beginning?"

"That's probably a good idea," Bekah laughed. "Are we starting already?"

"Oh," Evelyn said. This was why Bekah was better with people. Bekah wanted to be social. Evelyn wanted to disappear into the books. "Sorry, no, we don't need to start so quickly. I just got distracted by how many there are." She turned back to the books and skimmed through them, trying to glean anything she could just by touching them.

"Evie," Bekah called at her loudly.

Evelyn snapped back to the present. "What?"

"Oh, never mind," Bekah groaned.

George laughed. His laugh was joyful and had a deep warmth to it. "Let's not keep her waiting," he said to Bekah and Jackson. "She's clearly anxious to get started. It'd be cruel to make her wait."

Evelyn couldn't keep from smiling. She was very grateful to George.

Jackson helped Evelyn up from the floor. She chose to sit in the chair, leaving him to sit on the couch with Bekah and George.

"Wait," Evelyn interrupted soon after he began reading from Genesis. "God just spoke, and our world, our universe…everything was created?"

"He's a really big God," Bekah stated. "Really big."

Evelyn had a hard time grasping the grandness of her God. Jackson continued reading, and she was captivated by what she heard. She listened to him read about Adam and Eve, their sin and banishment from Eden, and Cain and Abel. She was just so tired. As Jackson began reading a list of genealogies, peace washed over her.

Jackson glanced up and saw that Evelyn had fallen asleep. No sooner had he noticed when he was elbowed in the side by Bekah.

"Let her sleep," Bekah ordered quietly. "She's been having nightmares; you can imagine why. Just let her get a little rest before we have to go home." She looked at George, "Perhaps we should excuse ourselves, so we don't wake her?"

George followed her lead. "Yes, I think you're right."

Bekah followed him from the room.

Jackson put the book of Genesis back on the table and retrieved a blanket for Evelyn. After he laid the blanket over her, he stood and watched her. She looked peaceful, but he wondered if she was battling nightmares beneath the calm facade of sleep. He wished he could save her from every nightmare, every horror that ever threatened her; but he understood that wasn't his job. He was not her Savior. He never knew it could be so hard to trust someone's safety to the Lord, even though He'd shown His faithfulness time and time again. He was still so weak in some areas of his faith. He wished he was like David as he faced Goliath, fully confident in the strength of God.

*Oh God, why do I doubt You? Who else loves her like You do? Who can protect her like You can? Forgive me for my weakness. I entrust her, and her safety, to You.*

He sat back down on the couch and let himself rest his eyes. He must have fallen asleep because he woke with a start. Evelyn had curled up in her chair, like a child trying to keep warm. Her head was moving, tossing about like she was trying to get away from something.

"Evelyn," he whispered at her side, praying he wouldn't startle her. "Evelyn, wake up."

Evelyn woke with a gasp. Her breathing came easier, steadied when her eyes locked with Jackson's. She stayed focused on his face for a moment before she laid her head back against the chair, letting herself relax with a deep breath. "I'm sorry. I didn't mean to fall asleep."

"You apologize for too much," Jackson said, kneeling down beside her.

The lights had been turned off in the room, and only a faint glow shone from the entryway. "What time is it? And where's Bekah?" Evelyn asked, looking around.

"It's just barely eight," came Bekah's voice nearby. "And I'm still here."

Jackson and Evelyn smiled at each other. "She's very good at keeping an eye on me," Evelyn sighed.

Bekah walked into the room then, followed by George. "So," she said as George turned on a light. "Who's up for a game?"

"Depends on the game," Jackson answered, noting the amusement in Bekah's eyes. He'd never known George to be one for mischief, but something told him that Bekah could bring it out in him.

Bekah smiled widely. "I've Never. But, we'll change the rules, because I don't drink."

"I don't know that game," Evelyn admitted.

"And I'm not sure she'll like the game," Jackson added.

"She'll love it," Bekah said, waving her hand about, dismissing Jackson's concern.

"How are we changing the rules," George asked, though Evelyn assumed he already knew the plan.

Bekah and George sat on the couch, and Bekah explained. "First," she said, "We'll just play until someone's lost five times. So, someone will say, 'I've never' and then say something that they've never done, that they think everyone else has done. If no one else has done it, then they lose a point. If someone else has done it, then they lose a point, and the person saying it doesn't. Make sense?"

"That sounds easy enough. But what happens if you lose?" Evelyn asked.

"The person who loses has to let everyone ask them one question of their choosing and," Bekah leveled her eyes at Jackson. "They have to answer honestly."

It sounded like a harmless game to Evelyn, and she figured that she had done far less than the others had; she had to be safe. "Okay, I'm in."

They all agreed to play. Jackson brought a chair in from another room, and Bekah started.

"I've never been early to a class," Bekah said, setting the tone of their game. Jackson and Evelyn lost points.

"I've never been caught past curfew," George said. Bekah lost a point and glared at George.

"I've never climbed a ladder at a library to get a book for someone else," Jackson said, smiling and looking at Evelyn. Evelyn lost a point.

"Well," Evelyn said, "I've never been drunk." The others all lost points.

"I've never gotten a tattoo," Bekah said.

To Evelyn's surprise and embarrassment, she was the only one who lost a point. Bekah was the only person, aside from the tattoo artist, who knew she had tattoos. The girl was up to no good.

"Seriously?" Jackson asked in surprise. "You have a tattoo? Where?"

"Uh-uh-uh," Bekah reprimanded. "No questions. She hasn't lost the game yet."

Evelyn's stomach twisted at the word yet.

"I've never worked at a library," George laughed.

"Now that's not fair," Evelyn protested. "You're all just ganging up on me now!" She only had one more point until she lost the whole game.

"Yes," Jackson laughed loudly. "And you're one for being fair at games; so no complaining from the cheat in the chair. It's my turn." He had to take a moment to think. He wasn't sure what he had never done that Evelyn had; though he never thought she would have had a tattoo either. "I've never worn a skirt," he said, smiling at Evelyn, who was presently wearing a skirt.

"Well I've never met such wicked people in my life!" Evelyn exclaimed. She couldn't believe she let herself get into this situation, and so easily.

"Oh, Evie," Bekah said, faking tenderness in her voice, "I'm so sorry, but the game's over. On to the questions!" She gave Evelyn a piercing stare. "And remember, you have to be honest. I'll go first. I've been wondering, how many tattoos do you have now?"

Evelyn glared at her friend. "You are a wretched, abhorrent person, Bekah." Bekah smiled proudly. "To answer honestly," Evelyn swallowed. "I have three tattoos." She saw Jackson's gaze go down her, intrigue written all over his face.

But it was George's turn. He sneered and rubbed his hands together. "What's the most annoying thing about living with Bekah?"

She could just kiss the man!

"That's easy," she laughed. "She knows too much. You can't hide anything from her."

And now it was Jackson's turn…and she was terrified of him.

Jackson couldn't get his mind off the fact that sweet Evelyn had not just one – but three hidden tattoos. But it'd be cruel, and probably inappropriate to ask to see them. And the poor girl looked so frightened. No doubt she'd noticed his interest in her body art.

"Don't worry, Evelyn," he soothed. "I'll behave. My question is: what did you think the first time you met me?"

Evelyn's brow furrowed as she thought back to that day. She'd thought a lot of things during that meeting. "You mean, besides the thought that I was going to fall to my death because you snuck up on me while on a ladder?"

"Oblivious to the world," Jackson teased.

"I had wondered if you were hurt. You carried yourself differently, and you favored your left side, even though you're right-handed."

Jackson stared. Aside from the fact that he'd never in a million years have thought that would have been what she'd been thinking when they first met, he was dumbfounded that she'd noticed so much in such a quick meeting. His silence stretched, knowing he couldn't enlighten her to the story of his injury…at least not yet.

George stood, breaking the silence. "You did well, Evelyn. You're a much better loser than Jack. I am impressed. Now," he said, addressing everyone. "Would anyone like anything to drink?"

They each told George what they'd like, and Bekah followed him either to help, or to flirt. Evelyn wasn't entirely sure. Jackson went to the brick fireplace to start a fire.

Evelyn watched his capable hands work. They were the same hands that held hers, that protected her from so much, that comforted her, that even tickled her playfully.

"I can't believe you have three tattoos," Jackson remarked, laying another log over the growing fire. "And that you never told me about them." He turned from the fire and saw her watching him. "You know I'm going to ask you to show them to me."

"Just because you ask something, doesn't mean you're going to get your way," she answered in jest and joined him by the fire. "And you said you would behave."

"Hmm…" He looked her over boldly; more boldly than he had the right to. "Three tattoos hidden away somewhere…"

"Jackson," she gasped, crossing her arms in front of herself and blushing with the heat rising in her cheeks. "Don't look at me like that!"

## Unspoken Words

"You look at me that way," he argued. He stepped towards her and placed his hands about her waist. He was tired of waiting. Or maybe he was just tired. But he was tired of just being *friends*.

Evelyn's heart was beating fiercely in her chest and she wasn't sure if it was because they stood near the fire, or if it was his touch that made her feel aflame. She looked up at him and spoke quietly. "You're scaring me."

He didn't let her go. "Evelyn, you never need to be scared of me."

"I'm always scared of you," she laughed nervously.

He kept his eyes on hers and could feel her body nervous at his touch. She shook slightly when she exhaled. "Why are you scared of me?"

Her eyes dropped. She didn't want to tell him why he scared her; that she loved him and was too afraid to tell him, that she was terrified of the day when he would fall in love with someone and she would lose her best friend. "You're not playing fair, Jackson."

"You never play fair," he argued, speaking softly. He slipped his right hand around to her back and her eyes closed with his touch. She pressed her lips and looked back up at him. "You're being mean." Even his frown was handsome.

"How am I being mean?"

"You're trying to intimidate me," she answered. "You're using your hands, and…" Evelyn let herself put her hand against his chest. "You're using your body, to tease me. It's not nice. I need you Jackson," she confessed. "I need to know I'm safe with you. You're the only thing keeping me from falling apart. I'm so scared, all the time. Please," she begged, "Please don't tease me…not tonight."

Jackson could see the fear in her eyes as she confessed to it. He cursed Tom for the fear he'd put in her heart, then asked God to forgive him for cursing him. His temper was a never-ending struggle. Tonight wouldn't be the night he told her how he felt. He'd have to wait. Maybe if they were alone he could tell her, or just kiss her until she was convinced; but they weren't. George and Bekah would return from the kitchen soon. So, he kissed her forehead and it drove him crazy when he felt her hands grip his shirt. He could feel her desire for him, but he would wait. She was worth the wait. He let her go. "You know you're safe with me. I didn't mean to scare you, or tease you."

She smiled weakly. "Thank you, Jackson."

Jackson kept her close, with his arms still around her.

"You never mentioned you thought I was hurt when we first met."

She didn't fight their closeness.

"Were you hurt?"

"I was." His mouth went dry at the memory, and the knowledge that he'd have to share what happened with her eventually. "Why didn't you ask me about it?"

"It didn't seem like a kind thing to do. I got the impression that you didn't want anyone to know, that maybe the story of the injury was worse than the injury itself. And," she added, "I was too scared of you to ask you anything…especially something personal."

"You really are something else," he smiled. "Do you know that?"

Evelyn was glad when she saw George and Bekah return with drinks. Her head was spinning.

Bekah was eyeing Evelyn suspiciously when she took her glass of water. "What were you two talking about while we were away?" she asked.

"Nothing, really," Jackson answered quickly. "I was just telling her I was surprised I didn't know so much about her."

"Mmm-hmm," George retorted. He clearly didn't believe Jackson. "Well, we had a more interesting conversation. Bekah agreed to go to the ball with me," he said proudly.

At nine thirty, George offered to walk them home. Bekah willingly accepted his offer, and his arm.

Before they left, Jackson gave her the book of John to take with her and he hugged her close. "Don't be scared," he had said. "God tells us He has given us a spirit of power, not of fear. He's with you. There's safety in His arms."

She thought about his words on their walk home and as she drifted off to sleep. George respectfully declined Bekah's invitation in, but the two stayed at the door and talked long enough for Evelyn to get to bed without any questions or conversation about the night.

*Lord,* she prayed, *please help me to know You're here with me, even as I sleep.*

She slept a wonderfully dreamless sleep that night.

# Chapter 31

Evelyn didn't see Jackson for the rest of the week; though she couldn't get him off of her mind. She caught herself slipping into daydreams, remembering how he looked at her by the fire. Hope began to grow. Maybe he hadn't been teasing her. Maybe, even for just that moment, he saw her as more than just a little sister. But such hope hurt, especially when George would come to visit Bekah with no word from Jackson.

Finals were a few days away now. Jackson would be done next week. Evelyn had a few days off from school, dead-days they were called, to study for exams and prepare their final papers due the week after. She still had work, but planned to spend the rest of her time studying and editing her essays so she could hand them in at her finals. But today was dress shopping day.

Bekah dragged Evelyn into a store through the double doors. It was, by far, the most elegant store Evelyn had ever been in. Crystal chandeliers hung from the ceilings and the sales staff waited to greet each customer, offering their personal assistance. Bekah had apparently been to this store before, because she hugged one of them and started talking a mile a minute about what they needed.

Bekah paused her monologue long enough for a simple introduction.

Maxine smiled and Bekah continued jabbering. Evelyn followed as they walked deeper into the store.

Maxine looked to be in her forties, maybe fifties, and had beautiful russet skin with black hair that, even tied back, hung down to her waist. She showed them to a dressing room, sat them down, and turned her attention to Evelyn.

"Now," she said. "Bekah has told me what she's looking for. What are you looking for?"

"Besides a dress?" Evelyn asked.

"I told you," Bekah said. "She needs our help, Maxine."

Maxine sat on a stool and crossed her legs. "You're going to the Officer's Ball, correct?" Evelyn nodded. "Tell me about this officer that you're going with."

"Well," Evelyn started. "His name is Jackson. He's a captain and well respected. He's tall, and strong, and handsome; and he's older than me...I'm not sure what I'm supposed to tell you about him."

Maxine had a kind smile. "How do you want him to see you?"

"And be honest," Bekah ordered.

She looked at her hands and thought. "I'd like him to see me as worthy to be on his arm. I don't want him to be embarrassed about having a younger girl as his date."

"Very good," Maxine said, and she stood and left.

"Where'd she go?"

Bekah laughed. "She's gone dress shopping for us," she explained. "Don't worry, she'll be back soon with the perfect dresses. She's amazing at what she does."

Evelyn wasn't sure how Maxine could have gotten anything from what she'd said. She also thought it was quite odd to have someone else doing her shopping. But sure enough, moments later Maxine was back. She had an armful of dresses for Bekah to try on, and one for Evelyn.

"If you don't like it," Maxine explained, "There are plenty more I can bring you. This just seemed to fit you when I saw it."

Evelyn looked over the dress while Maxine helped Bekah into one of hers. It was stunning, made of a silver-gray lace that hung in tiers down the body.

"Do you need help getting into it, dear?" Maxine asked.

"Oh, no thank you. I think I can manage." Evelyn changed quickly out of her clothes and stepped into the dress. After zipping it up the side she looked at her reflection in the mirror. The dress's thin straps sat delicately on her shoulders and the neckline fell modestly across her chest, but still plunged lower than she was used to. The dress was tight, but comfortable, against her body, until it met her hips where it draped close, but loosely, about her legs.

Bekah squealed from behind her. "It's perfect!"

Evelyn looked behind her in the mirror and saw Bekah, standing in her underwear, and Maxine looking at her.

"And it doesn't even need altering," Maxine added. "Fits you like a glove."

"Do you think he'll like it?"

"If he doesn't like it," Bekah said, "He's an idiot and you'll have officers lined up to take his place."

"I don't want a line of officers. I just want him."

Bekah laughed loudly. "It's about time you admitted that! Don't worry. The dress is perfect, and he won't be able to take his eyes off of you."

Evelyn looked at herself one last time in the mirror and turned around to face Bekah. "Have you decided on a dress?"

"Not hardly! I've only tried on one, and I'm not nearly as easy to figure out as you are," Bekah stated, stepping into another dress.

Evelyn changed back into her clothes and settled in for Bekah's exhaustive search for the perfect dress. Evelyn couldn't find a single fault with any of the dresses She wasn't sure if the search continued because Bekah was unsatisfied, or if it was because she was enjoying herself so much.

Whatever the reason, it gave Evelyn plenty of time to think things over.

Christmas was approaching quickly. When she lived in the government home, Christmas meant new clothes and a doll, if you were still young enough. Once she turned twelve, she enjoyed helping the Madames prepare the packages for the younger children. Since she'd been away from the home, Christmas had come to mean endless hours alone, just as every other holiday did.

But this year she'd be spending Christmas with the Monroes. She had no idea what their Christmases were like. The anticipation of it filled her with trepidation, but she couldn't deny the funny, tingling, slight-nausea-inducing feeling of excitement it brought as well.

She had wracked her brain over what she could give Jackson...and what would be appropriate. After almost tearing out her hair in frustration, she settled on sewing a quilt for him. He did so much for her, and this way, she could at least help keep him warm.

She had a lot of sewing ahead of her.

# Unspoken Words

All Jackson wanted to do was sleep. Between pulling double shifts to help cover Evelyn's building and his final semester quickly coming to an end, sleep had proven an elusive thing. It was the first of their three dead-days, and he had himself plopped at her library. The hope of seeing her kept him somewhat alert as he attempted to study.

She walked in just before he lost the battle against sleep, sending a surge of adrenaline through him. A surge he knew would die out too soon.

He took in the sight of her. Red tinted her nose and cheeks, but it didn't look to be the effect of tears. It wasn't snowing anymore, but it was cold, and the wind had a nasty bite. Her flush had to be from that.

He watched as she removed her jacket and gloves to set about her work. She never looked up to see him. He could sit there and watch her all day long and she'd never be the wiser. She was oblivious to the world.

He thought back to their Wednesday night together. George told him after he returned from walking them home Evelyn didn't remember him helping her after Tom's attack. George also reminded him that she'd been in shock and told him not to remind her of it.

As he thought on about that night, saying oblivious wasn't really fair. Evelyn, in fact, observed many things. He was frequently surprised at things she had noticed. But she was undoubtedly oblivious to him. That was something he intended to change.

Studying was a lost cause. If he couldn't focus, he decided going home to sleep was an acceptable course of action.

He wrote a note for Evelyn, tucked it in a book, and walked to her desk.

He smiled when she startled at seeing him.

"Jackson," Evelyn said, putting her hand against her heart. "You really need to stop that."

"It's really not my fault you're oblivious to me," he countered. "How are you, Evelyn?"

"I'm fine, thank you," she answered. "How are you?"

She was too polite, too withdrawn. He didn't like it. "I'm tired and headed home to sleep. I was wondering if you could return this for me," he asked, handing Evelyn the book. "It's a good read. You might want to flip through it first, though."

"Of course."

"I'll see you soon," he promised, and he left.

Evelyn held the book as she watched Jackson leave, wishing he would have stayed. She looked down at the book once the doors closed behind him. It was a bit befuddling that he requested her to return the book. And it didn't look like a good read. It looked very boring; but she opened the cover anyway and her heart skipped when she found his note.

*I'm coming over tonight.*
*Expect me at eight.*
*I miss you.*
   *Jackson*

Evelyn folded the note and tucked it away in her bag. Sarah was going out tonight and Bekah had plans with George.

She smiled.

# Chapter 32

George was over when Evelyn got home. He was becoming a familiar sight in their living room.

"Evie," Bekah pronounced before Evelyn even had the time to say hello, "We're going dancing tomorrow night, and you're coming. George says you haven't been socializing enough."

George gave her a look of apology.

"Tomorrow's fine," Evelyn replied, astonishing both Bekah and George. She smiled at them. "Don't look so surprised. I'm just too drained to fight." She decided not to include that she was particularly eager to send them on their way. "Where are you two off to tonight?"

"I'm taking her to dinner at The Thai House," George answered. "If we ever make it there," he called at Bekah, who had disappeared down the hall.

"I'm coming, I'm coming," Bekah announced, returning to the room. She had a dazzling royal blue dress on with black tights and ruby-red heels. "How do I look?"

George stood and took her hand, spinning her into him. "Stunning." He kissed her. Evelyn hadn't realized their relationship had taken that turn yet, or so quickly.

George helped Bekah with her jacket, while Bekah mouthed, "Oh my gosh, isn't he amazing?" to Evelyn.

Evelyn had to stifle her laugh. "What time will you be back?" she asked, trying to sound casual. Bekah shrugged.

"I'll have her home before eleven," George answered.

Bekah rolled her eyes. "He's a rule follower…I guess nobody's perfect."

Evelyn ate leftovers for dinner and sat down on her couch to pass the time studying until Jackson would arrive. As eight o'clock ticked closer, she became more and more aware of the fact that she and Jackson would be alone together. She also realized the last time she had waited for Jackson, Tom had shown up. She tried to fight the fearful memories away, but she still jumped when she heard a tap at the door.

Jackson smiled down at her when she answered.

"You look surprised to see me," Jackson said. "Did you not get my note?"

"I got it." Evelyn was too nervous to know what else to say, and her mouth was dry.

"Are you upset I came?"

"No, I'm glad you came." It was just Jackson, she reminded herself. He was safe. They'd spent lots of time together. But the thought of him, the sight of him, made her nervous.

"I'm sorry, Evelyn. I can see this was a mistake." Feeling completely defeated, Jackson turned to leave, frustrated at his own incompetence, unsure how to handle the situation.

A soft, delicately strong hand captured his.

"I'm sorry. Come in."

He looked her over skeptically. With Evelyn, there was always the chance she was just being polite.

"Please, Jackson," she said, speaking to his suspicion. "I've missed you too."

Her eyes dropped and Jackson knew she meant it. He followed her inside and closed the door behind him.

Evelyn let go of his hand and stood against the counter. "No one's home," she explained. No one was home. And she missed him so much. She missed the closeness they'd had before Jackson decided it was too dangerous for him to spend too much time with her, because of Tom. Missed how he hugged and held her at his parents' house.

His laughter surprised her. "So that's why you're so nervous," Jackson said, thinking he understood. "Don't worry. I promise I'll be on my best behavior tonight." He joined her, leaning against the counter, and knocked his hip against her playfully, trying to break the tension. "Are we just going to stand here the whole time?"

She didn't say anything, but she moved to the chair and sat down, tucking her feet under her and arranging her skirt to cover her legs. He sat on the couch. She could feel him watching her, even without looking up at him.

"Evelyn, are you mad at me?"

Finally, her eyes met his.

"No, I've just missed you. George's been here a lot."

"And I have not," he added with a frown. "I've been closer than you think. I've been working Patrols the last three nights. If you had looked out your window, you would have seen me pass. It'll be different soon. There'll be more time when I'm done with school."

"Jackson," she sighed, remembering how dead on his feet he looked at the library, and knowing it was because he'd been taking care of her instead of getting the sleep he needed. "You need to get more sleep."

"I sleep," he argued, smiling tenderly at her as if to show that watching over her was a pleasure and not a burden. "I slept today after I saw you. I'll sleep more after finals, when we go visit my parents and I know you're safe in the room next to me." He enjoyed how her cheeks turned pink in blush.

"I'll probably sleep better then too," Evelyn admitted. "The best sleep I've had since Tom attacked me was in your…" She stopped short of saying arms. Oh, her and her wretched inability to keep her mouth shut! Her embarrassment turned silly-school-girl when he winked at her admission. "It's hard to wake up from a nightmare here," she clarified, "where everything happened. It was nice to feel safe, and to not be alone."

Jackson leaned forward and took her hand…which wasn't quite right. He cupped her fingers, as perhaps a gentleman of old England may have taken a lady's in greeting.

"Please don't take this the wrong way, Evelyn, but you're always welcome in my arms. I wish I could always be here to face your nightmares with you, and that you'd never have to be alone."

"Thank you." His words were kind, innocent to be sure, but it fueled the hopes her heart held for more. Nervous energy began to course through her with each pounding beat of her heart. She was sure, almost sure, he saw her as the little sister he never had. But she hoped...

Hope hurt.

She needed to know.

His thumb swept over her fingers.

"I'm going to make some tea."

Jackson was accustomed to seeing her nervous, but he hadn't seen her like this. He didn't follow her. He'd give her the space she sought.

"I've been thinking…" Thinking a lot about the conversation they had, it seemed so long ago, in the theatre, before the mirrors, after he kissed her. They had spent a lot of time together since then, though less lately, and he had become her best friend. She was terrified to lose his friendship, but desperately hoped that he felt more for her, as she did for him. "…wondering…" She put the kettle on the stove. "Did you mean what you said?"

"When I said what?"

"Never mind."

Jackson decided it was time to join her in the kitchen. Something was troubling her, and he meant to find out what it was. She had become quiet and withdrawn since he arrived. "Evelyn, did I mean it when I said what?" He gave her a look to make it clear he expected an answer. He didn't enjoy using it on her.

"In the theatre, when you asked me what I saw in the mirror, and…" She trailed off, terrified of him.

Jackson loved seeing her like this. Nervous and trembling over something other women would blurt out without a thought to propriety. Evelyn was a lady. A sweet, kind-hearted, incredibly attractive lady.

"Yes," he said, smiling at her. "Of course I meant it."

That smile, it made her dizzy in the head. She had to remind herself to breathe. "Do you even remember what you said?"

"Yes. Would you like me to tell it to you again?" Her cheeks turned a soft pink.

"No!" She almost yelled. "I was just wondering, did you mean all of it?"

"Yes."

"Even…" she continued, and he waited. "Even what you said about how I look, and if I dressed differently, that I could have any man I wanted?"

His voice quieted, dropping involuntarily. "Yes, even those parts."

Her eyes stayed on his feet. "How should I dress then, to get his attention?"

His body drove him forward, putting his hand on her cheek. "If you have not caught his attention by now, then that man has no right to be around you."

She let her cheek press against his palm and looked up at him. "But what if I want to look nice for him? What if I want him to like looking at me? I think he sees me as a little sister…a child even. I just want to have a chance at being attractive to him."

Jackson's hand fell from her cheek. A child. She thought herself a child? He let her see him observe her. "You're far from being a child." Evelyn's cheeks went hot. His own heated slightly, surprising himself. "But," he continued, clearing his throat. "I thought you were the one who said being looked at and lusted after was different from being liked. Why are you so worried about this?"

Evelyn just shook her head.

He set his jaw. "Evelyn?"

She closed her eyes. "I honestly don't want to cause him to lust." She opened her eyes and looked into his. "But is it bad to want this one man to find pleasure in looking at me?"

"No." He smiled tenderly. "I don't think it's bad." If she only knew the joy she brought him, or saw herself through his eyes, she'd never be self-conscious again. "And just so we're clear, I never said you don't dress well. You're always beautiful. I only meant that you're modest, and a lot of men aren't looking for a modest woman, because they're only interested in a good time. I like the way you dress, and I'm glad you're modest. Now, are you going to tell me who this man is who's caught the attention of my Evelyn?"

*His Evelyn.* She thrilled at the endearment. "No," she answered. "I'm not ready to tell you yet."

Then he would wait, even if it killed him. She went willingly into his arms when he pulled her to him.

Things were changing between them. Even in the security of his arms, Jackson could feel her closing off from him. He just hoped this was a short season in their friendship – relationship – whatever they were, and she'd be ready to share her feelings sooner than later.

## Unspoken Words

Evelyn's dream was different that night. Instead of Tom attacking her, Jackson was with another woman. She had the same style and body as Sarah, but she had never seen this woman before. They laughed at Evelyn from across a room. It wasn't so much their laughter that bothered her, as much as it was their body language; it gave no question about their affections for each other. No question of their intimacy.

She woke alone, caged in by dread.

## Chapter 33

Evelyn had never been to this club, though that wasn't such a big thing. She'd only ever been to a few of them, and didn't care for any of them. This one was closer to campus than the others, which was why it surprised her that she'd never been. Bekah was the driving force that got Evelyn to go out with her and George. When Evelyn tried to get out of it, George insisted. She wasn't entirely sure how to argue with him. So there she was, leaning against a wall, watching her friends dance and wondering why they would force her to come out when they obviously wanted to be alone, when he slid next to her.

His name was Liam and his eyes were blue crystals lined with a forest of beautiful dark eyelashes.

"Hi," Evelyn said when he introduced himself to her.

He smiled. "Do I not get to know your name?" He was very good at using those blue eyes of his. Even as uninterested as she was, it was hard to keep her eyes off his.

Still, she wasn't biting. "Not tonight."

Her cold shoulder didn't discourage the man. Instead, he stood in front of her and trapped her between his arms, putting his hands against the wall behind her. She didn't feel threatened by him, but she was irritated.

"Don't worry, Evelyn, I'm only here to show you a good time. Dance with you, make you laugh, and sure, maybe flirt a little. But Jackson made it very clear that if I do anything more, he'll rip me limb from limb."

Evelyn was beginning to despise Jackson. Liam must have seen her frustration.

"Just think of me as a girlfriend." He took her arm and spun her towards the middle of the dancing crowd. "Who just happens to be incredibly handsome and charming," he added with a wink.

Evelyn couldn't help but laugh with Liam. He was charisma and charm all bottled up and bubbling over.

"So, tell me," Liam said, leading her to a table after they had danced for longer than Evelyn had intended. "Why isn't Jackson the one out with you tonight?"

Evelyn slid into the booth next to him and rested her elbows on the table. It was easier to talk in the privacy of the booth. The music wasn't as loud, and there was no one to overhear what was being said. "He's decided that people seeing us hang out will make them think that he likes me and will ultimately put me in danger. But," she added, rolling her eyes, "we never went out together before that anyway, so the motive for sending me out with *other* guys eludes me completely."

"You don't think he likes you," Liam asked, "even though he threatened me about even contemplating making a move on you?"

She laughed at what he was implying. "If you really liked someone, would you send someone else out with her?" Even as she laughed, her heart weighed heavily. She wanted Jackson to like her, but if he was still determined to make her hang out with other men, for whatever reason, how could he really like her?

"Well," Liam said. "I think the quickest way to get a man to make a move is to make him jealous. I know," he said, holding up his hands. "It's playing dirty, but all's fair in love and war, right? And come on, that guy needs a knock in the head if he hasn't made a move on you yet."

Evelyn smiled at him. "You're quite the charmer, aren't you?" Liam made a silly face.

Jackson already had her labeled as a cheat, and it wasn't a horrible idea. No, it was horrible, but it was horrible of Jackson to send other men to flirt with her! "It's a tempting idea," she admitted, smiling wickedly, "trying to make him jealous. Wait!" She realized she never admitted to even liking Jackson. "Why would you think I want him to make a move?"

Liam just shook his head laughing. "You don't get to argue that now, sweetie. Now what's your plan to get him to make that move?"

If the plan of having her flirt with other men was to convince everyone she wasn't interested in Jackson, it was failing miserably. Besides the fact that she wasn't interested in other men, she'd never been a flirt. She didn't know how and had never considered it an issue. Maybe it was because all the old novels she read as an English major painted a picture of a world so different from hers. A world where a lady didn't parade herself about, seeking the attention of men. A world where men had respect for women and didn't play games. But her world was not one of fiction and, if Jackson really did like her, her new plan was horribly wicked. "George is Jackson's roommate. I'm guessing he's been watching us, or has at least been glancing at us." Liam was nodding in agreement. "I'm tired, Liam. Would you mind walking me home?" She laced her fingers in his.

Liam laughed, hard. "You're evil. You know that, right?"

She shrugged. "You're the one who suggested we make him jealous."

"Whoa!" he stated, but left her hand in his. "I did not suggest that *we* do anything. Just holding your hand is putting me in the path of Jackson's wrath. But I'll play along. And if he doesn't make that move, I want a second date."

"Deal," she said. She didn't want to think about it, but there was a good chance she could end up on a second, real, date with Liam.

They walked hand in hand over to George and Bekah who both looked completely taken by surprise at their feigned affection for each other. Liam played his part well, keeping up his flirtatious ways.

"Liam's going to take me home." Evelyn tried to act infatuated with Liam. Smiling was easy enough to do; not laughing was another story completely. They didn't wait for a response. They just turned and left, grabbing their coats at the door.

Liam put his arm around her. A hearty laugh sang out of him. "You're a lot of fun, Evelyn. It's a shame this will be the last time I get to go out with you."

Evelyn laughed with him. She had changed so much over the past semester. It was completely comfortable to be walking closely with Liam and laughing about their scheme for Jackson. "Don't worry. If I know Jackson, it won't be the last time he lets someone else…wait, that's wrong. It will be the last time he tells someone to hang out with me. Do you know what it's like, having a grown man force people to be my friends? If he wants me out with other men, I think it's time I start deciding on who and when."

The ease she felt with Liam was bewildering. He seemed like a kind soul, and she couldn't deny she enjoyed his company as well. But she had to wonder if it had something to do with her frustration over being set up with other guys, by the one man she cared for.

"Well, I'd welcome another time out with you. But what am I supposed to say when he tries to kill me after this?" Liam asked, still with laughter in his voice, but also a hint of seriousness.

"Liam," Evelyn said, sidestepping his question. "Would you like to take me out next Thursday? School will be out and we can celebrate." She laughed at his confused expression. "You said you'd welcome another time out with me."

"Yeah," he answered, still looking confused. "I would, but I'm supposed to go out with Jackson and some other people that night."

"Oh." The realization that she wasn't being included as one of Jackson's friends stung, and seemed like enough evidence against his interest in her, further convincing her that he must see her as nothing more than a sister. What grown man would want a little girl hanging out with him and his friends?

"I'm gonna end up regretting this." Liam rubbed her arm roughly. "Alright. We're going to a tavern, and you're coming as my date. Taverns are loud with live music and noisy people, so don't wear what you're wearing tonight. Just wear jeans and something comfortable. They get hot, so dress in layers so you can add or remove what you need to be comfortable."

Evelyn was impressed that he explained it so well to her. "It must be pretty obvious that I've never been to one," she said. "I appreciate the heads up."

They got to Evelyn's apartment and Liam hugged her goodbye and left, whistling as he went. She closed the door and shook her head. Whatever results tonight would bring, at least she would know before Christmas if there was any hope for her and Jackson.

## Chapter 34

"I didn't do anything to her!" Liam yelled at him, pushing Jackson away from himself.

Jackson was fuming. He knew Liam was a flirt, but he had thought, George had promised him, he was a good guy.

"She was pretty mad when I told her you were the one who told me to go out with her in the first place," Liam shouted again at him. "She just wanted to arrange her own date, instead of it being arranged for her. You think she wants you treating her this way? Gosh, Jack, she's young, but she's not a child!"

Jackson needed to hit something. He wanted to hit Liam. He'd come to realize he had a big temper with a small fuse when it came to Evelyn. "Do you swear nothing's going on between the two of you?"

"Yes," Liam answered. "I swear. Just don't expect everyone you send out with her to keep their word to you and not make a move on her. She's gorgeous and a lot of fun. In fact, after Thursday, don't expect me to play by your rules either."

Jackson was glad that Liam left after that. He was preparing to say some things he knew he'd end up having to apologize for later. He didn't know what to think. Bekah and George both told him Evelyn and Liam were holding hands when they left. Just the fact that Evelyn was willing to be alone with Liam unnerved him. Bekah's confusion over Evelyn's behavior also ate at him. He knew, though, that he was being unfair. He had told her to show everyone there was nothing between them. If along the way she fell for someone else, it was his own fault.

He took his frustration out on his work. He trained with the officers and worked them hard in everything. At the shooting range he demanded perfection. At the gym, he pushed heavier weights, further runs, and harder punches. But at the end of the day his fire still burned, and his muscles ached.

Evelyn never left his mind. Nothing was going the way he had hoped with her. He'd told himself to use the time before Christmas to show her how he felt, and instead he'd barely seen her. And now she was hanging out with Liam of all people!

He prayed fervently for her. He missed her fiercely.

By Thursday, Bekah still hadn't asked anything about Liam. Evelyn wasn't sure if she didn't believe their act or if she did, but Bekah not asking meant Evelyn not explaining, and she was happy with that.

School was done now for the semester. She'd worked her last day at the library for the year and she'd managed to finish Jackson's quilt. To top it off, she'd found what she hoped was the perfect gift for Charles and Natalie. A shipment of used books had come into the library earlier in the week, and with it came a Bible. A real Bible. All sixty-six books bound in a beautiful navy leather binding and in almost new condition. She wasn't sure how it managed to find its way to the library, or how it managed to stay in such an amazing condition but, when she saw it, she knew she wanted Charles and Natalie to have it. It was against the law for the library to have the book, or for them to even sell it, so she tucked it safely in her bag and brought it home.

She had finished Jackson's quilt on Monday. She was folding it up and putting away her sewing things when Sarah walked in with Tom. It felt like time stood still, freezing her in a state of panic and terror when she saw him walk through her door. No one else was with them, and Sarah disappeared into her room. She said she needed to change, but Evelyn wondered if she was telling the truth.

Evelyn was alone with Tom. Gathering her things to retreat to her room was a failure. He had her cornered before she could take the first step. She wanted to look straight at him, prove she wasn't afraid, but couldn't bear his gaze and dropped her eyes. She didn't want to show any signs of fear, but she knew he saw it written all over her face.

"How are you?" Tom had asked her.

Her hands shook as she held the quilt against her like a shield. *Lord, help me.* "I'm okay." She had managed to put on a brave face for everyone; but the reality was she was drowning in her fear. Every time she left class, she worried Tom would be waiting for her. She'd wake from a nightmare and ache for Jackson. She would read the book of John now when she couldn't sleep, and she repeated Jackson's words over and over to herself that God had given her a spirit of power, not of fear, and that He was with her. But she was young in her faith and she needed help.

"I'm sorry, Evie. What I did, it was inexcusable. I feel awful about... about all of it."

Kind. Humble. This wasn't the Tom she knew. Even at his best, Tom had never been humble.

"Do you even understand what you did?" she asked quietly, speaking more to herself than to him. He did look sorry, though; he almost looked hurt. But his pain was his own doing, if he really felt pain, and her pain was worse.

Tom moved towards her. "Please forgive me."

It looked as if Jackson's plan was working and Tom apparently thought he had a chance of walking back into her life.

Evelyn praised God when Bekah walked in and saved her, making up a lie about needing her assistance on a paper and helping Evelyn carry her things to her room. Bekah stayed with her until Tom left, but the nightmares were worse than ever after that night.

She waited now for Liam to pick her up. Her bags were packed and ready to leave for Jackson's parents' in the morning, but tonight they were going out, celebrating Jackson's graduation. Jackson never did invite her, nor had he spoken to her in a week, but she had seen him. Twice she had woken from nightmares and looked out her window, just to see, and he was there. It was in those moments her hopes soared that Liam was right.

Bekah had left for George's house earlier, and Evelyn and Liam would be meeting up with them there soon. Jackson had arranged for a couple of cars to take them so they all could travel to the tavern together. Apparently, this tavern was some distance from campus.

Evelyn waited to choose her outfit until after she saw what Bekah was wearing. She decided on a pair of jeans with a plain white tank top, with a fitted brown leather jacket and boots to match.

"What do you think?" She asked, spinning for Liam when he arrived. "Am I dressed ok?"

Liam gave a low whistle. "Ok is not the word that comes to mind..."

She tossed him a reproving look. "Let me just go put my hair up and we can go."

He caught her waist as she turned and pulled her close. "Leave it down." He twirled a strand between his fingers. "It suits you. And I've a feeling ol' Jacky-boy's gonna love it," he added with a wink.

Evelyn wiggled from his arms, laughing and rolling her eyes, but she took his advice. He helped her into her winter jacket and then set off for Jackson's.

"So," she asked as they walked. "Do you regret agreeing to this yet?"

"No. At least not yet. Jack's good and angry with me though. I hope you're prepared to give him a little encouragement tonight." His arm found her waist. He knew Jackson was seriously emotionally invested in her, and tonight she was still technically off-limits. He'd respect that for her sake, not Jackson's. Even so, something was keeping Jackson from moving forward, and he wasn't entirely convinced Jackson would get past whatever was holding him back.

"What do you mean?"

Liam looked down at her. "Sometimes even Jack needs a little help."

She swallowed. "I thought the plan was to make him jealous?"

"Yeah, well," Liam said, giving her a small squeeze. "I've already been slammed into a wall over this, and I'd rather not get punched. Jack's a little bigger than I am, if you haven't noticed, and I don't want my pretty face to get messed up."

She laughed with him, but was shocked that Jackson had been so violent.

Soon, they were walking up to Jackson's house. "Alright," Liam said.

Evelyn knocked on the door. "Here we go."

Jackson was smiling, in mid laugh, when he answered the door. The humor left him when he saw Liam with his arm around Evelyn. Liam removed his arm to shake Jackson's hand.

"Hey, Jack," Liam said enthusiastically.

Jackson gripped his hand a little firmer than he needed to. "Hey, Liam." He held the door open for Liam and Evelyn to walk in. "The cars should be here any minute. Everyone's in the kitchen."

"Thanks," Liam said, and he left for the kitchen.

Evelyn stayed just outside the door. Jackson looked upset, but the fierceness of his expression trapped her eyes on him. He looked bigger, too. Once Liam had walked away, Jackson turned back to her. "Do you mind that I came?"

"Why would I mind?" Jackson asked. She tormented him, but he wasn't mad at her.

"You didn't invite me," she shrugged. "I thought maybe you didn't want me to come."

He heard the hurt in her voice. "Get in here," he ordered. He rolled his eyes at her as she walked in. "You know I always want you with me."

She swallowed and butterflies flitted in her stomach. Jackson took her jacket for her and hung it on a hook by the door. They stood facing each other for a moment; she was supposed to be encouraging him, flirting with him. She stood on tip-toe and kissed his cheek, then smiled. Tried to smile. "Happy graduation Jackson Monroe."

He would have taken her in his arms right then if she hadn't turned and walked away. It was going to be difficult to see her with Liam, instead of himself, tonight. Of course, it was his own fault.

It took an hour to get to the tavern. Evelyn rode in one car with Liam and four other people she didn't know. Jackson rode in the other car with George, Bekah, Everret, and two others. So far Liam's theory wasn't proving true.

Liam had been right, though, about the tavern. It was much different from the other places she'd been. She liked it. It was loud and it was bright. People were dancing and laughing everywhere, and it wasn't sectioned off like the clubs.

Liam held her hand as their group weaved their way to a couple of booths where they all left their jackets and other winter items so they could dance. Women noticed Jackson when he walked by them, as they always did. There was no doubt, Jackson was the prize they'd all be seeking tonight.

Evelyn followed Liam out to dance, and he was sure to stay in eye sight of Jackson. "Are you really sure about all of this?" she finally asked.

Liam spun her away and back to himself, making her giggle and her hair swirl. "Are you not having any fun with me?"

"I am. But there are a lot of women here, and so many of them keep looking at him."

"So?" Liam challenged. "There are a lot of men here too, and we're all looking at you. Besides, if he likes you, and he does, none of these other girls should matter. If they do, then he doesn't deserve you. If you really want to know how he feels, I can just kiss you. But you'd have to promise to keep him from killing me."

"No!" Liam laughed at Evelyn's panic. She was glad he was joking…hoped he was joking. "What about this whole encouraging him thing? I don't know how to do that."

"Oh," Liam laughed again. "You'll be fine. Now, would you please give me a break from all this and just have some fun?"

It was so easy to smile and laugh with Liam, so she obliged him, and they danced and laughed. She'd known him such a short while, but she was sure she'd found a long-term friend. How strange it was to have gone through most of life alone, and suddenly have friends.

Liam was attentive. Respectful. She'd never laughed like she did with Liam. He was a bit like Bekah, just a man.

But where Liam's focus remained on Evelyn, hers wandered, and after a few songs, she noticed a woman sitting at the bar, staring at Jackson. Jackson noticed her too.

Jackson had been watching Evelyn, and Liam's hands on her. Jealous wasn't quite the right word to explain his emotions. It was like watching someone else flirt with his wife. He just couldn't justify the pain or the violent anger, because he had no real claim on her. She was not his. So he laughed and smiled with his friends, but underneath those smiles he was boiling.

He noticed Evelyn's glancing to the bar. Interested in what was distracting her, he turned to see who it was. When his eyes met hers, she smiled and made her way over to him.

He had developed a coldness towards women who looked a certain way, who dressed like vixens and painted their faces with harsh makeup. But this woman was not like them. She reminded him of Evelyn, but she clearly was nothing like her. She looked to be closer to his age, her blouse was not buttoned all the way up as Evelyn's always were. She had short blond hair. Her lips and cheeks were painted pink, unlike Evelyn's natural color, and she looked straight at him, claiming him. Evelyn was never so bold. She was the perfect temptation, a mixture of sweetness and confidence. With his nerves already raw, he needed to be careful.

She leaned her hip against the end of the booth he sat at and smiled sweetly down at him. "You and your friends seem to be having a good time." Her voice was rough for a woman's, but not unattractive.

"We should be. We're celebrating." Jackson wondered if Evelyn was still watching this woman; or if Liam was watching. Would he wait to pursue her if he thought Jackson was flirting with another woman?

"Would you like to join us?" Everret invited her, breaking off Jackson's thoughts.

"I'd love to," she smiled at Everret.

Jackson stood to let her slide into the seat and sat back down. The booth looped around in a U shape, and she now sat between him and Everret. She slid only far enough to stay close to Jackson.

"So," she said. "Do I get to know your names?"

Everret answered for them. "I'm Everret, this is Jack, and Matt."

She smiled at each of them as Everret introduced them. "I'm Emma."

"And what brings you out tonight, Emma?" Jackson asked. So far so good; she didn't appear to be up to trouble.

"Same as you, Jack. Out celebrating."

Jackson didn't like how easy it was to smile with Emma, or that she kept his eyes off of Evelyn and Liam. But, it wasn't her fault he was in love with someone else, and that that someone else was currently dancing with another man and driving him crazy. "What are you celebrating?"

Emma perked up at his question. "My birthday."

Jackson took advantage of Matt and Everret taking over the conversation to watch Evelyn again. He wasn't completely convinced Liam was telling the truth when he said there was nothing between him and Evelyn. She smiled and laughed a lot with him. And now, her focus was off him and on Liam.

His attention was snagged back when Emma's hand slid onto his arm.

"You'll have to forgive Jack," Everret laughed. "He's busy pining for a girl who's here with one of our friends."

"Well that's poor luck." Emma didn't remove her hand. "But I'm sure there's at least one lady here who would be willing to distract you."

"I think it's about time you go dance with Jacky-boy," Liam suggested. Evelyn looked over at Jackson and saw the woman's hand on his arm. "I think he needs a little of your encouragement, and rescuing." He smiled and went off to dance with another girl who had come with them.

Evelyn tried to shake off her nerves as she walked to the table where Jackson sat with this other woman's hand still resting on his arm. It was hot with all of the people and dancing, or maybe it was her jealousy. She unzipped her jacket and tossed it on her other things and looked at Jackson. "Dance with me?" It was all she could manage to say, and she was pretty sure her voice shook with the fear and anxiety that filled her.

Jackson's heart began to speed up and his throat went dry when he looked at Evelyn. He took a big drink of water and when he stood, their bodies were almost touching. It gave him a strange pleasure that she didn't back up. He slid his hand around the small of her back and led her away from the table and out to dance. He knew it was rude of him to not say anything to Emma, but he didn't care.

As they began to dance, a moment of boldness overcame Evelyn and she moved closer to Jackson. She felt starved for his arms and the comfort he gave.

They'd never danced together before. Dancing with Liam was fun. Dancing with Jackson…fun couldn't describe it. Intense. Terrifying. She'd seen that look before, but in someone else's eyes. Jackson's thumb slid against her skin at that moment, under the hem of her shirt, just above her jeans.

She gasped and stepped back. Tom. She'd seen the same look in Tom's eyes.

Jackson put her shirt back under his thumb and gently pulled her close again. "You're scared of me, aren't you?"

"Terrified," she breathed. It wasn't the look that scared her, though, not when it was in Jackson's eyes. She had no fear for her safety with him. She feared the hope it lit in her.

A slow song began playing and he brought her closer still.

"You didn't look afraid of dancing with Liam," he commented with a huskiness in his voice.

"Liam's eyes weren't saying what yours are."

Jackson took her hand and kissed it before tucking it to his chest. "And what are my eyes saying?"

"Who was that woman?" Evelyn asked, dodging the question.

"Is that disgust I hear in your sweet voice?" he teased.

"She was claiming you." She didn't mean to say that, or use that tone. "That wasn't nice of me. I'm just surprised…I didn't know if…" And now she couldn't talk. Always too much yet somehow still too little.

Jackson laughed. "Jealousy is a bit attractive on you. Her name is Emma, and I only met her just now. I promise you, she has no claim on me, nor will she ever."

Evelyn meant to say something, but she noticed the tavern door opening and looked to see that it was Sarah who walked through the door, with Tom. Impulsively, she clung tighter to Jackson.

Jackson felt her anxiety and looked where she had just been watching. It was bold of Tom to be here tonight. Bold and stupid. He noted Sarah's attention on Tom. It was evident she wanted him. He looked indifferent. Jackson knew who he was looking for.

"He came over Monday night," Evelyn told him. "He asked me to forgive him. Told me he was sorry." She felt his body tense. Why did Tom have to be here, now?

"He wants you back." Jackson took her about the waist and swiftly walked her back to the booth and told her to slide in. She did as he said. He left.

Matt was dancing with that Emma woman and Everret was talking with people at another table, so she was alone until Liam returned and slid in next to her.

"So, how's it going with lover boy?" he asked smiling.

"I have no idea." She was amused that her irritation outweighed her concern about Tom. "How was your time without me?"

"It was good," Liam said, relaxing back against the booth. "Been meeting some new girls, having a good time, until Jack showed up." He looked at her from the corner of his eye. "He's a little bit intense, isn't he?"

Evelyn leaned against him. "I'm starting to get that impression. Too bad he's only intense about sending you at me. Sorry I'm ruining your night."

Liam chuckled. "Don't worry about me. I gave Jack an ultimatum. He either makes a move tonight, or you become fair game."

She blushed when he winked at her, suddenly feeling unsure about how close they were sitting. He had to be joking to make her feel better. "Did you really tell him that?"

"Yep; and I just reminded him of it too." Liam had put his arm around her and was watching everyone dance. He acted casual, but she wondered if he felt as laid back as the impression he gave. "Who's that he's dancing with?"

Evelyn looked in the direction he'd nodded and found Jackson. Jealousy and dread poured through her all at once. She was stunning and looked like a temptress; which was probably exactly what she meant to be. She stuck out like a sore thumb. Her dark hair was pulled back into a tight ponytail and hung straight down her back and she wore painted-on-tight leather pants and a black shirt that was completely backless. It hung lightly against her sides and came back together at the lowest part of her back, right where Jackson's hand was. They looked like they belonged together; both strikingly attractive and powerfully built, though her muscles were long and lean to Jackson's broader build. Out of all the women there, why did he have to dance with her? All of Evelyn's self-doubts plagued her as she watched him with her, and his hand against the bare skin of her back. Even at that distance, she could tell he was drawn to her.

"That's Sarah," she answered, feeling defeated.

Liam must have known her spirits had fallen, and they had, straight through the floor. He pulled her out of the booth and insisted they dance again. This time though, he held her close, and she let him.

Jackson was uneasy with Sarah and worried about Evelyn. He shouldn't have left her with Liam, now that he had no doubts that Liam was interested in her.

"You're very stiff tonight," Sarah's silky voice brought memories of another time with a different, yet equally lethal woman. Every movement of her body spoke to him, even as he tried desperately to fight it. She rubbed the back of his neck, but he quickly moved her hand back to his shoulder. "I was just trying to help."

He forced a tight smile. "I'm fine, Sarah." She smiled back. Even her smile was seductive. Such a contrast to Evelyn. Evelyn was far more beautiful than Sarah. Sarah only got more attention because Evelyn was modest, careful to never use her body against him, or anyone else, and quite frankly was completely unaware of the affect she had on men. Sarah, on the other hand, used her body and men's attraction to her as a weapon to weaken them. She was very good at it.

"You were spending a lot of time with Evie, but I haven't seen you around lately. Is everything okay between the two of you?"

"Yes." He saw Liam and Evelyn dancing. He locked eyes with Liam long enough to see him pull Evelyn closer. Then Liam's focus was back on Evelyn.

The deal was off.

He should be with Evelyn, not dancing with this woman. But he wanted Tom to see him dancing with Sarah. Dancing with a woman like Sarah would throw doubts into anyone's mind about his feelings for Evelyn; dancing specifically with Sarah would be sure to put doubts in Tom's.

"Did you finally realize you were wasting your time?" Mischief danced in her eyes.

"I don't think I know what you mean."

Sarah slid her body closer. "Hmm, I doubt that." She smiled at his obvious anger towards her. "I just mean, I know what she will and won't do for a man, and you're quite a man, aren't you?"

Finally the song ended, and he excused himself from her temptations. Sarah was up to no good, and he got the distinct impression that she had read his every thought while they danced. She knew their dance was meant to be a distraction, and he knew that information would get back to Tom.

Evelyn saw Jackson leave Sarah. They made eye contact for a moment when he spotted her, but she looked away quickly and back to Liam. She was beside herself with jealousy, and he saw it all.

"Excuse me," is all Jackson offered to Liam when he got to them.

Liam didn't argue. He did give him a warning look. He was a good man, Jackson knew that. He was a threat because of that, but a threat that Jackson welcomed in light of Tom. If Liam was willing to go against Jackson for her happiness, he'd stand against Tom for her protection.

Jackson put his arm possessively around Evelyn and walked her over to the bar. He was tense; Evelyn could guess why.

Jackson ordered two teas. The bar tender smiled at Evelyn, and he held her closer. He knew he was being absurd and that he shouldn't be claiming Evelyn the way he was. Tom was bound to see, but his patience had run out. He couldn't bear seeing her with someone else any more.

"I'm sorry I left you."

Evelyn sighed and leaned into his side. "You're back now." She felt him relax a little and his thumb began to stroke her hip; it was suddenly difficult to breathe. He took both glasses in one hand, keeping his other around her, and led her back to the tables where they joined a group of people she didn't know. He handed her one of the teas and gave his attention to his friends' conversation, completely unaware of her watching him, and loving him.

Evelyn didn't dance like Sarah did; she wondered if Jackson wished she would. She wondered a lot about the differences between her and Sarah and what Jackson preferred. But why did she have to have these questions at such a moment? She didn't want to upset him, but her thoughts ate at her until she had to ask. "Sarah's stunning tonight, isn't she?"

Jackson looked at Sarah again and looked back to Evelyn. "Not as beautiful as you." Her look said she didn't believe him. "I've been very jealous all night. I don't like sharing you; especially with Liam."

Her head was spinning and she found it difficult not to giggle when she spoke. "You? Jealous? I don't believe it."

"It's true. All night I've thought, what if he makes her fall in love with him and I lose her?"

"That would never happen. You know I adore you." It was always too easy to talk to Jackson, and she was always too honest. "And Liam's harmless."

"It's a nice feeling, being adored." Jackson laughed as she blushed. He was relieved she confirmed her absence of interest in Liam. "Really, though, you're very attractive."

Evelyn stepped back from him and set her drink on a nearby table. She was nervous about what she wanted to tell him, and didn't want to talk in front of his friends. She glanced up at him as she spoke. "I hoped you'd think so."

Jackson set his glass aside as well and stepped away from the others with her. Leaning against the wall, he grabbed her belt loop and pulled her to him. "Are you finally telling me who that man is you were hoping would notice you?"

She lifted her hands to one of the buttons on his shirt and played with it nervously, still only being able to glance up at him, but focusing mostly on his button. "I could be…"

Jackson was irritated when he noticed Bekah spot them from across the room. Now when he was finally going to get to tell Evelyn what he felt for her, Bekah was on her way to interrupt. "Here comes Bekah," he growled.

She came bouncing over to them, laughing, with George trailing behind her. "Jackson, I see you've stolen Liam's date. But I do understand; she is the loveliest girl here."

"I was just telling her that same thing, but she didn't believe me."

Bekah's mouth fell open, faking surprise at Evelyn's inability to believe him. "Well, you are, Evelyn. Even Miss Priss doesn't compare with you. She knows it too. She looked about ready to scratch Tom's eyes out when he was talking about you." She grimaced. "Sorry, we won't ruin our night talking about the scum of the earth. Now Jackson," she said, extending an innocently flirtatious hand to him. "Are you going to indulge me in a dance or not?"

Even though Evelyn was irritated with her friend for interrupting her and Jackson, she pushed him towards her. She and George laughed as they watched the two dancing. It was obvious Bekah was doing all the leading, and chatting Jackson's ear off.

George turned to Evelyn. "Well," he suggested, "Shall we join them?"

George was a welcome partner. He was lively and talkative, and a good dancer. It helped, too, that his relationship with Bekah made him the safest man in the room to dance with. Unfortunately, another man stepped in at the end of the song, asking her to dance, and George passed her over before she could decline.

Her new partner's name was Robb. He looked young, maybe even younger than she was, and seemed nervous; which was strange because she was always the one nervous and also because he was the one who asked her to dance. As they danced, he led her across the floor to the opposite end of the room. Evelyn had completely lost sight of Jackson by the time the song ended.

She thanked him and turned to leave, but he stopped her.

"Would you like a drink? You must be thirsty after all of your dancing."

She didn't like not knowing where Jackson was, especially knowing Tom was somewhere in the crowd, and Sarah. She couldn't forget about Sarah. "I'm fine, thank you. I'd really like to just find my friend."

"Jackson?" He didn't seem to want her to leave, and she wasn't sure how he knew who she was talking about; since he had seen her with George.

"Yes. How'd you know?" Fear jumped into Robb's expression, though not surprise, as his eyes shifted slightly past her. She turned around, assuming Jackson had found her, and found Tom instead.

"Hello, Evelyn." Tom sneered down at her. "Robb, don't worry, I'll help her find Jackson." He kept his eyes on Evelyn. He'd planned this meeting. A shiver ran down her spine.

Robb spoke quietly behind her. "It was nice meeting you, Evelyn." She didn't hear him leave, but knew he was gone.

Evelyn resigned herself to deny Tom the satisfaction of knowing he frightened her. She straightened her posture and lifted her chin. "Hello, Tom." Her insides knotted as he let his eyes wander down her body. "Tom, please don't…that makes me uncomfortable."

His sneer softened to a smile as he obeyed. "You look beautiful tonight."

Evelyn wasn't sure how to answer. She whispered a thank you and noticed a flash of, compassion maybe, go across Tom's face.

"I hear you're here with my Captain," Tom continued.

"There's a group of us. We're celebrating his graduation." Where was Jackson? "Technically, I came with one of his friends."

Something caught Tom's eye and his countenance shifted. "Have a good night Evelyn. I'm sure we'll see each other soon." With that arrogant gleam back in his eyes, he turned and left.

Evelyn looked around, frantic to find Jackson. They saw each other at the same time, and he started towards her. The band had begun playing a familiar song and everyone was singing with them. It was so loud. The chaos of the room began to press in on her. Before she had seen Tom, the people, band, and general festivities were fun. Now, they just clouded her mind. Jackson was almost to her when he was shoved, hard.

She had come out of nowhere and had him pinned with his back against the wall. Her body pressed against his as she grabbed his neck and kissed him passionately. There was nothing innocent in how her body moved against his.

Evelyn expected Jackson to shove Sarah away, to yell at the vixen who had her fingers in his hair. It must have only lasted a few seconds, maybe less, but it felt like an eternity; and it was long enough for her to see his lips soften under hers and his hands grip her hips, with his fingers pressing into the bare small of her back. She saw the anger in his eyes when he pushed her away, but it was too late. Evelyn turned and ran.

Jackson wanted to strangle the snake in front of him. Sarah stood smiling before him. The whole performance was for Evelyn to see, not from any attraction Sarah had to him. Tom! He knew Tom and Sarah were close; he had to be behind all of this, as revenge for his kissing Evelyn in front of him. And Evelyn, where was she now? He looked back to where she was standing just a moment ago, but she was gone. He could only assume she was running. He knew she'd want to get away from everything, but where would she run to? They were too far from campus for her to get back on her own at this hour. He left Sarah without a word and strode in the direction he hoped to find Evelyn.

Someone's shoulder knocked violently into him. When he looked back, he saw Tom, looking smug. That was confirmation enough. He wanted to cause him a great amount of physical pain, but finding Evelyn was more important.

"I could have followed her."

Jackson spun at Liam's voice. He held Evelyn's jacket.

"Next time I won't be a gentleman about it."

"There won't be a next time," he barked, taking Evelyn's jacket.

"Jack." Liam's tone stopped him. "That woman – Sarah – she has the mark of a huntress." Liam's eyes searched Jackson's for understanding.

Jackson didn't know there was a mark, but he knew what she was. Interesting that Liam knew about it.

"And what side are you on?"

"Not theirs," Liam answered. "Now go. She's outside."

He fought his way through the crowd and outside. When he saw her, his heart broke. She sat on a bench with her face in her hands. Her shoulders shook slightly and he knew she was crying, and he was the cause of it. She hadn't even bothered to get her coat. He had ruined everything and was in danger of losing her forever. What had he done?

At first, all he could hear as he walked towards her was the crunch of snow under his feet and a freezing wind blowing slightly. But as he got closer, the soft sniffling of her weeping sent knives through his heart. She didn't look up when he approached her.

"Evelyn," he spoke, draping her jacket over her shoulders. "Before I say anything else, or do anything else, or risk losing you any further, you need to know how I feel about you."

She looked up now, but kept her eyes off his. Her face was wet with tears and red with embarrassment. "I don't need to know anything. I have no right to act this way. You're not mine, and you have every right to be with whoever you want to be with."

"I don't want to be with Sarah. I want to be with you."

Evelyn meant to stand and leave, quickly. She only managed to stand, and slowly. Her body was shaking. She didn't know if it was from the bitter cold or crying. And where would she go to anyway?

"Tonight was a mistake," she confessed, trying in vain to compose herself. "I knew I cared too much for you. I thought… I hoped… But I know you don't see me like that. I don't mean to be ungrateful, you've done so much for me, but, maybe if you want to see Sarah, could you guys spend time at your house and not ours?" Her head was a fog, and her heart hurt.

"Evelyn! Listen to me." Jackson couldn't believe she still didn't understand. "I don't want to spend any time with Sarah. Ever. I want to spend all my time with you. You're my best friend, but you're more than that to me. Do you understand?"

Evelyn was dizzy now. She had dreamed of this, of him saying those words to her, but not after kissing someone else. Anger began seeping into her with the pain; anger she had no right to feel, but wasn't strong enough to fight. How could he kiss someone else if he really liked her? "I don't understand. First, you kissed me in front of Tom. Now, you're kissing Sarah in front of me. Is it a game to you?"

"I'm not playing a game," Jackson argued. "The kiss with Sarah didn't mean anything. It was a mistake."

She just looked at him, replaying what he had said in her head. *'It didn't mean anything.'* How could it not mean anything? How could saying so make it any better? His words just made it all worse. The pain. The embarrassment. All of it.

"I'm so sorry, Evelyn." He sounded desperate.

"You're sorry?" she whispered. "I wish I didn't care." Her sad eyes found his. "Do you know what it felt like to see you with her? I already had to watch you dance with her tonight. I saw how you longed for her, saw how low your hand rested on her back. And then you kiss her! And now you tell me it didn't mean anything, and you have feelings for me? Me, who you brought home to your parents for Thanksgiving and who you were going to take with you for Christmas, and spent hours upon hours with but never told this to before just now?"

Jackson had never seen her angry like this before. "She kissed me, Evelyn, I didn't…"

"You kissed her back, Jackson!" She was screaming now and didn't care. "Do you remember what I did when Tom tried to kiss me? I hit him, and I ran for my life. You weren't even around then, and still, I ran from him because he is poison. And just tonight Liam offered to kiss me to motivate you. Did I let him? No. Because he's not you.

"I saw you, Jackson Monroe. Don't you dare try and lie to me. You kissed her back! You let her rub against you! Your hands held her steady to do so!" She couldn't think straight she was so broken. Rage. Jealousy.

Anguish. They engulfed her as sobs ripped through her. She was going to be sick.

It was torture seeing her like this, knowing she was right. He had stopped thinking for a split second when Sarah pressed against him and he remembered all the sinful pleasures of his past. Now it seemed he had destroyed what he treasured most.

A Patrol officer passed by and called out to them. "Is everything alright, sir?" Even here his status was known. He was known.

Jackson forced his eyes away from Evelyn to answer the officer. "Yes, thank you." The officer left without even glancing in Evelyn's direction. When Jackson turned back toward Evelyn, her hands were trembling, though she tried to hide it.

Her head bowed and her gaze was cast down, unwilling to look upon him. "Everyone listens to you, don't they? They do whatever you tell them to."

"Not everyone."

"They do, Jackson," she nodded. "I've lived with Sarah a long time...long enough. I can't dance like her." She lifted her eyes to his, shifting her body to draw his attention to it. "I don't look like Sarah." She took a step towards him. "But I know enough to play the part." She closed the space between them and lifted her hand, meaning to run it up his chest...but touching him broke her. "But I don't want to be her. And I don't want you to ask me to do the things she does."

With her body, she meant to tease him, to mock him; but in her eyes there was no malice, only sadness. He took her shoulders. "I don't want you that way."

Evelyn's voice was quiet, full of the depth of pain she felt. "I think that is exactly right. You don't want me. You want her."

She was talking madness! She had to listen to him. "Evelyn, I don't want her, or anyone like her. I want you! I want you in every way a man can want a woman. Can't you see that?"

Evelyn could see that he meant it, but she'd seen how he responded to Sarah's lips, and her body. Tears were streaming down her face again. Her heart was broken. "I love you, Jackson, so much it hurts. And now it just hurts worse." She turned to leave but he caught her arm, pulling her into him. He wrapped one arm around her and cupped her face with his hand. His touch tore at her heart.

He spoke softly, his voice rough with emotion. "You love me." It wasn't a question, but she nodded. "Then forgive me." He kissed her forehead. "Please, Evelyn, forgive me." He kissed her temple. "And let me prove to you that you're the only one I want." He kissed her cheek and her chin. She was trembling now, and fighting sobs. His lips gently brushed hers and he felt her breath flutter. He pulled back, just enough to look in her eyes, and asked her again, "Please, forgive me." She nodded. "I love you."

A sob broke through Evelyn's chest when she heard those words, but Jackson fought it back, kissing her tenderly. His hand slipped from her cheek to cradle her head and she slipped her arms under his and around his waist, feeling the strength of his muscles as she hugged him closer. Reluctantly, she took her lips away from his and looked into his eyes again, as tears spilled from her own.

"I love you, Ayanna Evelyn Carter. I'll tell you so, and I'll show you, every day."

## Chapter 35

Evelyn knew she should eat something, but her mind kept wandering back to the pub. Jackson hadn't let her go the rest of the night. If his arms weren't around her, his hand was holding hers. She hadn't minded in the least. The one time he wasn't touching her was during an animated conversation with Liam, of all people, about some training routine she wasn't interested in. Spotting Bekah sitting alone, she'd hoped to use the opportunity to update her on Jackson. Jackson apparently had other ideas. Catching her about the waist, he tenderly stood her in front of himself, wrapping his arms around her. She had blushed at Liam's I-told-you-so wink, and Jackson held her tighter, pressing her back more firmly against his chest.

"You know you'll be fine," Bekah's voice broke through her daydream.

Evelyn looked her roommate up and down. Bekah's style of the day – ripped jeans, tucked in gray t-shirt, white blazer, and those heals. "How do you make that look good?"

"Nice try," Bekah laughed. "We're staying on you." Bekah sat next to her and smoothed her hand over Evelyn's, saving Evelyn's dress from being worried to shreds. "The only thing that's changed is now you know he likes you. I was starting to think he'd never tell you!"

Evelyn grimaced. "How long have you known?"

"I guessed it for a while, but he told me when he brought you home after Thanksgiving." Bekah smiled as a knock sounded at the door.

Evelyn's hands shook as she opened it. There he stood, terrifying and wonderful, dressed in his customary off-duty attire: flannel. He was unshaven. She didn't know why she liked him that way, but she did. Her soul ached to tuck herself into his arms.

Instead, fear paralyzed her. Her eyes skirted his. She would have blushed if she knew the thoughts running through Jackson's mind.

"Hey, Jackson." Bekah was getting good at breaking through Evelyn's dazes.

"Hey, Bekah." Jackson's eyes met Bekah's, but only briefly. His focus remained on his woman as he entered the apartment and shut the door behind him.

"Oh alright, I get it." Bekah hugged Jackson and looked at him seriously. "You treat her right, Jackson. And," she said smiling, "try to be patient…really patient."

Evelyn hugged her roommate tight. It was only ten days, but she really was going to miss her.

"First Corinthians, chapter 13," Bekah whispered. "Look it up. Maybe it'll help. And don't worry," she comforted Evelyn. "It's just Jackson. And you'll be with his parents. He has to be on his best behavior." She let her go and winked at Jackson as she disappeared down the hall.

Jackson studied Evelyn. He'd assumed she'd need guidance as they ventured onto this new road, but this was much more than a little inexperience. He wrapped his arms around Evelyn. "I'm scared too. I've never been in love before either."

"Oh my gosh," Bekah yelled from down the hall. "You're so cheesy!"

Jackson could feel Evelyn laugh. "How are you?"

Evelyn buried her face against his chest and took, what she had hoped to be, a steadying breath. It wasn't as effective as she had hoped because the scent of him was dizzying. "I think I'm having a nervous breakdown. But other than that, I'm fine."

*At least she's being honest with me*, he thought. "Why are you having a nervous breakdown?"

Evelyn backed away from Jackson and more collapsed than sat on her couch. "Oh, no reason. Just because you're," she waved her hand at him, "all that, and I told you all that stuff last night, and now I feel just a little bit exposed and absolutely vulnerable, and I'm still not entirely sure that I believe you." There, she said it. Why was he smiling at her? "What?"

"I'm going to enjoy convincing you that I love you." He reached out and pulled her back to himself. He slid his hands down her sides and kissed her behind her ear. She clung to him like she'd fall over if she let

248

go. He breathed in her scent and smiled. Yes, he was really going to enjoy convincing her.

It didn't surprise Evelyn that a car was taking them to the Monroe's. What did shock her was the absence of a driver in the car. "You can drive?" she gawked at Jackson.

Jackson put her bags into the covered truck bed and winked at her as he helped her into the passenger seat, sending her pulse racing. The man clearly enjoyed showing off for her. Or maybe it was her response to his touch that entertained him.

"One more first," Evelyn murmured as Jackson climbed into the driver's seat. The truck was old, though she didn't know enough about cars to determine its year. The outside paint was grey, and the interior followed in the same fashion. The dash didn't have an overwhelming number of knobs or buttons, but she still didn't know what any of the ones it did have were for. She did, however, know she enjoyed sitting in it. The seats were comfortable and it was spacious. The back seat seemed small; perhaps only large enough for children to be comfortable riding there.

At the turn of the key, the engine roared to life. Evelyn's hand flew to her chest at the shockingly powerful sound. "And it's not electric?" She tried to hide her giddiness. She failed. She had dreamed of riding in a gas-powered car, and there she was, sitting in the front seat of one. "How did you get someone to let you use it?"

There was unmistakable pride in his expression. "It's mine. I brought it back from New Mexico with me. I only drive it when I'm going to my parents' in the snow."

"Jackson, are you rich?" A smirk was his only reply. "You must be if you can afford a car and the gas for it. Are you rich, or just your parents?"

"So, you think the only reason I have money is because of my parents, huh?"

Realizing how her question sounded, she was glad he sounded amused instead of offended. "Just pretend I didn't say anything."

Jackson smiled over at her. "I'm not rich, but I don't want for much. Some of it is from my parents. They set up accounts and investments for me when I was young. A lot of it comes from my own hard work. I've been working, at least part time, since I was fifteen, and haven't really had any expenses until I bought this truck and then my house. I've only been a captain a little while, but they make a good living.

"And just so you know, most officers know how to drive. We'd be pretty slow getting to emergencies if we had to wait around for a ride."

Evelyn rolled her eyes. Maybe most officers knew how to drive, but the vast majority did not own their own private vehicle. And *she* wasn't in want. *He* had a surplus. There was a difference. A big difference.

She was glad she managed to keep those thoughts to herself.

It wasn't going to be a smooth ride to Jackson's parents' home, with the truck bouncing roughly at every imperfection in the road, but it was exciting. Evelyn was glad Jackson didn't press her further for conversation; it gave her time to think and get her nerves under control. They were coming to the cemetery when she finally spoke again. "Would you mind if we stopped up there for a minute?" she asked on impulse.

Though confused, Jackson complied, pulling over next to the sidewalk and turning the truck off. Worry gripped him when he saw how pale she'd gone. "What's wrong?"

Evelyn opened her door and slid out. "Will you come with me?" she asked, turning back to Jackson.

They walked through the frozen cemetery; the crunch of snow beneath their feet was all that broke the silence engulfing them.

Evelyn had never taken anyone with her to visit her mother's grave before, but she'd never loved anyone like she loved Jackson, either. Loving Jackson would require her to open up to him. She didn't know much about love, but that much she was sure of. This was a good first step. She thought about the scriptures Bekah told her about. Reading those, she decided, would be a good second step.

They finally stopped walking and Jackson watched as Evelyn knelt down to dust off the snow that had settled over the gravestone. Even before seeing the name, Jackson knew where she'd led him. But when the snow was cleared, he got a surprise he wasn't expecting.

"Your mother?"

"Yes." Feeling open and vulnerable, Evelyn stood and crossed her arms in front of her, not sure what else to say. She hoped she had imagined the displeasure she heard in his voice.

Their day had started off so differently than Jackson imagined it would. He had thought after she knew he loved her, she would be free of her fear of him. Instead, she was even more reserved. And now they were standing over her mother's grave, and her mother was Justine Thompson, wife to Harold Thompson, and an old family friend.

You would never find Harold's name in a history book, but a part of American history he was. He was the Secretary of State who fell in love with a woman from the Texas Republic and brought her home as his wife. Evelyn was right when she had told Jackson her father died from a fight with the wrong people. Extremists had hunted him down. Jackson's own father had been close friends with Harold, and Justine Thompson had lived with them for a short time, until her baby girl was born.

She had come to them terrified the same night Harold was killed. She had nowhere else to go and so she lived with them in secret. Jackson remembered her reading stories to him as a child; something Evelyn never got to experience. He would climb onto her lap and they would talk to the baby in her stomach.

Jackson wasn't allowed around when Justine went into labor, but he had been permitted to hold the baby, Evelyn, just hours after she was born. Memories were breaking over him. He remembered the feeling he had holding her, and Justine Thompson asking him, "You'll always protect my flower, won't you, Jackson?"

Flower.

Justine was gone the next morning. She didn't leave any information on where she was going, or what she named her baby. Jackson should have realized it all sooner. How was he going to tell Evelyn everything he knew? That she had been born in the home he grew up in? That he had known her mother? And then there was Tom and the other extremists. If they knew who she really was, she would be in more danger than her association with Jackson could ever cause her. Instead of telling her, he heeded the warning in his heart telling him to wait, put his arm around her waist, and kissed the top of her head. "Thank you for sharing this with me." He needed to talk to his father. *Oh God, please give me wisdom in this...or just, let me be wrong.*

## Chapter 36

Jackson pulled into his parents' driveway and grabbed their bags as Evelyn hopped out of the truck. She had missed this home, and his parents, so much; but the thought that they might not approve of her relationship with their son made her steps hesitant. She wished she had thought about that a bit sooner. As it was, it was too late now to worry about it. Jackson had opened the door and they were walking in, Jackson already calling for his parents.

The home had been transformed into a winter wonderland. Fresh garland and little white lights hung from every banister and doorway, with large red ribbons tying them securely in place. Every shelf and table had vases of ornaments or festively wrapped candies, snowman figurines, or some other special touch on it. A collection of figurines forming a beautiful scene of people, gathered in what looked like a hut or a barn of some sort, caught Evelyn's eye. She wasn't sure what the scene was, and she was pretty sure it didn't have anything to do with Christmas, but it was lovely. Evelyn had never seen anything so picturesque.

Natalie came bounding down the stairs, with Charles following behind at a less frantic pace. Jackson braced Evelyn with his hand against her back as his mother ran into her, hugging her tightly. His gentle touch took her breath more than the force of his mother.

"I thought I'd never make it these three weeks!" Natalie exclaimed, turning then to Jackson. "I'm so glad you're back!" She stood back after hugging her son. "You've grown! How is it possible that you've grown in three weeks?"

Jackson laughed and shook hands with his father. "I've spent a lot of time training with the officers lately. Had some frustrations I was working through."

"Was or are?" Charles asked, raising an eyebrow at his son.

"Was," Jackson answered smiling. Evelyn's brow furrowed at the unspoken conversation going on between Jackson and Charles. Her breath caught in surprise when Jackson slid his arm around her, holding her firmly against him.

Natalie rescued Evelyn from Jackson's grip, taking her hand. "You boys take the bags upstairs. We'll meet you in the kitchen." And she whisked Evelyn away. Once they were alone, Natalie turned, smiling widely at Evelyn with a twinkle in her eye. "So tell me, when did you two finally realize you liked each other?"

Evelyn had forgotten how blunt Natalie was. "How did you…" Oh. Natalie smiled as she saw understanding come over her. "I was his frustration. Um, just last night, actually. We haven't really talked about it, though." Evelyn just stared as Natalie's laughter rang out. Evelyn had no idea what was so funny. Things didn't seem funny at all. Confusing, yes! But not exactly funny.

"Oh, it's about time Jackson's had to wait for a woman," Natalie explained. "Good for you, making him wait. Now he's had a taste of what it's like for the rest of us. You're good for him. I hope you know that."

"What was Harold Thompson's wife's name?" Jackson wanted to talk to his father about Evelyn's parents as soon as possible, and it worked in his favor that his mother stole Evelyn right away.

"Justine," Charles answered. "Why do you want to know that?"

Jackson's shoulders sagged. How he'd hoped that he had been wrong. "Do you know what her maiden name was?" He could see his father was confused. A rare occasion.

"Carter, I think."

Jackson stopped his dad from going downstairs. "Evelyn's their daughter. She took me to her mother's grave this morning."

Even rarer than his father being confused was his father showing he was shocked; but this was one of those times. "Who else knows that?" Jackson heard the same alarms that had rung in his head sounding in his father's voice.

"I don't know. I'm sure I'm the first person she's taken to the grave, but I can't be sure no one else knows her mother's name." Jackson could see his father was thinking the same thing he was. This was dangerous information. "What would we even do if someone knew?"

Charles took a moment to think. "There's nothing to do about it right now, and while she's here, she's safe. After Christmas, I'll try to find out what I can. We'll pray no one else knows. What does she know?"

"She knows her father was murdered, but I don't think she even knows his name; She can't know much, if anything."

"You'll have to decide when to tell her. She needs to know, and it should come from you."

Jackson knew that too, but he wasn't looking forward to telling her. A weariness he didn't know he carried pressed in on him.

"I'm glad you, how'd you put it, worked through your frustrations with Evelyn," Charles teased his son as they walked down the stairs. "She doesn't look comfortable with you though."

"That'd be because I only told her how I felt last night." He might as well tell his father everything. It was always better when he did. "And it was after I kissed another woman." Jackson cringed when his father stopped mid-step. This conversation wasn't going to go down as one of his favorite father-son talks. "Go ahead and lecture me. I know I'm a complete fool. I could try to make excuses about how and why it happened, but I won't."

Charles began walking again. "It was a foolish thing for you to do, but I won't call my son a fool. We all make mistakes. Just be sure it's the last time you make that one. Evelyn doesn't seem like the forgetful type. I'd imagine she's going to struggle with that for a while. You're going to have to be patient, and humble. Those aren't your strongest qualities."

Jackson's laugh lacked humor. It hadn't crossed his mind that his actions with Sarah would leave scars on Evelyn.

Janna Halterman

# Chapter 37

*1 Corinthians 13:1-8a (NIV)*
*If I speak in the tongues of men or of angels, but do not have love, I am only a resounding gong or a clanging cymbal. If I have the gift of prophesy and can fathom all mysteries and all knowledge, and if I have faith that can move mountains, but do not have love, I am nothing. If I give all I possess to the poor and give over my body to hardship that I may boast, but do not have love, I gain nothing. Love is patient, love is kind. It does not envy, it does not boast, it is not proud. It does not dishonor others, it is not self-seeking, it is not easily angered, it keeps no record of wrongs. Love does not delight in evil but rejoices with the truth. It always protects, always trusts, always hopes, always perseveres.*
*Love never fails.*

Borrowing from the Monroe's personal library, Evelyn did as Bekah had told her and looked up First Corinthians 13 that night. She read and re-read the chapter, and as she read, she became more and more overwhelmed, crushed even, by the concept of love.

"Can I help you understand something?" Charles asked from his chair across from her in the library. Jackson and Natalie were cleaning the kitchen from that night's dinner, leaving Evelyn and Charles to their reading. They had been sitting, each reading from God's Word, in a very comfortable and safe silence.

Jackson had kissed Evelyn soundly on the mouth, and in front of his mother none the less, earlier that day. After that, she decided to stick closer to Charles. She didn't tell Jackson, because she wasn't entirely sure how to do so without hurting his feelings, but she wasn't prepared to be quite so open with affection. Part of that stemmed from the fact that they still hadn't talked about what exactly their relationship was, and part of it came from the fact that they had told each other they loved each other…but she really didn't know anything about love. Being so naïve about something everyone else knew so much about did nothing to comfort her or make her feel secure with Jackson. So Charles was her new best friend. He was the safest of the Monroes, and he was compassionate with her questions and hesitations.

"My roommate suggested I read this chapter," she explained. "She was hoping it'd help me understand some things, but I'm afraid it's just overwhelming me."

"What are you reading?"

Evelyn held up the booklet so he could read the title; First Corinthians. "Chapter 13."

"Ah," Charles said with a tone of understanding. "Love is a rather overwhelming subject. Why don't you talk through your thoughts?"

"Thank you, Charles, but I don't want to bother you with this."

"When Jackson was about ten years old," Charles said, "he would get very angry and Natalie and I couldn't understand why. One day during one of his moods, I had him sit down and I asked him what was wrong. He said that I wouldn't understand, but I got the impression that he wasn't too sure himself. So, I asked him a few other questions: who he had seen that day, what they had learned in class; just innocent questions to get him talking. He eventually got around to talking about what was bothering him. To this day he talks things out with me so he can figure out his thoughts. I will do the same thing with you, Evelyn, if you'd like. However, I am of the belief you have a less cluttered mind than my son and that you don't need nearly as much prompting. If you'd rather just talk through your thoughts and have me listen, without prodding, I'll be happy to be a silent participator in this exercise."

Evelyn was beginning to see why people didn't argue with Charles; there just wasn't any point. The man had a way of extending such kindness that it seemed rude to decline. "If Jackson comes in," she tried to explain, but how could she explain that she wasn't ready to talk to Jackson about everything yet?

But Charles could sympathize. "If Jackson comes in, we've been talking about how your finals went."

"Thank you," Evelyn smiled and then proceeded to explain her consternation. "Bekah, my roommate, suggested I read this chapter to help me understand this...whatever Jackson and I are." She could tell Charles was attempting to hide his smile. If it were anyone else, she would have been embarrassed, but not with him. His insuppressible smile communicated compassion and sensitivity. Amusement too, but she didn't mind. "I know what I feel and what I think about Jackson, and I know that Jackson says he loves me, but I'm not sure if our definitions of love are the same. I don't know if love has an exact definition or if it changes according to the person who feels it. Does that make any sense?"

"It does," he answered.

"I listened to Bekah and read the chapter, and according to this, love is a very specific thing. The problem is that the kind of love this describes is...well, it sounds impossible. Some of it sounds easy, like the not delighting in evil; but I'm sure I don't understand that fully either. You and your family are the best people I've ever known, and I know you love Natalie and Jackson. Are you always patient with them? Can you really forget every wrong they've ever done? But then it makes me think, if they've done something wrong, then doesn't that mean their love isn't the love described in this chapter?"

Charles sat with one leg crossed over the other with his ankle resting on his knee and his arms folded across his chest. It was a thoughtful position, with his dark eyes – the same as his son's – twinkling in contemplation. "I can see why you're overwhelmed," he said, taking his time to answer. Charles not only thought before he spoke, but he considered his words carefully. Evelyn appreciated it and admired that about him. It must have made him a valuable asset to the Patrols, especially when working with other countries over difficult situations. "Let me first answer your questions about me. No. I am not always patient and kind with them. I have not forgotten every wrong they've done. Every day, sometimes multiple times a day, I have to choose to forgive and I cannot forget unless God chooses to take a memory from me, but I can choose to let things go. I can choose to not hold things against them. I can choose to not bring up their pasts, their mistakes, for my gain. But it is still the love that First Corinthians describes. You're correct when you say that the love you just read about is impossible, but what you don't know is that nothing is impossible with God."

Charles' words rattled something deep inside her and a weighty burden came upon her unexpectedly. She took the stretch of silence Charles gave her to reflect on all he had said and to compare it to what she had read. The verses before her implied that love was something a follower of God didn't have a choice in; like it was a command and it needed to be resolute.

"God loves us this way, doesn't He?" she asked.

"He does."

"And we strive to be like Him?"

"Correct. In Ephesians it says to be imitators of God because we are his children."

He paused again and Evelyn noticed he chewed the inside of his lip when he was thinking. Charles had a verse for everything. It left Evelyn a little baffled, but also grateful for the plethora of Scriptures he could recall at any moment assuring her the Bible had guidance for everything. That was comforting for a girl who grew up having to learn everything the hard way, through experience and the embarrassment of her own naïveté. She now had an invaluable resource.

"Throughout the entirety of the Bible, we're shown the greatness of God's love for us. Then in First John, we're told that God is love. When you were born again, when you became a Christian, you received that love within yourself. As a child of God, you're called to this kind of love for everyone; not just for Jackson. In Matthew chapter five, we're told to love our enemies and pray for those who persecute you." Charles stopped.

"I'm sorry. I'm afraid I've taken this conversation to a topic you weren't prepared to discuss," he apologized. "You've been through more than your fair share of persecution. I know you were searching God's Word for insight on what is between you and Jackson, but you need to know there's so much more to love than the romance that our culture says it is."

"Are there any reference books or commentaries that categorize all topics, like love, in the Bible?" Evelyn asked.

A new stillness came over Charles, and Evelyn got the impression he was weighing something in his mind. She watched as his stillness transposed to movement and he stood and crossed the room to a bookshelf behind her. His hand disappeared behind a row of books as he reached for something she couldn't see. A faint click sounded and the bookshelf unhinged itself from the wall on the right side.

"You remember this, Evelyn," he said, pointing at the book his hand had reached behind. "If there's ever any sort of attack on this home, you come straight here and close the door behind you." He opened the door to expose a hidden room. Charles summoned her with his hand to join him and she obeyed immediately, driven by curiosity at what this secret room held.

The light from the library flooded the room completely. Even so, Evelyn noticed a small nightlight in a corner, along with a well-stocked supply of flashlights and headlamps. The hidden treasure of a room was lined on one side with a bookshelf and desk, with guns and ammunition on the opposite. It was rather impressive artillery. Between the two filled walls and directly behind the hidden door was a small opening. It was too dark to see where it led.

"That," Charles said, speaking to her unvoiced question, "leads to our basement and has connections to mine and Natalie's room and Jackson's, as well as a tunnel that will take you out to a cave by the lake. Your room doesn't have a door, so Jackson will show you how to get through his since your rooms are next to each other. But back to your question about commentaries. Here," he said, pointing to a section of old-looking books, "you'll find a few commentaries and other study materials for the Bible."

Evelyn's fingers ran over the spines of the books. She loved the feel of old books. "They're banned, aren't they?" Charles nodded. She gleaned that from the fact he had them hidden. "Do you have a full Bible?" she asked, hoping his answer was no since that was what she was gifting them for Christmas.

Charles relieved her worry. "Unfortunately, no. Those are harder to come by because everyone knows they're banned. I'm sure you know how that is, working at a library. When I was younger, I managed to get on an inventory check at a library in Louisiana and was able to grab these before the other officers found them and burned them."

Evelyn did know how that was. If there had been a Patrol assigned to their inventory this month, she would never have been able to smuggle the Bible out; unless the officer had been Jackson. A funny jolt ran through her at the thought of working an inventory with Jackson, alone in one of the back library rooms.

Charles selected one of the books and handed it to her. "This will probably be the most helpful for you." Evelyn began flipping through the book as Charles closed the secret bookshelf door. "I'm going to head up to bed," Charles said. "Natalie and Jackson should be done with the kitchen by now."

Evelyn closed the book to give Charles her full attention. "Thank you for talking me through everything. I would have still been staring at the page if you hadn't helped me."

"It's been a joy. Your questions challenged me and encouraged me in my faith tonight; so, thank you."

"Charles?" Evelyn asked just before he left the room. He stopped and turned to her. "Can you give me any advice on how to love your son? I mean how to love him the way God wants me to?"

Charles laughed, loud enough for the others to hear and Evelyn worried they might come in and ask what they were laughing about. "You're a wonderful young lady, Evelyn. You already love him better than you know." He stopped there and his lips softened in a smile, hinting at tenderness rather than amusement. "Natalie and I already see you as family. We've both prayed for you since before we even knew you."

Charles was well aware the full meaning of his words went over Evelyn's head. He and Natalie both hoped Jackson would marry her. But aside from her relationship with their son, they had prayed for her because of their friendship with her parents. For twenty years, there had been an unwavering burden on their hearts to pray for her, though without knowing her name, only knowing she was the orphaned daughter of their dear friends who had lost their lives. God was good. He had protected her and brought her into His kingdom just as her parents had always prayed. What a privilege it was to see God work, and how humbling. And this precious girl loved his son. None of them really deserved her. Well, Natalie did; but he and Jackson surely didn't.

"My advice would be to pray for him, and to be patient and quick to forgive. Jackson struggles with patience and he has been known to be quick to anger. He has his mother's temper." He winked at her and smiled wider.

"Thank you, Charlie."

"You're welcome. Goodnight."

"Goodnight."

## Chapter 38

*Love your enemies.*

Charles' words stayed with Evelyn late into the night. Jackson had walked her up to her room shortly after Charles had left. She brought an armful of books from the Bible, along with the commentary Charles lent her. Of course, Jackson carried them for her. In the book of Luke, she read again that she was called to love her enemies. The book of Romans said love must be sincere. She flipped through First John to find the verse about God being love and found in the same chapter that said there was no fear in love; that love drove out fear.

She needed to talk through her thoughts. She needed to talk to someone who knew more about the Bible than she did. She needed to talk to someone who knew what she had been through with her enemies. She needed Jackson.

With her arms full of books, she waited for Jackson to answer after she quietly rapped on his door. He was probably asleep. What time was it anyway? She was about to knock again, a little louder this time, when lips pressed into the curve of her neck. Her books clamored to the floor. Knowing it was Jackson didn't stop her from being startled. Without looking up at him, she bent down to the floor to retrieve her books. A smiling, bare-chested Jackson knelt down to help her. Why did he refuse to wear a shirt at night?

"I thought you were in bed for the night," he said, relieving her of the books she held and picking up the last few remaining on the floor.

"I need to talk to you," she blurted out. "I think I'm supposed to love Tom."

The color drained from Jackson's face.

# Unspoken Words

"No!" she exclaimed in panic and clamped her hand over her mouth hoping she didn't disturb Charles and Natalie. "Can we go in your room and talk, please? I need your help."

"He's done bad things to me, Jackson," she said as Jackson put her books on a small desk. "And he's hurt me…but I'm supposed to forgive him, aren't I? I'm supposed to love him."

Jackson's blood ran hot at the idea of Evelyn loving Tom. He had to remind himself that loving our enemies was exactly what God called us to do.

"Could you put on a shirt?" Evelyn asked, drawing him out of his brooding. Her cheeks were dusted with pink. He complied and pulled a sweatshirt over his head. "I'm right, aren't I?" she asked, bringing the conversation back to her loving Tom.

"Yes," he choked out.

"Does that mean I have to be friends with him?"

"Absolutely not," he answered. He was almost certain he growled it out.

"I'm sorry, Jackson. Your dad was helping me research a topic with the Bible. I thought you would be a good person to talk to since you know so much about the Bible and because you know me, but this isn't fair to you. I didn't think about how it would make you feel." She turned to gather her things again.

Jackson watched her preparing to leave his room. The sight of her in her nightclothes always made him smile. They showed off nothing. Nothing. It was something else. When he saw her like this, or like when he had joined her for her run, it was just her. And he loved her.

"Hang on," he said and took her books. Just as in her room, there were two chairs that faced each other. His pair had a small table between them. He placed her books on the table and drew it closer to one of the chairs. They were large, comfortable looking, chairs. He sat in one, the one he had moved the table close to, and motioned her towards him. He was quick to grab the back of her pants when she passed him to take the other seat. "Uh-uh," he said with one of his roguish grins and pulled her into his lap. "If we're going to talk about you loving that man, I'm going to need you close." He trapped her chin in the pinch of his fingers and kissed her lightly. Then a little not-so-lightly. "Ok, on to love…"

They hunted through the scriptures into the early hours of the morning. The commentary was a great tool. Jackson was grateful his father lent it to her. When she had questions about the context of different verses, he tried to explain for her. The Scriptures he had memorized seemed to help her a lot.

He held her as she sobbed through the final realization that she was being asked to love someone who had bullied her throughout her whole life, tried to corrupt her innocence, and brutally sought to take her purity. He held her with his own heart breaking, and prayed over her for healing from the all the hurt she'd experienced at Tom's hands, and for wisdom in how to handle her situation. He prayed strength and love over her as she faced this difficult road of forgiveness. And he prayed for himself too, that he would walk the road of forgiveness and love and mercy with her, and that he would keep his heart and his hands clean of the violence he harbored towards Tom.

"Jackson?" Evelyn whispered after their prayer.

"Hmm?"

"I'm tired." Her head lifted from his chest to look into his face. Tired was an understatement. Still, tired had never looked so beautiful.

"You should go to bed."

She nodded. He noted little lines of – was it sadness – forming on her brow.

He gently kissed her forehead. "I love you, my brave, beautiful girl," he whispered, before touching his lips to hers. He had intended to kiss her then, harder, longer, but Evelyn stole her lips away.

"Jackson..." Evelyn started, wrestling with her timidness and desires. "I'm not..."

It felt natural for him to hold and kiss this woman he loved, so natural that he frequently forgot she didn't feel the same way. He tugged a strand of her hair playfully, wanting to ease her mind. "It's late, Love. Let's get you to bed."

## Chapter 39

Their first two days with Charles and Natalie flew by in a whirlwind and Christmas Eve was upon them. Evelyn dressed hurriedly in her excitement to hear more from God's Word but stopped in her tracks when she found Jackson waiting outside her door as she opened it. He smiled mischievously and stole her back into her room, leaving the door open only a crack.

She had managed to keep a safe distance between the two of them over the past few days. Jackson had thought after their late night together talking about love, she would have been less guarded with him. If anything, she'd built her walls higher. Had she not still trembled at his touch, he would have thought she had changed her mind about him. When he managed to be near her, he could feel her attraction to him. But she had kept him away for too long now. Every day since he met her, he had wanted to kiss her. After tasting her lips, the desire was overpowering.

Evelyn's innocent wide eyes and red cheeks made her all the more beautiful to Jackson. She knew what he was there for and she stood frozen waiting for him to take it. "You're still so scared of me."

"Yes," she said, trying so hard to swallow that fear. She was scared of him, but he also made her head swim with the love she had for him.

"I love you, my Beloved." Jackson tilted her chin up, making her look at him. "May I?" Her cheeks bloomed crimson, but she nodded, ever so slightly, and he kissed her. He kissed her gently, knowing the passion he felt, if expressed, would scare her more. Her fingers dragged against his chest as her fists closed gripping his shirt. He took his lips away, sighing and letting his lips brush her neck.

Evelyn's knees gave out under her. Jackson locked his arms about her, keeping her on her feet, letting a little chuckle escape him…until she pushed out of his arms.

## Unspoken Words

Evelyn pressed her hand against her heart, trying to get it under control and her breathing back to normal. However, the wretched thing was determined to pound a wildly unsteady beat within her. Once she was stable, she looked up at Jackson and offered a small embarrassed smile. The mischief that played in his eyes a brief moment before was gone, replaced by a great deal of concern. "Just a small panic attack. You can be a little overwhelming."

"I am trying to move slowly."

Evelyn laughed softly. "Before Thursday I was convinced you weren't moving fast enough. It's not you, Jackson. This is all so new to me. It just happened, and now we're here, and I have no idea what you want from me or what we are."

"But you still love me…" Jackson asked, a smile playing on his lips.

"I love you." Evelyn watched him walk towards her and slide his arm around her waist.

"And you enjoy me touching you?"

"Yes." Her heart was racing again. "And trying to get used to it."

"And kissing?" The mischief was back in his eyes, and the fire.

She wrapped her arms around him and rested her head on his chest, needing his comfort more than the pleasure of his lips. "Your kiss takes my breath away. But can we talk about us before we do much more of that?"

They did have a lot to talk about, and every kiss he took before that conversation was a stolen one. The truth about her parents' identities and the circumstances of her birth was enough to jeopardize her readiness to be in a relationship. But every moment he kept those details to himself was likely to increase the betrayal she would feel. Then there was a good deal about himself he still needed her to know; shameful details he would have to confess to the woman he loved. He hugged her tighter knowing these blissful embraces could be among their last. "Yes. We'll talk tonight."

Church, at a glance, was much the same as the last time Evelyn had joined them. They started with prayer and hymns, Charles read and they discussed, and they ended again in communion and prayer. Evelyn sat in the back and listened intently to everything being read and said. It was a miracle, though, that she could think of anything other than Jackson's arm possessively wrapped around her back.

They were reading the Christmas story. Evelyn had no idea Christmas had to do with the Bible. Everything from the virgin mother to Jesus being born in a stable and being hunted by a jealous king was new to her. Evelyn's heart trembled for Mary, thinking of how terrifying it must have been to have to run for her son's life. This time, when communion was offered, Evelyn partook and felt the humbling honor of being able to do so, in being God's child.

After church, Jackson kept his arm around Evelyn as they talked with the others. It had no logic, being in a room where he was the only single man, but he was determined to show everyone Evelyn was his. She didn't seem to mind. He knew he didn't deserve the way she looked up adoringly at him whenever he spoke, or how her eyes smiled every time he looked down at her, but he cherished it.

"I see things are different from the last time we saw you two," Claire said, moving toward them with Nathan and their three children.

"Yes." Jackson smiled down at Evelyn, making her heart leap. "Took us a little while, but we finally figured things out."

"I'm glad. You looked pretty frustrated last time," Claire teased, and she and Nathan laughed at Jackson.

Jackson laughed sardonically at his friends. "Well, I was going to invite you all to stay for lunch, but I think I'll just forget to do that now."

"I hate to disappoint you," Claire smiled, "but your mother already invited us, and we accepted."

Before long, Natalie had an elaborate lunch of roast beef, vegetables, potatoes with gravy, and hot rolls spread across the festive dining room table. Natalie and Claire did most of the talking, taking turns teasing Jackson and Nathan with childhood stories. As she listened, Evelyn got the feeling Jackson had liked Claire at one point. If she was right, she wondered why Claire chose Nathan. Even if she was wrong, Claire had said she was the one who pursued Nathan.

Claire was beautiful. Not in a seductive way like Sarah, but the best way Evelyn could describe it was that she was not just a natural beauty, but a vision of nature taken human form. She had brown hair with a wonderful, almost curly, wave to it falling just past her shoulders. Her green eyes were the color of a spring-time meadow, and she had adorable freckles dotting her face giving her a youthful look. Evelyn guessed she'd be one to age with grace. Looking between the three childhood friends, she wondered again why Claire hadn't chosen Jackson.

Everyone but the children had finished their plates and the conversation finally made its way around to Evelyn and Jackson.

"Evelyn," Claire asked, "How did Jack manage to win your affections? He's sitting pretty proud over there next to you, so I'm guessing you were a hard catch."

Jackson smiled at Evelyn as he put his hand on her knee. Evelyn's cheeks warmed. "No, it wasn't hard for him to catch me. He had my attention from the moment we met. Actually, I almost fell off of a ladder the first time he talked to me." Evelyn laughed but was frustrated with herself. Never having been in a relationship before, she wasn't sure how much was appropriate to tell them.

"Jack always did have a way of affecting girls," Claire said.

Evelyn wasn't surprised that the sight of Jackson had captivated other women before.

"So, if she wasn't a challenge for you, why were you so uptight at Thanksgiving?" Claire asked Jackson.

Jackson kept his eyes on Evelyn for a moment, then turned to Claire. "It wasn't as easy as she thinks. She doesn't know it, but I thought she had forgotten me as soon as she turned back to the books the first time we met. It took over a year for her to speak to me outside of the library. And as for my frustration...I'll just say I didn't know what to do or say around her."

"I told you she's good for him!" Natalie laughed. "She's the first girl I've ever seen humble my son. She's a miracle, and she doesn't even know it." Everyone laughed, except for Evelyn. She couldn't understand what was so funny, nor did she like all the insinuation of a parade of women through Jackson's life, even though she knew there had been others.

"Then how'd you finally get together?" Nathan asked Jackson.

Evelyn looked at Jackson, and for once, he looked unsure. That was unexpected. Everyone else saw it too. "Oh no, Jack, what'd you do?"

"Remember that night, right after we graduated high school?" Jackson asked. Evelyn had no idea what he was referring to, but the shame and embarrassment shrouding Jackson implied something bad had happened.

"No," Claire breathed, breaking the awkward silence. "Jack...you didn't..."

It took Nathan just a moment longer. "You kissed someone else again?" he almost choked.

*Again?* Evelyn thought, trying to push it from her mind. Whatever, or whomever, was in the past, would stay in the past.

"Gross." Everyone looked at Ryan, whose face was contorted in his disgust at the mere thought of kissing a girl as he pushed his vegetables around his plate. Laughter exploded around the table. This time Evelyn joined in, and Charles all but choked on his water.

"Yes," Jackson confessed. "It was gross."

"But that was after I made her go out with two other guys," Jackson added sheepishly.

"Jack, Jack, Jack," Nathan said, shaking his head. "You have to explain."

"Yeah, the Jack we know would never send someone else out with the girl he liked, even if you couldn't have her...especially if you couldn't have her," Claire explained.

Jackson's dark eyes focused on only Evelyn. "I don't know what I was thinking."

Evelyn had seen that look before, and she still couldn't quite grasp its depth, but she knew now there was love in it. "That's not true," Evelyn countered, letting his eyes entrap her. "You were trying to keep me safe."

"Now, wait just a minute...Jack kissed someone else. Evelyn, what possessed you to forgive him for that? And Jack, didn't you learn your lesson the first time?" Claire questioned like an exasperated mother.

"I was out with another man that night," Evelyn suddenly stated defensively, wanting the matter cleared and over with. "He had every right to kiss whoever he wanted to. He did nothing wrong, but he still asked for forgiveness. He followed me out into the snow, even after I said some very unkind things. He looked scared and broken. I know what that feels like. I love him. How could I leave him to face those things alone, especially when he always protects me?"

Jackson realized his mouth was gaping and closed it. Looking from Evelyn to the others, he had to blink to see if the challenge in her eyes was really there.

It was.

He almost laughed. No one dared one more word on the subject.

"Well I think you'll be preaching next week," Charles said, breaking the silence. "You're the youngest Christian here, and you probably understand love better than any of us. I'm impressed."

Natalie had been watching the way her son and Evelyn looked at each other throughout the meal. She had seen plenty of girls look at her son, and she'd seen her son look at plenty of girls…too many for her liking. But something was different this time. There was more than just attraction, that couldn't be denied; there was respect. She smiled to herself, as mothers often do when they see something pure and good in their child's life. Evelyn was that something.

## Chapter 40

Once Charles and Natalie had gone to bed, Jackson asked Evelyn to wait for him to come and get her. After showering, Evelyn waited in the kitchen wearing her nightclothes - grey linen pants and a matching loose-fitting long-sleeved grey shirt. Leaning over the sink with her elbows resting on the counter, she sipped a glass of water as she drank in the view of the dark starry night. A quick, shallow gasp escaped her as familiar hands slid around her. She smiled, happy to have Jackson with her again.

"I like your tattoo." Evelyn straightened so her shirt once again covered the small of her back, and turned quickly in Jackson's arms. "Why are you embarrassed?"

"It's embarrassing…It's just, I've seen you…" The memory of her referring to him as a candy shop flushed her with heat. "I don't look like Sarah. I see how men…" *I saw how you…* "are attracted to her. I just don't want to…It scares me…" Why was it so hard to talk to him? She cleared her throat. "I'd just rather keep myself covered."

Jackson shook his head. "Thank you for what you said today at lunch in my defense." He kissed the tip of her nose. "It meant a lot to me to hear you say what you did."

Evelyn smiled and rested her head against his chest as he pulled her into him, her hands unintentionally gripping his shirt.

"Do you know its torture when you do that?"

"When I do what?" She asked, looking up again.

"Grip my shirt that way."

She dropped her hands from him. "Sorry. I only do it because I shake so badly around you."

He gave her a curious smile. "Is that the only reason?" Her blush gave her away. "I didn't think so." Jackson let the subject drop and led her up to the sunroom.

The only lights on in the room were the ones twinkling on the branches of the Christmas tree. The couches had been pushed back to make way for a bed of blankets and pillows just below the tree. She obeyed Jackson when he told her to sit and watched as he retrieved a tray she hadn't noticed when she looked over the transformed room.

Jackson set the tray of cookies on one side of Evelyn and handed her a cup of hot chocolate, then sat on her other side. "I made it all myself, as a way to say I love you. I made the hot chocolate while you were showering. You shower very fast by the way."

Evelyn smiled and drank her hot chocolate. Stars shone through the wall of windows and the moonlight reflected off the snow covering everything outside. After what seemed like a long time, she put her cup down and lay back against the pillows behind her. "Who am I that I get to be here with you, to be served hot chocolate and cookies, and somehow be loved by you?"

Jackson lay back next to her and turned on his side to face her. "You're the woman I'll never deserve." Even in the dim light, he could see her blush. "I know you want to talk about us, but I need to tell you some things first. There's a lot I need to tell you."

Evelyn sat up again, too nervous to recline as she was. Jackson appeared very uncomfortable. The change in his demeanor happened so fast, it worried Evelyn even more than she already was. She held her breath as she waited for him to continue.

"There are two main things I need to talk to you about. The first concerns my past." *God, please guide my words, and please let her forgive me.* "I haven't been completely honest with you about my past with women.

"You asked me on our drive home after Thanksgiving about how many girls I've dated...and if I had loved any of them. I wasn't lying when I answered you. I only had four girlfriends in college, but you should know I dated frequently and, if you asked any of them, I was just the same as every other man, just the same as Tom." He saw the terror flash across her face, but forced himself to continue. "Girls have always sought me out, and I knew what they would let me get away with. A lot of them were like Sarah, but some of them were nice girls who just had too much to drink. I promise you, I never crossed any lines like Tom did, or anything remotely close to it, and I have never used my uniform against a woman, nor would I ever. My interactions with women, when I was off-duty, however, were anything but pure."

Evelyn felt something strong, but she didn't think it was anger. Maybe jealousy, though she wasn't sure. She'd never experienced this particular emotion before. "When was the last time you dated a woman besides me?"

"The night I got attacked in New Mexico."

"What happened there?"

"Four men attacked me on my way to work after being at a..." he hesitated being honest with her, and hated himself for it, "after being at the home of the woman I was dating. I was shot twice and had a few of my ribs broken...to say it was a bad day would be a gross understatement." The details of his story were gruesome, and still difficult to remember. Now that he was physically healed and the pain from his wounds no longer afflicted him, it was easier to pretend like he could forget what had happened that morning.

"Why did you stop seeing her?" She saw pain flash across his face briefly. If she had blinked, she would have missed it.

"She was in on it. She told the men where and when to find me." Evelyn looked like she was about to break apart, and Jackson hated that he had to go on. "She was what extremists call a huntress...an assassin. I don't know why God protected me, even while I was living in sin. Most huntresses do the killing themselves and people don't typically survive their attacks. But it was good that she was involved. I wouldn't have had the strength to leave her if she hadn't betrayed me. And anyway, she's in jail now."

"What do you mean by living in sin?"

Jackson cringed. He'd hoped that one, slipped-in, comment would explain his relationship with the woman. He was such a coward. And he'd forgotten how foreign God's Word was to Evelyn...no one outside of the Church would understand his cryptic comment.

"God made marriage for..." He felt like a schoolboy blundering through his explanation. "That is, He was very specific..." He had to take a breath. This was embarrassing and he was pathetic. "I'd always planned to save myself for my bride."

Evelyn looked utterly confused.

"I planned to not have sex with a woman before I was married. I slept with the huntress. For three months I 'lived in that sin.' It's why I had been at her house before the attack. I went to her like a dumb puppy and turned my back on everything I ever believed…including God. I haven't been with anyone since, and I will not cross that line again until I'm married."

Evelyn's heart broke for Jackson, even while it ached over what his confession meant for her. She'd actually assumed he'd been with women before…almost everyone but herself had. Hearing it still hurt. "But that was a long time ago. You haven't dated anyone since her?"

"No. I guess you could say that after getting my ribs broken and getting shot, God got my attention. Then I met you, and I already told you I couldn't think about anyone except you after we met."

Tears were swelling in Evelyn's eyes. "Were you scared?"

"No," Jackson answered honestly. "I was very angry." There was still more, worse. "Evelyn, you need to know I killed two of them." He frowned when he felt her shudder and shift away, ever so slightly. "I didn't want to; I swear to you I didn't. But it took me a little while to care about the lives I ended. I justified it by telling myself there were four of them, and only one of me, so I had no choice. But it eventually caught up with me. I know now that I did have a choice, and I chose selfishly." He had taken two men's lives. Nothing could justify that.

"Those men would have hurt others if you didn't stop them," she said, and meant it, too. No one would have come through her door to save her from Tom if he had died that night. "I'm sorry you had to experience that, all of it." Distress still lined Jackson's face. The words from Psalm 32 filled Evelyn's mind as she sat there with him. Charles had suggested she read it yesterday while she was avoiding Jackson. She had it memorized now. "'Oh, what joy for those whose disobedience is forgiven, whose sin is put out of sight. Yes, what joy for those whose record the LORD has cleared of guilt, whose lives are lived in complete honesty.'" She inched closer to him and squeezed his hands. "Your dad said it was one of your favorites. I think I see why now."

He truly would never deserve her. Evelyn frequently humbled Jackson, but never more so than now. He wished there was nothing more they needed to talk about, that he could simply hold her until the sun came up.

But there was more, and there was no easy way to tell her. "The second thing is about your parents. But you have to understand, I didn't know any of this before Friday." He saw the depth of her confusion in her eyes. "We – you and I – we've met before, a long time ago…twenty years ago. Your parents and my parents were friends before you were born."

Evelyn wasn't sure how to hear what he was saying. "Jackson, I don't even know who my dad is. How could you know?"

"I didn't know until you took me to your mother's grave. Your father, Harold Thompson, was the Secretary of State and good friends with my father. He met and married your mother on a business trip to Texas. Extremists murdered your father, and your mother came to my parents looking for safety. There was no way to get her back to Texas after that. Extremists were looking for her, and she was pregnant with you. The morning after you were born, we woke up and both of you were gone. We didn't even know your name, where she was going, or any of her plans."

Evelyn felt as if she should be freaking out, having an emotional breakdown of some sort, but she wasn't. No doubt it would come later. "So…I was born here?"

"Yes."

"And you knew my mother?"

"Yes."

"And she wasn't a drug addict?"

"No."

"My files say she was."

"Your file says whatever story she told them. She probably lied about it to keep you safe. No one would be looking for a drug addict's daughter. My father's going to look into it after Christmas." He forgot he hadn't told her that his parents knew this information too. "My parents only found out Friday as well. I needed to talk to my father to make sure I wasn't wrong. But your mother was not a drug addict before you were born. She was a soft-spoken, kind-hearted woman who loved you very much. She called you her flower. I don't know what happened after she left, but I wouldn't blame her for anything after losing your father and then you too. But before then, she was as pure as you are."

"Thank you for telling me." Evelyn's mind refused to think about what she'd just heard about her parents. Jackson's past was a needed distraction. "What was her name?"

"Whose?" Jackson asked. He worried about the glassy look in Evelyn's eyes. "Your mother's? You know that."

Evelyn shook her head. "No. The woman you had sex with." She hadn't meant to say it so plainly.

Jackson hadn't spoken her name since he visited her when he got out of the hospital. Even locked in a cell and dressed in criminal's clothing, she was enticing, and he hated her for it. That first night he met her, she had made him a slave to his fleshly desire for her body and kept him shackled for three months. He still struggled with hatred for her, but prayed against it every time it rose in him again. "Alice."

"How did you meet?"

Jackson noted her fidgeting hands. Not a good sign. "At a gym. She sought me out."

"How long did you date her?"

Jackson wasn't accustomed to talking about himself. Aside from the report he had to write, and the trials he had to attend, he didn't share these details of his life with anyone; not even his parents. They knew the basics, but not every intimate detail like Evelyn sought. But he knew she deserved an answer to every question she had, so he tried not to let his anxiety show. "Three months."

"I thought you said...never mind. I must have misunderstood."

He knew what she meant. He had already admitted they slept together for three months. "No, you didn't. I took her home with me the first night."

Oh. That shocked Evelyn out of the daze she was in. "You walked away from me when we met. She must be very beautiful, to captivate you so quickly."

Jackson was glad to see life back in her eyes, but knew he needed to affirm her. "She had her charms, but she is nowhere near as beautiful as you. And she didn't captivate me, you do. She ensnared me. I would let men talk about Alice. I didn't respect her enough," *or myself,* "to keep people from saying things. I've never let men talk about you, even before I really knew you. Maybe I shouldn't tell you, but I want you more than I ever wanted her. And, if you will remember, I did not walk away; you did."

Evelyn smiled sadly. "Do you mind if I go? I just want to go to bed." She was standing even as she spoke, not waiting for an answer. She left Jackson sitting alone and when she knew she was out of sight, she ran to her room to get away from everything she'd heard.

As soon as her door was closed, she collapsed on the floor and cried, though she wasn't entirely sure what she was crying about. It was good news that her father had been a good man, and that her parents had been married, and that she had been loved and not the accident she always assumed she had been. And it was good news that she now had a connection to her past through the people she loved most. But something still tore at her heart.

As she cried, she tried to discern her feelings about Jackson's past. She knew she didn't judge him for what he had done; his actions against those men were in self-defense, and she'd seen Sarah dig her claws into the hearts of enough men to know how easily they could fall prey to seductive women. She discovered her hurt in her own shortcomings. After being with that Alice woman, how could she ever be enough for Jackson? She wasn't sure how it was possible to be jealous of the woman who hurt the man she loved; but she was. So she cried and cried until she couldn't cry anymore. When she had shed every last tear, she finally crawled into bed and tried to sleep.

# Chapter 41

Evelyn wasn't sure what woke her up. There wasn't a noise. No nightmare. It was too dark to be morning. She checked the clock. Three o'clock. She lay restless for a few minutes until she decided she would get a drink of water. As she passed the sunroom she looked in and saw Jackson.

He sat on the floor with his legs crossed and his head in his hands and his lips moving, though she heard no sound. She couldn't understand why he wasn't in bed. She whispered in to him, "Jackson?" He became rigid at the sound of her voice. "Jackson, why are you still up?"

"I just lost track of time." He didn't look up at her.

Something told her to go to him, so she did. Kneeling in front of him, she could see the agony on his face. She forgot about her own pain, her insecurities; she forgot about herself completely. She climbed into his lap and wrapped her arms around him, hoping she could love the pain out of him. The strength of his arms around her fought against the fear in her heart and, after some time, she could speak. "I love you, Jackson." She thought she felt him laughing, but when she looked at him, she saw he was crying.

It wasn't fear; it was absolute terror that swept through her. "Jackson!" She would have jumped away from him if he wasn't holding her still. "Please tell me what's wrong."

Jackson remembered the last time he had cried. He was seven, and he had learned that Justine Thompson and her baby girl were gone. And now that precious child was back, grown and beautiful, and she loved him. "Everything's wrong," he admitted. "I am an adulterer, and a murderer, and I've rejoiced in seeing you open your heart to me when I should have made you close it and lock it away from me. I tried so hard to protect you from everyone else, but it's me who puts your heart in real danger."

## Unspoken Words

She shook her head and smiled. It was her turn to speak against the lies in his heart. "Do you want to know what I see when I look at you?" she began, remembering how he spoke against the darkness in her own heart. "I see a man, a very handsome man, who has had to endure some terrible things." She spread her hands over his chest and ran them up to his shoulders. "I see a man who is built for battle, who has never backed down. I see a man who will make tough decisions to protect those who need protecting, and who will sacrifice himself for those he loves. I see a man who loves deeply but judges himself too harshly." She took his hands in hers and kissed them. "I see a man with strong hands that have saved me so many times and arms that hold me together when I'm breaking apart. You are fierce and strong, and you are kind and just.

"You could break others, but you choose to build them up." She let his hands go and draped her arms about his neck. She forced herself to look straight in his eyes. "Jackson, you brought me into your family and your home. You've fought for me, you've protected me, and you were willing to let me go to keep me safe. You're walking a path of selflessness, even though I know you don't see it that way. You're my hero." She bit her lip nervously. "When you look at me you send chills through me, the touch of your hands makes me tremble. Since the first time you kissed me, I haven't been able to stop thinking about it." She leaned in and whispered against his lips: "That is what you must see in yourself." For the first time, she kissed him.

Jackson was dangerously close to losing control. Emotions raw from the agonizing hours not knowing if his past had pushed her away, his body ached for her comfort. He could feel her pulse matching his, racing under his palms as he cupped her face. Gasping for air to clear his mind, he pushed her out of his lap.

"I'm sorry," he spoke, his voice deep and rough with his emotions. These feelings, yearnings, were all too familiar. He had been praying unceasingly for her since she left him earlier that night. He prayed for her comfort, for understanding, and for healing. And he prayed she'd return. He couldn't let himself use her this way.

He kept his eyes closed and his hands tight around her arms as he tried to calm down. Weakness against his flesh was his shame. He couldn't have her any closer, but he didn't want her to leave either. When he opened his eyes, he wasn't surprised that Evelyn's were downcast. He let go of her arms and tipped her chin up. "I'm sorry I pushed you off my lap, but I had to get you away from me. I was losing control." He smiled weakly at her. "You can be a little overwhelming." Seeing her blush at her own words repeated back to her made him smile wider. "I think it's time we talked about us."

Evelyn moved to sit next to Jackson and, continuing in her newfound boldness, held his hand as they talked. "So, you're my boyfriend, and I'm your girlfriend, right?"

Jackson lifted their hands and kissed her fingers. "Yes. That's what we are, for now."

Evelyn shifted slightly at those last words. "What do you want from me, as your girlfriend?"

Jackson took his time answering. He'd thought about what it would mean to have Evelyn in his life this way, but he hadn't thought about it in the way she was asking. "Hmm," he started, and smiled as she laid her head on his shoulder. "I guess what I want from you is honesty. Honesty and a lot of help keeping me accountable."

"I don't understand what that means."

"Well," he tried again, "I want you to always be honest with me about what you're thinking and feeling; especially if I hurt you or scare you, or if you decide you don't want to be with me anymore." He felt her laugh, but he was very serious. "And as far as accountability goes, I'm going to take you into my bed if I don't have your help fighting temptation. I'm sorry to be so blunt. After this I won't speak so plainly about it and I will only bring it up if it becomes absolutely necessary, but this one time I just need to be honest. I want you that way, but not until we're married…if you decide that's what you want. Until then, I need to protect you from my desires, and I'll need your help doing that. Being alone will be difficult, so it wouldn't hurt for you to let Bekah know when we're going to be together. She seems rather protective of you, and I have a feeling she'll be keeping an eye on us anyway. If I scare you, or you are uncomfortable or nervous, you need to tell me. I never want to hurt you and I don't want us to have any regrets. You being honest and open with me will help me behave." Evelyn sat quietly next to him and he wondered what she was thinking, if he had been too bold in what he said.

Evelyn spoke softly when she finally spoke. "Why did you bring up marriage?"

"Why wouldn't I, if we're talking about us?" She sat quietly, appearing unsettled. Jackson felt her despair. "Do you know why I'm dating you?"

"Because you say you love me," she whispered.

He let go of her hand and took her in his arms. "Look at me, Beloved." When she did, he kissed her lightly. "I want to marry you because I love you. I'm dating you so I can try and convince you to marry me. I've known for a while now that I want you as my wife, and I'd marry you this second if you'd say yes."

Evelyn didn't say anything. She already felt the embarrassment and shame of her unladylike forwardness, kissing him the way she did just moments ago, and now Jackson was talking about marriage. She didn't know anything about how to be a wife…she had only scratched the surface of love just a few days ago! But even though she was terrified of marriage, she knew she would say yes if he asked. "I love you, Jackson."

"I love you, too."

## Chapter 42

Natalie found her son and Evelyn asleep in the sunroom. She was relieved they were sitting up against the couch. If she'd found her son lying down with this sweet girl, she would have had to kick him in the shins. She was so glad her son had fallen in love with Evelyn. She had worried about her son's choices when it came to women; he didn't know how much she knew of his life away from their home. She saw the pain in his heart when he came home from New Mexico. It hadn't been the first time she saw shame in her son's eyes.

God taught Natalie how to pray through mothering Jackson. She learned how to trust Him when her boy left for college and was sent to New Mexico, and she rejoiced seeing her son choose life in Christ after he had been through hell. And now he had found his bride; though she wondered if he knew that. She couldn't have hand chosen a better wife for her son. She had already seen her son strengthened by Evelyn's presence in his life. She humbled his pride and encouraged his heart.

Natalie didn't want to intrude on them, but she was impatient for them to wake up. She knelt by her son and squeezed his arm gently. His eyes shot open, but he remained perfectly still. She mouthed, "Merry Christmas," tapped her wrist, as if she wore a watch, smiled, and left.

Evelyn was learning quickly holidays in the Monroe home meant food, and lots of it. She had woken up that morning with Jackson nuzzling her cheek and the smell of breakfast making her stomach growl.

The morning was cheerful and splendid in every way and Evelyn couldn't contain the excitement from bubbling out of her. It was, after all, her first real Christmas and all the childhood magic of the miraculous day was fresh and new to her. Unlike their first days with Charles and Natalie, Evelyn welcomed Jackson's affections. Even as they sat across from each other eating breakfast, their feet touched under the table. Jackson noticed that even though she didn't run from him anymore, there was a new shyness about her, a shyness that welcomed his pursuit.

Evelyn eagerly offered him her assistance when Jackson volunteered to do the breakfast dishes. The look she saw pass between Charles and Natalie made her think that they were either very glad to have some time to themselves, or they were laughing about something to do with her and Jackson. She didn't mind not knowing; the look that passed between them was filled with kindness.

Since Jackson knew the kitchen better than Evelyn, she opted for the washing portion so Jackson could dry and put the dishes away. They worked in a comfortable silence for some time, but Evelyn's mind was far from quiet. She was still digesting all that she'd learned from the night before, and more than a few unfamiliar emotions continued to run through her. An odd sense of feeling at home for the first time floated in and out as she thought about the possibility of standing where her mother had once stood, wondering if her mother had ever hovered at this sink washing dishes as she was now.

But last night's conversation was more than pleasant revelations about her mother and reassurance of Jackson's love for her. There were difficult things too. Knowing her father had been murdered and her mother forced into hiding, and that there was someone in Jackson's past who may still have her claws in his heart gave her pause. Then Jackson's hand would brush hers–an intentional touch–and wonder would come upon her. Somehow his touch made her pulse quicken and gave her a wonderfully overwhelming sense of safety at the same time.

"Evelyn?"

Evelyn's mind focused. She wasn't sure how long she had been washing that same dish, but Jackson had finally taken it from her, and alarm now lined his face. It wasn't like her to be inattentive.

"I'm sorry, Jackson," Evelyn apologized, trying to sound light-hearted. "I spaced out for a minute. What were you saying?"

Jackson set the dish down and turned her towards him. "I wasn't saying anything." He took a towel and dried her hands. "I was asking what you were thinking about."

Evelyn knew her blush gave her away. She'd been thinking about that Alice woman, and not in a good way. Her thoughts were embarrassing, even to herself. "Nothing," she said quickly, too quickly. Jackson raised a brow at her. He didn't believe her. "I was just thinking about last night."

"A lot was said last night. What part were you thinking about?"

She wasn't ready to talk about the thoughts preoccupying her mind so completely. She hugged Jackson, feeling somehow smaller in his arms than she normally did, and pressed her cheek to his chest. One thing she did know, and that she was willing to share. "I love you."

Jackson's heart swelled the way she said those three simple words. He knew there was more she had been thinking about, but somehow knowing she loved him, and that he loved her too, was enough right now. She'd share whatever she was wrestling with when she was ready. He wasn't blessed with an abundance of patience, but for her, he'd learn it.

*Love is patient...love is patient.*

# Chapter 43

After the dishes were finished, Evelyn and Jackson followed Natalie's youthful laughter and found her and Charles at the piano.

"Evelyn dear, *you* want to sing carols before we open gifts, don't you?" Natalie asked, pleading with her eyes and her tone for Evelyn to say yes.

Evelyn smiled only a small smile. "I'm afraid I don't know any; but I'd love to listen to all of you." Evelyn could see her comment had caught Natalie off guard. She understood though; who didn't know Christmas carols? There were a few that she could hum, and even knew a few words too, but none she knew well enough to feel comfortable singing along with Jackson and his family.

"Well then, young lady," Charles said with a wonderful twinkle in his eyes. "It's about time you learn some." He took Evelyn's shoulders and led her to sit next to Natalie on the piano bench. "You can read along as Natalie plays and, when you feel you've got the hang of it, you join in with us."

Evelyn smiled pleasantly enough at Charles' encouraging words, but inside she suspected she wouldn't be joining them in song any time soon, if ever. But Charles, like his son, was very good at reading her thoughts.

"We'll just keep singing through the song until you join us."

Jackson appreciated his father handling the situation so well. He knew Evelyn had been embarrassed to have to admit she didn't know any carols, but after today she surely would. With a wink from Charles to his wife, Natalie began to play *Deck the Halls*. It was a joyful noise, to be sure, and Evelyn surprised herself as she quickly learned the tune and joined in chorus with them. As they followed with *Go, Tell It On The Mountain* and then *Joy To The World*, the Monroes found it difficult to keep singing. In fact, Jackson had quit singing all together. He had heard Evelyn hum a hymn quietly during their last stay with his parents, but he'd never heard her sing outright before now. He was sure even the angels must have been leaning down from heaven to hear her song.

Natalie flipped through her music and Jackson smiled when he saw the next song she stopped at: *O Holy Night*.

"Evelyn?" Natalie paused. "I wonder if you would bless us and sing this for us?" Evelyn's alarm was apparent, but Natalie pressed on. "We could sing it through once, so you could get a feel for it. You're catching on so quickly and you have a beautiful voice."

"I –" Evelyn was choking on her words as fear gripped her, tightening her chest and closing her throat. She had been having so much fun singing with them, she hadn't noticed them admiring her voice.

"Natalie," Charles spoke calmly to his wife, as he smiled reassuringly at Evelyn. "You can't expect her to put on a private concert for us just because she has the voice of an angel. But Evelyn," he now spoke to her, "would you be willing to let Natalie break from this song? Jackson stopped singing two songs ago, but I'd be honored if you'd sing with me."

*Oh Charles*, thought Evelyn, *what would I do without you?* With a calming breath, she nodded. "I think I can do that. But could we still do as Natalie said, and everyone sing through it once so I can learn it first?"

Natalie's face lit like a child's on Christmas morning. Being as it was Christmas morning, it was very fitting. "Of course, my dear."

Evelyn looked up at Charles and Jackson felt her panic. "You promise to keep singing with me, right?"

Charles placed his hand gently on her shoulder. It didn't surprise him that she was shaking some. "I'll sing constant and loud if you promise to do the same." She nodded nervously, then turned to the music as Natalie began to play.

Evelyn was pleasantly surprised the song was a melody that she knew well, so she only had to read the words. Natalie and Jackson sang it through twice before falling silent. Charles kept up his part of the deal, as she knew he would, and sang constant and strong. Evelyn let the words rain over her, feeling every word she sang.

## Janna Halterman

*O holy night!*
*The stars are brightly shining*
*It is the night of the dear Savior's birth!*
*Long lay the world in sin and error pining*
*Till he appear'd and the soul felt its worth.*
*A thrill of hope the weary world rejoices*
*For yonder breaks a new and glorious morn.*

Oh, how she knew the truth in those words! Her whole life she'd lain in sin and error, and when she found Him, she felt its worth: the worth of herself in Him, and His worth! And hope had thrilled her then, as it did now, and as it had all the days in between.

*Fall on your knees*
*O hear the angel voices*
*O night divine*
*O night when Christ was born*
*O night divine, o night*
*O night divine*

Evelyn wanted to fall on her knees, but she stayed seated on the bench with her eyes closed now, singing to the Lord. She sang the words with Charles but not as he did. Harmonizing instead and adding inflection and pauses and even words where her heart sang them. The scene they sang out in praise was painted in her mind; a beautiful scene of the birth that changed the world. It was a divine night, she was sure of it, and she sang it from the depths of her soul and her heart. She and Charles sang it through twice together. She wasn't aware of her tears until Natalie's playing stopped and Evelyn opened her eyes.

Silence hung around them for a few moments. Evelyn's cheeks burned in embarrassment. "I'm sorry," she said timidly, wiping her cheeks dry.

Natalie put her hand on her knee in a motherly way. "Evelyn dear, don't you ever apologize for worshiping our Lord or being moved to tears through it. You sang beautifully and it was a blessing to hear your voice." Natalie's eyes stung from her own tears pressing forward. "That was your mother's favorite. She sang it with Charles too, almost the same way you did just now, and it was mine and your father's favorite thing to listen to. Your poor father," she smiled at the memory, "he couldn't sing at all. But your mother…" She had to pause to steady her emotions. "Well, I can hear your mother when you sing, and it's a beautiful sound."

Natalie purposefully lightened the mood after that. Though she felt it was important to share with Evelyn about her mother, she also knew that Evelyn was weary with emotion. She needed some light-hearted joy that Christmas morning. After a few laughter-filled songs, they gathered in the sunroom to exchange gifts.

Jackson had been waiting anxiously to give Evelyn the gift he'd purchased for her. He had found it the day after Thanksgiving. After his run with Evelyn, he quickly showered and left the house while his mother expertly kept her busy until he returned. He knew then there was a chance they would still be nothing more than friends by the time Christmas came, but he hoped. She was precious to him, and she needed to know it. Her reaction upon receiving his gift had been of some concern to him if their relationship had remained the same; but recent developments eased those fears and he now waited with great excitement for her to open it.

Evelyn's enjoyment was obvious as she watched the others exchange gifts, her face glowing with wonder and joy. Jackson cherished watching her, and particularly enjoyed seeing her delight at opening the cookbook from his mother filled with all their family recipes.

Evelyn was thrilled that he liked the quilt she made for him. He sat with it wrapped around him while they continued to exchange gifts, giving him a childish look Evelyn found endearing. Father and son each got the other a new gun, making Evelyn and Natalie laugh and tease them for being excessively masculine in their gift choices. And when Natalie and Charles opened their gift from Evelyn, she was overjoyed to see they loved it as much as she'd hoped they would.

Natalie's gift to her son was a mystery to Evelyn. She watched as Jackson read a letter from his mother and was curious at the emotion she saw run over his face. He tucked the letter away and thanked his mother politely, but Evelyn felt like there was much more depth to what had passed between them than they were letting on.

Jackson saved his gift for Evelyn last. He smiled as she tenderly undid the bow and peeled back the wrapping paper to reveal an ivory box with the words *Worth Far More Than Rubies Jeweler* written in crimson lettering on it. He knew she wouldn't recognize the name of the jewelry store, or the Biblical reference, but her eyes made it clear she was enraptured by what she held in her hands. The lid flipped up easily revealing her gift.

The fine box held perfectly beautiful pearls. Evelyn's fingers trembled as she touched the multiple strands of pearls creating the necklace. It was the most beautiful thing she'd ever seen and, most assuredly, the most beautiful thing she'd ever owned. She had never shopped for jewelry before, but there was no doubt this cost him a great deal. Afraid she'd break it or damage it in some way, she closed the box and placed it gently next to her. All she could manage was a simple thank you and a trembling smile. She thought, she hoped, Jackson knew how much she loved it. She would be sure to tell him later, when her emotions from the shock of his gift weren't stealing her voice.

## Chapter 44

Evelyn looked herself over in her mirror, anxiously smoothing the front of her gown. Wearing this dress meant vacation with the Monroes was over.

Her time with them had been so precious to her. After Christmas, the family fell into a comfortable routine, the kind only a family could enjoy, and one Evelyn had never experienced before. They just folded her right into that old, time-tested, love-formed routine. Morning yawns over steaming cups of coffee. Laughter and good food filling their stomachs and souls. But her favorite was the quiet, still moments of peace that she and Jackson shared, sitting close on the sunroom couch, reading God's Word.

Jackson had managed to curb his antics. Aside from the few kisses he stole when he found her alone, he restrained his affection and only held her hand gently, wrapped a protective arm around her, or played with her hair. Her favorite was when his fingers skimmed over her skin on her neck as they ran through her hair.

But that time was over now, and they were back in Syracuse. Charles had a driver lined up to take him and Natalie home after the ball. Though Natalie was disappointed they were leaving so soon, no one argued. Charles was the respected leader of the family.

Dear Charles. Never had Evelyn known a man so strong nor so gentle and kind, and full of love. Her heart broke a little wondering what her own father had been like.

The pain snapped her out of her thoughts, and her eyes refocused on the reflection before her. She had never worn so lovely a dress. Though it was surprisingly comfortable, she was far from comfortable in it. Bekah had assured her time and time again that it was modest, but Evelyn wasn't so sure. The neckline was much lower than she was accustomed to, and she felt strange being wrapped in such elegance.

She smiled at the sight of her necklace. The low neckline of her dress, and her hair pinned up in curls, exposed enough bare skin to create an uncluttered backdrop for showcasing its beauty.

Just as Evelyn buttoned her jacket's top button, the expected knock sounded. Evelyn laughed as Bekah flitted to the door to open it. She was a woman of joy, and that joy made her radiant.

Bekah spun for George as he entered their apartment, and George displayed well his pleasure at seeing her. Bekah's gown was cherry red and sported a deep V at the bust. If Bekah was at all voluptuous, Evelyn thought it would have looked very indecent; but as her figure was, it was darling. The gown was tight down through her hips and then flowed away from her legs mid-thigh, producing a fluttering swirl of fabric about her as she twirled.

Evelyn tried to steady herself as Jackson entered, following George. Her heart fluttered at the sight of him. His suit was tailored to him perfectly, emphasizing his muscular physique and causing Evelyn to become slightly short of breath. She made no effort to try and hide her nerves from him; he wouldn't miss her eyes skirting his or her hands playing at the fabric of her coat. Her fluttering heart jumped when he took her hand and pressed a kiss to it.

Evelyn tried to ignore the chaos of emotions inside of her, and, of course, failed miserably. Thrill was tackled by anxiety, who was then shoved back by happiness, who then was immediately drowned by doubts…over and over the emotions raged, and those were only the ones about Jackson.

Somehow invading the mix with the others were fears of Tom, who, no doubt, would also be at the ball. She held tighter to Jackson as they walked. It still felt strange to be so bold with him, but she needed him, and he steadied her.

Charles and Natalie joined the foursome as they walked to the ball. It only took an introduction to send Bekah and Natalie into merry chatter. Jackson and Evelyn followed silently. Jackson's thumb ran softly over the top of Evelyn's hand that he held firmly. The chills running up her arm had nothing to do with the cold surrounding them.

It was then Evelyn realized Jackson had been quiet their entire walk. Something was wrong.

"Don't worry, dear," Natalie said as they arrived at the door, putting her arm about Evelyn's waist. "You're going to have a splendid time. Jackson's going to have to learn to share, because everyone's going to want to dance with you tonight."

Evelyn forced a smile and let herself focus on other things as they walked into the ball. Beautiful gowns and handsome suits filled the building. Walls and tables were decorated in silver, reds, and white, sparkling fabulously in the dim light. Music sang through the rooms, louder than she had expected; not so loud that you had to shout to be heard, but loud enough to keep conversations private.

Jackson gave his winter jacket to a man just inside the door and turned to take Evelyn's. His hand clutched her coat, but his eyes locked onto her.

"Do you like it?"

He handed over her jacket without as much as a glance at the man who took it. "I do. It's ... you're beautiful." He looked over the curves of her body, and the delicate lace that gently clung to her. He smiled seeing his gift adorning her neck, and forced his eyes up to meet hers. "You're incredibly attractive. If my parents weren't with us, you just might get into trouble in that dress." He laughed at the alarm in her eyes and kissed her forehead. "You know you're safe," he chuckled, taking her arm. "Now, come and dance with me. I promise I'll behave."

After dancing for some time, and enjoying every moment, Jackson and Evelyn joined a group of officers. "Bekah said she moved out," Jackson whispered in Evelyn's ear, nodding towards Sarah and Tom.

Evelyn very much enjoyed the way his lips touched her ear when he was saying something for only her to hear. It made paying attention a little difficult, but she managed.

She nodded. "It makes me nervous not having her there. I worry about Bekah becoming a casualty now, when someone's sent after me." Jackson's hand tightened around hers when she said it, confirming her suspicion that it was just a matter of time before she was attacked. "She sure is something, isn't she?" she asked, speaking of Sarah again. With her black hair, gold jewelry, and practically painted on gold dress, she looked like a goddess from an old mythological tale.

Jackson knew what she meant. Sarah caught almost everyone's attention as she passed them, but his own heart was cold to the snake. The only reason he tracked her was to be sure she was nowhere near his Evelyn.

"Jackson...what's wrong?"

He had been silent for too long. His thoughts were too busy with other things and he was letting it show. "Nothing," he lied. Now wasn't the time for him to tell her what his father had found out from the Madames at her government home or that he himself was being sent back to New Mexico for six months. A letter had been waiting for him when they arrived home earlier that day. Extremists had declared open war in New Mexico, and he was being promoted to Colonel. He had two days to get his work and private affairs in order, and then he had to leave. He didn't want the job, but he had no choice in the matter.

Evelyn looked like she was going to say something when a loud boom and flying debris stopped them in their tracks.

It was a small explosion on the other side of the room, but they felt the heat of it. The resulting chaos did more than irritate Jackson. These were officers, they shouldn't panic. He took Evelyn's arm and led her to a back door. "Wait here for Bekah, then go to your apartment and wait there for me and George. Do not leave this building without Bekah at your side, and don't open your door for anyone but me or George. Do you understand me?" He knew he was speaking sternly, but there wasn't time for gentleness. She nodded and he left, proud of her calmness, and amazed at the lack of fear he sensed.

Evelyn stood watching the chaos. The explosion had frightened her, but Jackson's cool demeanor steadied her own emotions.

A fire had resulted from the explosion and, with all the smoke, she couldn't see if anyone had been injured. But she was sure there must be casualties. Busy looking for Bekah, she didn't notice the door opening until he had his arm around her, and his hand clamped over her mouth. He held her against the wall, just outside the door. She had tried to fight him off before and failed, but still she fought.

"Be still!" Tom insisted. "I'm not here to hurt you. Please, Evie, be still for a moment." She obeyed, but couldn't keep fearful tears from spilling over. "I'm going to take my hand away from your mouth, but only if you promise not to scream." She nodded and he removed his hand and slowly stepped away from her, releasing her from his grip. Pain lined the eyes of the once cold man. When she dropped her gaze from his face, she saw he was holding her jacket. "Evie, I'm here to warn you. You're in danger; more danger than before. Certain people have learned things about you. Do you know who your parents were?" She nodded again, unable to find her voice. "Don't go home tonight. There are men there searching your apartment. I need to know Evie, are they going to find books from the Bible in your room?"

She looked up at Tom, wiping her cheeks dry and feeling absolutely dumbfounded. "Just one. They won't have to search for it. It's next to my bed." She still had the book of John that Jackson had lent her. She was surprised when Tom cursed.

"Go to Jackson's. You and Bekah both need to stay there tonight. I'll make sure Jackson knows that's where you'll be." Her jaw began to chatter from the cold. "I'm sorry, here." Tom helped her into her jacket. There was something heavy in the pocket. "It's a gun," he explained when she felt to see what it was. "Can you shoot?"

"No."

"You need to learn. Bekah's a good shot. If you run into trouble on the way to Jackson's, just give it to her. She'll protect you." Tom put his hand on her cheek, and she froze. "I really am sorry. I'm going to try to keep you safe now, I promise." He gave no other information or explanation. He turned and left.

Evelyn stepped back inside the door just as Bekah was approaching. There was something fierce about Bekah's demeanor.

"Why were you outside?" Bekah asked hotly, taking her back out the door she'd just entered, and began walking in the direction of their apartment. Conveniently, it was also the direction of Jackson's house.

"You're not going to believe what I'm going to tell you," Evelyn started. "But first, we can't go home. We have to go to Jackson and George's. Tom was here. He said men are searching our apartment and that we need to stay away from it."

"What else did he say?"

Evelyn paused at how well Bekah accepted this information. "He said I was in danger, asked if I knew who my parents were, and said if we run into trouble, I should give you the gun he put in my jacket pocket." That part brought a reaction. "And he asked if they'd find any books of the Bible among my things."

"Evelyn Carter, you're carrying a gun right now?"

She nodded. "How does Tom know you can shoot?"

"We need to talk when Jackson and George meet up with us. I think it's time we get everything on the table."

## Chapter 45

"We trained together, me and Tom," Bekah explained hours later as they sat around Jackson's kitchen table. Charles and Natalie had stopped by only long enough for Natalie to see with her own eyes that the girls had made it to Jackson's home safely. With the night's events, Charles had even more work waiting for him than he'd anticipated. Midnight had passed, but no one acknowledged the new year. The ladies were still dressed in their gowns and the men were covered in soot and rubble from their work helping in the aftermath of the explosion. They looked like quite the scene.

Jackson wouldn't look at Evelyn. Even when she retold her encounter with Tom, he kept his eyes away from her.

"It's not a coincidence that I'm your roommate, Evie," Bekah continued. "I've known who you are since before I met you. My family works with government homes to keep children like you safe." She turned to George. "I trained with Tom when he was joining the extremists; undercover, of course. I was planted there to watch him. His dad's been searching for Evelyn for years now. I shadowed him long enough to get the information I needed, then I got out. After that, I was assigned to Evie. My job was to keep watch over her until she was eighteen. But we were friends by then, so I stayed."

Evelyn looked around the table. George was looking at Bekah as though he didn't know her. She supposed that was partially true. It was a rather important thing she'd kept to herself. Evelyn wasn't entirely sure how she felt. Confused probably summed it up best. Her eyes landed on Jackson. Poor Jackson was struggling to keep the reigns on his anger.

"Why didn't you tell me any of this?" Jackson growled, his hands balled tightly in fists.

## Unspoken Words

Bekah didn't break under the intensity of his stare. For some reason, that didn't surprise Evelyn. She looked straight back at him with her answer. "I didn't tell you because I didn't trust you with it. I'd be hunted down if the wrong people found me out." Jackson looked as if he had more than a few words for Bekah, but instead he stood and left, leaving an almost visible trail of rage in his wake.

Bekah turned back to Evelyn. "I'm sorry I never told you. I honestly thought if you never knew the truth about your parents, then you'd always be safe…or at least safer. There's so much more going on than any of you realize. The extremists we have today are different than they were twenty years ago – or even ten. They're not driven just by their hatred for Texas and its supporters. It's Christ and His people they hate. There's a deep evil hunting people down now."

Maybe Evelyn should feel betrayed that her friend hadn't shared any of this with her before now, but as she searched her heart, she found gratefulness instead…and more questions. "Did you know I was born in the Monroe's home?" Bekah nodded. "So you were assigned to me, and you've known everything about me and never said anything. I guess that explains your protective side. I am grateful you stayed with me, after your assignment was over."

Bekah smiled her relief.

"Jackson's got more to talk to you about, Evelyn," George spoke, breaking the silence. "And I need to talk to Bekah. So, we're going to excuse ourselves for the time being."

They stood and George led Bekah to another room, closing the door behind them. There was something about George that Evelyn liked very much. He was a man of peace, but from what Jackson had shared with her, she knew he wasn't a push-over either. He was clearly angry with Bekah for withholding so much, but Evelyn didn't fear for Bekah. George would be rational and thoughtful about it all. Maybe, she thought, he was like her when it came to hearing the truth. Perhaps knowing the truth gave him peace, no matter what that truth was.

Jackson, however, was not a man of peace…not naturally. He always had a fire burning in him. It was something she hadn't noticed about him at first, and when she did, it worried her some. It worried her now. There were times she'd see it in his eyes when he looked at her and it made her blush. Or she'd hear it in his voice when he discussed things with his father. She'd seen it the night that Tom attacked her, too. She was glad Jackson had Jesus. Without Him, the fire would consume him. But with Him, he was safe, and she loved that fire in him.

Now, if he'd just come back so she wasn't sitting alone at his table. But who knew how long that would take. So, she took her situation for what it was, an opportunity to pray.

Jackson ran his hand through his towel-dried hair. The shower had calmed him down some, but his blood pressure was quickly rising again. He wanted to shake Bekah for withholding so much from him, but he couldn't blame her. He'd have done the same thing. The fact that Tom had gotten to Evelyn so easily, and while she was supposed to be in his care, was what boiled his blood. He'd failed Evelyn, and Tom protected her. That more than chafed his pride.

All he found when he returned to the others was Evelyn, asleep and alone. His ego wanted to blame George and Bekah for leaving her, but the reality was he'd failed to be there for her…again.

"Hey, Jackson," Evelyn whispered in the silence.

"I thought you were asleep." He smiled. "How'd you know I was here?"

Evelyn slowly lifted her head. "You're not as stealth as you think you are."

"Hmmm," Jackson smiled again, closing the distance between them and pressing his lips to her exposed shoulder. "I doubt that very much. What were you doing here all alone?"

"Praying."

"Good answer. About anything specific?"

Evelyn turned to face him. "For you."

"Me? Why for me?"

"It's been a long night for you."

Jackson shook his head, once again humbled by her. "Come on," he said, holding his hand out for her. "We'll see if I have anything you can change into."

He found a shirt and a selection of pants and shorts that he thought she might be able to cinch tight enough to keep up and handed them to her, and she disappeared into his bathroom. She reappeared with his pants rolled multiple times over, and still hanging baggy on her.

"You look adorable."

"I look like a boy," she said, embarrassed. "And the pants won't stay up."

"There's nothing you could do to make you look like a boy," he laughed. "Just take the pants off. My shirt's a dress on you anyway."

Evelyn cringed but complied.

"You're amazing," Jackson told her when she reappeared in his knee-length shirt. Evelyn rolled her eyes. "I'm serious!"

"And what is it exactly, that makes me amazing?" Her tone rang with skepticism.

"The way you function in stress, for one. Like tonight. There were women in tears, screaming after the explosion. Even some of my officers…too many of my officers…ran around in confusion and panic. You, on the other hand, let me bark orders at you and stayed calm and coherent."

Evelyn sighed a laugh. "That doesn't make me amazing. Your instructions gave a clear plan. All I had to do was follow it."

"Evelyn. Think about tonight's events," he argued. "You were nervous wearing that dress…which just so you know, is my favorite dress ever… You had to be in a room with Sarah and Tom, experienced an attack from terrorists, were confronted by Tom, given a da…" he cleared his throat. "I'm sorry. Given a gun. Were told you had a hit put out on you. And learned your best friend is someone you don't know as well as you thought you did."

"I wasn't near the explosion. Tom confronted me for my own protection. I made it to your house safely, with my best friend who I found out will do drastic things to protect me. And now I get time with the man I love." Evelyn raised her eyebrows as if to dare him to even try to argue.

"Thank you," Jackson smiled slyly, "for arguing my point so perfectly."

Evelyn blushed under his stare. "George said you had more to discuss with me."

"Very nice change of subject," Jackson teased. "But yes, there's more. There always seems to be more." He leaned against the edge of his bed and waited for her to sit in the chair at his desk before continuing. "I'm being sent to New Mexico. I leave the day after tomorrow."

After all the events of the night, even after Tom's warning, this news hit Evelyn like a bat...no, an avalanche. "How long will you be gone?"

"Six months. I'm hoping it won't be any longer, but I can't be sure. I thought the extremist presence here would secure my position, and in a way it has. I'm being promoted to Colonel and I'll be stationed here afterwards, but I have to go there first." Jackson watched Evelyn carefully. He wanted to hold her when he told her these things, but he didn't think she'd like that; though he'd never offered, either.

Evelyn nodded slowly. "I know there's more, so just tell me everything."

"My father visited the woman who ran your government home when you were brought there. She had a lot more information than we thought she would. Your mother lived with you at the government home until you were five. She only left because Tom's father showed up looking for information on a baby with your parents' last name. So, to keep you safe, your mother and the head Madame falsified your papers, and she left. You could never be adopted because any agency would have discovered the altered papers, putting you in too much danger. She also said your mother visited often after that, but she kept her distance from you." He wasn't looking forward to sharing the rest. "Evelyn, your mother didn't overdose. She was poisoned. I'm so sorry."

Evelyn sat quietly for a number of minutes before she moved. Jackson couldn't even begin to guess at what she was thinking. Without a word, she stood and walked to him. She wrapped her arms tightly around him and pressed her cheek against his bare chest. "Promise me you'll come back. Promise me you won't fall in love with someone there and leave me here alone. I know that's not fair, but I need to know I'll see you again if you leave."

Jackson's heart broke discovering her biggest fear was him forgetting her. "Beloved, as long as God doesn't take me home, I will return to you. I promise." He watched as she moved her hands to his chest. She began tracing over the scars from his last trip to New Mexico. He swallowed hard when she pressed her lips to those scars, kissing them one by one. It was a tender gesture, but it made his pulse quicken and sent a spark through him he knew wasn't going to be easy to extinguish. She saw what he was feeling when their eyes met, and hers widened in understanding, flushing her cheeks red. "I love it when you blush."

"You just like knowing you affect me."

"That is true," he admitted, cupping her face. "But I also love it because it reminds me how modest you are, and how sweet." She overwhelmed him in the best way. "I love you so much."

"I'll leave you the combination for this in case you need anything while I'm away," he said, suddenly leaving her to open his safe. He needed the envelope his mother gave him on Christmas.

Late Christmas night, after their joyous day of celebrating had come to an end, when he was alone in his room, Jackson had taken out the envelope holding the letter from his mother. He took the letter out and tipped the envelope letting the concealed ring fall into his palm. Justine Carter's engagement ring.

The letter was, actually, from Justine and had been addressed to his mother. She left her ring with Natalie, explaining that she had to hide, but if anyone found her with her ring, she'd be found out. She also couldn't leave the ring with Evelyn because it could be stolen or lost so easily, or bring her trouble. Justine expressed her hopes that one day the ring would find its way back to her daughter, though she put no responsibility for that on his mother. It was just one new mother sharing her hopes with a friend she knew would understand. In one line, she even joked about Jackson putting her ring on her daughter's finger, one day.

Now, Jackson took the letter out and handed it to Evelyn to read.

He saw the emotion of reading her mother's letter wash over her. Her right hand pressed against her heart, her left shaking slightly as she held the paper. When her eyes lifted to his, they were filled with tears.

"I know it's too soon, Evelyn." Jackson could barely speak. "I know you're still scared of me and I'm leaving for six months. It's too soon, but time has run out." He slid the ring out of the envelope and dropped to his knee, holding it out to her. "This ring is yours, regardless of your answer to me. And if your answer is no, I understand, and it won't change anything between us. But I have to ask you. I can't leave you and not ask. Ayanna Evelyn Carter, Beloved, will you marry me?"

Evelyn felt her blood pressure drop as quickly as the tears from her eyes. Jackson was up and had her in his arms just before her knees gave out. Marriage. He'd asked her to marry him. She pressed her cheek into his chest, breathing deeply, trying to think through the shock.

"Have I told you that you're completely overwhelming?" she smiled up at him once her head had stopped spinning.

"So, what's your answer?"

"Oh, Jackson," she sighed. "I love you, but I don't..." she felt defeat rise up in him, and for the first time it was his eyes that dropped from hers. "Deserve you, Jackson. I don't deserve you."

"That's the biggest lie I've ever heard."

"It's true, Jackson. You –"

"Ignore the voice telling you that," he fought back. "It's a lie. The truth is I have no right to your heart, but by some miracle you've let me in. Evelyn, please marry me."

Shock overtook him when she pressed her lips hard against his. He could feel her smiling and tears washing down her cheeks. "Yes!" she whispered against his lips. "Of course, I will."

He held her away from him long enough to slip the ring on her finger. A perfect fit. He scooped her up in his arms and stood kissing her. He didn't deserve this woman, or her joy, but he thanked God for both.

Evelyn's heart felt as though it would explode, thinking she'd never have enough of this man. And then panic and fear slammed her. Marriage would bring intimacy.

Jackson put her down gently. He'd felt her mood change as her body tensed. "What's wrong?"

She looked at the perfection of his build. Even with his scars, he was beautiful. Marriage would bring an openness and intimacy that absolutely terrified her.

"Don't worry," Jackson said, tipping up her chin. "We're not married yet. And I'll be patient. And gentle. I promise."

# Chapter 46

## *January 14 - Sunday*

Evelyn never knew that Bekah carried a gun until Tom stopped by the second Sunday Jackson was away and found himself staring down the barrel of her quickly drawn pistol. To Evelyn's surprise, he didn't look the least bit shaken. He slowly took his own gun out and handed it over to Bekah. She kept him at the end of her gun for another moment before she finally decided to let him in.

"Well?" Bekah demanded. "What do you want?"

"I just wanted to check in with you two," Tom replied. His voice sounded like he was trying to control his temper. Evelyn didn't think he was used to not being in charge. "I know Jack's going to be gone for a while." He looked at Evelyn for the first time that night. "I just wanted to make sure you were safe."

"We have other officers seeing to that," Bekah shot at him.

Evelyn sighed. The change in her heart towards Tom was astonishing. She had hated him so strongly before and feared him to her very core; but now things were beginning to change. She tried to understand him instead of judge him; though he still made her uncomfortable, and the memories of his attack continued to haunt her. "Bekah, could you excuse us for a little?" Bekah's look could kill. "Take his gun with you. Then you can shoot him with both hands if he tries anything." That seemed to pacify her once docile roommate.

When Bekah was gone, Evelyn turned back to Tom who still stood at the door. "Hi, Tom." It was all she could manage to say now that they were alone. She wondered what Jackson would think of her letting him into her home. It hurt to think of Jackson.

"Hey, Evie."

They both stood in silence for what felt like a long while. "Would you like something to drink? Some tea? Or coffee?" She was surprised now by the look Tom gave her.

Something akin to what others had described as shame rose in Tom's stomach. "I attacked you. Why would you offer me something to drink?"

Evelyn knew she had a decision to make: hold on to her hate and her hurt, or give everything to Christ and follow Him in loving Tom. Hatred would ruin her in the end, but loving him…her strength alone wouldn't be enough. "You're not attacking me now. Today you're a guest in my home, and I intend to treat you as such. So, what will it be, tea or coffee? I have water and milk as well, if you'd prefer one of those."

"A glass of water would be nice, thank you."

She knew he was watching her and she tried to keep her hands from shaking. She did intend to treat him as a guest, but she still feared him. She wasn't sure if there would ever be a day she didn't. When she handed him the glass, his eyes fell to her hand. He saw the ring.

"Jack moves fast, I see. He's a lucky man." He spoke as a man defeated.

"Thank you, Tom. You can sit if you'd like." She sat in the chair, and he followed sitting on the couch.

"When did he ask you to marry him?"

Evelyn looked at the promise she wore on her finger. "The night of the ball, after we all made it back to his house. Thank you, by the way, for helping me that night."

"Please don't thank me. After everything I've done, it's not right that you'd thank me for anything. Evie, about that night, I am sorry."

"I'm sure you didn't come here to talk about that. May I ask why you did come by?" She knew he was being sincere, but she couldn't talk about that night right now or maybe ever.

"Yes," Tom said, clearing his throat. "My father found out who you are, along with the rest of the extremists. I tried to argue that it didn't matter who your parents were, since you never knew them, but when they found that Bible stuff here…well, I lost that argument. So, I came to see…I'm wondering if there's anyone, any men, you trust? You can't be alone anymore. I know Jack set up a tighter Patrol route on your apartment, but walking to work, or after class… If it's light out, you'll be safer, but after dark, you just can't be alone anymore. They won't hit your home again for a while, but it doesn't mean they won't try and grab you if they find you."

A chill ran up Evelyn's spine. "I trust George."

"Besides George. He's too busy as it is with Jack gone."

"Liam." She felt guilty even thinking about asking him and suddenly had déjà-vu rush over her. Just a short while ago, she sat in her apartment with Jackson while he explained that she needed to be with other men. At least this time she didn't have to pretend to flirt. Tom looked at her like he expected a longer list. "I don't have many guy friends."

"That's fine. Liam's the one you were sitting with at Jackson's party?" Evelyn nodded. "He'll do alright." He looked at her for a long moment, wishing he had been more patient, that he hadn't drank as much as he did that night, wishing everything was different between them. "I could be there for you too, if you'd let me…if you could forgive me."

Tom wasn't one to apologize, Evelyn knew that; and he'd asked for her forgiveness twice now. "I forgive you, Tom," she whispered out. "But I'm still so scared of you. I've had nightmares about that night, so many I've lost count. I don't hold it against you. Truly, I don't. But it's taking every ounce of self-control to be in this room with you, even with Bekah just down the hall." She wasn't sure why she was telling him all that, but she knew it was the right thing to do. He needed to know she forgave him, and she needed to say it out loud to make it real. She saw the hurt in his face. "I'm not telling you this to hurt you. I just want to be honest."

Evelyn couldn't have known the pain she saw on his face came from the depth of his heart. From the first time Tom met her, she had found her way into his heart and kept a small part of it soft. He knew the rest of his heart was as hard and cold as stone, but as her words of forgiveness washed over him, it was as if she had struck him deep inside his heart, sending cracks through it from the inside out, letting blood pump there for the first time. It was painful, to say the least.

"I'm not sure how you can forgive me, after everything I've done," he said, standing. "I'll keep my distance from you. But if you see me, please don't be afraid. I just want to keep an eye on you and make sure you're safe. Bekah," he called down the hall. "I'm leaving. I'd appreciate my gun back." Bekah appeared with her gun in her right hand and Tom's in her left. She handed it back to him, barrel pointed away. Tom tucked it under his shirt and left without another word.

# Chapter 47

Jackson had a foul taste for all of New Mexico, but Las Cruces was unbearable. He wanted the cold of a New York winter, not the tepid air he now breathed. He didn't know how a desert could ever be a desirable enough place to build a city. At one time, Las Cruces was just smaller in population than Syracuse, but now it was almost double the size. Everything about the desolate landscape made him thirst, physically, mentally, and spiritually. He fought that thirst the only way he knew how, by engrossing himself in prayer and God's Word.

Of all his torments, none were worse than his fear and longing for Evelyn. Thoughts of her did keep him safer at work, though. He was more apt to take extra precautions to protect himself and his men than he had been during his last trip to New Mexico; but his thoughts of her also kept him awake at night, depriving him of sleep. He prayed all hours of the day and night for her.

He'd received five letters from her in the almost six weeks he'd been away. He knew Tom was back, and though he was grateful someone was keeping an eye on Evelyn, he didn't like that it was Tom. Liam was another threat entirely. He knew Liam wouldn't hurt her, wouldn't pressure her into anything, but he also knew Liam would be all too eager to comfort Evelyn while he was two thousand miles away.

Work kept him busy. He worked seven days a week, and after every shift he collapsed in exhaustion. But busy was not necessarily good. Murder was on the rise; violent, heinous murders. No matter how many Patrols were sent out, they couldn't seem to get control of the war the extremists waged. In Las Cruces, it was easy to see that Bekah's information had been correct. The war was against Christianity now, not just Texas. That accounted for the chill he would feel all the way to his bones sometimes, as if something unseen was oppressing him. Praying memorized scriptures became an invaluable weapon against the invisible enemy, the real enemy. Satan.

God had blessed him in his friendship with his partner, Rick. Rick was an older man, and if he weren't a widower, Jackson thought he'd be long retired by now. But as it was, his wife had gone to be with the Lord fifteen years back and they had had no children, so he was alone. He was a wonderful man of God.

Rick counseled Jackson on and off their shifts, speaking truths through Scriptures and his God-given wisdom. When Jackson was particularly anxious about missing Evelyn, Rick would encourage him to share stories of his times with her, and would share his own stories about his Rosie. When Jackson was with Rick, life was a little easier. But he couldn't always be with his friend.

God is in control. Jackson was reminded of this as verses from Matthew ran through his head.

*Don't be afraid of those who want to kill your body; they cannot touch your soul. Fear only God, who can destroy both soul and body in hell. What is the price of two sparrows – one copper coin? But not a single sparrow can fall to the ground without your Father knowing it. And the very hairs on your head are all numbered. So don't be afraid; you are more valuable to God than a whole flock of sparrows.*

As was his normal routine, tonight he lay in his bed – his mind wide awake but body exhausted to weariness – praying for Evelyn. Something else was eating at him this night as well. As the Scriptures ran through his mind, it felt more like God was speaking to him about himself, not about Evelyn. As his eyelids became heavier and heavier, he was relieved to know he was finally finding sleep that night, but then his eyes shot open. He hadn't noticed the smoke in the air. It had come so gradually, while his mind had been elsewhere.

Jackson ran to his bedroom door and opened it, just to find the rest of his apartment catching fire. It was too much to put out on his own or for him to leave through the front door. He closed his door again and quickly holstered his weapons. He thought twice about jumping quickly from his window onto the fire escape and was glad he did. As he peeked through the curtains, he could barely make out two men below. They were watching the front door though, not his window, so he slowly and quietly made his way out and up the ladders lining his building.

As he climbed to the next story, he realized his fire alarm hadn't gone off. His attackers must have disarmed it before setting the place on fire. Other apartments would catch without any warning. He'd have to get them out. Maybe a rush of people would scare his attackers off, but it could also result in innocent people becoming targets for these men. Unfortunately, he didn't have the luxury to weigh every outcome; they needed to get out of the building.

He'd met the family below him; a young couple with kids. Jackson climbed quickly back down to the window below his and tapped lightly, praying the husband would be the one to look out. He was. Jackson held his finger to his lips and motioned for him to open the window, which he did. Jackson climbed in, quickly explaining they needed to get out. The husband and wife scooped up their young children and waited for Jackson to lead the way.

Jackson's pulse began to quicken, realizing blood was sure to be shed tonight. But it couldn't be this family's. There was no fear, just determination to protect innocent people. As Jackson had instructed, they went out their front door and the parents ran their children to safety behind the staircase's rails, shielding them with their bodies.

Jackson's gun was already up when his two attackers saw him. If he hadn't been ready to shoot, he'd already be dead. But he was ready. One attacker was down, hopefully still breathing. Thankfully, the other was a bad shot and his gun clamored to the floor when Jackson's bullet went through his knee.

The shots were enough to rouse curious neighbors and, before long, the evacuation was complete as the Fire Patrols assisted in putting out the flames. But his letters, and his quilt, were gone.

Both extremists made it to the hospital alive, but the one Jackson had targeted first only made it a few short hours. One more life to add to Jackson's list of lives taken, but the young family and the rest of his neighbors were safe. Their children had been completely hidden from the violent scene by their parents' bodies, and Jackson was grateful for that.

## Unspoken Words

After a long night of finding lodging for the other apartment tenants, the sun was rising, and Jackson's shift was starting. Twelve grueling hours to go before he'd have another chance at sleep.

## Chapter 48

Evelyn had seen a lot of Tom since Jackson left for New Mexico, but aside from his visit that first week, he had kept his distance, until today. It was a Wednesday, and Liam always walked her to and from work on Wednesdays. She had only asked him to walk her home, but he insisted on both. She still felt guilty relying on him.

It had been an awkward conversation when she had to explain her situation. It was embarrassing to admit she was, again, being told how to take care of herself and that, again, she'd been instructed to ask him for help. It didn't seem fair, or right, but Liam was very serious in his agreement to help her.

"Tom's been around a lot today," Evelyn commented as they left the library. "I thought he'd know by now you're with me on Wednesdays." Liam's soft laugh surprised her. "What's so funny?"

"I think that's why he's hanging around today," Liam said with a sly smile.

"He's the one who said I should ask you to babysit me." She couldn't keep the humiliation she felt out of her voice.

"No one's babysitting you, Sweetie."

"You sound like you're talking to a child."

"Anyway," Liam said, steering away from the subject. "I think you need to come out with me tonight for some fun."

"Thanks, Liam, but –"

"You haven't gone out once since Jackson left. Don't you think he'd want you to have a little bit of fun?"

"Do you really need me to explain what Jackson would feel if I went out with you? He already doesn't trust you…well, he trusts you. He just worries. Besides," she said, stealing her thoughts away from Jackson, "I know you, and there are plenty of girls you'd rather be out with tonight."

"You can't be alone on Valentine's Day. It wouldn't be right."

Valentine's Day. She didn't know how she had forgotten or been able to ignore the telltale signs of it all day. "Even more reason for you to go out with someone else. There has to be some pretty girl you want as your Valentine. Go out with her."

"Come on, Evelyn," Liam argued. "It'll do you good to dance and laugh. You need to have some fun."

"No," she stated sternly. "Thank you, really, but no. Besides, I haven't been sleeping well…really at all. I just want to stay home."

Liam was silent the remainder of the walk to her apartment, but when Evelyn turned to thank him, he spoke. "May I come in?" She shrugged and moved to let him in.

Evelyn never felt threatened by Liam, but the thought struck her that maybe she should. He walked past her and leaned against the kitchen counter. Liam was a very attractive man, and his charm and wit made him a favorite with the ladies. It was a shame he had agreed to spend so much of his time with her. There were so many other women who would enjoy his attention and time. Not that she didn't appreciate him; she did. She just felt guilty.

He watched her now with a strange seriousness she'd never seen on him before. "Evelyn, I know you love Jackson. I know you're engaged and that nothing's going to change there. You never complain or confess to any weakness, but I know you're scared. You're not the girl I met that night dancing and now you've admitted you're not sleeping. You don't have to be so alone. I care for you. We're friends, and it's torture seeing you like this. Can't you just have one night of fun? Forget about your fears for a night? You know you'd be safe with me, that I wouldn't try anything; I won't hurt you. Or if you won't go out, just let me stay a while and talk to me."

Before she could say anything, there was a knock at the door. Evelyn couldn't think who would be knocking. They never had visitors except for George, and George had a key now. She looked wide-eyed at Liam, but he wore a crooked smile.

"I wondered how long it would take him to check on us. You'd better answer it. He'll probably shoot me if I do."

Tom stood tense when she opened the door, his eyes shifting between her and Liam, who still stood against the counter. "I just wanted to make sure you got home safely."

"Yes." She didn't have to force a smile. She was so relieved someone had interrupted their conversation. "Liam was just teasing me about not being any fun anymore. Maybe you can tell him how I've never been any fun." She thought it was funny. The guys apparently didn't agree. They just stood in uncomfortable silence, until it became clear neither of them was going to speak, or leave without the other.

"Well, Liam, thank you for walking me home. And Tom, thank you for checking on me." Liam hugged her, a little too close and left, waiting just behind Tom. She assumed to make sure Tom didn't stay. "Really, Tom," she said just as he started to leave. "Thank you. Jackson and I both appreciate you. And you don't need to stay so far. I know you watch me walk home from classes. I won't be angry if you walk with me." He nodded and left. Tom had become a timid man before Evelyn.

Bekah was already out with George for the night, so Evelyn was alone. She had no appetite, so she showered and dressed in her nightclothes and, by eight o'clock, she couldn't think of a reason to be up any longer, so she headed to bed. As she went to double check the lock on the door, there was a knock. She assumed it was Liam again, and as she unlocked the door, it sank in how unwise that decision was.

Two men came crashing through the door as soon as she turned the lock. The larger of them backhanded her across the face, sending her falling to the floor. They didn't even bother closing the door behind them. She scrambled to her feet as quickly as possible. There was no way she would be able to get away, but she couldn't just lie down and give up.

"You get one answer," the man who hit her growled. "Who do you serve?"

Evelyn stood, facing off with her two attackers and prayed. It was an odd question to her, but instinctively she knew her answer. "My Lord Jesus Christ." She wished that she felt no fear as she saw the men's faces harden, that her faith was unwavering, and that she could face this trial without her knees knocking. But she was scared. Yet, not once did she consider renouncing her faith. This fear was worth facing. Still, she hoped to get away. Her only chance was to run out the open door, but even as she glanced at the door, the men knew her thoughts. The smaller man flipped his gun in his hand and struck her on the side of the head with the handle. Things weren't quite black, but her vision was starry, and her head ached worse than when she hit the table during Tom's attack. She felt a sharp pain in her side, and again, and again and quickly lost the ability to breathe.

Two explosions sounded and the pain in her head was even worse, but it stopped the violent assault on her stomach and enabled her to finally draw a deep, ragged breath in.

With each painfully drawn inhale, her vision began to clear until she could finally make out Tom. He was kneeling over her and fiercely whispering her name. She was quite sure she should be dead, but wasn't so sure why Tom would be there with her, or why she still hurt so badly. Eventually it became clear that she was not dead. She was on her apartment floor, and in a lot of pain, but very much alive.

"Evie, we're out of time. We have to go. Am I carrying you or can you walk?" Tom's voice was low, but urgent.

"I'm not sure." She let Tom wrap his arms around her and lift her to a sitting position, where dizziness set in. She felt her head and her hand came away wet with her blood.

"Don't worry," Tom tried to assure her. "It's not as bad as it looks. Do you want to try and stand?" She nodded, slowly and painfully, and he helped her to her feet. It didn't take long to discover she wasn't in any shape to walk yet. Tom wrapped her in a coat and sat her on the couch to help her with her shoes. When she stood again, she was a little steadier.

"Where are we going?"

"You won't be coming back. Is there anything you need?" Tom saw that what he said wasn't making sense to her. "Evie, you can't come back here. Tell me what you need."

"I'll get it." She kept her eyes up, not allowing herself to comprehend what happened to her two attackers, and made her way, unsteadily, to her bedroom. She put her new copies of the books of John and Romans, the necklace from Jackson, his letters, and the cookbook from Natalie in a bag and returned to Tom.

Evelyn's stomach lurched. The sight of two men with bleeding gunshot wounds in the backs of their heads forced its way into her line of vision, so much so she couldn't look away. They were two men who had been living just minutes ago. She knew they had been sent to kill her, but they were now lost for forever. Her heart cried out to God. She wondered what Tom felt, if he felt anything at all, over taking the lives of these two men. She recoiled when he took her hand.

"I'm sorry," Tom said, grabbing her hand more firmly. "But we have to go now." He pulled her out the door just as another man was ascending the stairs. There wasn't enough time for Evelyn to look away, so she watched as Tom raised his gun and shot him. There was no hesitation in his movements, and even as the man was falling in death, Tom was pulling her forward.

Evelyn lost her ability to focus as Tom dragged her along behind him. She just wanted to lie down and rest, and maybe throw up. "Tom," she rasped out. "Tom, I have to stop." It shouldn't surprise her anymore, but Tom cursed when he looked back at her. They stopped and she collapsed to the ground, hoping in vain to regain her steadiness and her breath.

Tom took a knife from his pocket and cut off a strip of his shirt and pressed it against her wound. "Hold this firmly against your head, okay?" She nodded and he lifted her into his arms. The sway of his stride made her even drowsier. "Evie. You have to stay awake." He must have known she didn't want to stay awake. "I swear I'll kiss you if you fall asleep, so you'd better stay awake to make sure I behave."

She didn't know where they were going, but his threat managed to keep her awake. Soon they were across campus knocking on another apartment door. A familiar male voice cursed. Why was everyone cursing tonight? He carried her in and laid her on a couch. Liam was there. Evelyn watched as Tom grabbed Liam's arm violently and pulled him across the room. He spoke too quietly to be heard, but Liam looked horrified. After a minute, Tom knelt by her side.

"I'm going to go find George and Bekah. I'll be back soon. Stay awake. If Liam tells me you fell asleep, I'll still kiss you." He smiled sadly, knowing his threat was indeed enough to keep her awake, and he left.

Liam approached her then. He sat on the edge of the couch and checked her head. He wore an expression of deep sadness. Evelyn had never seen such a look on his face.

"We need to clean you up." He put her hand back over the cloth pressed against her head and disappeared for a few minutes. The sound of running water filtered down the hall and moments later he was back, scooping her up and carrying her into his bathroom. He sat her in a chair he had placed in his shower and began gently rinsing the blood out of her hair and off of her face and neck. He cleaned her until the water ran clear. "I'll get you a clean shirt." He left and returned with one of his shirts folded neatly. "Take yours off and try and wipe any blood off of you that you can. Let me know when you have my shirt on or if you need help."

Her stomach and ribs were already yellow and black from the beating and it hurt dreadfully changing from one shirt to the other. When she called for Liam, he scooped her back up and carried her to his bed and laid her against propped up pillows. "I'm going to have to go into hiding when you tell Jackson you were in my bed."

"I'll make sure to give you advanced notice." He made her laugh. It hurt, but it was good too. "Are you going to tell me what Tom told you?"

"He said you were attacked," Liam began, sitting on the edge of his bed. "He said you could have a concussion so you can't sleep right now. And he said he was going to go find Bekah and George, but he told you that too."

Evelyn laid her head back against Liam's pillows. She was so tired; all she wanted to do was sleep and escape this pain she was in. "Why do I get the feeling you're hiding something from me?"

"You'll just have to pretend I'm not. You know, you should have let me stay with you tonight. You would have been safe."

"No," she said, closing her eyes. She may not be able to sleep, but no one said she couldn't just shut her eyes. She felt less pathetic not seeing the look on Liam's face. "You would have just been hurt, too. Besides, I'll heal from this one fast; it'll be easy to get over. It's not the worst attack I've suffered." Maybe she got hurt worse, but this pain was much easier to handle. There were more terrifying things than being threatened with death. The deaths she'd witnessed, though, those would stay with her.

"What do you mean it wasn't the worst attack?" The shock in Liam's voice reminded Evelyn he didn't know Tom had attacked her before. Perhaps it would be better to leave his name out of it.

"I was attacked back in November, over Thanksgiving break. Same thing, extremists hunting me down. Jackson found me that night. No one died then, but I guess there was only the one attacker, and he wasn't aiming a gun at me."

"How was it worse, if he wasn't going to shoot you like these men were?"

She opened her eyes. Pain and more pity stared back at her in Liam's eyes. "It was just worse. I don't want to tell you why." She watched his eyes harden. He had figured it out.

"And Jackson didn't kill him?"

"He got there before...I don't want to talk about it." She closed her eyes again.

"That's fine. I wish you would have told me though. Sometimes talking makes things better."

"And sometimes talking makes things worse," she stated plainly, closing the subject.

"I'm sorry I made you uncomfortable earlier today," Liam said into the heavy silence. "Back at your apartment. I only wanted you to know that I'm your friend, and friends rely on each other. I'm really happy for Jack, that he has you. I've always respected him, and I'd never do anything to hurt our friendship. It's the same with you. I think you'll be leaving for a while and I don't want you thinking there's any weirdness between us. I care for you, but because we're friends. If, however, Jack never made his move on you," the playing tone she appreciated so much was back in his voice, "then perhaps I'd care for you more. But I won't embarrass you with any of that."

She smiled easily with him again, as easily as she could with as much pain as she was in. It was nice to have her friend back. They spent the rest of their time together talking. He insisted Evelyn do most of the talking, to make sure she didn't fall asleep. By two in the morning, Tom finally returned with George and Bekah.

Evelyn insisted Liam and Tom leave the room when George inspected her head and stomach. She didn't want either of them seeing her bruised stomach, and certainly didn't want them seeing that much of her skin, or her tattoos. It was bad enough George would see it. Liam reluctantly left his bedroom, Tom refused to move. With Bekah sitting next to her on the bed and Tom seeming to stand guard at the door, George pressed on her stomach and ribs to make sure it wasn't worse than bruising. He determined she'd be fine, though he suspected she'd be dizzy for at least a few more hours with any quick movements or standing or walking too much.

"Tom's taking you to your family," Bekah explained. "You have family in Texas."

"How do you know that?" Evelyn asked, looking over to Tom who still stood at the door, but he didn't seem up for answering questions.

"He's been a great help to us, Evie," Bekah explained. "His father has – had – copies of your birth records and documents on your family, too. That's how Tom knew to go to your apartment tonight. He found them and the orders to kill you. He's going to get you home now."

"Texas isn't home. Jackson's my home. Wait…" Last she'd heard, Charles was the one with her birth records. "How did your dad get my records?" Tom looked reluctant to talk. "Tom, are Jackson's parents okay?"

"Yes," Tom finally answered. "There were two copies of your records. Mr. Monroe only got one of them."

"You're sure they're okay?"

"They're completely fine. None of us will go near Mr. Monroe or his wife. He's much too dangerous, like his son. But unlike his son, Mr. Monroe's weakness is near impossible to touch because she lives with him and never leaves the house without him. It'd take an army of us to go against him."

Evelyn breathed relief. Charles was indeed very protective of his wife. "Why can't I just go to them, if they're so safe?"

"Tom will explain it all later. But you have dual citizenship, which is pretty much unheard of. So along with you being a Christian and the daughter of your parents, you're also a citizen of the Texas Republic. I guess you could say you're a threat to the modern and traditional extremist. You have to leave."

Evelyn looked at her roommate. "Jackson. I can't leave him."

"He's coming back," George said, joining the conversation. "We've received intelligence reports that extremists are going to declare war here within the month, so we've got him coming back to help here. We'll tell him where you are. If he is able to follow you, we'll help him get to you. If not, well, we'll make sure you're informed. You're just going to have to trust God right now, Evelyn. You need to leave, give your future to Him."

She nodded. She could trust George's words. He was rational, and he wouldn't advise her on something Jackson wouldn't agree with. Still, tears burned at her eyes. "When do I have to leave?"

"Almost immediately," Tom informed her. "We need to catch the four thirty train. There needs to be distance between us and Sarah as soon as possible." Tom saw the confusion on Evelyn's face. "I'll explain everything once we're on the train."

"I brought you clothes," Bekah added, "so you won't have to travel in nightclothes, or Liam's clothes." The men gave her privacy and Bekah helped her change. "I guess we won't be running the school race this year." Her voice held the tone of a joke; a failed attempt to cover her sadness.

It was hard to believe just earlier that same school year they had been chatting so light-heartedly about the race and about the cute trainer who turned out to be a Captain named Jackson. "You're like a sister to me. I'm going to miss you terribly."

Bekah hugged her tight, making her hurt but she didn't show it. "Just get to Texas," she insisted. "Get there and enjoy a life away from the trouble you've inherited here. If we don't see each other again here, I'll see you when we're with our Lord."

# Chapter 49

Evelyn followed silently behind the man who was once, so recently, her enemy. She agreed to run in hopes of finding a safety she could never know if she stayed. Each step weighed more than the last. Each step took her further from everything and everyone she loved.

Ahead of her was Tom. Behind her was Jackson, and so many unspoken words.

Dear Reader,

Thank you so much for reading my book, Unspoken Words. I know time is a precious thing, and I hope that you enjoyed the time you spent in these pages.

This is my first novel, and though the writing process wasn't exceedingly lengthy, it took more years than I'd like to admit getting myself to publish it. Now that this task has been completed, I am on to book 2!

I wrote Unspoken Words in response to a dream I had one night. From the very start, and all the way through to the completion, I've had two goals…two prayers. The first, that God would be glorified in what I write. More than anything, I love my Heavenly Father. He is so good, so full of grace and love. In storms and in the quiet, my favorite place is holding tight to Him. He is my place of peace. When I opened my computer that first day to begin writing, I knew I wanted to write for Him.

The second prayer is that whoever reads these words I've typed would know the love of God. Dearest reader, whether you've heard it a million times or never, you are so dear to God's heart and He loves you so very much.

I'd love to connect with my readers. Social media is all the rage these days, so if you'd like, you can follow me on Instagram or visit my desperately in need up new content website:

Instagram @JannaHalterman
jannahalterman.com

Blessings,
*Janna Halterman*

# Acknowledgements

There are so many amazing people I need to thank for encouraging me and supporting me through the writing and self-publishing of this book, and I won't do any of them justice by this.

Thank you to my husband for putting up with my crazy stories and dreams, for allowing me to disappear into my land of make-believe, and for loving me through it all.

Thank you to Ashley, BaCall, and Kate for reading and rereading, for encouraging and pushing, and not letting me chicken out of seeing this through to the end. I love you girls and couldn't have done this without you.

Thank you to Jennae for letting me talk to you about characters like they were real people and for traveling across the country with me to see their world. What an adventure!

To Cara, thank you for our many writing coffee-times and getaways. I cherish those memories so dearly. You knew my characters and what made them tick, and helped me get them on the page.

To Liz, thank you for taking your time and using your amazing talent to edit this book! You are such a blessing.

And Luke! Thank you for helping me with all the tech stuff that hurts my head.

There are so many more people: all the ladies on my launch team and those who read earlier manuscripts and gave feedback…thank you to each and every one of you.

Of course, it is only by God and His grace that allowed me to write and be surrounded by such amazing people. My greatest thank you is to Him.

Made in the USA
Monee, IL
30 July 2020